STOLEN

THE STOLEN SERIES
BOOK ONE

MARLENA FRANK

To my parents,
John & Connie,
for teaching me how to
wonder, persevere, and question.

PREFACE

Way back in February 2012, over on a Livejournal community of all places, I posted a short response to a photo challenge on fantasy. It was about a little girl losing her way in a garden and needing a kind stone lion to lead the way. It got a couple of encouraging responses since it was a fairly small community, but that's all the motivation I needed. Now ten years later, I'm writing this. Stolen has been brought to publication after several ups and downs along the way, including living at a small press for three years.

I never would have guessed that the little snippet of a story would go so far or get so much love. I dreamed, but never dared to hope too much that others would love these unique characters or this colorful world as much as I did. In 2012 I wrote the first draft for Stolen, then in 2013 I pieced it apart with tweezers and wrote it all over again. I scrapped characters and added others, flipped some characters completely around, and found Shaleigh's true character.

Fast forward to 2017 where a small press took a risk on not only me and my debut novel but also on my first ever series. I was so excited; I had to walk out of my shared office so I could jump up and down in the empty hallway. It's hard to explain that level of excitement, to work on something for so many years and finally see your hard work rewarded.

After a few successful years, the small press got a new owner, downsized, and reverted the rights to this series. I was devastated, but I knew I had the experience to publish these books on my own. I didn't want to lose this series I had worked so hard to build. With the tools I learned last year creating my first indie publication, I was able to move on and create the book you hold now.

It's been a difficult, but I'm more determined to bring my books to the world than ever before. It all started with this book, with these characters, and this incredible story.

I hope Stolen steals your heart like it stole mine years ago.

Marlena Frank
September 9, 2022

CONTENTS

Part I
FREEFALL

1. An Embarrassment ... 3
2. The House Rituals ... 28
3. The Treehouse ... 42

Part II
EQUAL FOOTING

4. The Ruins ... 59
5. The White-Haired Gentleman ... 78
6. The Mark ... 98
7. The Overlook ... 152
8. The Tour ... 182
9. A Party in the Clouds ... 218
10. A Performance to Play ... 242

Part III
MISSTEP

11. The Lure of Power ... 279
12. A Promise ... 309
13. The Ruler of the Garden ... 342
14. The Violet Eye ... 369

Also by Marlena Frank ... 389
Mailing List ... 391
Support Me On Ko-Fi ... 393
Acknowledgments ... 395
About the Author ... 397

PART I
FREEFALL

AN EMBARRASSMENT

Shaleigh didn't think about how much concrete and steel stood over her head as she stepped carefully down the decaying hallway of Ferris Factory. The building had been abandoned for so long that the mildew and fungus ran rampant from the moisture that crept down the crumbling walls, so a respirator was a requirement. Ferris Factory was only two stories tall from the outside, but the floors underground felt endless. The elevator shaft only went down three floors when it had been operational; the rest of the floors could only be reached with the stairs. She doubted any of it had been inspected by the fire marshal.

Her best friend, Kaeja, walked so close behind that she could feel her warm breath on the back of her neck. The only sound that echoed up and down the hallway, besides their footsteps, was the snap of Shaleigh's camera. The photos were why they risked their lives to explore dangerous places: to document the decrepit. It was thrilling to explore a place that nobody else would see.

Eventually all the walls would fall, and Ferris Factory would decay into memory. Shaleigh and Kaeja would have the only remaining proof it even existed, especially since it was clear that nobody was supposed to know about this section of the factory.

A rat skittered out of a heap of moldy paperwork and Kaeja took a deep breath until it passed. "This is the worst one yet. By far." Shaleigh grinned, though her respirator concealed it. "Come on, we had to come back and take the stairs down. We couldn't just end it at the base of the elevator."

"Do you see that?" She swung the flashlight to the side. "I couldn't even hang a picture on that wall. Four floors down was enough, five floors is just begging to get hurt."

Kaeja was right, the walls of the hallway curved inward like a bow string. Shaleigh hadn't noticed how bad it was until she mentioned it. "We'll be quick."

She snapped as many photos as she could while Kaeja held the flashlight. It illuminated a good portion of the hall, but the beam had little effect against the thick, sick air. The light ought to have made the place more inviting, but it only made the shadows darker. It was hard for Shaleigh to keep her hands steady for the photos; fear and exhilaration kept combating within her. Sure, this place was terrifying and could collapse at any moment, but the thought of capturing a world that would never been seen again, of documenting the forgotten before it disappeared, made her tap the shutter button of her camera faster. "I wish we had more time. I'd love to look inside some of these rooms."

"Not me," Kaeja said, her eyes shadowed by the reflections of the flashlight on her mask. "These halls are creepy enough, thanks." The light flashed across some metal scraps against the bowed wooden wall. It was hard to tell if it had been left behind by the workers, or if it had fallen from the ceiling. "Didn't they used to make cars here?"

"Sure, that's it." Shaleigh snorted as she tapped on a dirt-encrusted sign that warned visitors that the hallway was a high security corridor. "Whatever helps you sleep at night."

"It's an old building, but that doesn't mean they were hiding anything down here."

"Then what's with the high security? They had to be doing something illegal down here. The maps we found don't even show these floors. I heard it used to be a hospital," Shaleigh glanced back to her with a smile. "Dad heard it from a colleague at work. They used to keep dangerous people here." Kaeja stared at her, the beam from the flashlight in her hands trembling.

A high-pitched squeal of metal echoed down through the insides of the building, as though the entire structure was shifting under its own weight. The squeal turned into a groan that shook the very floor beneath their feet. Both teens froze, barely daring to breathe as debris fell from the ceiling. Seven levels of exhausted steel, wood, and plaster shifted over their heads. They stood in silence waiting for the walls to give way, waiting to be buried beneath the rusty metal beams, discolored linoleum floors, and rat-infested insulation; but the building remained steady.

The noise stopped. Particles drifted in the air.

"It doesn't sound very good, does it?" Shaleigh whispered.

"I don't like it. I don't care what you say, this is the lowest I'm going. Five levels below ground is far enough."

Shaleigh stifled a laugh, "That's what you said when we found the stairs."

A high-pitched noise erupted down the hall causing both teens to jump. It didn't sound metallic...it didn't sound like the building at all.

Kaeja stared down the hallway with wide eyes. The noise broke into a whimper, and then there was silence. It only lasted maybe a few seconds, but they both knew what they had heard. Someone was down there with them.

Shaleigh turned to look behind them, but without the flashlight beam it was too dark to see anything. "Was that —was that behind us?"

Kaeja spun around, temporarily blinding Shaleigh in the process. "I don't know. I thought it came from in front of us."

The darkness felt like a cage all around them. The beam of the flashlight, darting forwards and backwards down the hall, seemed so small and insignificant now. Someone was in the darkness. Someone was watching them. Shaleigh stepped around Kaeja and started back toward the stairwell. "We should go."

Kaeja grabbed her arm and Shaleigh could feel her clammy fingers through the sleeve of her jacket. "Are you crazy? You said that's where it came from."

"How else are we going to get out of here?"

Kaeja could give no argument and shook her head. "Shaleigh..." she whimpered.

"It's okay, we'll do it together." She put her camera around her neck and took Kaeja's hand. They walked slowly towards the door of the stairwell, side by side, fingers clasped in a death grip.

For a moment, Shaleigh thought she saw movement ahead of them and stopped. Kaeja must have seen it too because she swept her flashlight left and right, searching for whatever it was. Just before the beam of light reached one of the doors, Shaleigh was certain she spotted a shadow move into one of the rooms.

"Ow..." Kaeja whispered giving their joined hands a tug. Shaleigh realized she had been gripping too hard and loosened her hold but didn't say a word. Her eyes were fixed on where the shadow had been. As they drew closer, an arm stretched out, hairy with long, black fingernails, and pulled the door closed. There was a splash as though something heavy had fallen into a pool of water from behind the door.

Kaeja screamed. A bolt of adrenaline hit Shaleigh and she grabbed Kaeja's arm. Together they ran. As they passed the door, the knob began to turn with a creak. She wasn't sure if Kaeja had seen it or not. "Keep going!" she yelled, all pretense of caution forgotten.

Once the stairwell came into view, they sped up. Shaleigh slipped on a wet spot and her foot skidded. She would have sprained her ankle if she hadn't grabbed for the wall. *What a stupid way to die,* she thought as she regained her footing. She had to keep her head straight, because panicking in an old, decrepit building was a sure way to get hurt or killed by whatever was after them. She forced them to slow down to climb over a pile of broken boards and nails. Shaleigh had thought it odd to have it so close to the stairwell when they'd first come down, but now she saw it as a marker, a warning perhaps, to keep trespassers out. As she helped Kaeja down the opposite side of the rubble, she heard limping footsteps approaching them.

"It's coming!" Shaleigh cried and together they sprinted for the stairwell. The flashlight bounced beams off the walls.

They hit the metal door like a battering ram, shoving it into the rusted railings of the stairs, causing it to reverberate like a gong up and down the concrete shaft. Shaleigh gripped the metal rail, feeling the flecks of paint come off on her hands, and the raw rust beneath. She exchanged a glance with Kaeja, both trying to catch their breath. The respirator was humid with her breathing and she couldn't wait to rip it off when they got outside. She looked up the dark stairwell above them and grimaced. There were too many floors between them and safety.

Kaeja gasped and reached out to grab Shaleigh's arm. Shaleigh stared at her. She thought she could make out footsteps from the hall they just left, but it was so faint it was hard to make out. It could have just been the sounds of the building, but she didn't want to take any chances. Taking a deep breath, Shaleigh led the way as they started up the stairs.

One floor, two floors, three floors.

Was that the sound of the doorknob beneath them being turned? Kaeja hurried to her side as they continued to climb. Both were audibly gasping now. It wouldn't take much for their pursuer to know where they went. Shaleigh's thighs were burning. She could sprint up a flight or two of stairs, but this was tough. It didn't help that she was already out of breath before they even started climbing.

"What if it's locked us in?" Kaeja asked between sucking in gulps of air.

Shaleigh didn't respond. She didn't want to even consider that option.

They climbed two more flights of stairs. Kaeja reached the door first. They both let out a sigh of relief when the door opened. Panting, they jogged to the main exit, a pair of massive iron doors that looked like they belonged in a mausoleum. Neither of them said a word as they descended the short flight of broken steps to the grass. Shaleigh ripped off her respirator, Kaeja did the same, and they both exchanged grins as they crossed the grass-pocked concrete walkway. It felt good to feel the heat of the day on her skin too. The sun was sinking in the west, but the air was sweet with wild honeysuckle and a light breeze rustled the old oaks. Shaleigh relaxed a bit but could tell by Kaeja's expression that she wouldn't be able to relax until they had left the property completely.

The concrete walkway fell away to tall grass that came up to their hips, as they sidestepped small pine trees that were beginning to take over the lot and moved further away from the building. The chain link fence that surrounded the property sported multiple warning signs for trespassers, though they were faded from exposure. Kaeja pulled back the corner of fencing they had used to get in, and they both climbed through without saying a word. Kaeja paused, took a deep breath, and relaxed her shoulders.

"I know you'll hate to hear this, Kaeja," Shaleigh started. "But I think I'm done with Ferris Factory for a while."

Kaeja laughed. "No complaints here. I'm going to add that we never go underground again either. I am not running up that many stairs again, no matter how great you say the pictures will be." Shaleigh couldn't help but laugh. The downtrodden path through the woods made it a short walk to reach the bus stop. Shaleigh unwrapped the scarf from around her head and shook out her twists. The breeze felt wonderful on her scalp. They dropped everything into Shaleigh's backpack as they walked. The main road was surprisingly empty for a Sunday after-noon. After exploring inside of decomposing buildings for a while, she had new respect for even the simplest things. The bench for the bus stop, covered in graffiti and bearing a single broken board, looked like a luxury.

Kaeja sprawled across the broken wooden bench and covered her eyes with her arms. "Wow, what a rush!"

"I know!" Despite her smile, Shaleigh still glanced over her shoulder, as though expecting the person from the building to be slinking toward them through the woods. "What do you think it was?"

Kaeja stared up into the sky. "Someone crazy, I'm sure. It's a good thing they made some noise. I don't like the thought of them sneaking up on us like that." She sat up and patted the bench beside her.

Shaleigh obliged, her legs were still shaky. "Did you see that hand?"

Kaeja shuddered, "Looked like he hadn't seen the light of day in forever." She stretched her arms over the back of the bench. "This is exactly why I don't like the big ones. There are too many hiding places."

"The small ones aren't much better," Shaleigh added. "Sometimes it feels like a shot right out of Texas Chainsaw Massacre, you know?"

Kaeja nodded and the two grew silent from their own nerves. Kaeja's leg jumped up and down, as though at any moment she would jump up into a sprint. Shaleigh kept resisting the urge to look over her shoulder once more. The bus couldn't come fast enough.

"Ugh, I need to think about something else." Kaeja said with a tense smile. "You've got a party coming up tonight, don't you? You get to get all dolled up. I know you don't like the people much, but I do envy you getting to go."

Shaleigh sighed. "I had almost forgotten about it." She checked her watch. It was a good thing they had left when they did because she still needed to get home and clean up. "If you like it so much, you can totally go for me."

"Your dad would never let me. He needs you there."

"Unfortunately."

Kaeja scooted closer and put an arm around her shoulders. "I'm sorry. I guess that is pretty hard on you. Do they ask you a lot of questions about him?"

Shaleigh nodded. She hated the tight feeling she got in her chest whenever she thought of those stupid parties. She hated the fact that she had to go. Why in the world did Roseworth College have so many of them anyway? It was like they wanted to torture her.

Deciding to change the subject, she picked up her camera from around her neck. After checking to make sure nothing had been damaged in their mad dash, she asked, "Want to see the pictures?"

Kaeja nodded but looked concerned. Shaleigh ignored it.

The brilliant light of the flash somehow made the dark halls of Ferris Factory less frightening, less dangerous. If only people were so easy to strip of fear.

WITHIN THE DARK hallways of Ferris Factory, a shadowy figure, one that might resemble a strange young man if seen in the right light, listened to the footsteps of two teen girls echo up the stairwell and out of earshot. He heaved a great sigh in frustration. It had to happen eventually, he reminded himself. Nobody was perfect. Still, failing stung. In his defense, this was the grossest location he had ever had to deal with. He dropped his furry hand from the doorknob and bent down to unravel the scrap metal that had tangled up his leg earlier. He had fallen into a disgusting puddle of water because of it, and barely had time to pull the door closed before they passed by.

His nose drew too close to his own body and he winced at his own stench. He needed to find a place to take a bath, but then he would try again. Next time he wouldn't fail.

~

EDDIE HAMMOND'S home was at the top of a hill with a driveway that wound around the base. It was more lavish than he would have normally been able to keep on a college dean's salary, but his wife, Vera, paid for most of it with her legal work. Neither had the time to decorate such a big home, so the decor was done in patches by different designers, which explained why the ballroom had sleek, modern chairs and the backyard garden had Grecian fountains and statues. The normal faculty attendees had shown up, with a few new faces sprinkled throughout. Shaleigh walked through the crowd with a forced smile, nodding, waving, and saying all the right things for about twenty minutes. That was her social limit.

Her dad had gotten wrapped up talking to a faculty member that Shaleigh didn't recognize. She could have been in the history department though, because she occasionally caught words like *Gaelic* or *Sidhe*. Shaleigh inched away, then escaped out the back door and into the garden. At least the dean always hosted parties at his house. Shaleigh had gotten good at finding quiet areas to get away from the crowds of people inside when the parties began. Branches of enormous oaks swayed overhead, and the air smelled of fresh rain. The sky held only the dim remnants of light far in the west, but most of it glimmered with stars. Spotlights were placed in various areas to highlight the best spots of the garden. The water from the fountain helped to drown out some of the party noise. She took a deep breath of the humid air and felt the tension ease out of her. She pulled her camera out of the messenger bag on her hip and started taking pictures of the statue that stood atop the large hexagon-shaped fountain. Looking through the lens, she could forget about the person who chased them that day at Ferris Factory, could ignore the people at the party, it was just her and her camera.

The big statue in the middle of the garden was quite ugly, especially considering how much money the dean had probably sunk into creating the little oasis. It depicted a child spitting water into the fountain, her face locked into an uncomfortable *oh!* of surprise. The artist seemed to have been unable to decide if the girl should be a cherub or a fairy, and instead turned it into a bizarre mixture of the two. The face was very boyish for a girl, as though the statue's gender had also been a point of contention. Shaleigh had taken pictures of it before, but it served as a good excuse to busy herself. She walked the entire garden about five times before collapsing onto one of the few dry benches beside the ugly statue. She had a good view of the steps that led up to the front door from there and saw several groups leaving. In a few minutes she would head back up, collect her father, and escape while she could. It was funny how much more comfortable she had been in the condemned factory earlier.

"Getting any good shots tonight?"

Shaleigh turned to see Eddie Hammond. She had been so busy eying the front steps that she had neglected the steps to the back porch. He was a broad-shouldered man, and the white suit against his dark skin only made him look bigger. People who didn't know him thought he was intimidating when, in reality, he was probably the kindest person in the entire department. He sat down beside her.

"I had to get away for a bit." She nodded to the statue, "Besides the fountain is lovely."

He chuckled, "It's hideous. Vera says I hired the designer but I'm pretty sure it was her."

He clasped his fingers together and they sat in silence for a moment, watching the wind move through the oak branches high above their heads. Another round of storms was on its way.

"You know, I remember when you came to our first Spring Fling. Do you remember when that was?"

"Years ago."

"Six years actually. You were so excited to be here and nobody could keep up with you. You simply had to see everything. You were easily the life of the party."

Shaleigh laughed, "I was ten! I broke a glass and almost destroyed one of your paintings if I remember right."

He smiled, "I still don't know how you made it into the attic."

"To be frank, I don't either."

He turned to her and there was concern in his eyes. Shaleigh steeled herself for what she knew was coming. "I'm worried about you two. How has he been doing?"

She shrugged, "The same."

"And the sessions? Please tell me he's been attending them."

"He went to one, but he said they were trying to brainwash him and quit. They gave him some medication, but I don't think he takes it. He said they made his brain not work right."

He nodded with a heavy sigh. "I'm sorry, Shaleigh. You really shouldn't have to deal with this on your own."

Shaleigh pursed her lips. She understood the implication even if Dean Hammond didn't fully realize it. He was referring to her mother, Kristen, who had abandoned them when Shaleigh was a baby. These conversations were always the same. The dean did the bare minimum of what he thought was required to get her father help, but he never tried too hard. Shaleigh had concluded years ago that the only reason he tried at all was to appease his own conscience. He probably had complaints from other faculty members about it on a regular basis. While she was sure some faculty understood, many of them couldn't condone a colleague who lied so readily. They didn't care if it was due to mental illness or not. She stifled a sigh and looked away. No, that wasn't it. That wasn't what made the dean try every year to help. Her dad had known him since they met in college, when her dad had also met Shaleigh's mother. He had been merely Eddie Hammond then, not the dean of the History Department.

"You could say something to him," Shaleigh said, knowing it was pointless. "He respects you."

The Dean sighed and leaned back against the bench. "I don't want him to feel like I'm threatening him again. Last time he didn't speak to me for weeks. I don't want to alienate him."

Shaleigh closed her eyes and let the silence stretch out again between them. She knew he meant well, but his good intentions felt caustic after so many years of hearing them. Their conversations always came back to her father's mental health, and try as he might, Dean

Hammond never had much interest in Shaleigh. To him, she would always be Haki's daughter and never her own person. Four times a year they came to these faculty parties, which her father insisted on attending. She hoped she could find someplace to be left alone, but Hammond always found her. She wanted to think he cared about her, but somehow the warmth never came across. She startled when he put a hand on her shoulder.

"Come on. You shouldn't be out here moping all night. Come back inside and enjoy yourself. Everyone has been asking about you; some even thought you had left."

"I wish. I still have a learner's permit, remember?"

He forced a chuckle as they walked back up the long steps to the back deck. She could hear the jazz music playing through the glass doors and the lilting of a woman's laughter. He paused and looked down at her.

"Talk to him," he whispered. "See if you can convince him to go back to his therapy sessions. He would benefit from them."

Shaleigh managed a small smile. "I'll try."

SHALEIGH THOUGHT the party had died down, but she was wrong. The party was even more crowded than when she had left earlier. Professors, staff, and every other person in the department appeared to be stuffed into the three rooms that Hammond put aside for his parties. Shaleigh had put on her nicest black dress and applied coconut oil on her twists to make sure they looked nice. Even though she hated wearing dresses, she always felt underdressed at these parties. She turned to ask Dean Hammond where they had all come from, but he was already engrossed in another conversation. On her way to the punch table she barely avoided a collision with one of the wait staff, who seemed just as anxious about all the people as she was. She sipped on her punch and eyed a corner where she could disappear to when she heard her father's voice over the hum of conversation.

"I'm sorry, have we met?"

A woman's voice responded with humor, "I don't mean to stare, but you look so familiar!"

"That's alright, it happens. Dr. Haki Mallet." Shaleigh looked to see her father shake the woman's hand, adding, "but you're welcome to call me Haki. I'm afraid I'm usually cloistered up in my office, so I doubt we've met before."

"Did you come alone?"

"No, I came here with my daughter. I believe she stepped outside. Her mother couldn't make it, you see, so she was good enough to come instead. I'm afraid Kristen's been home sick the last few days."

"I'm sorry to hear that!"

Shaleigh felt her stomach drop to her knees. She studied the serious woman with bleached hair and didn't recognize her. She must be a new hire who hadn't been deterred by the rumors of her dad. At least, not yet.

"How sweet of your daughter!" The serious woman gave a small smile. "I know my son Charles would never come with me to one of these. He's more mechanically minded. Would likely be bored stiff."

"Shaleigh loves these parties. She really looks forward

to them. I'm just concerned about Kristen. When she's home sick, it's difficult to think of much else."

Shaleigh ground her molars together to hold back a snarl. She had to get away from them or else she might get dragged into his stupid lies. She darted to an adjoining room and found a chair in a corner opposite the stairwell. She didn't want to hear him continue. She couldn't stand to hear it all again.

Nursing her punch, she overheard another conversation between two men near the doorway. One of the voices sounded familiar and she looked up to see Dean Hammond's positively irate expression. He was talking to a bald man with a bushy red beard. She strained to listen in.

"I assure you, Red, Haki is hardly getting special privileges. He works twice as hard as many of the faculty in this department and has brought in more funding than almost anyone else. In fact, you could take a few pointers from him."

The bald man gave a nervous laugh. "I don't think making a guest appearance in a single documentary gives him any more clout than—"

"That single documentary brought in more funding than your research has all year. They've already lined him up for two more series and he's becoming a household name. Do you know of any other expert on ancient European mythology who could do what he's done?"

Shaleigh recognized the bald man then. It was Roger "Red" Dawkins, who had been a full-fledged professor for years, even chaired multiple committees, but somehow his brisk personality didn't quite catch on with television executives. He'd been passed up by multiple chances according to her dad.

"I could have. I may not have as many books under my belt, or look as good on television as he does, but I keep busy with the *multiple* committees I'm on. Perhaps if I could get out of a few of those I could help out with some of these documentaries myself." He polished off his drink. "It just seems like the more work I do, the less research I get done. Haki, on the other hand, somehow manages to get paid more. There's obviously more to it than merely the work. Something I'm missing."

Dean Hammond shook his head and searched the crowd, hunting for an escape. "You need to be more professional, Red. You sound jealous."

"Of course I'm jealous!" Red spat, "For all the praise he gets, you think he could share a bit of the limelight with the rest of us. Perhaps contribute to the department instead of squirreling away all his funds and contacts for himself. We both know he's a time bomb, and when he does blow it'll affect everyone in the department. The man's a regular loon. He can't be trusted with that kind of responsibility. One day he'll simply snap, and that'll be it. I can only imagine the headlines..."

Shaleigh had never seen Dean Hammond draw himself up to his full height, but the way he stood now with his shoulders blocked off and the anger burning in his eyes, she understood how he had become the dean. "That's enough, Red. Kindly keep your coarse rumors in check."

"No! It's a goddamn fact and everyone knows it. What is it this time? The wife's home sick again, I hear. It's no secret she up and left him fifteen years back. He's a loon and a dangerous liar, Eddie. Everyone knows she's dead after all."

Shaleigh's fingers were freezing on the glass of punch clutched in her hands, but she couldn't move them. Her face and ears burned with rage. She wanted to believe it; she wanted her mother to be dead. As terrible as it was, it would be easier to accept than if she had willingly abandoned them.

"You know what I think?" Red swam on, ignorant of Hammond's obvious ire. "I don't think she ran away. That's nonsense." He scoffed. "I think he killed her. That's why he's so messed up. Something clicked in his head after that, and he'll never be right. I'm just afraid of what will happen should news get out, Eddie. What would they say if a crazy, lying, murderous professor who has become a household name on television was suddenly dragged out into the light with a murder investigation?"

He was trying to blackmail Hammond. Right here in the middle of a party, right here where anyone could see, where anyone could hear, Red Dawkins was trying to blackmail him using her father. The heat from her face had moved through her body like fire coursing through her veins. She barely felt her frozen fingers as she got to her feet and walked towards them.

At the sight of her, Dean Hammond's stony expression faded as he realized she must have overheard their conversation. "Shaleigh, don't..."

Red, on the other hand, had been drinking and was completely oblivious. He gave her a cocky grin. "Ah Shaleigh, there you are! How are you enjoying the party?"

Without a word she tossed the icy punch into Red's face and dropped the glass onto the wooden floor. It shattered on impact. A hush descended over the room, numerous pairs of eyes turned towards them, and a scarlet flush lit up Red Dawkins' bearded cheeks. "Don't you dare say another lie about my father," she growled, keeping her voice low.

The cold drink to the face seemed to have sobered Red up; he glanced around at the eyes watching them and stammered incoherently. Shaleigh didn't give him a chance to collect himself, but turned to face Dean Hammond, whose fury had subsided into bemused calm.

"Sorry for ruining your party, Mr. Hammond."

"That's not a problem, Shaleigh." He glanced over at Red, who was mopping up his face, then back to Shaleigh. "You certainly didn't ruin a thing for me." He gave her a warm smile and Shaleigh took her cue. It was time to leave. The crowd parted for her as she stalked across the room and back into the previous room. The chatter picked up again as she hunted for her father. Both of them had outworn their welcome.

She found him still chatting with the serious blond woman near the punch table, oblivious to what had happened. Shaleigh looped her arm around his and tried to steer him to the exit.

"It's time to go, Dad."

"Just a moment," he nearly spilled his drink and gave her a confused smile. "Amelia and I were discussing the conflicting evidence around Stonehenge." He managed to place his glass on a side table as Shaleigh dragged him to the exit. "What in the world is the problem?"

Amelia, the serious blond woman, called out, "Do give my regards to your wife."

Shaleigh didn't look up to catch the smirks or the hidden laughter around them, though she knew they were there. Her father, as usual, was completely oblivious as she pushed through the large wooden door and down the steps to the front driveway lined with cars. There must have been dozens of them, parked anywhere they could get an inch of cement, and more were piled nearby, cluttering up the grass yard. Shaleigh was sick of them. She was sick of all of them. She was so focused on reaching their vehicle near the end of the turnabout that she barely noticed her father slip out of her grip.

"Goodness, I suppose I'll have to continue my conversation with Amelia on Monday." He sighed as Shaleigh continued onward. "What in the world happened back there? Do you plan to tell me?"

Shaleigh hopped into the driver's seat of the silver SUV, avoiding her father's concerned stare as he climbed in on the passenger's side.

"I don't know if I like you driving at night. You do have your learner's permit with you, don't you?"

"Yes, Dad." She grunted as she turned on the car, "Besides you've been drinking." He didn't argue, and she took off down the driveway; her dad barely had enough time to buckle his seatbelt.

"You can't drag your father out of a party without some kind of explanation, young lady. Did someone make you uncomfortable? Did someone hurt you?"

That last question hit too close to the issue, and

Shaleigh paused for a moment before turning onto the street. "I did something I...probably shouldn't have."

He nodded, his glasses gleaming from the passing headlights. "Let's hear it then."

A LIGHT MISTING BEGAN and darkness settled in as they merged onto the freeway. The windshield wipers squeaked, the wind rattling the car as they sped up, but Dad still hadn't said much. All he did was stare at her through his spectacles. She couldn't tell if he was fuming mad or judging her driving skills. He had been disturbingly quiet ever since Shaleigh had told him what happened at the party. She checked her speed one more time and tried again, "Dad, please talk to me."

He shook his head. "You threw your drink into Red Dawkin's face. What can I possibly say?"

"I had to do something. You would have done the same thing if you heard the lies he was saying about you. I couldn't just sit there and listen to that trash!"

"No, you couldn't just sit and listen to it. You had to make matters worse. Red has always hated me, honey, but now you've added wood to the fire. You'll be a part of his slanders, his venom, and I was trying to keep you out of his way, but now he has even more ammunition to use against me."

"What are you talking about? I threw it in his face, not yours."

"You're my daughter, Shaleigh. Everything you do

reflects on me, and today your actions reflected my poor parenting."

Shaleigh rolled her eyes. "I can't believe you."

"It's alright, it's hardly something you could control. I don't want to argue with you about it any further. You were in the wrong and that's simply the end of it."

For her father perhaps, but not for Shaleigh. She couldn't let go of her anger like her father could, nor could she forgive and forget like him. She couldn't live in some happy little delusion. "Do you know what he said about you? I don't just go around tossing drinks into any jerk's face, Dad."

"Oh, I'm sure he has some new theory, some new pompous speculation. I couldn't care less what nonsense he flings at me, and I would prefer you not—"

"He said you killed Kristen."

Her father froze in mid-statement, his breath catching in his throat. The windshield wipers squeaked against the glass in the silence. The mist turned into a light rain as Shaleigh turned off onto their exit.

"Dean Hammond says you should go back to your sessions. Have you thought about doing that, Dad? It might help, you know."

He didn't say a word and his silence was maddening. She was worried that perhaps by telling him what Red had said, it had only triggered another episode, another delusion. She was relieved to hear him choke back a sob as she pulled the SUV into the garage.

His voice cracked as he spoke, "Don't ever believe such lies, Shaleigh. I did no such thing to your mother. Once she gets back from her business trip—"

Shaleigh knocked her head against the headrest. "Why do you make me do this?" She asked, "Why can't you just admit that she's gone?"

Her father continued as though she hadn't said a word. "Once she gets back from her business trip, you'll find all that nonsense is simply ridiculous."

Shaleigh slammed her palm against the steering wheel. "There is no business trip! She isn't coming back!"

His voice faltered, and she turned to see streaks of tears running down his cheeks in the yellow light of the garage. "That's enough," he whispered. She could hear the strain in his voice, the desperation. She knew that tone well. It meant that the conversation was over and that he wasn't going to budge an inch about it for the rest of the night. Shaleigh was in the wrong and he was in the right, case closed, analysis complete, problem solved. The last time she really tried to push him, he locked himself in his room for days, sobbing for hours on end.

Shaleigh parked the SUV and slammed the door as she got out. Without a glance back, she fetched the mail and closed the garage door. She passed her father as she headed into the house. He was still buckled in the SUV in the passenger seat, bent forward and crying.

She knew she ought to feel pity for him, and a long time ago she had. Now all she felt was frustration and something else: a trapped feeling, as though the walls around her were falling inward. She couldn't stand it when he cried. It made her angry and she couldn't really explain why. She let herself into the dark house. They had forgotten to leave any lights on again.

It wasn't until she had sorted through the mail, put the

bills for her father to pay beside a fairy statue of a man with flaming red hair, hung up the keys for the SUV, and headed upstairs that she started to feel guilty for her words. There was no telling which of them was left more broken when Kristen abandoned them fourteen years ago: the husband or the two-year-old.

THE HOUSE RITUALS

"You know what I want to do? I want to be one of those street photographers," Kaeja stated right before she stuffed a French fry in her mouth. She grinned and swallowed before adding, "I want to take pictures of people in their natural state. I want to show them in a way that nobody's ever seen before. You know what I mean?"

"Uh-huh," Shaleigh muttered as she sipped her drink and stared out the window at the old train tracks that disappeared into the grass. Rick's Place was a dingy little diner, but the food was good and the prices affordable, even if the booths were busted and the décor was outdated. It also was only a ten-minute bus ride from their high school.

Kaeja had been excited ever since they met up at the bus stop, and Shaleigh knew she shouldn't have accepted the offer to get dinner before going home. She just wasn't feeling talkative today, and she certainly didn't want to discuss anything about the future. No matter how she looked at it, she would always be caring for her father and his delusions.

"You aren't even listening, are you?" She looked up to see Kaeja glaring at her.

"I'm just not in a good mood today." It wasn't a good excuse and Shaleigh knew it.

"Don't mind me," Kaeja said with a frown. "I'm just revealing my life goals, you know, no big deal."

They ate their greasy food in silence for several moments before Shaleigh finally admitted, "The party last night didn't go very well."

"Oh," Kaeja put her drink down and pursed her lips. "That's right, I forgot about that. Did your Dad end up in tears again?"

"It was worse than that," Shaleigh muttered, keeping her eyes on her food. Kaeja motioned for her to continue and she caved, telling her everything from the conversation she had overheard between Dean Hammond and Red Dawkins, the drink she had thrown in Dawkins' face, her father's outrage, and finally how she left him last night—sobbing in the garage.

"Jeez, I'm sorry, hon." Kaeja sat back, her eyes wide. "I thought it was getting easier for you two."

"Not with Dawkins around. He's determined to ruin Dad and drag his problems into the light. He tried to force Hammond's hand in the middle of the party and I don't know what to do. I guess he hates both of us now… especially since I tossed punch in his face."

Kaeja chuckled, a thin smile on her lips as she asked, "Any idea where he lives?"

"No, I don't," Shaleigh stated. "Even if I did, I wouldn't

say. I don't need to get Dad into any more trouble."

"This has you too worked up. It's your Dad who has the problem here, not you."

Shaleigh swallowed the immediate denial that came to mind. She kept messing things up.

Kaeja frowned, "You need to get away from this, girl. It'll drive you nuts."

"I can't."

"We should go do something together. You don't have any plans for tonight, do you?"

"Just homework, I guess, but—"

"Good! We'll go to my house and watch some movies." Kaeja reached across the table and took Shaleigh's hand in hers when Shaleigh stayed silent. "Just the two of us. Come on, it'll be fun!"

Shaleigh couldn't help but smile as Kaeja's lime lacquered fingers dragged over the back of her hand in comfort. It was one of the things that she really appreciated about Kaeja and why she was her best friend and confidant. Kaeja actually cared about her and wasn't afraid to show it. Her father wasn't very keen on hugs or any kind of physical contact really, and Kaeja was just the opposite. She was always putting an arm around her, or whispering in her ear, or holding her hand. It made Shaleigh feel not only appreciated but loved. There was more to the world than living in the crazy cage with her father.

"I wish I could," Shaleigh whispered. She stared down at her barely-eaten sandwich and fries, trying to find the courage to talk about it. She never spoke to anyone about her problems other than Hammond, and only in a weird disconnected way, like analyzing a situation in a textbook, not her real life. She took a deep breath and let it out again, grabbing at her necklace and twisting the little metal bird pendant between her fingers. "I'm worried about Dad. I didn't see him this morning, and I want to make sure he actually got to work." Her words hung in the air as she struggled to continue. "I'm afraid I'll go home and he's going to be curled up in bed with the curtains closed again."

Kaeja sighed. "You shouldn't have to deal with him alone. It's not fair to you."

"I don't have a choice. He doesn't have anybody else."

"Not even friends? I mean, I know he's a standoffish guy, or at least he was at the art show I met him at."

Shaleigh sighed. "He only has friends who he never invites over. He doesn't want anyone at the house."

Kaeja furrowed her eyebrows. "Do you think he'll be mad if I'm there?"

"No, I mean he likes you. He says you have a good sense of humor."

She grinned and drummed her nails on the table with excitement. "That settles it then, I'm coming with you."

"What?"

"You can check on your Dad and I don't have to be stuck in my room bored all night."

Shaleigh could have hugged her.

IN A NORMAL FAMILY, coming home to a dark house with all the lights out meant nobody was home. In the Mallett house, that wasn't always the case. If her dad was in one of his moods, he would have gone throughout the entire house, turned out all the lights, pulled down all the curtains, and spent the day in bed being depressed. He hadn't had that mood in a long time, but after his break-down in the car last night, Shaleigh wouldn't be surprised.

"Dad? Are you home?"

The house was silent, but again that too didn't mean much. He might be asleep or at least pretending to be. She closed the door behind Kaeja and locked it behind them.

"What are we going to do if he's still here?" Kaeja asked keeping her voice low as she scanned the area. Shaleigh smiled despite her nerves. For urban explorers like them, it became habit to get a layout upon entering a building, and it was funny to see Kaeja scan the place as though looking for all the quick exits.

"I'll set him up with another appointment with his therapist. He won't like it, but I'll make him go if he's been here all day." Shaleigh said. "If he's fallen into this mood again then he's going back. I don't care what he says."

Kaeja opened the curtains in the living room, letting in light from the setting sun to illuminate the many paintings that lined the walls. She turned around and her eyes went wide at all the colors and figurines that surrounded the room. Shaleigh couldn't help but smile a little wider at her surprise. It was a common reaction when people saw Dad's fairies. He was an avid collector of them, regardless of style, color, age, location... he collected it all. There were metallic sculptures of fairies surrounding flowers, abstract paintings of fairies in dazzling light, fairies wielding daggers and swords covered from head to toe in blood, and bare-chested female fairies bounded in vines and rosebuds. Her dad didn't see them as lewd or disturbing, nor did he find his bookshelves of figurines eccentric. To him, they were examples of how a tale could be manipulated over hundreds of years. The fairy was an archetype, like the trump cards of a tarot deck or the bishops in a chess game. They were reflective of the human spirit simply in how many different ways they were interpreted. They were creations molded by human hands, carefully crafted by expert artisans, storytellers, academics, and anyone else who had a hand in their making. They could be fighting warriors, powerful magic wielders, queens in armor, or dangerous seductresses. They were whatever the human imagination wanted them to be, for good or evil.

Shaleigh had no problem with her father's obsession nor did she mind the paintings that were stacked in storage bins alongside a hundred other figurines. It was one of her father's few oddities that she actually appreciated. Growing up, she made up all sorts of stories about where the fairies came from and what battles they had won. She laughed as Kaeja continued to gape turning in a circle. "They're pretty cool, aren't they?"

Kaeja nodded and moved closer to examine a painting of a fairy dressed in a great golden crown. "There are so *many*. I know you said he was a collector, but I had no idea..."

"If there's one thing my father loves almost as much as my Mom—it's his fairies."

Kacja turned and gave her such a heartbroken look

that Shaleigh regretted her words instantly. "That's terrible."

"I know...that's not what I meant, you know that." Shaleigh pulled her elbows in, feeling defensive. "I actually would prefer to see more fairies around instead of Kristen's old clothes and makeup."

"What?"

"Oh yeah, he keeps all of it." She lowered her voice just in case her dad was upstairs listening to them, "He keeps them up in their old room."

Kaeja gave a nervous laugh. "You do realize you have the weirdest family."

Shaleigh didn't answer and settled on a shrug of indifference. Until she knew the house was empty, she didn't want to take the risk of upsetting her dad further. If he was having one of his moods, she didn't want to send him spiraling into a deeper depression. Plus, while she appreciated Kaeja being there with her, it didn't mean she wanted to embarrass her father in front of her.

They crept upstairs and Shaleigh gave a light rap on her father's closed bedroom door. "Dad? Are you home?"

There was no answer. Kaeja had followed her up and was examining the family pictures on the walls. In all of them Shaleigh was less than a toddler, when she appeared in them at all. The rest were of her parents, Kristen with her carefree smile and her father beaming so hard you would think his eyes were about to pop out of his skull. The older Shaleigh got the more she looked like her mother. She even had her slightly lighter brown skin tone which she hated. She didn't want to look like her. She didn't want to be reminded of her.

Shaleigh pushed the door open after knocking a second time and receiving no response. The curtains were drawn, the lights were out, but the bed was empty. It was unmade though, which wasn't like him. Normally he was more of a clean freak.

She felt the pit of anxiety in her chest deflate. "He's not here," she said with a loud sigh. "Let me check the rest of the house just to be sure first."

Kaeja nodded but Shaleigh could see the confusion in her eyes. She didn't understand the house's rituals. She didn't get why Shaleigh had to make sure her father wasn't anywhere else in the house before she herself could relax. She didn't know that sometimes Shaleigh woke up to nightmares of finding her father dead from a gunshot to the head in the guest bathroom, foaming from the mouth from a bottle of pills in the kitchen, or hanging from a rope in the garage. It wasn't that her father had ever tried to commit suicide, but the threat of it was enough to make Shaleigh check every single room in the house before she could fully put her fears to rest. The guest bathroom was empty, the kitchen was clean, and the garage still housed the SUV from last night. That was a little odd, but Dad had probably taken the bus to get to work and he did that sometimes if he didn't feel like driving.

After checking the house, she climbed the stairs again. Kaeja was still milling around her dad's room, holding one of the fairy busts in her hands. She jumped when Shaleigh poked her head in and nearly dropped the metal woman.

"He's not here," Shaleigh said with a smile.

"Good!" Kaeja said placing the bust back on the stand. "You know you said he kept your mom's old clothes and makeup, but I don't see any of that around."

She said it so casually, as though he would just leave it out for anyone to see.

"No, that's in their bedroom."

"Wait, so this isn't his bedroom?"

Shaleigh shook her head, her nervousness rising. "No, this is his bedroom. They shared that room." She pointed to the closed door beside them.

Kaeja stepped over to it, grabbed the handle, and turned it. Shaleigh couldn't get her pulse to calm down. This wasn't some abandoned building they were searching, this was her home. Worse yet, she was sharing her father's most private secrets. If he was here, he would have stopped Kaeja in that instant, but Shaleigh couldn't.

It was almost like she wanted Kaeja to see it. If she was being honest with herself, she wanted to share her pain with someone.

IT WAS ALWAYS strange stepping into their old bedroom. The curtains were always open and inviting, with a couple of dresses laid out on top of the bed, hangers still attached, and a pair of white heeled shoes poking out like mice from just underneath them. It always smelled of gardenias, a scent that Kristen had apparently loved. She was pretty sure her dad would come up and spray Kristen's perfume around to keep the scent, though he would deny it.

As far back as Shaleigh could remember, her dad had his own room and had been careful to remove any trace of himself from the room he had once shared with Kristen. But ever since she had left, he had kept the room tidy and ready for her return. It made him happy to do things to make it look like she still lived there. It gave him something to look forward to. He eventually fooled himself into believing his own delusion. The pantsuit that hung from the top edge of the open closet door was one that he placed there, freshly dry-cleaned. It was to give the impression that Kristen had left it hanging there in her rush to get to work that morning. Today's pantsuit was yellow but Shaleigh had seen other pantsuits and dresses there. Without taking the outdated fashion of the clothes into account, it was difficult to say that the room wasn't lived in. Every surface was well dusted, the clothes were regularly washed, and even the clock on the nightstand was kept running—the seconds passed by even though the room itself was frozen in time.

Based on Kaeja's expression, she had known what to expect from Shaleigh telling her about her dad's problems for years, but seeing it was very different. She couldn't conceal the shock or keep herself from stroking the blue silky fabric on one of the dresses on the bed. Shaleigh stood rigid and watched Kaeja carefully even as she leaned against the dresser. Seeing Kaeja's reaction made her think of Red Dawkins' rage from the night before. How would he react if he could see the extent of her father's delusions? Would he relish bringing her father's madness to the light? Would Kaeja ever tell anyone? It was a silly thought really, because Kaeja would never do anything to hurt her. It was normal to be shocked. Normal people would be shocked...but the longer Kaeja stared in awe, the more Shaleigh felt her trust growing thin.

"I warned you," she said as she gripped the edge of the dresser. "I told you it was bad."

"I know, but..." Kaeja's face was unreadable. She must have heard the distress in Shaleigh's voice, and now was trying hard to come up with something to say.

"You can't say I didn't warn you!" Shaleigh's hands were slick with sweat and her legs were trembling as she shouted this.

Keaja looked at her with pure pity. "I know you warned me. I know it, okay? Quit saying that."

Shaleigh stood as still as she could, not sure why this was so difficult. She had never brought anyone to her mom's room before, it was just a silly old room. Why should it make such a big difference? She felt like she would break into tiny pieces. "Say something," her voice was hoarse.

Kaeja's eyes went wide. Her mouth opened but no words came out.

"Say something, damnit! What do you think?"

She had never seen her friend at such a loss for words. It worried her more than anything she might have said. If her father came home and saw them here, would he be mad? Would he start feeding Kaeja the same lies he told Amelia last night? It would certainly push him deeper into his delusion, maybe another attack, or maybe something worse.

"What— do— you— think?"

"I don't know!" Kaeja snapped. Her eyes narrowed. "You want to know if I think he's crazy, but I have no idea. Do I think he has problems? Yes. Do I think he's weird? Of course I do, but I can't say if he's crazy or not, hon. It's not exactly an easy question."

Shaleigh dug her fingernails into the wooden dresser. Her fear and embarrassment were quickly turning to anger, and she hadn't the faintest idea why. The room felt too hot. The scent of gardenias was scratching at the back of her throat, and Shaleigh suddenly couldn't stand the sight of the room. She ran out, down the hall, and around the corner to her own bedroom. She slammed the door so hard that one of her architecture books fell out of her bookcase.

THE LIGHT RAP on her bedroom door had Shaleigh looking up from her body pillow. She was sitting with her back against the edge of the bed with her arms and legs wrapped around the enormous pillow as she tried to stop her tears. She wasn't sure how long she had been holed up in here, long enough that her eyes felt puffy from crying.

"Shaleigh? Are you okay?"

She sighed. If it was anyone else at the door, she would have ignored them. Her father would have just walked in, it wasn't like she could lock the door even if she wanted to. None of the doors in their house had locks except the exterior doors. Shaleigh had locked herself into a room when she was a child and her dad had decided to take away all the locks instead of training her how to unlock a door. It made her appreciate Kaeja's decency to knock. She even had the respect to ask to come in.

"I'm okay," Shaleigh muttered into her pillow.

"I come bearing apologetic Milk Duds."

Shaleigh smiled. "Where did you find those?"

Kaeja came in and tossed her a box. "From the gas station across the street. They're your favorite."

She popped one in her mouth, the sweetness cheering her up a little. "You have a good memory."

"Only when it matters." Kaeja knelt next to her and pulled Shaleigh's clawed fingers into her own. "I'm sorry about what I said. I guess I just panicked."

"It's okay, I shouldn't have pushed you. I probably shouldn't have even let you into her room."

Kaeja gave a warm smile and sat down next to her, putting an arm around her shoulders and pulling her close. Shaleigh leaned into the hug with a sigh. She hadn't realized how much she needed one. "Why not? Afraid I'm going to try on some clothes?"

Shaleigh gave a weak smile.

"Your mom had some good taste in clothes though." Kaeja glanced down at her own cleavage. "Though I don't think I could fill out some of those dresses as well as she did."

Shaleigh couldn't hold back a laugh that time, and Kaeja gave her a squeeze.

When she spoke again, her voice was low. "Shaleigh, I wanted to ask you something...important." She bit her lip.

Shaleigh pulled away so she could look at her easier. She expected some joke, but Kaeja's face was too serious. "What is it?"

Kaeja was studying her hard and her bottom lip trembled just a little. "I— I want to take you somewhere. Out of here for a bit, I mean..." She gave a sheepish grin and the fear that had been in her eyes disappeared. "Want to go to the park?"

Shaleigh blinked, "The park?"

"Yeah, I think you need to get away from your dad for a bit. Maybe we could pick up some ice cream while we're there or maybe go for a walk or—"

"No thanks," Shaleigh sighed, leaning back against the bed. "I'm not really in the mood."

Kaeja gave a heavy sigh. "Well I was going to save this for a special day, but I think you need it." She messed with her phone for a moment then held up the screen.

It took a minute for Shaleigh to recognize what she was seeing. It was an aerial view of a wooded location off a curvy dirt road. But when she spotted the name of the road, her eyes lit up.

"Mockingbird Lane? The treehouse?"

Kaeja grinned.

"I thought you said it was off limits cause it's condemned."

"Well...I mean it's condemned, but it's way smaller than that stupid factory."

Shaleigh pulled her into a tight embrace, "Oh, thank you! You're the absolute best."

Kaeja squeezed back, so much so that Shaleigh had to gently pry her off after a moment with a laugh.

"Did you want to go now?" Shaleigh asked.

"Why not? You got a date or something?"

Shaleigh rolled her eyes.

THE TREEHOUSE

"Are you dressed?" Kaeja called from inside the closet. It wasn't much of a walk-in closet since the best you could do was go inside and spin around, but she insisted on not being able to see Shaleigh when they changed. Neither of them wanted to get their nicer school clothes dirty, and since Kaeja was a bit taller, she could fit into some of Shaleigh's baggier clothes.

Shaleigh had just pulled on jeans and a black sports bra. "I'm decent, but the shirt I want is in there with you."

Kaeja emerged in an old tie-dyed shirt and an older pair of jeans that looked more like capris. She had pulled her locks of hair up into a high ponytail and looked like she had stepped out of the eighties. The look accented her high cheekbones and Shaleigh's heart skipped a beat. If anyone could take a bunch of old, ragged clothes and somehow make them look amazing it was Kaeja. She had a head for fashion like some people had for cardinal directions. She arched her eyebrows at Shaleigh, "Only barely decent! I hope that's not how you plan to appease the homeless down there."

Shaleigh pushed past her with a playful glare. "Give me two minutes and I'll be done. Promise." She had just yanked a T-shirt off a stubborn hanger when Kaeja gasped.

"What's that?"

"Hm?" Shaleigh turned to see what she was talking about but froze when she realized how close Kaeja had gotten. She felt the girl's fingers probe her lower back and a chill went up her spine. Embarrassment rose to her cheeks and she turned her back to face the closet. "What are you doing?" The outrage that filled her voice melted at Kaeja's concerned look when she looked over her shoulder.

"I'm sorry," Kaeja backed away. "There's some weird mark on your back. I thought it was something stuck there, but it's not."

Shaleigh put her hand to the patch of skin that still tingled from Kaeja's touch. She didn't feel anything, and half expected that Kaeja had put something there just to make her jump. With a huff she went to the mirror above her dresser and turned, craning her head around to look.

She expected to see the smooth dark flesh that she was used to seeing; instead she saw a pale white blotch as big as her palm, just above her hips. She rubbed at it, "What is it? Did I sit in something?"

Kaeja was standing next to her looking worried, "I don't know. Want me to look at it?"

Shaleigh's discomfort from earlier was gone as panic slowly settled in. She nodded.

Kaeja dragged her over to better lighting under her lamp then crouched down behind her. Shaleigh tried not to let her hear the quaver in her voice as cold fingers probed at her skin. "What do you think it is?"

"I want to say it's a birthmark," Kaeja said after a few seconds.

Shaleigh shook her head, "No, I've never had one there." She held up her forearm and showed a barely visible birthmark she had watched move from her shoulder down the length of her arm from when she was a little kid. The skin wasn't nearly as white as the patch on her back; a bit paler than her normal dark tone perhaps, but not white.

Kaeja got to her feet and came around to face her. "Don't take any offense at this, but you don't bleach, right?"

Shaleigh blinked, "My hair?"

"No, your skin. Do you bleach it?"

"No! Who does that?"

Kaeja shrugged and sat down on the edge of the bed, "I knew a girl from Nigeria who used it all the time. I think she moved though. I haven't seen her in a year or so."

Shaleigh rubbed at the mark obsessively, before yanking on a random T-shirt and pulling it down to make sure the mark was hidden from view.

"What are you doing?" Kaeja asked sounding concerned.

She checked herself in the mirror to tuck in the shirt to completely conceal the mark, pull back her hair into a ponytail, and make sure nothing was hanging off her that could get snagged in the building. "Getting ready. What does it look like?"

"Wait a minute. Let me at least look up what that mark might be."

Shaleigh clenched her teeth. "Don't. I don't want to know."

Kaeja smirked, "Don't give me that. Let's see what the interwebs have to say." She started flicking through her phone. "Okay are you cold, stressed, coughing, or sneezing?"

"What?"

Kaeja held up her phone, "That's just what it asks, okay? It might have brought on the color change, is all."

"No, look it's nothing, okay?"

Kaeja nodded but went back to her phone. "Look, if a weird mark shows up on my best friend, I want to know how it got there."

Shaleigh groaned and moved away, "You are over-reacting."

Kaeja frowned, "Hey, come here, let me feel it again."

"You've felt it enough, just get off your phone." Shaleigh crossed her arms, "Unless you didn't really want to take me?"

That got Kaeja's attention. She slipped the phone into her pocket. "Alright, no need to get nasty."

Shaleigh led the way out, hopeful that this would be the last she heard of her strange mark. Of course, as soon as they boarded the bus, Kaeja was back on her phone researching different symptoms and causes. It took a force of will to keep from flinging the damn thing out the window.

Shaleigh's first addiction was exploring buildings that were being built. Most were kept unlocked until the really expensive pieces were brought in, like showers and sinks. Anything copper would be kept under lock and key. Until then the framework was left open, and she loved guessing what each room was for and slowly watching it transform. After three or four houses though, it got boring. She knew the styles, she knew the rooms, she knew the basic layouts to expect. It just wasn't as thrilling anymore.

Then, three years ago, she discovered a forum for urban explorers online, and her entire perspective changed. She would spend hours looking through photos taken of places that were forgotten or dangerous. Sometimes it was just a simple picture of a rundown building from the street, other times it was from abandoned mine shafts in Russia. The explorers' main three mantras were to look but not touch, leave places as you found them, and be safe. Those rules had saved her butt multiple times, especially that last one. Even after three years though, she still got giddy whenever she and Kaeja embarked on a new exploration. The larger locations were easier to scope out. It was obvious that they were abandoned and usually there was already some weak point, either in a fence or a back door, that allowed access without having to rely on bolt cutters or other illegal methods. Residences were a different story. You really had to make sure that nobody lived there before you ever set foot on the property. Plus, the farther out of town it was, the more dangerous it got. She knew that neglecting to do proper research could lead to a bullet in the leg or worse.

The old house that Shaleigh had affectionately dubbed the Treehouse was an exception. The bus had taken a back road six months ago when the normal route was blocked off by a parade. Later on, after some digging, they found out that the road was called Mockingbird Lane. There were no street signs for it, and it weaved down a gravel road beneath an almost constant canopy of trees. It had been a bumpy ride and Shaleigh had nearly shoved Kaeja in her excitement. She couldn't help it though—as soon as she had seen that the roof had been lifted up off the house by a tree that was growing through the middle, she knew she had to put it on their list. It was obvious the building was abandoned—the enormous pine tree that had taken residence there didn't leave much in the way of shelter. The main concern was safety; the place being condemned made it an even higher priority.

Kaeja insisted on packing cigarettes and candy bars just in case they ran into a homeless person, a can of mace in case they ran into something worse, and, of course, their respirator masks. By the time they walked the handful of blocks from the bus stop, the sky was beginning to turn orange and the shadows were stretching out across the sidewalk. Shaleigh almost wondered if they had been too hasty in pushing out so late and almost regretted accepting Kaeja's offer; but then she turned the corner and saw the roofless house again and all her fears were put aside.

The eager tree had just poked up through the wooden roof, lifting off a chunk of it like a baby chick emerging from an egg. Beams of sunlight caught perfectly through the windows and even from the street she could see that the foundation hadn't yet been destroyed. The place was condemned but it looked a hell of a lot better than the factory from yesterday.

Kaeja took a step forward. "It's beautiful, isn't it?"

Shaleigh nodded, not quite able to find her voice.

"I don't think we'll need the respirator masks. It looks pretty dry." She turned to take Shaleigh's backpack and broke into a smile at her friend's wide-eyed look, "Are you okay?"

She nodded slowly, "Yeah I just...I've wanted to come here for months."

Kaeja took the backpack and looped her arms through it, then came over to rub Shaleigh's shoulders. "It's okay. We're here now, right?"

Shaleigh took a deep breath to calm herself. "You're right." She pulled the cap off the lens of her camera that hung around her neck. "I don't think we'll have long though."

Kaeja gave her shoulders a final squeeze before stepping forward, "That's okay, we'll be quick. It's smaller than I thought it was from the street. Looks like it only has a few rooms."

It was obvious as they descended downhill that they hadn't been the first to visit the place. There was a down-trodden path of grass that led to the door that was littered with cigarette butts and at least two beer cans. Shaleigh was glad to run through a few spiderwebs along the way. That meant that there likely wasn't anyone still in the house or that had visited here recently.

Still, it was better to be safe than sorry. "Hello?" Shaleigh called out, stopping shy of the front door. "Is there anyone here?"

"We don't want to bother anyone," Kaeja added. "We just want to take a few pictures is all."

The front door had fallen off, or maybe had been yanked off, it was hard to tell which. Either way, it had been dragged across the small clearing in front of the house for some reason. The front of the house was completely covered in graffiti, from half-hearted drawings to unknown phrases, to weird faces. The door had been taken off sometime after the graffiti visitors though, because it too was decorated in the bright yellow, blue, and green paint that made up the now indecipherable words on the front. It also still had a sign that declared it condemned. Kaeja stopped to take photos, but Shaleigh moved inside.

"Hello? Anyone home?" she called again. The front door led straight into the kitchen and living room. There was a couch that had fallen against the wall, its back facing the tree trunk which had split through the center of the room. Floorboards buckled throughout the room as the roots of the tree pushed up from below. The kitchen sink was discolored and had a knot of pine straw in it as though a bird had been trying to turn it into a nest. She looked around. It was indeed a small house, but there were more rooms inside than there originally appeared. One hallway moved off to the left, another to the right. There was no second floor to the building, which was probably the reason it hadn't fallen apart after the tree bisected it.

Kaeja walked up behind her. "What a cool place." She stepped forward to take a picture of a large wooden cross on the wall behind the tree trunk. The ground was littered with magazines that, at one time, may have been stacked neatly in a corner, and now were just paper mush that bloated and flaked with the weather. The lovely light blue wallpaper had mostly peeled from the walls, but pictures still hung there. The photos hadn't withstood the stress though, and most were cracked, with only the ghost of a face or a pair of eyes occasionally discernible. Kaeja went over to take a close-up of one, peering into the tattered pieces under the glass to try to see who had loved this place so much. "What do you think happened to the people who lived here?"

Shaleigh moved down the right hall toward what she guessed was a bedroom, judging from the corner edge of a dresser she spotted poking its way into the hallway. "Probably died. With all this stuff left behind? That's probably what happened."

She could hear Kaeja snap another picture before moving away, likely towards the other hallway. "That's what estate sales are for."

"Nobody wants to buy magazines or old family photos though."

Kaeja went quiet.

Where the living room had been letting in lots of lovely afternoon light, this room was terribly dark. There was only one small window Shaleigh could see and it was completely draped in fabric. It was perhaps the only place so far that smelled of mold. It wasn't terrible, but she knew better than to try to move it. She wished she had brought a flashlight. She didn't think she would need it since the place had the roof taken off, but here the roof was still attached. As strong as that pine tree was, it hadn't taken off the roof completely yet.

She stopped cold in the doorway, thinking back on the hallways from the factory the day before. Her heart was racing but she knew it was all in her head. She hadn't realized how much the factory had shaken her until now. Shaleigh looked over her shoulder and considered turning back. They brought supplies for homeless people and for potential attackers, but no flashlights. She did have one flashlight though, didn't she? She had her camera.

She could get a few shots in the dark and then try to see if there was another window available. One that wasn't hidden by a moldy curtain. The scent of wet wood and humid air got worse as she went farther into the room. She put her T-shirt over her nose as she continued. It did help some. She felt her way over to a corner, noting that the floor buckled in odd places much like the living room, but it felt sturdy enough to stand. She bumped her knee against a rocking chair by the far wall and decided to use it in a shot. She turned it around, wincing as it squeaked against the wooden floor.

"You okay in there?" Kaeja called from the distance.

"Yeah, just moving in."

Kaeja laughed and Shaleigh grinned. This room wasn't so bad. Even in the dark the worst she had come across was an old rocking chair and a large dresser. Now that her eyes had adjusted, she determined there was the only window available, but that was alright. It gave the photos a moody atmosphere.

She had just crouched down in front of the rocking chair to take a few photos when a hand covered her mouth. At first, she thought it was Kaeja, and didn't scream. But when she tried to pull it loose, it didn't budge. That couldn't be Kaeja, she would never take a joke that far. The attacker tugged her back against their body— his body— and began pulling her deeper into the shadowed room, opposite the wall she had been near. Shaleigh tried to form a plan of attack. She screamed, hoping Kaeja would rush in, but her voice was muffled by the hand over her mouth. Was he a homeless man, angry that two teenagers were nosing around his hideaway? Was he a psycho who planned to kill her first and ask questions later?

The image of her body lying cold in the dirt in front of the Treehouse, tossed aside like the front door had been, forced Shaleigh to act. She elbowed the man as hard as she could wherever she could reach. She was pretty sure she got him in the stomach and felt a small surge of triumph as his body jerked, but he didn't let go.

"Damn!" Her captor snapped in a boyish voice. She was desperate and was about to elbow him again or even kick if she could get the leverage, when she realized he was now playing a wooden pan flute— right into her ear no less. She felt the heat from his breath against her skin and shuddered. Was this guy high? Surely Kaeja heard it too and would come running in here, mace in hand ready to spray this jerk.

He played the tune again, a simple five note song, and

she felt her eyelids growing heavy. The song seemed to melt into her mind. It was all she could hear, all she could think, until she couldn't tell if she was hearing the music, humming it to herself, or just thinking about it. Either way, she no longer cared if she was awake or not.

MUSIC WAS PUMPING through her veins, filling her breath, and clouding her thoughts; but the repetition was driving her mad. It felt like her head was stuck inside of a bell and the same notes kept reverberating through her skull. What made it worse was that she knew it wasn't real. Occasionally she would catch scraps of noise that didn't make any sense: the squeaking of metal gears, the flapping of wings, or the mutterings of a male voice she didn't recognize. The dissonance put her on edge even as the song attempted to relax her.

She couldn't stay like this. She needed to know where she was and what was happening. Every time the unfamiliar voice filtered through, she fought harder against the thick syrup of music in her mind. She had to escape and clung to those odd sounds she couldn't explain. Slowly she began to sense more: the roar of wind in her ears, the tight grip of an arm around her waist, her chapped lips trembling in the cold. The melody began to grow distant like a music box moving into the next room. She felt her heart thudding in her chest as she attempted to open her eyes.

The light was blinding, and her eyes snapped closed.

She stared at the reds of the back of her eyelids until they no longer hurt.

She swallowed hard and tried again, forcing her eyes to stay open against the wind and light. The sky was the color of a robin's egg with strips of white clouds off in the distance. Shaleigh squinted as her eyes began to water. All she could see, it seemed, was the enormous sky until a great white, feathery wing dipped into view and her heart leapt to her throat. She stared as it dipped again and again and realized that it didn't belong to a real bird. The wings shook and rattled as they flapped, feathers sticking out in odd places, and occasionally they even got stuck midway. She was flying…

She looked down to her feet and saw a sea of trees beneath them; the canopies stretching as far as she could see in every direction. They had to be at least a mile up in the air. Shaleigh panicked and struggled against the grip around her waist. A scream broke free as she began kicking her legs out in a mad impulse to get free.

"Crap," a now familiar boyish voice muttered. "You aren't supposed to be awake yet."

Shaleigh froze and turned her head so she could look at her captor. What she saw made her wish she hadn't. Whatever he was, he certainly wasn't human. His long brown hair did little to hide the curved, furry ears that sat on either side of his head. At first, she thought they were a headband, but they kept twitching from the wind. He also had a tail, a black-tipped tail that swung this way and that as he looked down at her with eyes a tad too big for his skull. Her first thought was that he looked like he was part rat.

"What are you?" Shaleigh gasped, her throat as raw as a wind tunnel.

"Take it easy now," the rat-boy said with a nervous grin. "No need to get upset." He was riding something akin to a bicycle which was squeaking mercilessly; it also looked to be what was powering the wings. It didn't look very complicated; it also didn't look very safe. She was in a basket at his side, and he was holding her there with one arm while he steered the bike with the other. Shaleigh didn't want to find out where her captor was taking her. She didn't know what he was, but she wasn't about to be his lunch.

Suddenly she thought of the fairies her father studied, and of the changelings she had read about in one of his books. They were creatures who stole children and left doppelgängers behind to take their place. Was that what this thing had done to her?

"Are you a changeling?" She asked through chattering teeth.

"Oh boy, you are asking too many questions and we haven't even landed yet."

He seemed to be getting nervous and Shaleigh wondered if he could play that pan flute again while he flew a bike through the air. That was the last thing she wanted. She decided to keep him talking while she tried to find a way to take control of the bike.

"Where are you taking me?"

He ignored her but then muttered, "We've only got a few more hours ahead of us, don't worry now."

The rat-boy was pretty scrawny and Shaleigh thought she might have enough strength to unseat him from the flying bike. It would be risky but at this point, what wasn't? If she died in the fall, at least she would be away from this creature, and she didn't want to even think about where he was taking her. No, given her options she had to fight back now or maybe never again get the chance. She pursed her lips to build up the nerve, then grabbed the hand around her waist and yanked it up to her face.

"Wait, what?"

Trying her best not to notice the fur that covered the hand or the small black claws on the tips of his fingers, she bit down as hard as she could.

"Shit! You bit me!" The creature cried and tried in vain to pull his hand away. The bike lurched to the side. One of the wings creaked to a halt and the bike tilted further. Shaleigh tried to reach for the edge of her basket as she fell over the side, but she couldn't grip anything. Soon she was lurching toward the trees. Maybe she hadn't thought this through completely. Her scream was ripped away by the roaring wind. Rat-boy was also in a panic as he let go of her to mess with the gears and switches along the handles of the bike. Shaleigh began to fall.

Rat-boy turned back to her, originally in a panic to fix the bike's gears, and with wide eyes, a look of horror appeared on his face. With that look Shaleigh knew that there was no way he could catch her, not with that ramshackle bicycle.

PART II
EQUAL FOOTING

THE RUINS

The trees were much closer than she remembered—that was her first thought as she fell toward them. Perhaps the bike had lost more altitude than she realized when she attempted to hijack it from the rat-boy. Of course, that was little consolation once she hit the trees. She had tried to cover her face with her arms, especially her eyes, but there was little she could do once she began slamming into branches. Limbs whipped at her body. Her left leg swiped through a heavy branch, and she felt a pop of warm pain burst near her calf. She cried out, but the breaking and snapping of branches, twigs, vines, and shrubs crowded out her cry. She didn't think she would ever land, but she knew it was coming. She tried to brace herself, tried to prepare for the pain.

She hit cold water with a loud slap but kept falling. She couldn't tell which way was up and had to resist the urge to take in a breath and inhale water. Slimy fish darted against her, trying to get away from her sudden arrival. Her descent slowed and her lungs ached with the urge to breathe. She had to find the surface. She needed air, but her body didn't want to obey. Her joints were stiff, her left leg throbbed in pain, and she couldn't tell which way was up. She hung there for a moment, squinting into the murky water, feeling curious fish move against her skin. While she floated there, motionless in the cold water, her body found the surface for her. It naturally began to rise with what little air was left in her lungs. That's when she forced herself to move.

Everything hurt as she swam upwards. Her lungs convulsed, her eyes stung, but she could just make out the sunlight along the surface. Seeing it gave her renewed energy and she clawed upward, no longer able to focus on a proper swim. She didn't care if she was disoriented, or rational, or focused, she had to reach it. She let out a snarl as bubbles raced ahead from her lips. Finally, she broke through the surface and dazzling sunlight warmed her skin.

She gulped in as much air as her lungs could take: fabulous, sweet, warm air. White stars danced across her vision as she took in another breath and another. She breathed as if she had never done it before and savored each lungful she took in. Moving to float on her back, Shaleigh stared up into the incredible blue sky with a smile on her lips. A lake, she realized, taking in the distance shoreline, had saved her. Fortunately, it was deep, otherwise she might not have survived the fall. A shallow creek, barely visible at the far end of the water, must flow into it when it rained, but when it was sunny, the water was relatively still.

A hanging limb caught her attention as it swung helplessly above her head. That must have been where she had crashed down through the trees. She swallowed the fear that ran through her. For as painful as the trees had been, she was lucky to have hit them. Not too far away was a rock formation with only a few bits of grass growing through the cracks. She was lucky to have hit the water. She was lucky to be alive.

The trees, the logical part of her mind pointed out, were not ones she recognized. In fact, she was pretty sure that trees with spiraled leaves shouldn't exist at all. Her brain was foggy, but she forced herself to pay attention. She would rest soon, she promised herself. Her tired smile left as she looked at the other trees. There were others with leaves she recognized, like oaks or maples, but the colors were wrong. One of them had bright leaves the color of raspberries. Another had more muted colors, an aqua-gray that looked more appropriate for a dragonfly. It was all very wrong.

The lake that had only a moment ago brought her so much joy suddenly felt dangerous. She felt exposed floating in the middle of this alien place. She looked around at the murky water and wondered what her noisy entrance might have disturbed or attracted. She couldn't stay here. She didn't want to survive the fall only to be gobbled up by some enormous fish. She had to get to land. It might not be any safer there, but at least she wouldn't drown.

As she began to doggy paddle over to the edge, the pain in her leg flared up. Each kick to move forward aggravated it, and as she swam exhaustion began to creep up on her. She was running out of energy and switched to a backstroke instead. It eased the pain in her leg a bit, but it was a bad sign that she couldn't even manage a simple swim. The woods, she noticed now, were alive with sound. There must have been hundreds of birds from what she could hear, though she couldn't spot any movement above her. She had to hope they were small songbirds and not violent primates or anything else that might find her a threat or some gruesome play toy.

When her fingers struck the bank of the lake, relief swept over her. She flipped herself over onto her stomach, reeling at the pain in her leg. Shaleigh dug her fingers into the cold, wet mud, and dragged her bruised body onto land. She laid there for a moment, one foot dangling in the edge of the water, until she thought of alligators, or worse, and decided she couldn't stay there. Her vision hazy, she saw a large, overgrown bush. It wasn't much in the way of cover, but by the time she dragged herself the ten feet it took to reach it, she was completely spent.

Collapsing in the shade, she listened to the multitude of birds overhead and gazed at the lake. It was then that she realized that the back of her neck hurt, and when she rubbed it, remembered her camera was missing. Had she dropped it back at the Treehouse? Was it dropped while she was being flown through the air? She didn't remember. She didn't even know if she had it when she woke up. Suddenly she felt naked, like she had forgotten to put on a shirt. It brought on a pang of frustration, but she was too tired right now to think on it more. She could barely keep her eyes open. The lake looked so peaceful and serene at a safe distance. A warm breeze swept through the trees and across her skin. She closed her eyes and smiled as she remembered the look of horror that had flicked across the rat-boy's face as she fell.

It felt really good to be alive.

THE RAT-BOY WATCHED in absolute horror as the girl from the Human World fell toward the ground. There was no way he could catch her, not on his slow bike. How did she even wake up? That music was supposed to make humans sleep soundly for hours.

He righted the bike and circled for a bit, but the trees were too thick. It looked like she fell somewhere near The Ruins. He shook his head. There was no way she could survive that. If the fall didn't kill her, the predators would. He turned the squeaky bike back in its original direction and pedaled over the forest below.

His hand stung where she bit him. Did humans have diseases? He pursed his lips and resisted the urge to lick at it. He didn't know how in the world he was going to explain this to his boss, or worse yet, to Madam Cloom.

SHALEIGH'S SLEEP was of pure exhaustion and she didn't dream. At one point she felt a deep rumble that seemed to shake the ground, but her body was too tired to care. When she woke up she found herself still on her back, staring into a dark sky filled to the brim with stars. Shaleigh had never seen so many in her life, and it took her a moment to realize that she wasn't still asleep. Then she realized that the rumbling noise was still with her and her eyes went wide as she realized it was coming from right beside her.

She turned her head to see that her view of the lake was now blocked by a very large statue of a lion. It was as though some artist had arrived while she slept and built it right beside her. It must have been four times the size of a normal lion. Shaleigh pushed herself to her elbows, wincing at the pain in her arms and across her face. She knew better than to try to stand yet. Even in her sleep she could feel her leg throbbing. She thought maybe the statue had been dragged there in the night, perhaps someone had set up camp nearby, however the clearing around the lake looked empty.

"Ahh, you're awake," a deep voice boomed, and the rumbling noise diminished.

Shaleigh's entire body tensed. She turned around left and right, then stopped to stare at the statue. Its eyes were open now and its tail hit the ground with the force of a jack-hammer.

"I was wondering when you would wake."

The lion was talking to her. The statue of the lion was speaking to her. She opened her mouth but no sound came out. The lion stood and stretched with the grace of a house cat. Then he looked at her a bit closer.

"My apologies, I don't mean to frighten you. You are a Human girl, are you not? From the Human World?"

Shaleigh nodded, not quite knowing what she was nodding to. It sounded right, it sounded safe at least; really what in the world do you tell a curious, talking statue? Anything it wants to know of course. Maybe she hit the water harder than she thought.

"I fell," she managed through trembling lips, "and landed in the lake."

"Yes," the lion smiled. "I heard something crash through the trees and heard the splash. I thought," he clawed at the ground and twitched his serpentine tail. "I was afraid that you might be dead."

Shaleigh took a deep breath, trying to straighten her thoughts. "Almost," she managed, "not quite though."

"What is your name, child?"

"Shaleigh."

"Are you hurt, Shaleigh?" He seemed honestly concerned now and began prancing his front paws.

"Just my leg I think. I'm not sure what's wrong with it."

"I have just the thing." He nuzzled towards her a makeshift sled. It looked like it had been made by people, because she had no idea how a stone lion could make such a thing. It had the top of a gurney with handles attached, but without the legs or wheels on the bottom. "Do you think you could get on? I can drag you."

Shaleigh bit her lip. It was tempting to say yes...but she really didn't know what this thing was or what it wanted. "I think I'd rather stay here." The lion gave her a disappointed look and she added a, "please."

"Oh, no, you can't do that. This place is dangerous." He looked around and Shaleigh noticed how dark and quiet the forest had become. "The wolves prowl these woods at night, you see." Shaleigh shuddered, and he added with a paw outstretched, "Don't worry, I don't think they'll come near me, but I can't stay all night. I have the library to think of."

She blinked. "You have a library?"

The lion smiled a big, toothy grin. "Oh yes, a big library! Dozens of books, in fact!"

Shaleigh nodded. She didn't expect the stone lion to have a library, but if there was a library, then maybe there were people. If there were people, then maybe they could help with her leg. "Alright, let me see if I can climb on then."

Getting on the sled was more difficult than she had thought it would be. Her leg had gotten stiff while she slept, and everything felt much more difficult than before. She felt exhausted and her stomach growled incessantly. The lion leaned down after watching her struggle for a few seconds and offered a paw to help her onto the sled. He was surprisingly gentle considering how easy it would be for him to crush her. By the time she laid down she was tired, but grateful to be pulled around without having to move more.

"Thank you," she sighed, breathing hard from the exertion.

"I'm just glad you're okay. I wasn't sure what I would do if you hadn't moved by morning."

The surface beneath her was flat and cushioned, discolored, and covered in dust. He picked up the rope that had been tied around the handles and looped it around his tail; his claws were as dexterous as fingertips. Shaleigh watched him curiously.

"I assure you it's safe. We'll go slowly so you don't

catch any rocks. These sleds at one time carried many people into the city from the battlefront."

She stilled. "Did you say battle?"

The lion gave a concerned look at the dark trees in the distance. "You can't see them now, but there are groves of Pello Pines that, at one time, devoured most of my countrymen. They pose no danger now, mind you, but by the time Master Cathal stepped in, the great city of Aife was already destroyed." A streak of darkness marred his stone face and he turned away from the woods.

"Everyone is dead then?" Shaleigh asked, her hopes of getting help for her leg diminished.

"All but me," the lion responded sadly. They didn't speak as he dragged the sled away from the lake. She thought about asking more about the pines, even the battle, but the dark forest around them made her decide against it. The sled jostled quite a bit until they reached the grass, then it became a far smoother ride. The lion seemed to know the best path to take in order to provide as little discomfort as possible.

Soon they came to a wall of hedges that stood like silent sentries at least twice Shaleigh's height. Her heart pounded as they approached it for they seemed to loom out of the starlight. The lion went to a tiny gap in the wall of limbs that she could barely see and dragged his massive body through it. The sled didn't have the slightest problem, nor did she jostle around, when she followed. Once they were through, Shaleigh gasped in delight.

The city of Aife felt like the Greeks themselves had breathed life into it. Tall marble buildings stood cold and dormant in the darkness like pale ghosts lamenting their lost lives. The air smelled of wild lavender and the starlight from above made it feel surreal and magical. Trickles of water could be heard everywhere, and she spotted several stone fountains fitted with large statues. A woman smiled with exhilaration as water shot up from her fingertips and back onto her head; another had three children locked in an eternal battle, their faces frozen with mischievous glee. They passed by homes that had been buried by their rose bushes and columns run through with ivy.

"The library was once known as the jewel of Aife," the lion said in the silence. "There were scholars and magicians from across the land who came to mine its words." The building they approached had half a dozen Grecian columns before it with ramps that came up on either side, almost in a heart shape. Between the ramps stood a tall flat pedestal that stood empty. Shaleigh had to squint as they passed it and was surprised to find she could read the words.

Mawr the Guardian

Protector and Keeper of the Grand Library of Aife.

"Mawr the Guardian," she whispered and noticed the lion look back in her direction.

"That is the name they gave me." He gave a sheepish smile and paused on the ramp to eye the pedestal. "I used to have lines of children coming to see me each day. Let us visit the library, they would say. Let us ride upon Mawr! They were so precious to me, those little ones, because they were so thirsty for knowledge, so innocent of the world, and so eager to make change." He lowered his head and shook his mane. "I miss them so much sometimes." Wet tears fell to the ramp and Shaleigh felt a pang of guilt.

"I'm sorry," she fumbled. "I didn't mean to bring it up."

"It's not your fault, little one. You didn't ask to be thrown into this sad land." Shaleigh said nothing more as he dragged the sled through the large wooden doors of the library. They must have been quite impressive at one time, but now only three of the six doors remained. Once inside the scent of mildew struck her so hard she groaned.

"What's wrong?" He asked pausing to look at her in concern.

"The smell!" She grabbed her shirt and pulled it up to cover her nose, it didn't help much. "I can't stand it! Please take me back outside."

He frowned and took her back out into the city. He pulled her around behind his pedestal so that she could lean against the wall of the building. Shaleigh had started coughing and found it difficult to stop. Mawr ran off and returned with the handle of a bucket locked in his mouth. "Here, drink," he said through his teeth.

"What?" She coughed again, and he put the bucket of water down beside her.

Shaleigh hesitated. Despite her thirst and despite the scratching in her throat, she knew better than to drink just any water. Mawr seemed kind-hearted, but this city was bereft of people, and for all she knew it wasn't battle alone that had destroyed them.

"Please drink!" He insisted, nudging it closer to her with his nose. "I assure you it is safe. Our well water is quite clean."

Shaleigh didn't have much of a choice as she wheezed

again. Casting aside all her knowledge on dangerous water, she cupped her hands in and drank. It tasted cool and crisp; she shuddered as it went down her raw throat. Then she couldn't stop drinking. By the time she had finished, Mawr was at her side again, this time holding a tree branch in his sharp teeth. She blinked up at him, "What is that for?"

He shook his head and nearly swiped her with the branch. "'Erries," he muttered.

Shaleigh looked at the branch for a long moment before she realized there was another plant hanging off it. Blackberries. She plucked one and put it in her mouth, ready to spit if she didn't know the taste. The burst of tart flavor made the sides of her mouth ache from salivating. She gorged herself and plucked the entire branch free of the fruit. With a contented sigh, she laid back against the wall of the library, her belly and thirst finally satisfied. Mawr had climbed up to his pedestal, his paws curled over the lip of the edge as his eyes bored into her.

"Feel any better?"

"Much better," she stretched. "Thank you."

He leaned back with a wide smile and the low rumble of his purr started up again. Shaleigh leaned back further to look up. The moon was high overhead, nearly full, and it put a ghostly gleam on the empty stone and marble city. She spotted colors on the back of Mawr's pedestal as they glittered in the light. It looked like graffiti that was left behind, yet it wasn't like what Shaleigh was used to seeing. These were the markings of children. A carica-tured lion done in cheerful yellow with a large wobbly grin was surrounded by stick figure children, all with smiling faces.

She turned to study the city and tried to imagine what it looked like with people living in it. They certainly loved their gardens, their books, and their statues, but it looked like they enjoyed shopping too. One building had wooden doors that had been carved in the shape of dresses, done up in pinks and whites which had faded over time. In the moonlight they looked surreal against the dark interior of the building, as though a woman's head, legs, and arms would appear at any moment. Another smaller building had a wooden sign that was propped up against its doors. She couldn't tell if it had fallen that way or if it had been left in such a state. It had been nearly shattered in two during whatever raid the city had faced, and the words were indecipherable, but she thought some of the debris in the corner might have once been tables and chairs, possibly belonging to a restaurant. Then she spotted another garden beyond the restaurant which housed a marble pedestal as large as Mawr's.

"Was that another lion?"

Mawr looked in the direction and his purring stopped. "The Lady Sphinx used to sleep there. She was a good friend of mine." He trailed off and curled his tail around himself as he turned his back to Shaleigh.

"I'm sorry. I keep bringing up painful topics."

He managed a smile over his shoulder. "It is alright, child. I told you, this was not your fault."

Shaleigh stared at the empty pedestal. "Was she a Guardian like you?"

He sighed and faced her with a nod. "She was the

Guardian of the Awakened Mind. She and I were the last of our kind before she died."

"What happened to her?" Shaleigh asked before she could stop herself.

"It was after the humans were gone. The Lady Sphinx and I believed we could take care of Aife by ourselves." He nuzzled his muzzle between his paws. "We couldn't have been more wrong. The Pello Pines came and tore the roof from the library. She tried to protect it, but they ripped her out of the sky. I was so distraught that I didn't have time to repair it before the storms came. Now, I've lost the Lady and the Library. I do not deserve the title of Guardian!"

Shaleigh remembered the horrible stench of mold inside and reached out a hand to touch one of Mawr's great paws. "I'm so sorry, Mawr. It must have been a lovely library at one time."

He leaned his cheek against her hand and sniffled. "It was," he whispered. "She was even more beautiful though."

Shaleigh leaned back as everything went blurry. She didn't realize she had fallen asleep until the sun was winking in her eyes. Mawr had curled up around her in the night and despite the fact that he was made of stone, she hadn't felt the slightest chill. She listened to his deep breaths, like wind traveling through a cavern. With a slight smile on her face, she tried to move and carefully escape his hold, only to have pain shoot up her injured leg and she let out a yelp of pain.

Mawr's large stone eyes slid open in an instant. "Shaleigh," he muttered, still trying to shake off his sleep. "Are you alright? Is something wrong?"

Shaleigh kept a hand on her thigh, waiting with clenched teeth for the pain to subside. Mawr was on his feet, moving his great head side to side, prancing in place with worry. "Is it broken? It might be broken. Oh goodness, I don't have anything for that around here."

Slowly, the pain eased up and Shaleigh leaned on the bed of the sled for support. She hadn't noticed it in the darkness, but the dirtiness of the bed looked quite a bit like dried blood in the daylight. She tried not to think too hard about it. "Calm down, Mawr. It might not be broken." She sat up and decided to give the leg a proper look over. She had no clue what she was doing but she needed to do something. Despite exploring abandoned buildings for years, Shaleigh had never broken anything. Sure, she had tripped down some steps a few times, gotten scuffed up or bruised on occasion, but she had never realized until now how lucky she had been not to have broken anything.

She needed to roll up her pant leg in order to see the wound, but her jeans were too tight. That likely caused the jolt of pain that made her wake Mawr.

"I need to cut this somehow."

Mawr brought his paw over. "Can I help?"

Oh wow, that's a big claw, she thought, and her leg was already swollen. "Just…be careful."

He nodded, dragging a single claw gingerly up her pant leg. He didn't cut her once and she let out a breath of relief as the pressure lifted.

"Thank you," she whispered. "That's twice now you've helped me."

She pulled the fabric apart and realized just how

swollen it was. Her knee was about twice the size of what it should be. For as precise as Mawr was when he was cutting her pants, he went into a full-blown panic when he saw her leg.

"Oh dear, that doesn't look good at all." Mawr peered down at her leg as though it was fatal. The big stone cat had seen battles and death far more than Shaleigh had, and his panic was infectious. "Can you move it at all?"

Shaleigh tried to wiggle her toes and another jolt of pain shot up from the arch of her foot all the way to her thigh. "No...I don't know." Sweat broke out on her forehead and she tried to keep her breathing calm as her leg continued to throb. "Everything just hurts."

Mawr paced back and forth, his stone paws scraping on the walkway with each step. "This isn't good at all!"

Eventually the pain receded some and Shaleigh leaned against the wall again. She was covered in sweat and knew it wasn't from the heat of the day. Her entire body was shaking and Mawr's commentary didn't help. "I know it's not good. Do you have anything here to treat it?"

He shook his head. "All of the supplies were used up in battle." He was staring hard at her, as though he could already imagine what her corpse would look like. He had been quite kind to her and he obviously wanted to help, but Shaleigh thought of the Lady Sphinx and the Library. She didn't want to be another of the lion's sad stories. She didn't want to be just another tale told to poor travelers who would listen.

"Okay so we don't have any supplies. Surely there are other people around, other places besides Aife, right?" She shuddered at the memory of the strange rat-boy in the flying machine from before. "Someone kidnapped me from my home and brought me here. He had to be taking me somewhere and I got the impression that he didn't want me to be lost. I don't like the idea of seeking him out, but he might have some medical supplies at least."

Mawr narrowed his eyes. "You were kidnapped?"

"Yes," Shaleigh whispered. "He played some kind of flute and it sort of put me to sleep or something. I don't know what it did to me. Next thing I knew I was flying over the trees. When I fell, I thought I was dead."

"You said it was a flute?" Mawr pranced.

She nodded.

"I've heard of a powerful Faerie that rules The Garden. It is the only city that is close, but we would have to travel through the forest." He turned away. "But that's far too dangerous. We shouldn't try it."

Shaleigh cocked her head to the side. "Mawr, I can't stay here. If I don't get this looked at, I could die."

He wasn't meeting her gaze and his prancing turned to pacing. "You're badly wounded and there will be wolves out there."

"You're a powerful stone lion," she smiled. "I'm pretty sure you could frighten away any wolves that gave us trouble."

"You don't understand! I'm not powerful and I'm certainly not brave. When the battle started, I hid in the library instead of helping my humans. I let all my children die. When the Lady Sphinx was slain, I was inside, cowering under bookshelves." Tears streamed down his gray cheeks. "The title of Guardian must have been given to me as a joke. I've never been able to protect anyone or anything."

"Mawr..."

He looked up at the doors to the library with a scowl. "All my precious books, they're all gone. They're all molded now. I couldn't tell because I can't smell," he sniffled. "And I couldn't see because I lost my glasses ages ago. If I can't even protect my books, how can I possibly protect you?" He fell to the ground and great sobs tore through him. His moans were so deep that the ground reverberated beneath her. A part of her began to harden, to solidify, but she knew that wasn't right. That was how she felt when her father cried, but Mawr needed her help. He had been trapped in a city of death and memories for too long, and if she wanted to get help for her leg she needed Mawr's help.

It wasn't just that though. Mawr had saved her from the wolves once already by staying with her at the lake and bringing her to Aife, he had fed her and gave her water, and he also helped cut open her pant leg. He had saved her life many times now, and what had she done for him? Start to feel anger when he started crying. She felt the hard part inside melt at that realization, and almost wept with him. Shaleigh couldn't stroke his mane or hold his paw since she couldn't crawl over to reach him; so, she sat as Kaeja used to do and whispered words of kindness as she listened to his pain.

When Mawr was finally spent, he looked up at her with a face darkened with tears. "I'm sorry, Shaleigh."

"Don't be sorry. You lost the ones you loved and you can't ever get them back."

"Because I'm a coward," his voice cracked.

"No, you were afraid, but you don't need to be. You're not going to this place alone, you'll have me with you."

He whimpered, "But if we're attacked—"

"Then we'll fight them off together." Shaleigh stared into his eyes until Mawr gave a weak nod.

"You're right of course."

"Okay," she said. "So...what can I use as a weapon around here? Surely something was left."

Mawr gave a small smile at that. "Actually, I think we do have something."

THE WHITE-HAIRED GENTLEMAN

It was odd to see the lake again during the day when she was fully conscious. It was smaller than she remembered and looked far more beautiful reflecting the clear aqua blue of the sky. The trees were still full of birds and the air was filled with their calls. There were trills, caws, chirps, and songs that blended into something she had never heard before. Then there were the trees themselves. Their spiral leaves bounced like springs in the wind, their massive branches towering over their heads. They were far taller than any of the structures within Aife; she and Mawr were like dolls compared to them.

Mawr slowed his pace once they entered the woods, but Shaleigh didn't see anything out of place. These trees didn't look dangerous, but she kept her eyes open for any signs of wolves. They had tied her to the sled and turned the rope into a makeshift harness that went around Mawr's chest. Shaleigh dragged her fingers along the special dagger that rested on her hip in a leather sheath.

Feeling the grain of the wood's handle made her feel more powerful. Mawr had told her that if they did run into any wolves, she wouldn't need to use the dagger, merely wield it. Shaleigh wasn't entirely sure what that meant. Would it spout fire at her enemies? Would it kill them on sight? Despite Mawr's warnings, she was kind of hoping she would get a chance to use it.

The farther they got from the lake, the darker the forest seemed to become, despite the sun that was still high in the clear sky. She thought maybe there was a thicker canopy above them, but the tall, spiral-leaved trees were thinning out instead. Soon she noticed the sky was growing darker and when she saw a few stars poking through the twilight, Shaleigh could no longer contain her curiosity.

"Mawr, what's happening?"

The cat turned his head so that she could hear him but kept his voice low. "We're approaching the graveyard of the Pello Pines—where the great battle ended. Their husks are still with us."

That didn't make any sense. If the great battle had ended, and if it was as long ago as Mawr seemed to imply, why was the sky turning to night? She held the handle of her dagger, not quite ready to unsheathe it, and searched the woods around them for movement. Just as the sky turned to complete darkness, she saw the first husk.

It looked like black tendrils had shot out of the earth like a giant leviathan and wrapped an enormous tree up so that Shaleigh could barely see the grey wood beneath all the coiled layers. The twin trunks of the captive tree appeared like two legs in mid-stride, with roots shooting out near the ground.

"What is that?" she breathed.

Mawr stopped and the forest seemed maddeningly quiet compared to the brilliant noise that had filled the woods earlier. The lion took a deep breath. "That tree was one of the Pello Pines. They were greedy trees with a taste for the living. Master Cathal encased them with Daegonrúsc, a cruel plant bred by the Fae."

There was a slow creaking that emerged through the silence and Shaleigh thought she saw the black tendrils tightening their grip on their captor. Her heartbeat thundered in her chest. The black tendrils of the Daegonrúsc were alive. Suddenly this excursion became far more dangerous than she had expected. She thought they would be dealing with wolves, not these hideous, frozen giants.

"He made the day into night and put all the Pello Pines into a deep slumber, forever dreaming of battle and victory. It is all an illusion of course."

Shaleigh glanced toward him, "So they're still alive too?"

He nodded as the creaking began again. A small gap around one of the Pello Pines' legs was soon covered with more inky black tendrils. A shudder went through her as Mawr ducked his head, starting forward at a faster pace. As they moved deeper into the forest, more and more Pello Pines swathed in the thick encasement of Daegonrúsc emerged under the eerie glow of starlight.

They came to an area that was so overwhelmed by the dark tendrils that tangles of them went as far as she could see in all directions. The path they were taking grew narrower until Mawr was having trouble pulling the sled around the vines.

Then Mawr came to a sudden stop and Shaleigh had to push herself up onto her elbows to see what was wrong.

"Oh dear," Mawr groaned. A Pello Pine must have tried to cross the path at the time of its capture. Its base was split into at least three different limbs that were now covered in black, shiny tendrils. Their path was completely blocked, without even room to squeeze around it. Mawr turned to her with wide eyes, "What should we do?"

Shaleigh was shaking and couldn't tell if it was from the injury or fear at this point. "I thought I saw another path behind us," she said, feeling meek in the darkness. "Can we turn around?"

Mawr nodded. He was a large lion though, and with the path so narrow, it took him a few minutes to get his body turned. They had almost turned around completely when she heard a hissing laugh.

"What a lovely gift you bring us, Mawr."

Shaleigh felt a shiver go down her spine. She could hear others whispering the lion's name like a chant, though they were still hidden.

"Mawr... Mawr... Mawr..."

The lion pranced his paws and looked around, obviously trying to see where the others were hiding, but like he had said earlier, he was blind without his glasses. Shaleigh held her breath as pairs of orange eyes, angled and without pupils, appeared from within the tendrils. She spotted one set, then another, and another. There must have been at least ten of them and soon it was clear that she and Mawr were surrounded. Her hands went slick with sweat as she clutched the handle of the dagger on her hip.

"Are those—" she started to ask.

"If you ever want to leave these woods, foolish little statue, you will leave her with us," the voice hissed.

"Yes, with us...leave her..."

"Mawr," Shaleigh urged. "What are they?"

"If you know what's good for you," Mawr said in a simpering tone. "You'll leave us alone or else I'll squash you. Like an insect." The poor lion's purrs were more menacing than his threats.

The trees broke out in fresh laughter. A long dog-like muzzle emerged from the black tendrils in front of them, its mouth open as it laughed, letting Shaleigh see its sharp teeth. As it crawled forward, it was perhaps the biggest wolf she had ever seen. Its chest looked more like it belonged to a greyhound and its arms were as long as a human's. Its body was covered in a thick wrapping of dark fur. A cold numbness fell over her as the creature descended the black tendrils with the gait of a canine but the grace of a primate. Its glowing eyes were not focused on Mawr; they were focused on her.

"You can't outrun all of us," the wolf greeted with a toothy smile. "If you don't hand her over, we'll simply have to take her from you. Think of all that blood, Mawr. Do you really want it to stain your stone skin?"

Mawr hunkered down to the ground, planting his paws on either side of his head. His entire body was shaking. "No," he groaned, adding, "I won't let you touch her."

There was absolutely no fight in him and the wolves could see it. The others were joining the first, forming a tight circle around them.

"Stay back!" Shaleigh cried and pulled out the dagger. She held it into the sky as though it was a lightning rod and waited. She was expecting fire, magic, something to shoot out of it, but it merely reflected dully in the starlight. She held it up higher, trying to keep her voice steady, "Kill them already!" The dagger didn't do anything.

The wolves broke out into more laughter while the leader moved onto his hind legs to sniff Mawr's side. It smiled at Shaleigh as it took hold of the harness around Mawr's neck. The lion whined.

"That's a lovely knife you have there, girl." She could feel the heat of its rancid breath as he leaned closer. "Do you expect that to hurt us?" More of them moved closer, all on two legs, all with their eyes aimed at her.

Shaleigh's heart was thundering in her chest and her hands were shaking. The leader gave the harness a tug, taunting her, but when it tried to take it off completely, something within the stone lion snapped. He lurched away from the wolf, gave a cry to the sky that sounded much like the echo of an avalanche, and then knocked the leader aside with a quick strike of his paw. Suddenly they were moving and Mawr was racing down the path from where they'd come.

Shaleigh sat up as best she could and pointed out a path, "Take a right, Mawr, a right!" But the lion kept going straight. She pointed out another and again Mawr stayed straight.

"We can't slow down!" he cried, "They'll catch us!"

She turned, seeing orange eyes sticking close behind them, and worse yet, even more were joining them. She shuddered, wondering just how many wolves there were in the forest.

Mawr gave a yelp and the sled spun to the side. Shaleigh cried out and braced herself. More of the wolves were in front, cutting them off. Mawr stood panting, his head turning from side to side looking for an exit. The sides of the path were blocked by the slumbering husks of the Pello Pines and the dark tendrils of their captors. The leader stepped forward again, a clawed hand to his jaw.

"That was a foolish move, little statue. Now we'll have to grind you to dust." Hissing echoed throughout the woods.

"I'm sorry, Shaleigh," Mawr whimpered. "I did my best."

Shaleigh held the dagger tight in her hand, trying to figure out which one would lunge first. Even if it wasn't a magical blade, she could at least slice through a few before they got her. The leader moved closer and Shaleigh held out the dagger, both hands shaking as she clutched the handle.

A brilliant white light flashed suddenly, illuminating the woods and the wolves that surrounded them. Shaleigh blinked, covering her eyes as the others whimpered and moaned. It took a moment for her vision to clear after the white light had faded.

"What was that?" The leader snarled, but the light came again, and this time Shaleigh could hear the mechanical sound of her camera as the flash dissipated. It seemed to be coming from above them.

She looked up to see a man dressed all in crimson sitting with his legs dangling over a branch of the vine canopy. His white hair was so long that it fell over the edge of the branch with him, but the weirdest thing, to Shaleigh, was that he had the biggest grin on his face.

"My, my," he said cheerfully. "The great wolves of the ruins must be starved indeed to pick on such weak prey." In his hands he held Shaleigh's camera—she thought she had lost it forever when she had fallen. He twirled the neck strap with one hand as he held the camera in the other. Where had he gotten it though? He hit the flash button again with a laugh. "What's wrong? Do you have some aversion to the light?"

The wolves, Shaleigh realized, were backing away. The bright light of the flash must have hurt them. She heard their snarls of protest but knew they wouldn't be held back forever.

The white-haired gentleman leapt down beside Shaleigh and held the camera out for her to take. "I'm afraid this isn't the best time for introductions. So…might we instead simply trade?" He eyed the dagger in her hand. Shaleigh didn't have much of a choice in the matter. She had to keep hitting the flash button or else those wolves were going to kill her. She gave him the dagger and turned to snap another photo, aiming this one at the leader. The woods filled with light and the leader grimaced.

"I can lead you out of here, but you'll have to follow my instructions," the white-haired gentleman said to Mawr, then turned to Shaleigh with a smile as the wolves inched back. "You, my dear, will need to hold onto me."

Her throat didn't want to obey her, so she nodded instead and took his hand in hers when he held it out. His skin was paler than anyone she had ever met.

He reached out with his free hand and patted Mawr rather rudely on the rump. "Alright then my good friend, onward!" He pointed in the direction they had originally been headed, but Mawr's poor eyesight wasn't helping them. They had barely moved an inch before the lion stopped.

"Which way?" he cried, prancing in place.

"He can't see," Shaleigh blurted out. "Go straight, Mawr!"

In an instant the lion obeyed but, in his panic, bull-dozed straight through several of the wolves. Shaleigh felt herself tilt and almost go over the sled's side as they bounced, but the gentleman pulled her back at her sharp cry.

"My apologies, m'lady," he nodded, letting her hand go before moving to the front of the sled. Shaleigh gripped the rope tighter and turned around to look behind them. The wolves were still coming. Feeling trapped, Shaleigh flashed her camera over her head in an attempt to dissuade them. She felt a hand on her shoulder and tensed, "Best not waste that light. We may need it yet. Let me know if they get too close though, yes?"

Shaleigh didn't have the chance to answer.

The gentleman, unperturbed by the bouncy, rough terrain beneath them and the wolves tracking them, began giving Mawr orders. Mawr took a sharp turn and the sled slid off the edge of the path and scraped across the black vines. There was a terrible creaking over their heads as Mawr was forced to slow. Shaleigh stared as the vines began to unravel from their prey. She saw the slumbering tree within twitch and tried to hold back a scream. The black vines were unraveling, trying to wrap around Mawr's head while the gentleman was cutting them off. With each slice, they jerked back like snakes, but there were so many Shaleigh wasn't sure if he would be able to get rid of them all.

Then something tried to yank the camera out of her grip. "No!" she cried and turned to see a wolf's glowing eyes directly in front of her face, jaws wide and teeth so close she could smell its breath. One clawed hand gripped the camera while the other gripped the sled for balance. She hit the flash button at least five times and the entire forest lit up with light. The wolf winced but didn't let go. Black claws dragged over the metal casing and it snapped wildly in the air. She went to hit the flash again, this time with the lens directly in the wolf's eyes, when the white-haired gentleman appeared beside her, and with almost imperceptible speed, slammed the dagger up through the wolf's bottom jaw. Blood poured out of the wound, down the gentleman's pale hands, and onto his crimson sleeve as the camera's flash illuminated the gory scene in vivid detail.

"Miserable mutt!" the gentleman muttered before dislodging the blade and kicking the creature off the sled. The vines he had been fighting earlier returned to wrapping themselves around the Pello Pines, but they moved slowly as though wounded. "We must keep moving!"

The sled jarred into motion and Shaleigh watched the wolf fold into a motionless heap. The others stopped and approached it, distracted from their pursuit by their fallen comrade.

"You killed it," she whispered.

"Of course, m'lady. I didn't have much choice." He wiped the blade on his sleeve. "This is a silver blade after all. It was made to kill these beasts."

Shaleigh swallowed down the dry lump in her throat at the mournful howl that broke the silence. Her stomach still quaked as they moved farther and farther from the wolves. The gentleman knelt beside her and put a hand on her shoulder to keep her steady. That was when Shaleigh noticed his unusually pointed ears.

He shook his head at her surprised look, "Children from the Human World do not belong here."

Shaleigh certainly agreed.

SHALEIGH KNEW they were safer as the starry sky changed back to twilight. No one relaxed until the black tendrils became less frequent. Shaleigh heard the chirping of birds and had to force herself to take deep breaths to calm down. She let go of the rope, her fingers stiff and palms sore from how tightly she had gripped it. She laid her head back on the sled and let her eyes slide closed. When she opened them again, the brilliant blue sky greeted her. She smiled as spiral leaves bounced in the breeze. They had only been in the forest for a few hours, but it felt like days. Mawr pulled the sled into a copse of trees and flopped down in the grass, his chest expanding from his deep breaths.

"We did it!" Mawr cried and his deep purrs vibrated around them.

"I thought we were goners," Shaleigh remarked as she pushed into a sitting position. "Thank you by the way." She held out her hand to the white-haired gentleman, who arched his white eyebrows in surprise. "We would be dead without you."

He shook her outstretched hand with both of his. "Possibly, but I couldn't have done it without this little contraption," he said in a silvery voice, moving his dark brown eyes to the camera which hung like a medal around her neck. Now that she could see it in the daylight, it looked terribly banged up. The lens cover was missing and there were long scratch marks along the casing. She wasn't sure if she could take proper photographs with it again, but at least they were alive. A pang of regret hit her, but she pushed it away. It was just a camera, she told herself, but the feeling quelled only a little.

"How did you find it? I thought I lost it." she asked to distract herself.

"This might sound rather far-fetched, but it fell from the sky." The white-haired gentleman grinned at her laugh. "I saw it catch the light as it fell and thought I might retrieve it. Might I ask how in the world it got up there?"

"I was...kidnapped."

He pursed his lips but gave a slow nod, as though flying kidnappers were a regular nuisance. "Is that why you can't walk?"

"We're going to the Garden," Mawr interjected as he got to his feet again. "I'm sure they can help her."

"The Garden?" He sucked in a breath. "Are you sure that is wise?"

Mawr's smile fell. "It is the closest city. Is that not a good idea?" He sat back down.

"I suppose that depends on your allegiances," The gentleman pushed a strand of hair behind a pointed ear. "I, for one, would like to go there, but unfortunately that's—"

Mawr suddenly jerked in horror and leapt to his feet. "You're—you're—" He pranced the same way he had in the forest surrounded by wolves. "You're a Faerie!" he blurted, trying to back away slowly, but too panicked to notice the way the sled jolted with each step.

The gentleman laughed outright. "You've just noticed? You poor thing, your eyes must be terrible."

Mawr shook from his mane to his tail. Shaleigh didn't understand what was wrong.

"Calm down, Mawr. He saved our lives, remember?"

Mawr wouldn't even look at her. His big eyes were fixed on the gentleman, who was beginning to get annoyed the longer the lion stared.

"Come now, this is ridiculous. Don't you have a thanks for me, you silly lion?" He made to stand and Mawr bolted. The sled swung to the side and banged into a tree. Shaleigh felt a jolt of pain reverberate up her leg and hissed. The rope had slid across the gentleman's legs, knocking him to the grass. He jumped away just in time as Mawr took down the path.

"Mawr, stop! You're being ridiculous!" Shaleigh cried and tried to pull on the harness, but Mawr was so panicked he would be hard to stop even if he wasn't made of stone. She thought about cutting herself free, but the Faerie still had the knife. She looked behind them to see him jogging to catch up. He was surprisingly fast, and she was reminded of how quickly he had killed the wolf with the silver dagger.

The trees parted, and the path moved toward a brick bridge built over some rapids. There must have been quite a drop over the edge from the sound of the roaring water below. Mawr couldn't see where he was going and barreled toward the edge of the drop instead of the bridge.

"Mawr, stop! You're going to get us killed!" Shaleigh screamed and finally the lion skidded to a halt. The sled slammed into his back legs and Shaleigh yelped as more pain shot down her leg. She curled forward, two hands pressing on her thigh, waiting for it to cease.

"I'm sorry," Mawr whispered. He must have heard the rapids below and backed up awkwardly, nearly missing the sled with his enormous paws.

"There's a bridge..." Shaleigh said with a shaky breath, but Mawr wasn't paying attention to her.

"Faeries can't be trusted," Mawr muttered in a meek voice more to himself than her. "Their magic is danger-ous!" He jumped at the sight of the gentleman catching up with them. "He could turn us into toads if he wanted, or cut our heads off with a look, or throw us into the river—"

Mawr fell silent as the Faerie approached, but surpris-ingly the gentleman's brown eyes were wide and fearful. He looked like he expected a monster to emerge from the bridge, but there were only fields of grass on the other side with shoots that would probably come up to

Shaleigh's thighs. She wasn't looking forward to getting dragged through them either.

The gentleman seemed to see something else and stepped back. "Trust me, child of the Human World, you do not want to go in there." He paused when he saw how panicked Mawr was becoming in his presence. "Madam Cloom runs that city and she's been collecting your kind. There are many rumors about what she does with them… and none of them are good."

Shaleigh swallowed hard, marveling at how dry her mouth felt. Her leg was throbbing and Mawr nearly careening over the edge didn't make her feel any safer. She looked at the grassland, not sure if the gentleman was speaking the truth or not. Mawr, on the other hand, was ready to bolt at a moment's notice. The Faerie advanced slowly, his hands out as though he were facing a wild stallion.

"Please," he whispered, his brown eyes watching her intently. "You would be far safer coming with me. Those heathens—they can't be trusted. There's no telling what they'll do to you inside."

Mawr stiffened.

"You're injured," the gentleman insisted, ignoring the lion. "You need help. I can take you to someone who—"

"I don't even know your name." Shaleigh said, cutting him off, "I don't know where you came from or anything about you."

He bowed low at that. "I am Talek and I come from lands far beyond here." When he rose, he was smiling. "I am a Faerie, as Mawr so eloquently pointed out, but I do not wield the power that he speaks of. That would belong to—"

"Back away from the girl!"

Shaleigh blinked and turned to see a short-framed woman with a long black braid aiming a crossbow at Talek's head. She might have been Hispanic if she were from the Human World, but her copper eyes were a color Shaleigh had never seen before. She wore full metal armor and her chest plate had the strange emblem of a rabbit on it. She moved the crossbow a hair and fired a bolt straight past Talek's head. Mawr jumped and Talek backed away as other soldiers came up behind her.

"Easy, Captain!" Talek shouted in a smooth voice, "I don't want any trouble."

The Captain advanced and Talek had his back to a tree with his hands raised. The Captain stood mere feet from him, her crossbow aimed at his chest. "Why else would you be slinking around the gates of the Garden? Aren't you usually more interested in Faeries? What interest do you have in an injured human child and—" She did a double take at Mawr who, even huddled on the ground, was taller than any man. "…and a lion?"

Talek made the foolish decision of trying to use the distraction to get closer. The Captain, however, didn't lower her guard for long and raised the bolt to his face again. "Oh, please give me an excuse," she smiled. "Any excuse for me to rid the world of your sick kind." She stepped forward and pulled the silver dagger from his belt and flung it to the ground behind her.

Talek eyed the blade with a frown. "That's rather rude,

don't you think?" Despite the confidence in his voice, Shaleigh could see his raised hands were trembling.

"Don't kill him, he helped us," Shaleigh pleaded. "We were attacked in the woods by a pack of wolves."

That didn't do much to help Talek's position. The Captain put the bolt to his throat. Surely if he could turn the Captain into a toad with a word or lop off her head with a look, as Mawr had said, he would have done it by now. Instead he looked as helpless as anyone else would with a weapon at their neck. "What were you doing in The Slumbering Forest? Answer me!"

"I—I was helping."

"For that matter, why were you with a pack of shadow wolves? Looking for new friends, or planning an attack on the city, you disgusting little roach?"

One of the guards came up behind her. "Captain Briar?"

"What is it?" she spat.

"What should we do with the girl and the statue, sir?"

The Captain didn't drop her weapon and Shaleigh had to bite her lip to keep from speaking up for Talek again. She had no doubt that he had been telling the truth, especially now. She wished she had accepted his offer when he had given it.

"Detach her from the statue and get her to the Healers. As soon as they're done with her, bring her to me. I want to take her to the High Faerie myself. As for the lion," she glanced over to Mawr's huddling form. "He can come inside, but I want four soldiers to keep an eye on him. We may need to question him."

"Yes, sir."

The guards moved around Shaleigh, cutting through the ropes that attached her to Mawr, and paused to figure out how to pick up the sled without causing her more pain. Shaleigh kept her eyes on the Captain and strained to overhear their conversation past the guards' mutterings.

"Isn't it illegal to kill innocent civilians outside of the Garden gates?" Talek asked as a trail of blood ran down his shirt. "Last I heard, your authority ended at that bridge." The guards had lifted the sled and were carrying Shaleigh towards the bridge.

Shaleigh sat up straighter. "He was helping us!" she cried out to them, but only Talek and Mawr glanced to her.

Captain Briar dug the bolt in harder and Talek winced. "I don't know what you've done, but I will find out." The guards and Shaleigh were on the bridge and heading towards the other side.

"If you're wise," the Captain snapped. "You'll put as much distance between yourself and my city as you can." She wasn't finished, but Shaleigh couldn't hear any further. Over her head a stone archway suddenly appeared, adorned with vibrant green flags emblazoned with a strange, black, crescent moon marking. The air was suddenly full of the sounds of the city.

"What?" she gasped as she looked around. It was as though the place had popped out of nowhere. She could see now that the bridge was actually a drawbridge that led into the hidden city.

A two-legged ox stood just beyond the end of the bridge and snorted at the guards as they passed carrying

Shaleigh. His big black eyes landed on her and he flicked his pierced ears in warning. Shaleigh's breath caught. It looked like a minotaur, the kind mentioned in the old legend of King Minos and his cursed child. A set of thick leather straps went across its chest and attached to the front of an old-fashioned carriage. As they moved further into the crowd, she could spot at least half a dozen more of the beasts intermingled with a ton of people. At least, she assumed they were people. Some had unusual eye colors, while others had weird silvery or golden gleams on their skin, and a few had vibrant pink or blue streaks in their hair. Of course, this could be written off as wearing contacts, having on tons of makeup, or enjoying multicolored hair dyes, but somehow having minotaurs walking around made things different. Regardless of what they looked like, all of them had their eyes on her. She felt her face grow hot and cracked a small, awkward smile.

A high-pitched squeal from the crowd made her jump. It was the only warning she had before an apple was thrown right at her face. She moved aside, barely avoiding it, and winced at the pain that flared in her leg. Why were they throwing things at her now? The guards around her didn't seem bothered in the least. They didn't even notice.

A tusked, furry striped boar that was tall enough to come to her knees erupted from the crowd. With its pointed tusks raised, it squealed again and darted straight for her. Shaleigh's eyes went wide. First, they threw fruit at her and next they sent beasts to hurt her. She brought up her arms, hoping that she could defend herself, but then she was being lifted into the air. It wasn't an even lift, one of the men nearly dropped her and was trying to keep his footing. She sucked in a breath as pain reverberated up and down her leg, reaching her thigh. The boar darted beneath her and emerged on the other side. It headed straight for the apple on the ground then returned to its master: a child dressed in little more than rags. There was chuckling from the onlookers and even the guards were chiming in with a few smiles and shaking their heads. They were laughing at her, Shaleigh realized. Here she was with a broken leg and the entire group was standing around mocking her for it.

Her eyes locked on the gate entrance, hoping that Mawr would come through behind her. He might be clumsy sometimes, but he was the only real friend she had here. If he walked in now, their laughter would stop and she would at least feel a little safer, but no one else came through. She thought back to Captain Briar's reaction to him, how shocked she had seemed. Would he be considered some abomination? He was the last of his kind after all, and Shaleigh wasn't sure what they would do with him here in this strange place.

The crowd closed in around them, moving on with their daily activities. The minotaurs pulled their carriages, and she could see glimpses of eyes peering out from the carriage windows. She was an oddity, a strange newcomer. She could hear their laughter, see their smirks, and caught some of their remarks as she passed. Despite all she'd been through, this was the first time since she awoke in this strange world that Shaleigh felt truly alone.

THE MARK

shadow fell over her and Shaleigh twisted around to stare up at the enormous building the guards were carrying her towards. Sections of it stuck out at odd angles, like a Jenga tower forced to stand regardless of gravity. It might have originally been made of wood, but each new section that was forced on was connected using stone where metal joints would normally exist. Doors and windows in a variety of shapes were painted in vibrant colors, making the whole building look like it had been plucked from a child's head and planted in the ground. There were round green doors, pink rectangular ones, even a purple one in a weird zig-zag shape. The stained-glass windows gleamed in the sunlight, and near the top of the building she could almost make out faces and scenes. It was perhaps the most confusing structure she had ever seen. It spoke of unrestrained eccentricity and dripped with madness. As they approached the double door entrance, a feeling of dread gripped her. More than ever she wished Mawr was with her. Somehow it was easier to be brave when someone else was so frightened.

She turned to the guard next to her, a short man with a cappuccino complexion, a thick black beard, and a red sash over his shoulder. She recognized him as the guard who had spoken to the Captain earlier.

"What's going to happen to my friend, Mawr? They won't hurt him, will they?"

"The lion? Is that his name?"

"He's from Aife," she said, and the bearded man frowned. "I know he looks dangerous, but I promise he's very gentle. He risked his life to bring me here. I just don't want anything to happen to him."

"The city of Aife has been deserted for nearly a century. You're telling me he's been living there all that time?"

Shaleigh nodded. She was taking a risk talking so openly about Mawr, but she was worried that they would jump to conclusions about him. He was quite an imposing statue and even the Captain seemed nervous at the sight of him. She didn't want him to be harmed for helping her.

The guard dragged his fingers through his beard for a moment. "I'll make sure they know that he poses little threat, though his actions will probably speak more than your words will."

"Will they let him stay? I don't want them to send him back to Aife. There's nothing left there."

"I'm afraid I can't say one way or another, child. But I can put a good word in for him and that should help in his favor." He narrowed his eyes as he studied her. "What's your name?"

"Shaleigh Mallett," she whispered feeling defeated. She had hoped she could do more than just put in a good word. She wanted Mawr safe at her side.

The bearded man smiled and tipped his hat. "Lieutenant Varg. If you want, I can keep you updated on his status. The Captain has put me in charge of you until I pass you off to the High Faerie, so I imagine we'll be seeing a lot of each other."

Shaleigh managed a small smile. The Lieutenant was pulled away to sign some paperwork as they stopped at the entrance just before the intimidating double doors. The doors were a thick, dark wood and each one was carved with a medieval-style tree whose limbs spiraled out onto the rest of the walls. It looked like something out of her father's fairy pictures. Above the doors was a carved placard that read: The High Castle of The Garden. If this was supposed to be a castle, it was unlike any that Shaleigh had ever seen. It didn't follow any of the architectural book designs she had at home, couldn't even be called fortified with all those doors. A few of the guards shifted arms and Shaleigh had to close her eyes as the pain in her leg resurfaced. She appreciated them carrying her, but every slight change sent needles through her.

Lieutenant Varg signed scrolls with a quill. She watched the black feather switch back and forth with his sloppy signature. She had never seen someone use a quill before and a strange queasiness came over her. It was bad enough being in this surreal world but having objects from history used as though they were common place made her feel disjointed. She didn't have a chance to dwell on it for very long though. The doors creaked open and they headed inside. It took a moment for her eyes to adjust to the darker corridors. But at first sight of the walls, all the discomfort she felt fled.

The halls were rounded and spiraled left and right, in ways that didn't always make sense. They were made of polished dark wood similar to that of the front doors and gleamed from the sunlight coming in through the stained-glass windows. The hallways split off in different directions from the entrance like the outer edges of a spider-web. Candelabras forked out of the walls like long-fingered talons, and Shaleigh got the impression they were walking up a gradual ramp. There were no signs or labels on anything, no arrows to point visitors in the right direction. At least the guards knew where they were going. It would be too easy for a stranger to get lost in a place like this.

After traversing down several spiraled halls, they finally came upon a rather boring-looking room with its door wide open. It was a plain square shape with plain white walls, and a dull gurney had been haphazardly shoved into a corner. Along the far wall were three basic beds that only consisted of a mattress and a pillow, no sheets. The room didn't belong alongside the gorgeous hallways. It felt like a quickly thrown together addition meant to meet some requirement. One of the soldiers reached out and knocked on the open door as they brought Shaleigh inside.

A man and a woman sat at a pair of simple wooden desks, both hunched forward and scribbling madly with their quills. All along their desks were piles of scrolls tied up with string or sealed in wax, either made of pristine white paper or old yellow parchment. Some were curled while others were crumpled as though a child had tossed them there. The guards eased Shaleigh onto the closest bed and Lieutenant Varg turned to the pair, clearing his throat. The scribbling didn't cease.

"This is Shaleigh. We have reason to believe she's from the Human World, based on her attire." The Lieutenant turned to Shaleigh and gave her a small smile that was meant to be reassuring but caused her stomach to clench. "There seems to be a problem with her leg."

The pair didn't even lift their heads. Shaleigh wondered if they were deaf.

The Lieutenant shifted awkwardly. "Captain Briar sent her along."

The woman finally turned and peered over a set of rectangular spectacles. "Captain Briar?" she asked in a nasal voice, then looked at Shaleigh, blinking rapidly as though only now realizing she was in the room. She turned to the man next to her, "Franklin, he said it's from the Human World."

"Hmph," the one called Franklin muttered, not in the least bit interested.

The woman gave a thin-lipped frown. "You lot can head along. We'll take care of her."

The Lieutenant nodded and motioned to his fellow guards, who exited the room first. Just before he reached the doorway, he turned and gave Shaleigh a concerned glance. "I'll be back later to fetch her. The Captain plans to take her to see the High Faerie."

"Yes, yes." The nasal woman waved away his concerns. "Come back in a half hour and we should have her ready."

Shaleigh didn't like the sound of that. She wasn't a medical expert, but she was fairly certain her leg was broken. Bones didn't mend in half an hour. The Lieutenant seemed satisfied though and gave a warm smile before pulling the door closed behind him.

Shaleigh sighed and turned to the pair. "I'm pretty sure it's broken. It happened last night when I fell..." She trailed off, thinking it best not to mention the business about getting kidnapped and falling from a winged bicycle. These two didn't seem too trustworthy or friendly.

The woman just stared at her, blinking, before she turned to Franklin again. "I said it's a *human*. Last I checked, they were in your area of expertise."

The man groaned. "Yes, I know." He sounded like a kid being forced to take out the trash rather than a skilled physician.

Shaleigh tried to calm her nervous heartbeat. "I'm sorry, but aren't you two supposed to be doctors?"

Franklin gave a snort and the nasal woman turned back around to her scribbling. He turned to look at Shaleigh, wiping his ink-stained fingers on a dirty looking cloth. He got to his feet and hitched up the waist of his pants with a grunt. "Let's have a look at you then." He strolled over and pulled out a monocle from the breast pocket of his blue coat. He didn't look at her leg, rather he looked at her face, particularly her eyes. He took hold of her chin and turned her face left and right, "Mm-hmm. Yes, definitely a human."

Shaleigh rolled her eyes. "Of course I'm a human. Would you mind looking at my leg instead?"

He frowned and pocketed his monocle before pulling

up the leg of her jeans that was still shredded around the wound. Shaleigh laid back on the bed, shuddering at the agony that went through her. She felt his probing fingers move gently around the flesh and forced herself to try and relax despite the pain making her jump.

"Yes, it sure does look broken," he chuckled, and she bit her tongue to keep from saying something terrible. Franklin already seemed reluctant to help, if she pissed him off...well he might use it as an excuse to avoid helping her altogether.

"Can you fix it?" she asked as kindly as she could.

"Absolutely," he said, heading towards a nearby table with supplies. "Might be a bit painful, but nothing a human can't handle. Let me see, I don't know who's going to cover the cost though. What do you think, Mel?"

"He said the High Faerie, so you'd best not cut corners," the nasal woman responded without looking up from her papers. "Give her the best for now. Someone will be forced to pay for it."

Franklin nodded and came back to where Shaleigh was resting. He put down a thick belt and her mouth went dry at the sight of it. She bit her lip to stop herself from asking what he would use it for. He gave a grunt and pushed the bed at an angle with the wall, then stood back, holding out his hands as though lining up a photography shot.

"What are you doing?" she asked, hopeful that Mel might say something if this was also considered cutting corners.

Franklin seemed to find her question amusing and chuckled. "Giving you the best." He went over to the wall and eyed a series of strings that were hanging from it. Shaleigh didn't want to know what those did either. He finally chose one and pulled it down hard. She heard something mechanical cranking above her head, and a wood slotted paneling dropped down with circular shards of glass molded into it. There was a red one, a blue one, and an orange one, the paneling turning as though it was attached to a wheel before stopping on fourth color - a yellow glass. It lowered closer to her, and the light from the windows filtered through the colored glass, encompassing Shaleigh's bed in a golden glow. Music began to play. The deep tones vibrated through her, making her teeth chatter together. The pain in her leg started to fade, her vision went hazy, and the world began to spin.

"What are you—" she tried to ask but her tongue stopped working.

Franklin nodded in satisfaction, a tiny grin on his face, and headed to the opposite side of the room. "Quit asking so many questions."

Shaleigh glared before falling into a fearful, golden sleep.

SLOWLY SHE AWOKE and saw the stained-glass windows moving. There was a persistent squeaking noise, like a broken wheel, and her first thought was of the flying bicycle she had found herself in before. Her eyes snapped open. Something felt wrong. She was moving, being pushed up a hallway on a gurney. She could feel the weight of a bed sheet on her injured leg, but that wasn't right. It needed to be put in a cast or brace. She wasn't ready to leave the Healers yet. Those two idiots probably got confused and sent her somewhere else. They seemed the type to find any excuse to not care for a patient. She tried to push up into a seated position.

"Easy now." Lieutenant Varg said, putting a hand on her shoulder as he smiled down at her. He continued pushing the rolling bed. His smile pushed aside some of her panic. At least he seemed to know what he was doing.

"My leg," she muttered, her words slurred. Her mouth still didn't want to obey. All she remembered was that warm, golden glow coming down around her. What had they done to her?

"I know," he reassured. "It probably still bothers you a bit. The Healers said there might be some lingering, memory pain."

Shaleigh blinked, trying to make sense of his words. "No, that's not it. They didn't do anything. They just put me to sleep."

He arched his eyebrows. "Oh? You sure about that?"

"Positive," Shaleigh stated as she sat up completely. He pulled aside the rolling bed and waited as Shaleigh pushed down the bed sheets to expose her ripped, bloodied pant leg. "See?" She said as she triumphantly pushed aside the torn jeans. "They didn't even—"

She paused and stared at her leg in silence. It was completely whole, completely repaired. There were large, dark blotches where her skin had stitched together. The skin felt sensitive but looked fine. She tried bending it, angling it in weird ways, always bracing for a bolt of pain, but there was nothing. "I don't understand," she muttered. "How did they do it?"

Lieutenant Varg rubbed his beard. "The Healers have a powerful magic. They specialize in repairing broken limbs and shucking out infection." He took hold of the gurney and began pushing it again, the smile never leaving his lips.

"I guess you're used to seeing people be amazed, huh?"

"Used to it? No. I just think it's grand. The Healers were imparted with magic from the High Faerie himself. They might not be the best company, but they're good at what they do." He moved the gurney around a pile of crates that were piled against the wall. "Besides I don't see why you're so surprised. After befriending a Living Statue and getting attacked by the shadow wolves, I don't see why a mended leg should come as such a shock."

She turned to him, "So you spoke with Mawr?"

"Oh yes, he seemed quite forthcoming, just as you said. I daresay there were several soldiers who weren't exactly keen to approach him though."

She nodded, remembering her reaction when she awoke to see him lying beside her. Even asleep, he was intimidating. "What's going to happen to him?"

"We're going to find out. We're meeting up with the Captain and then we'll present you to the High Faerie. I'll ask him about Mawr while we're there I suppose." The Lieutenant's smile fell when he spoke. It made her uncomfortable knowing this Faerie was going to be doling out, not just her future, but Mawr's as well. She would have to be on her best behavior to make sure that Mawr wouldn't be forced out of the city. Talek's words returned to her, *"Madam Cloom runs that city and she's been collecting your kind. There are many rumors about what she does with them, and none of them are good."* Shaleigh shuddered.

Captain Briar was waiting for them at a hallway junction with a sour expression on her face. "You certainly took your time, Lieutenant."

"My apologies, Captain. The Healers were—"

"Don't blame them for your delays," she snapped and led the way down another hall. Lieutenant Varg gave a heavy sigh but didn't speak further. They followed in silence and Shaleigh noted multiple guards passing by. They stopped and either nodded at the Captain or saluted as she passed. Then there were the people who Shaleigh assumed worked at the castle. A flustered, wheezing man appeared around the corner, wearing a large straw hat and pulling a wagon piled with bushels of orange and yellow flowers. As he passed them, the hall was filled with a lovely sweet scent. Surely a place that grew such wonderfully perfumed flowers couldn't be terrible. All the same, Shaleigh swallowed a lump in her throat and rubbed her hands together nervously. After a second her hands fisted at her sides as her stomach tightened.

They were traveling upwards. The hallway was inclining ever so slightly. She could make out the sound of birds echoing in the distance and wondered if they were going outside. Soon they walked through a wide archway that opened into a lush garden. The humidity and heat hit her all at once, making her gasp, but she also caught the smell of flowers—the same scent from the hallway. The walls were plated with hexagon glass windows that reached up to a glass domed ceiling. She realized they had traveled far higher than she had expected. Tall grasses shimmered with the wind in the distance. The field looked similar to the one she had thought existed across the bridge, but this one was full of steep hills and deep valleys. Vines with large coral-colored blooms grew up the sides of the walls as though determined to encompass the room in their vibrant color and heavy aroma. The floor had turned to cobblestone and opened into a rounded patio with an elaborate gazebo at its center.

A tall man with red, shoulder-length hair and dressed in an elaborately tailored black suit stood with his back to them. He waved his white-gloved hands around as though conducting an orchestra, only he was instructing the flowers instead of musicians. Shaleigh strained forward to get a better look. Big flower heads were lopped off at a flick of his fingers and hovered over to a series of baskets pushed against a wall of hedges.

"Teagan," the Captain said in greeting. "We've brought the girl from the Human World."

"Excellent," he stated in a silky voice. He dropped a few more flowers into their respective baskets and turned to face them. Both Captain Briar and Lieutenant Varg bowed low. Shaleigh was hyper-aware of how uncordial she was, lying partially under the sheets of the gurney, especially now with her leg healed. She tried for a small bow. Teagan came closer, a playful smile on his lips. His skin was a caramel brown but had a golden sheen when the sunlight touched it. Golden trails that looked like they had been penciled on spiraled outward from his cheekbones to his hairline. She couldn't tell if it was makeup or part of his skin and had to remind herself to breathe.

"Do you have a name, child?" he asked. His dark eyes seemed to pierce through her and Shaleigh found herself at a loss for words.

"Shaleigh Mallett," Lieutenant Varg answered for her after a pause. Shaleigh gave a mental sigh of relief.

"Her leg has been taken care of then?" Teagan asked, turning to him.

"Yes, sir," he said.

"And how long did it take them?"

"A little over half an hour, sir," Lieutenant Varg stated. "They took a while to figure out whose job it was to take care of humans."

Teagan gave a wry chuckle. "It's good to hear their training has paid off so well." He glanced to the Captain. "Has Madam Cloom seen her yet?"

She sighed and crossed her arms. "You said any human children are to be brought to you first. Unless those orders change, those are the ones I'm going to abide by."

"Good," he said, his face growing darker. "I wanted to make sure you didn't try to go around me. Like last time."

Captain Briar grunted but looked unsettled.

"What have you found on her so far?"

"Nothing yet," the Captain said. "I merely brought her in. The checking, I understand, is your job."

"Following your orders to the letter, Captain?"

She shrugged.

"Surely you understand the importance."

The Captain put her hands on her hips. Her lips curled into an unwelcoming snarl. "Look, that's not my area. I couldn't care less if she's got the mark." She looked Shaleigh up and down. "Besides if she is some powerful leader, she certainly doesn't show it. I wouldn't lay my sword down for her."

Teagan rubbed his forehead. "Of course, she wouldn't show any signs right away. That is why we're collecting them after all."

"Yes, but why are they always so young?" The Captain approached and Shaleigh tensed. "How old are you, girl?"

"Sixteen," Shaleigh whispered.

She laughed. "I've got rookies with more experience." She turned around and walked back to Teagan, staring him in the eye. "I understand Madam Cloom's position in this. She has no choice but to search because of how superstitious most of the civilians are in this kingdom." She crossed her arms. "But don't expect me or any of my soldiers to give credence to such madness. I have far more urgent matters on my hands than to waste my time chasing prophecies. Did you hear the shadow wolves last night?"

"Yes, I did," Teagan muttered, his posture faltering. "I imagine they were testing the defenses. They do that from time to time, as you well know."

"They came too damn close to the gates this time, Teagan. With a couple dozen soldiers, we could go into the woods and hunt them down for good. All I need is your approval."

"They keep to their territory, and we'll keep to ours."

Captain Briar stepped back in disgust. "Fah! That's Faerie logic if I ever heard it. We have trade lines you know, caravans that transport goods to the north. What am I to tell the merchants?"

Teagan looked toward the flowers. "Tell them to have faith in the Garden to take care of them."

"Like that's going to—"

"And send along an escort."

She took a deep breath. "How many are we talking about?"

"No more than twenty every two weeks. They'll have to organize times to travel as a group with the other traders, and if they don't like that, well—" He gave a sly smile. "Then they are certainly welcome to put up funds to hire a few off-duty soldiers or Seekers to accompany them. Those Seekers could stand to stretch their legs a bit more."

"That's ridiculous! None of them will want to—"

"Now if you'll excuse me, Captain, I have business to attend to."

Captain Briar gave a heavy sigh but turned away. "Come, Lieutenant. We have letters to write."

Lieutenant Varg turned to Teagan, "Sir, Shaleigh came in with a Living Statue called Mawr."

"Really?" Teagan cocked his head to the side, "Does he seem formidable? Would he be good in a fight?"

"No, he's easily frightened," Shaleigh blurted out. She had held her tongue for most of the visit, but with the mention of shadow wolves near the gates and dangerous trade lines, she feared him being used to carry goods or something. Teagan looked bemused, and Lieutenant Varg kept looking nervously at him as if waiting for him to snap.

"Please continue," Teagan said. "You seem to know this Mawr rather well. I was told that all the Living Statues had been eradicated centuries ago. I'm pleased to hear there may be some still alive and well."

Shaleigh swallowed hard. All three of them were staring at her and it reminded her of the uncomfortable stares she got at Dean Hammond's party after throwing her punch in Red Dawkins' face. Her face went hot, and she was suddenly fishing for words. "He...likes books."

"An avid reader then? Excellent. We could use an actual scholar on the Garden grounds for once!"

"Only he can't see. He used to have glasses, but they were broken."

Teagan turned to the Lieutenant. "Varg, isn't it?"

Lieutenant Varg went rigid. "Yes, sir!"

"Bring me a bit of glass, a bit of metal, and the measurements for Mawr's stony head. I'll see what we can do."

He gave a stiff nod, and the Captain chuckled dryly. "So, we make spectacles for giant cats now. I had no idea." She turned and headed for the hallway behind them, raising her voice so that it echoed throughout the glass room. "Before you start measuring that cat's head, we have the security of the Garden to take care of."

Shaleigh listened to their footsteps echo down the walkway behind her, mingling with Captain Briar's grumblings.

"Don't mind her," Teagan said with a wince, as though he could hear every word the Captain said under her breath. "She and I don't see eye to eye on many things, but her intentions are good."

Shaleigh nodded, looking anywhere but at him. She wasn't sure if this High Faerie was trustworthy or not, and she certainly didn't like being left alone with him.

"Thank you for helping Mawr."

He bowed, surprising her. "Certainly. Until we know whether you bear the mark of Master Cathal, you are considered a guest in our halls."

Shaleigh didn't want to think about what would happen if she didn't bear this mark. "What do you mean by a mark?"

"Ah, yes," he chuckled. "You're probably confused. Tell me, have you noticed any unusual changes lately? Some skin sensitivity, perhaps? Unusual pigmentation, maybe even recurring pain anywhere?"

Shaleigh had a sinking feeling as she recalled Kaeja's cold fingers against the small of her back. She didn't know where that blotch of skin had come from. It didn't hurt or anything, and she had completely forgotten about it until he asked.

She must have looked surprised because Teagan nodded. "I thought as much."

"How—?" she started to ask, but he cut her off.

"Never mind that." He turned her bed around and started carting her back down the hallway. "I'll need to examine it more closely to see if it matches what we need."

Shaleigh clutched at the bed sheet. She wasn't sure she wanted him or anyone else examining her back, regardless of how attractive he was.

"So, tell me, how did Shaleigh of the Human World make her way to Land of the Fae?"

"I was kidnapped." Her voice was shaking, and she had to clear her throat to continue speaking. "It looked like some kind of rodent person. He played a flute or something. Next thing I knew, we were flying through the air."

"Flying, you say?" Teagan smiled. "That does sound dangerous. Perhaps you can tell me more in the guest chamber?"

THE GUEST CHAMBER was rather plain and square, with only a small window that looked out over a bustling street. The bed was drab like the gurney she was brought in on. Teagan pulled out a small wooden flute and played a few minor notes and then put it back into his breast pocket. He must have seen her trepidation at the instrument because he said, "You've seen this used before, I take it?"

She nodded. "My kidnapper used something similar, only it was a pan flute."

"Ah, a pan flute! I haven't seen one of those in nearly a year." He gestured to a side room, "If you would step into the closet there and put on the smock you see clipped up inside. It's a simple thing, but it should fit you."

"What for?" Shaleigh didn't like where this was headed. Even the Healers didn't make her change clothes.

Teagan arched an eyebrow. "So I can examine the mark you clearly have somewhere."

"What if I don't have one?"

He smiled, "Oh, you do. We wouldn't have sent Colin to fetch you if you didn't."

Shaleigh gaped at him. "You sent someone to kidnap me?"

The door to the room opened and there stood her kidnapper. His hair hung in his eyes, his black, rounded ears poking out on top of his head just a tad. He slid into the room and clicked the door closed behind him, appearing to stand on his tip-toes with his large fur-clad feet. His eyes landed on Shaleigh and he jumped.

"You found her!"

Shaleigh turned to Teagan, glaring. "You sent this animal to kidnap me?"

Teagan looked absolutely shocked at her reaction, as though kidnapping people was a perfectly respectable profession. "Yes. When we learned that you might bear the mark, we sent someone to fetch you. Colin was our natural choice. He's quite...skilled."

Colin gave a bashful smile. "I don't know about that, sir. I lost her after all." He stepped forward with a grin, as though he was meeting a long-lost friend instead of a lost captive. "How did you survive? I thought you were crazy when you jumped. We were over the Ruins too! I figured you had some kind of death wish. I hear folks in the Human World get that pretty often."

"You thought I jumped?" Shaleigh couldn't hold back her rage any longer. She rushed forward, grabbing Colin by his white shirt, and pushing him against the wall. "I didn't jump, you idiot! I thought you were going to eat me!"

Colin put his hands up in fear, his eyes darting from her to Teagan and back again. "What? Why would I eat you? Are all humans from your world so paranoid?"

Shaleigh couldn't tell if he was dense or just trying to rile her up. "You kidnapped me! You've got claws!"

"So? What part of that makes you think I wanted to eat you?" He wasn't fighting her. In fact, he looked more shocked and terrified than angry. Shaleigh knocked his head against the wall as she released his shirt and walked toward the closet, trying to calm her temper. Teagan's laughter wasn't helping.

"I even asked you where you were taking me. You ignored me!"

Colin cowered in his spot against the wall. "How could I possibly hear you over all that wind?" He held up his bandaged hand. "Besides, you're the one that bit me, remember? Some of us can't afford to go to the Healers for every little scratch."

"That's enough, Colin," Teagan managed amid lingering laughter. "Try to treat Shaleigh with a bit of respect, won't you? In a few hours, she may well be on her way to ruling this land."

Shaleigh rolled her eyes. She got the impression the words were supposed to pique her curiosity, but it didn't work. "I don't want to rule anything. I just want to go home."

Teagan's voice lost its humor. "That is out of the question, I'm afraid."

"Why? You brought me here. Why can't you take me back?"

"Let me go ahead and make this clear for you." Teagan clasped his hands together and stepped forward as though about to deliver a eulogy. "You can't ever go back to the Human World. Regardless of whether or not you have the mark of Master Cathal, we simply can't allow that. If others knew of our world and found a way here, there would be no end to our troubles."

"But I promise—" She looked from Teagan to Colin, who was sitting on the floor avoiding her gaze. "I won't tell anyone. Not a soul."

Teagan sighed. "I'm afraid we've heard that before. That is in fact how many humans found their way here in the past. You can imagine how difficult it was for those of us living here. A flood of humans unfamiliar with our world and its dangers, attempting to steal something of value to take back with them. Only those few who survived and returned to their homelands met even worse fates. They were fortunate not to be locked up or slain for their supposed witchcraft." Teagan pursed his lips. "To be fair, the rules are as much for your sake as for ours."

Shaleigh was at a loss for words. Would she never get to see her father again? What about Kaeja? There was no telling how she had reacted when Shaleigh disappeared from right under her nose. Shaleigh didn't want to believe it. She couldn't believe it.

"Don't fret," Teagan added hastily. "We'll check for the mark first, and if it matches, then we'll present you to Madam Cloom herself."

Shaleigh felt a pit form in her stomach. "And if I don't have it?"

"Don't worry about that right now," he said with a dismissive wave of his hand. "We'll cross that bridge when we reach it."

~

THE SMOCK, as Teagan called it, felt more like an old potato sack. It itched her skin everywhere it touched, and she was pretty sure she could make out faded lettering on the front. She stared at herself for a long moment in the mirror, frowning under the layer of grime. Her hair was tangled with bits of grass, twigs, and something that might have been dried blood. She really hoped it was hers and not the wolf who had been killed in front of her. Her eyes were wide and she looked haggard; the potato sack really wasn't helping.

She stepped out and Teagan gave her a blanket in case she needed it. She wrapped it around her legs, grateful for the additional warmth. At least the blanket was soft.

"Alright then," Teagan said. He had taken off his jacket, hanging it on the inside of the door, and rolled up his sleeves. "Tell me where it is."

Colin blinked, "I never saw it, sir."

He sighed, "I wasn't talking to you. Shaleigh?"

She swallowed to ease the dryness in her mouth and a shiver went down her spine. She pulled the blanket closer around her and closed her eyes. "On my back," she whispered. "On my lower back."

The two men were silent for a moment as Shaleigh sat down on a chair with her back facing them. "Go ahead then, you want to see it so badly."

"Colin, perhaps you should step out."

"Of course, sir," he muttered and Shaleigh heard the door open then close. Teagan sighed, and the bolt of the door locked into place. Shaleigh tensed. She understood that with the power Teagan had, he could probably prevent her from leaving the room if he wanted to, and here she was sitting in a potato sack.

"I am sorry about this," he whispered, and she felt him roll up the back of the sack exposing her bare flesh.

Shaleigh tried to treat it like an uncomfortable doctor's visit, although it was anything but. She focused her gaze on the wall, trying not to think too much about the fingers that probed her lower back. Her breath came in short bursts and she could feel her pulse throbbing in her temples. She wrapped her fingers around the edge of the sack and twisted a spare thread between her thumb and finger.

"It's remarkably similar," he muttered to himself and got to his feet, not bothering to roll down the sack. She shivered as a cold breeze hit her from his movement and felt goosebumps spring up on her arms. She watched Teagan move beside the bed and stare up at a painting on the wall. It was the first time Shaleigh had noticed it, but the way Teagan studied it got her attention. An older man with white hair and a cheerful grin sat in an elaborate chair with his arm awkwardly placed across his chest. It looked like a weird position for an artist to use, at least until she saw the strange pale mark on his bronze skin. It looked like a crescent moon with a three-pronged burst coming off the back-end. It was the same symbol she had seen on the flags outside of the castle. She had to admit, remembering back to her own mark, that it looked disturbingly similar.

"The flare isn't quite the same, but I've never seen another so close."

"What does it mean?"

He clasped his hands behind his back and turned to her. "I'll need to take you to see Madam Cloom right away. We'll need to get you clean first, and properly dressed. She'll never admit you in your current state."

He pulled out his flute and played another tune, higher pitched than the last. That must mean someone else would arrive soon. Shaleigh rolled down the sack just in time before the door opened. A dwarf woman entered dressed all in blue and white. She smiled at Shaleigh and little crinkles formed on either side of her eyes.

"How are you, dearie? You must be Shaleigh." She put out both hands to shake hers.

"This is Meryl, one of the imps who work for the High Castle," Teagan introduced.

Meryl did a short curtsy. "I'll be taking care of you." She glanced at Teagan. "I assume she'll need a good scrubbing?"

"Definitely." Teagan smiled and put a hand on Shaleigh's shoulder. "Take good care of her, won't you? She's had a rough time of it."

"Yes, I heard about the—" Her eyes went wide. "Oh my goodness! Look at your poor leg!" In Shaleigh's current dress, her legs were exposed, and the skin around her knee was dark and blotchy from healing. Meryl leaned down and stroked it like a cat. "You poor thing," Meryl fretted. "Don't worry, I'll make sure you're ready."

"That's okay," Shaleigh said, not liking the way Meryl pawed at her and drew back her leg. "I can bathe myself."

"Are you sure?" she asked, clasping her hands together. "I can help if you—"

"I know how to take a bath, thank you very much."

Teagan chuckled at her abrasive tone. "Very well. Meryl, you'll probably still need to draw her a bath, but let Shaleigh wash herself up if you would."

Meryl gave a heavy sigh. "If you say so, but she probably won't be very thorough. No offense, dearie, but I've never seen anyone from your land who knows how to do a proper scrubbing."

Shaleigh decided not to respond to that. It was bad enough being presented to Madam Cloom like some prized farm animal. Already she dreaded whatever outfit they would choose because she was certain it would have to be open in the back for her mark to be examined. She could do without all the sidelong insults too. They made it sound like her world was full of barbarians.

~

COLIN HAD BARELY STEPPED out of the room before Lieutenant Varg dropped a ball of paper into his hand.

"What's this?" he asked, trying to unroll it.

"Measuring tape. Come with me," the Lieutenant said with a sly smile.

Colin could make out the tiny numbers along the edges. It was hard to recognize at first because it was knotted up as though it had been flung and balled up multiple times. He thumbed back at the room.

"Master Teagan didn't tell me anything about—"

"And we don't need him to know about this, alright? Look," he gave the closed door a look before gesturing down the hall. Colin thought the secrecy was silly. Master

Teagan knew everything that happened in the Garden, or so they said, so why was he trying to sneak around?

The Lieutenant pulled him around a corner and put a hand on his shoulder. Colin had never seen the man act so little like a soldier, though now that he thought about it, he usually saw him when the Captain was around.

"We have a situation. That Living Statue that came in with Shaleigh? We need to take measurements of his head."

Colin narrowed his eyes. "And?"

"And none of our soldiers have been able to do it yet. I was hoping that you could—"

Colin put up his clawed hands. "Nope—nope, I did my part here. I brought her into our world, and that's the end of it for me. Besides, Master Teagan is my boss, not the Captain."

The Lieutenant sighed and stroked his thick, black beard. "That's the thing. If we can't do the measurements ourselves, then we have to get the Captain involved. You know how she is. I don't know how she'll try to take measurements then, and I don't want Mawr to get hurt. He seems nice enough, and he's probably the last Living Statue."

Of all the soldiers, it would be Lieutenant Varg who would try to pull on Colin's heartstrings. "Mawr? That's his name?" Even as he said it, he knew he would help. It was easier not to help somebody if you didn't know their name.

The Lieutenant started down the hall, keeping Colin beside him as they walked. "That's right, and he's a friend of Shaleigh's. So, you know, if you help out here…maybe you can try to get on her good side if she ends up being the reincarnation."

"We don't know that yet. She just got here."

The Lieutenant's dark eyes fixed on him. "And what if she is, Colin? What then? Who do you think she's going to take her anger out on first?"

Colin rubbed the back of his head. "You've got a good point. Okay, I'll help."

Lieutenant Varg slapped his back. "Excellent!"

BATHING WAS NOT AT ALL like Shaleigh had expected it to be. She thought when Meryl was ordered to draw her a bath, it merely meant she was going to heat the water up and let Shaleigh wash, but it was nowhere near that simple. There was a fireplace in the corner of the bath-room that must have been lit earlier. Over it hung a great black pot of water that was hot enough to give off steam.

Shaleigh paused midway into the room. "I'm just taking a bath, right? What the heck is that for?"

Meryl clucked her tongue and held her hand over the pot. "It's not quite warm enough yet, dearie. I'll need to tackle that hair of yours first."

Shaleigh clutched at her hair, frowning at the bits of grass and dirt that came free on her fingers. "I can wet it in the tub," she said, backing away as Meryl came toward her.

"Nonsense! We'll have to take out all those..." She waved a hand around her head. "All those things!"

Shaleigh tensed. "Those are twists, and they took

hours to put in." They were also rather expensive. Kaeja had offered to put them in months ago, but her well-intentioned attempt made Shaleigh look like she was balding in places. Ever since then, Shaleigh had gone to a hair dresser to get them done.

"Now don't fight me on this," Meryl scolded, her voice dropping low. "I don't want to fetch Master Teagan and have him force you to let me do my job. You can't be seen by Madam Cloom looking like a wild child who just crawled out of the forest. That wouldn't look proper for either one of us, now would it?" She had looked like such a sweet old lady at first, but now there was something about her that made Shaleigh nervous.

Shaleigh pulled a twig out of her hair and noticed that many of her twists had already been removed anyway, probably from the fall into the lake earlier. With a heavy sigh she sat down on the edge of the tub in defeat.

Meryl laughed, "Oh come sit down beside me on the floor, dearie. There's no way I can reach you up there."

Shaleigh did as she was told and tried to push aside a pang of guilt as Meryl began unwrapping the twists piece by piece.

"Don't be so upset." Meryl patted her cheek like a child. "You've really got a chance now that you're going to see Madam Cloom. Unlike most humans in these parts."

It felt weird to be congratulated on a skin anomaly that Shaleigh wanted nothing to do with. "What would have happened to me if I didn't have the mark?"

Meryl's expression grew strained. "Well you certainly wouldn't be in here with me." She forced a short laugh.

Shaleigh waited for her to finish before pressing again. "So, what would have happened instead?"

Meryl was silent a moment, then sighed. Her fingers worked quickly against the snarls of her hair. "A strong girl like you would have probably been sent off to the Pasture. Or maybe with your good manners you would work as a shopkeeper's assistant in the Marketplace."

She frowned. "I got the impression it didn't always end up in a new job position."

The short woman let out a long breath. "It all depends on Madam Cloom's mood. She knows what the Garden needs after all, and if we have a shortage of farmers or shopkeepers, she would send you there. Otherwise, she might use you for a bit of entertainment." She turned to glance at the door to the bathroom and lowered her voice. "Sometimes they'll get traded as servants with the kingdoms to the north, or if you're lucky, you might get chosen to be in one of those human harems I hear they collect up there." Meryl's eager expression made Shaleigh's jaw drop in horror. For some reason, the squat woman interpreted that to mean she should continue. "If no one has any use for you, you could be chosen to be a villain in a play. That way the suffering looks are even more realistic for the crowd."

Shaleigh's eyes went wide. "And people know about this?"

Meryl cleared her throat, "Of course they do. Sometimes they'll get angry if there hasn't been a real bloodletting in a while." The excitement that entered her voice sent a shiver down Shaleigh's spine. As kind as she might appear, there was far more to little Meryl than Shaleigh had expected. She would have to be careful.

Shaleigh sat in silence as the rest of her hair was untwisted and soon the pot was boiling and hissing. "Perfect timing," Meryl said and rolled the tub over to the black pot. She picked up a long metal pole and pulled a latch to pour the boiling water in.

As the room was filled with steam, Shaleigh asked, "We're going to let it cool off first, aren't we?"

"Of course, dearie! I wouldn't want you scalded now, would I?"

SHALEIGH LET the hot water wash over her and closed her eyes. The steam filled her lungs and she leaned her head against the side of the porcelain. Meryl had put in rosehips and some oils into the water that filled the room with a fresh, flowery scent. It made her think of the fountain in Dean Hammond's garden. Had that party really only been a few days ago? It felt like years.

The room was quiet other than the muffled voices from the next room. She had to push Meryl out so she could get into the tub without the woman watching critically. Despite what Teagan had told her, Meryl acted as though Shaleigh didn't know how to bathe herself. Shaleigh closed her eyes and dipped underwater a few times, enjoying the feel of the hot water rolling down the back of her neck.

She couldn't remember the last time she had taken a hot

bath. The bathroom she had at home only had a shower and a toilet; the only bathtub she knew of was the one in the master bedroom that was attached to her mother's room. A chill crept up her arms and Shaleigh slid deeper into the water to fend it off. She hadn't allowed herself to think of home, not since the first day when she passed out beside the lake.

She thought of her dad now and could almost envision the look on his face when Kaeja told him the news. His jaw would drop, and his eyes would bulge; his glasses would slide down and go crooked on the bridge of his nose. Then he would excuse himself, and go lock himself up in his room or his car and then...

The air felt heavy and thick, and her eyes snapped open as she pushed up into a sitting position. "Please Dad," she whispered to the empty bathroom. "Please don't kill yourself."

She hugged her knees tight, knowing full well that he wouldn't be able to hear her, and it could already be too late. He had always teetered on the edge though, hadn't he? He had always been a little unsteady, a little off. He might even think Shaleigh had run off, just like her mom. She pressed her palms against her eyes, using the hot water to wash away the tears.

A knock at the door made her jump, and the water sloshed around her with a mind of its own. "Yes?" She hoped she didn't sound upset.

"Just making sure you're doing alright in there." She could imagine the toothy smile on Meryl's lips. "Did you find the soap alright? The towels too?"

Shaleigh heaved a sigh. "I'm fine. I'll be out in a minute." She tried not to sound short, but it was difficult when she felt so frazzled. She splashed water on her face, more to make the sound for Meryl's benefit than to wash up. She couldn't let herself get dragged into those thoughts. She would end up no better than her father, thinking of the same problems again and again until they consumed her, and right now she needed to focus.

Meryl was the second person who had warned her about Madam Cloom. First Talek and now her. At least now Shaleigh knew precisely what to expect. If she were lucky she might be turned into a laborer in the fields or a shopkeeper...or put in somebody's harem. Otherwise she could end up killed for sport in the middle of a play. She had to hope that the weird blotch of skin on her back meant something to someone. That was her ticket to survival. Madam Cloom was the person she had to impress, however terrible she might be. If she could earn her respect, perhaps she could even find a way back home. Teagan had the ability to do it, but wouldn't. Maybe she needed to try to get in touch with Talek instead. He had offered to help, but it would be limited. He couldn't behead soldiers with swords aimed at his throat, but maybe he knew of something.

She stared up at the wood-paneled ceiling looming over her. She thought of her dad lying back in a tub similar to this one with pictures of the two loves of his life on either side and a razor in his hand. She shuddered, muffling a cry against her hand. No, she had to get back to him. Regardless of what Madam Cloom, Meryl, or anyone else thought, she had to get back. Her father needed her.

Shaleigh picked up the soap and washcloth and bathed

herself carefully, mindful of Meryl's words. The water was tepid now, but she felt more focused and confident than she had in days. She had a direction, though it was a cloudy one.

~

SHALEIGH STEPPED out of the tub, not quite certain what to do to let it drain. She dried herself off but then couldn't find a robe or anything to put on. She had to settle for wrapping the towel around herself and poking her head out the door to ask for help. Teagan and Meryl were sitting opposite each other on a set of chairs nearest the window.

"I'm done," Shaleigh called. Meryl popped to her feet and hurried over. "I couldn't find anything to wear though..."

Meryl frowned as she approached. The expression went from kind to menacing in an instant, and it caught Shaleigh off guard. "Oh, do you really call that drying off, girl? You silly people from the Human World. It's amazing you can even walk straight!" She chuckled, but Shaleigh didn't like the look in Meryl's eyes. The little woman tried to enter the bathroom, but Shaleigh kept her foot planted on the door, blocking her. Shaleigh was only wearing a towel, and—worse yet—it didn't quite cover her butt. Meryl hadn't done anything dangerous yet, but there was something in her words and the way she moved that left behind a haze of unease.

Shaleigh gave a weak smile trying to stall. "That's okay, just give me what I need to wear, and I'll put it on."

Meryl looked up at her, that plastic grin not meeting the hardness in her eyes. "You probably wouldn't have the slightest idea how to put it on. Let me in and we'll get you dressed in a jiffy." She pushed again and Shaleigh's foot slipped slightly against the moist floor of the bathroom. The door opened a couple of inches further. Shaleigh wouldn't be able to hold her towel and keep the door jammed for much longer. Meryl pursed her lips.

"Such a rude girl!" Meryl snapped. "Just let me inside already. Your kind are always making me work even harder to do my job. As though cleaning up after you isn't difficult enough." Meryl's voice lowered to a snarling menace and her sweetness melted away completely. "Quit making me look like a fool in front of Master Teagan, girl, or you'll regret it!"

"Meryl." Teagan was striding up toward the bathroom door, towering over the tiny woman. Meryl's eyes went wide and her lips curved back up into a meek smile as she backed away.

"I'm sorry, sir, but she won't let me attend to my duties."

"Your duty is to make sure Shaleigh is happy. Does she look happy to you, Meryl?"

Meryl glanced upward in sourness. "No, sir." She added hastily, "But my duties also include her being well-kept. How am I supposed to do that when she won't even let me near her?" The menace was coming back into her voice and Shaleigh planted her foot in case she tried to force her way in again.

Teagan kneeled to look her in the eyes. "Must I remind you, Meryl, that your duties are whatever I ask of you?"

The squat woman shrank away from him. "I'm—I'm sorry, sir. I just—"

He smirked, "You just thought you could determine your duties on your own?"

"No, sir! I just—"

He lifted her chin and Meryl rattled like a dried leaf. "Such shameful work will have you outed from High Castle, Meryl. Keep that in mind the next time you decide to bully any human in my Garden."

Meryl's big eyes went glassy with tears. When she spoke, all the fire had left her voice, and she looked more like a child than a grown woman. "Yes, sir."

"Now get out of my sight. I don't want to see you for the rest of the week."

She nodded, too choked up to speak, and hurried out of the room.

Shaleigh stood frozen, uncertain what to do. Her hold on the door loosened while she waited for Teagan's anger to turn on her next. Instead he gave a long sigh when he stood up.

"I am sorry about that. She's always had a distaste for humans, especially ones from your world, but I had hoped she could work through it by now." He turned and frowned at her towel. "Hmm, let me see if I can find you a robe in here. Just a minute."

He went to the closet and Shaleigh let out the breath she had been holding. She leaned against the door, letting her forehead rest against the wood. The humidity of the room had made her break into a sweat, or perhaps it was Meryl's doing.

"You're not too upset, I hope?" Teagan said as he

rummaged through the closet.

"I'm alright," Shaleigh reassured. Her heartbeat was speeding, but Teagan's calm demeanor helped to put her at ease. Unlike Meryl, he didn't seem to have that layer of danger hiding under the skin. She needed to be careful though. Everyone seemed terrified of this man, and it was probably for good reason.

Teagan emerged with a black cotton dress and handed it to her. "Put this on. I truly am sorry for her behavior."

Shaleigh took it and closed the door again. "It's alright. She just...took me by surprise I guess."

She slid the dress on, annoyed at the fresh dampness on her skin and how it made the simple cotton cling to her body. When she stepped out of the bathroom, Teagan was spreading outfits on the bed.

"Meryl is usually assigned to keeping the rooms and helping guests, but I'll make sure she keeps her distance from you."

Shaleigh dragged her hand along the edge of the bed, thinking suddenly of her mother's room and of her father. She dragged her fingertips across the soft fabric, thinking of home. "You ordered Colin to kidnap me, right?"

Teagan paused and turned to her. "Come now, kidnap is such a harsh word."

"Why can't you have him send me back then?"

He stared at her for a long moment, then held out his hand. "Come. Let's have a seat and talk."

Some part of her wanted to refuse him, but then again, she was asking for his help, wasn't she? With reluctance she pushed down the threatening anger and took his hand. Teagan led her to the chairs where he had been sitting with Meryl a few moments before. Shaleigh curled her legs underneath her and watched as Teagan clasped his hands together, searching for the right words. She had seen this body language before. Dean Hammond had used it often when dealing with angry colleagues.

"I know this is difficult for you. I know this world is very different from yours and that you probably miss your family."

"And friends," Shaleigh added pointedly.

He gave a small smile and looked away. "Madam Cloom would never want you to leave. She's afraid if someone returned to the Human World again, other humans would come and try to conquer our lands. It may sound far-fetched to you, but they've attempted it before."

"I wouldn't do that," Shaleigh insisted. "I wouldn't. I have no interest in bringing anyone back here, I just want to go home. I don't belong here. My father, he—" Her voice caught in her throat and she had to swallow. Teagan watched her closely; there was sympathy in his dark eyes, or perhaps pity. Shaleigh pushed through, "I'm worried about him. I used to take care of him and I'm worried about what will happen to him if I don't come back. He might hurt himself." The words hung heavy in the air. Somehow saying it aloud gave the possibility even more power.

Teagan took a heavy breath, looking uncomfortable and at a loss for words. He stood and walked over to the window, clasping his hands behind his back, staring out into the busy street. "I'm sorry, Shaleigh. Please know that I understand your concerns." He turned back to her, "But we need you to do this. Madam Cloom is merely a temporary ruler—a caregiver, you might say—but she is not our true leader." He paced back and forth, his gaze distant. "She has very little compassion and is quite vicious. Your mark is the closest to Master Cathal's that I've ever seen. If you're not his reincarnation, then you're the closest I've seen in nearly two hundred years."

Shaleigh looked back to the painting on the wall with the white-haired man in the chair. "Is that him?"

Teagan nodded, "Yes. Master Cathal founded this city. It was his magic and his skill with a blade that ensnared the Pello Pines as you saw them in the Slumbering Forest."

She thought back to those inky black vines that coiled like snakes around their slumbering victims. She thought back to the sky that had gone from day to night in only a few paces. "That was Master Cathal?"

"Yes. He foretold that he would return to guide the Garden again one day, for it was his life's work to bring hope back to the lost lands that had once been ruled by those killing trees. He said we would be able to recognize him by his mark." He nodded toward her. She placed a hand on her lower back and fancied that she could feel it beneath the dress.

"I thought I had skin cancer."

"That is a possibility, of course. Master Cathal wasn't nearly as detailed as I wish he would have been, though he was always unpredictable. Many a night, I've wondered if he didn't simply tell us that as a farce." There was a soft-ness that came over his words when he spoke of the man, and he didn't meet her gaze.

"So, you knew him then."

Teagan gave a bitter laugh, "Oh yes. I knew him quite

well. He is the magician who bound me to the Garden, and inadvertently to Madam Cloom."

Shaleigh looked back up at the white-haired man in the painting. He looked nothing like her really—his skin was a golden bronze where hers was a dark brown. His jaw was square-shaped and hers was straight. She was tall and gangly, where he looked short and muscular. Even his lopsided grin looked nothing like her smile, and it was utterly out of place in such a fancy portrait. There was a cheerfulness in his expression that Shaleigh had never worn herself, nor had she ever seen in her father.

"It's definitely not genetic," she said. "If I do this, if I prove to be his reincarnation, could I order you to take me home?"

He smiled. "If you become our new leader, I will take you wherever you wish."

It was a long shot at best. Shaleigh had never considered herself a leader. She certainly didn't put any faith into that silly reincarnation story. She just happened to be lucky enough to have a mark that looked like Cathal's—or unfortunate, enough depending on how she looked at it. But this was her only ticket back to her world unless she could get in touch with Talek somehow. That would be difficult, but at least if this reincarnation mess fell through, she could hopefully rely on Talek's assistance to get home. Whatever it took to get back. She had to; her father might die otherwise.

She took a deep breath. "So, it all goes back to Madam Cloom then."

"Oh yes, nearly every path in the Garden goes back to her."

"What do I need to do?"

"Impress her." Teagan walked over to the bed and motioned to the outfits he had laid out. "That begins with an appropriate outfit. I wasn't sure what you would prefer, so I picked a few different options."

Shaleigh walked by them, letting her fingers drag over the fabric as she studied them. The first was a gown with shimmery red fabric that looked fairly modest from the front, but the back was a steep V.

She frowned as she picked up the garment. "To show off your mark," Teagan added noticing her look. "She will want to see it prominent on you at all times."

Shaleigh sighed. She wasn't a fan of wearing dresses to begin with, but the red dress also looked like it would be a tight fit and restrict her legs. She didn't like the idea of not being able to run if she needed to. The second was a light teal color that looked like a jigsaw puzzle of wraps and ties.

She picked up a strap and turned to Teagan with a snort. "Is this even an outfit?"

He shrugged. "My apologies. As I said, I wasn't sure what you would prefer, and your mark is in a very... unusual location."

"At least it wasn't on my boob."

Teagan put a hand over his mouth to keep from snorting.

The final outfit Teagan chose had a leather skirt that she liked because it reminded her of the armor that Captain Briar wore. The top, which looked more like a workout bra than a shirt, was made of the same leather fabric. The skirt had a belt attached, and both the skirt and the top had laces that went up the back. Her midriff would be bare, but at least it would be comfortable. At least it would stay on. If Kaeja were here, she would be able to pick something out and explain exactly what all the parts and pieces were, but Shaleigh's eyes would always glaze over when she spoke about fashion.

"Didn't you say Master Cathal wielded a sword too?"

"Yes, he was very talented."

"Then this one is appropriate, isn't it?"

Teagan nodded. "Yes, I would say so. It just isn't as protective as true armor."

"It doesn't have to be," Shaleigh said. "It just has to give the impression of a warrior."

Teagan held up the red gown again. "Are you sure? These gowns are rather nice as well, and both are colors that Master Cathal rather liked."

"That red one is too restrictive. I'd barely be able to walk in it, and that one looks like a cat toy. This outfit is at least sensible."

He laughed and shook his head. "You make a good point. Now I'm almost embarrassed to have pulled them out for you."

"Don't be. The only reason I know anything about this is because my friend Kaeja back home was into fashion. She wouldn't approve of any of these, but I can only do so much, you know?"

He gave her a sad expression. "Believe it or not, I do know precisely what you mean." He turned away to put the other outfits back in the closet. Shaleigh headed to the bathroom to change. To be honest, she was actually looking forward to trying on her new clothes. Yes, it wasn't real armor, but it felt like it, and she would need all the confidence she could get.

WHEN SHE EMERGED from the bathroom, a little uncertain, Teagan was waiting for her. He gave a wide smile as he saw her, and said, "It fits you quite well!"

"You think so?" She paused. "I don't know, I feel out of place in it."

"Then perhaps it's appropriate, considering your situation." He walked around her, stopping at her back. "It could probably be tightened a bit. Tell me if it's too much." She waited as he tied everything again.

"Does my mark show?"

"Oh yes, it's quite clear." He grabbed a pair of shoes he had placed by the bed and set them before her. "Judging by your taste in clothes, I thought those would work well for you."

Shaleigh wasn't sure what to expect. Sandals would have made her look like a Roman gladiator, but heels would have also looked strange, though they might be expected in such a regal meeting. Teagan had chosen a pair of flat boots, whose laces matched the rest of the outfit and somehow just worked.

"I don't expect you to be in a real battle," he said, and she could hear the amusement in his voice. "However, I thought it best for you to be steady on your feet."

She pulled on the boots and laced them up, only to frown when she noticed they were too big. "I don't think they fit me."

"Oh?" He stared at her feet for a moment. Shaleigh blinked as the shoes shrank down until they fit perfectly. "How about now?"

"That was crazy..."

He grinned, "I suppose it was, wasn't it? Come, I'll tie your hair back to finish the look." He pulled out a black ribbon and pulled her hair into a short pony tail. It was weird, not really doing anything to it and leaving it hanging loose. It made her feel underdressed at first, but Teagan's approving gaze helped. "Excellent. Won't you see for yourself?"

He took her back towards the closet where a full-length mirror was mounted on the wall. Shaleigh was amazed at what she saw. She didn't look like a city girl who was used to crawling around old buildings in her off-time, and she certainly didn't look like someone who had been dragged through a cursed forest behind a stone lion and chased by wolves. Her boots came up to her mid-calves and even though bits of her hair stuck out from where Teagan had pulled it back, it gave her an intensity she wasn't used to seeing. She looked like a fighter, a warrior, perhaps even a leader. She turned around and saw the blotch of pale skin on her lower back, so similar to Master Cathal's. It almost looked like a beacon against the rest of her outfit, but she didn't feel ashamed of it anymore. Instead, the sight of it gave her more resolve.

"Let's get this over with."

～

COLIN DIDN'T KNOW what to expect when Lieutenant Varg said Mawr was a Living Statue. He thought perhaps it would be a little stone boy or like those gargoyles they sometimes have in the Human World. He didn't expect anything so *big*.

Mawr was curled up in the corner of his stone cell with his tail wrapped around him and his head buried in the corner, as though he thought he could hide. It was the biggest jail cell they had in High Castle, and Mawr barely fit. It was certainly tall enough, but even curled up he took up a quarter of the space. Colin swallowed down the dryness in his throat.

"That's Mawr?"

The Lieutenant nodded. "You see why we had trouble. I think he's mostly scared of us, though nothing we say can really calm him down."

His words made Colin sympathize with the lion. It had to be frightening being in such a strange place. It was worse knowing that you were the only one of your kind— he understood what that was like. He took a deep breath. "Let me try to talk to him."

"Be my guest. Good luck." The Lieutenant crossed his arms and took a step back. At least Colin wouldn't be alone.

He tossed the measuring tape up and down in his hand as he approached the cell door. "Hi there, Mr. Mawr," he said, trying to smooth out the shakiness in his voice.

"Go away!" Mawr said, his shoulders tensing. He sounded like he had been crying. Could Living Statues cry? How did that even work? Colin pushed the thoughts aside.

"I know you don't like any of us right now, and I'm sorry about that. It sounds like you and Shaleigh barely survived the Slumbering Forest." He crouched down outside the cell.

The lion turned his head to look at him when he mentioned Shaleigh's name and Colin could see that his cheeks were stained with tears. His heart hurt. "Is she alright? They took her away and nobody told me what happened to her."

"She's fine," Colin reassured him. "They took her in and healed her leg. She's doing much better. Now Master Teagan is looking at her mark and she can go see Madam Cloom shortly."

Mawr shuddered. "I've heard of her. She's scary."

Colin cracked a smile. "She sure is. I think most of us agree with you there." He glanced back to Lieutenant Varg. "Even though some won't say it." The Lieutenant avoided his gaze.

Mawr turned around to face him, pushing his butt into the corner and wrapping his tail around his paws, making scraping noises as he got comfortable. He squinted at Colin. "You're a strange one, aren't you?"

Colin laughed, "Now that's not very nice! If we're being honest, we're both strange, aren't we?"

Mawr hunched down. "Oh, I'm sorry! I didn't mean to insult you. I just thought you looked different from the others. I'm so sorry."

He waved it away. "No worries. I get that a lot. I'm not exactly human, but I guess neither one of us are, are we?"

Mawr gave a small smile. Colin breathed a sigh of relief. "Look, my friend, Lieutenant Varg over here told me that none of his soldiers have been able to get measurements of your head today."

Mawr cocked his head to the side. "Measurements? I thought they were trying to strap harnesses on me or something!"

Colin laughed at that. "No, no, measurements! Master Teagan wants us to measure your head for..." He glanced back to the Lieutenant.

"For glasses," he hissed.

"For glasses!" Colin repeated cheerfully, then gave Lieutenant Varg a quizzical look.

"Oh, that would be wonderful!" Mawr said getting to his feet. "I haven't had glasses in so very long, and I miss them so much. I used to read ten books a day, and not being able to do that has been so painful."

Colin smiled as the Lieutenant unlocked the cell door and he carefully approached. He couldn't help but tremble at the sheer size of Mawr. With a single swipe, he could easily knock Colin out, but somehow he didn't seem the type. "What kind of books did you like to read? I used to drop by the library all the time before I came here."

"Everything really, but history was one of my favorites."

"You like history too?" Colin asked as he leaped up onto Mawr's back. The stone lion seemed wary for a brief moment, then relaxed as Colin deliberately dropped the tail of the measuring tape down so Mawr could see it. Colin guessed he couldn't see very well, but at least the tape looked nothing like a harness.

"Oh yes, I liked reading about dragons like Tanwen. I

never wanted to meet her, but I really liked her. She was so brave and strong—nothing like me."

In the distance, Lieutenant Varg gave Colin a thumbs up as he wrapped Mawr's head with measuring tape.

Colin grinned. "Tanwen, the dragon that eats people?"

Mawr shrugged and Colin had to hold on with his claws. "Nobody's perfect."

IF ALL PATHS led to Madam Cloom, then Shaleigh thought she must live at the very top of the city. It felt like they had been climbing steep hallways for the past ten minutes. She was beginning to wish there were stairs instead of ramps; at least then she would be able to see the ending.

"Here we are," Teagan said at last. He had been leading the way, but didn't seem the least bit phased by the climb. Shaleigh, on the other hand, was panting. His eyes narrowed in concern. "Are you alright?"

"Yeah," she muttered, leaning against the wall. "Just let me catch my breath a moment."

Teagan turned to the massive archway before them and Shaleigh followed his gaze. Ivy ran up the walls and a sweet, familiar scent wafted out from the chamber. It took her a moment to recognize it as the flowers that Teagan had been cutting earlier; the same ones that had been carted by when she was being escorted by Lieutenant Varg. She pushed away from the wall in an attempt to get a better look inside, and that was when she noticed the guards. They stood on either side of the archway with spears held in front of them, looking almost like statues.

They were each outfitted in armor similar to what Lieutenant Varg had worn, only without the red sash. Their arms were bare and judging by how built they looked, she imagined they were both quite skilled with their weapons.

She turned to remark on them to Teagan, only to notice how tense he had become. His warm demeanor from the guest room had fallen away. He stood tall with his hands clasped behind him, taking on the same persona that he had with Captain Briar back at the gazebo. It was more than that though—he was frightened. His dark eyes darted toward her. "Are you ready?"

Shaleigh nodded, unable to think of anything to say.

He held her gaze for a moment before stepping forward. "You'll need to speak up more than that if you plan to impress her." Shaleigh glared as he approached the guards. "Hail! I bring Shaleigh of the Human World to have an audience with Madam Cloom."

The man on the right, who had a dark bushy mustache, stepped forward with a smile, relaxed his hold on his spear. "There's no need for such formalities, sir. You're welcome at any time, as you know."

Teagan smiled tightly. "I realize that; however, Shaleigh needs a proper introduction to the way things work here." He waved a hand at them. "Present arms to her as you would to Madam Cloom, please."

The mustached man hesitated for a moment, then stepped back into position. "Yes, sir!" He bellowed out a series of commands that Shaleigh couldn't quite understand and then the two men thrust their spears into the air and crossed them at the center of the archway with a metallic clang.

Shaleigh jumped, but Teagan's warm smile returned as he gestured her into the chamber. "After you, my lady."

She took a deep breath and lifted her head. She hoped she looked confident as she strode into the chamber, and not like a fool. As soon as she was through the archway, the scent of the flowers was everywhere. She appreciated the smell in the hallway, but it was overpowering here. The chamber was about the size of a small concert hall, and every wall was lined in green ivy. The greenery poured upward like a volcano spewing ash to the sky. Woven amid the ivy were the pink- and orange-hued flowers she recognized; it was like a tapestry of vegetation. Tendrils of the vine crept upwards toward the domed glass. With a racing heart, Shaleigh turned to the ornate marble stairs that led to Madam Cloom.

The steps were tiered into four groups, and after climbing the first set, she could set eyes on Madam Cloom, perched atop her throne at the highest point in the chamber. She was smaller than Shaleigh had expected, with a large nose but keen, darting eyes. Even at this distance, she could feel her gaze on her, judging everything from her outfit to her hair to her stride. As she went up the final flight of steps, Shaleigh could feel heat from the late afternoon sun on her back and glanced backward. The glass dome of the room, she realized, was more than mere decoration. At this level Madam Cloom could see almost every point in the city. Sunlight streamed across the marble floor, making Shaleigh's shadow look like a fearsome gladiator. If only she felt like one.

There was another shorter set of steps that would lead directly up to Madam Cloom's throne, but Shaleigh knew better than to climb those. She stood for a moment, not quite certain what to do, then spotted Teagan a few feet from her side. He glanced down to the floor, and Shaleigh dropped down to a crouch.

"Madam Cloom," Teagan announced. "May I present to you Shaleigh Mallett of the Human World."

"Stand up, child," the woman's voice creaked like a well-used rocking chair. "I want to have a look at you."

Shaleigh got to her feet and tried her best to put on a stern expression, but based on the amusement in Madam Cloom's face, she must have looked rather foolish.

"Aren't you a dark little human. Young too, I bet you haven't seen your twentieth year yet, have you?"

"No—" Shaleigh started to say, but Teagan cut her off.

"I believe she is merely sixteen, Madam, but surely that is of little importance. We've had potential incarnations far younger than that."

Alright then, so Teagan needed to do the talking. She could handle that, though she wished he had said so to her earlier instead of discussing outfits.

Madam Cloom got to her feet. Shaleigh could hear the rustling of her skirts. She had her gray hair up in a loose bun on top of her head; her gown was a deep emerald that sparkled when it caught the afternoon light. Her gaze continued to judge and the thin smile on her lips made Shaleigh shift with discomfort. "I thought she was supposed to be Master Cathal's reincarnation, the great uniter, the kind leader, the gentle ruler; instead it seems you have brought me a warrior in training." She barked a laugh. "I doubt any of Captain Briar's troops would have anything to do with this scrawny whelp, and I don't see why I should either."

"I assure you, she is capable of calling upon the most unlikely of allies. It seems she found a Living Statue amid the Ruined City of Aife."

The woman shook her head and walked over to the window, leaving only her head silhouetted before it. "So," she shrugged, "she can befriend pathetic statues. From what the Captain tells me, he's hardly any threat. I don't see what's so impressive about that."

Teagan wore a strained expression and looked like he wanted to retort, but took a moment to compose himself. "The statue helped her escape a pack of wolves within the Slumbering Forest."

That seemed to pique her interest. Madam Cloom turned back toward her with a hint of disapproval in her expression. "Mingling with statues and wolves? You do know how to make an entrance I suppose, and build an army; a useless army, but still." The woman scoffed and Shaleigh grimaced. "You do have that in common with him." She settled back down into her chair, her gaze fixed on Shaleigh. "What of her mark?"

Teagan gave the barest smile. "It is indeed the closest I have ever seen to that of Master Cathal."

"But it is not exact?"

"No, Madam, but it is very close."

The woman was silent for a moment. "Have you no tongue, child?" she barked and Shaleigh jumped. "Can you not speak for yourself?"

Shaleigh glanced at Teagan, who looked concerned. Perhaps she misread him earlier. Perhaps she should have been the one talking this entire time. "Yes ma'am, I can speak." Her voice sounded small in this enormous chamber and it annoyed her.

Madam Cloom chuckled. "Your outfit is but a costume, isn't it? You certainly don't sound like a warrior."

"But I—"

"Oh, let's see it anyway. Bring her up, Teagan, let's have a look at this famous mark."

Teagan was at Shaleigh's side instantly, holding out his arm for her to take. She took it, grateful to have something to hold onto. She glanced at him, but his expression was unreadable, his eyes fixed on Madam Cloom. Any hints or tips he could give her were finished. She was on her own now.

Madam Cloom pulled out a thin set of spectacles as Shaleigh came up the steps. Teagan let go of her and motioned for her to continue to the throne. She stared down at her boots noticing how her bare knees poked out beneath the leather skirt, and the dark blotches that still speckled across her healed knee. Madam Cloom was right. This outfit was just a disguise. She wasn't a warrior, she was a high-schooler who liked to go on adventures with her camera. She was a teenage delinquent whose curiosity sometimes got her in trouble with the authorities. She was a daughter who was forced to take care of her sick father.

"Turn around and have a seat, child." Madam Cloom twirled a finger in the air when Shaleigh reached her. "Let me have a look at this mark that dear Teagan is so enamored with."

The woman had a sickening smile. Something about

the glee of it mixed with that holier-than-thou stare made a flicker of rage flare up inside her. Shaleigh crouched down on the floor, her knees squeaking across the cold marble and echoing throughout the chamber. She felt Madam Cloom's spongy fingers probe her lower back and an impulsive shudder went down her spine. She didn't mind Kaeja's fingers, or even Teagan's—but having Madam Cloom touch her in such a vulnerable spot made a frown tug at the corners of her mouth.

She understood now why the woman's smile bothered her so much. It was a smile she had seen before. It was that arrogant look that Red Dawkins had worn as he was spouting all the hatred about her father. It was the same smile that had made her ultimately toss her drink into his face. Shaleigh squared her shoulders, willing herself to be calm. She couldn't lose her head here, not in front of Madam Cloom. Not when so much of her dad's future and her own relied upon this moment.

"Turn around."

Shaleigh spun, mindful of her skirt, mindful of her noisy knees, mindful of the fact that her nails were digging into her palms with the effort it was taking not to lash out. Madam Cloom up close was no pretty petal, and her keen eyes picked up every single flaw Shaleigh had. She took Shaleigh's chin and moved her head this way and that, then that cocky smile came back.

"I don't think you're pretty enough to be Madam of this Garden. You don't look at all like a leader," she chuckled.

"I'm more than you think," Shaleigh said in a low voice

unable to keep silent any longer. "Perhaps you're too cowardly to deal with me?"

Madam Cloom's eyes went wide and Shaleigh heard Teagan take a couple of steps forward from behind. "Madam? Please, she doesn't—"

"Stay out of this, Teagan," Madam Cloom ordered without tearing her gaze away from Shaleigh. Her sickening smile was gone and Shaleigh thought she saw just the tiniest flicker of fear. "You've definitely got guts, girl. I'll give you that."

"I've got more than that in me," Shaleigh said, straightening her spine. "I've got Master Cathal's spirit in me. If you plan on killing me, I think you'll have a tough time doing it."

Shaleigh got to her feet and, for the moment, enjoyed towering over the short woman on her throne.

"Perhaps I misjudged you, child." Madam Cloom said with venom, "If nothing else, I suppose you will provide excellent entertainment. Teagan, prepare her to compete."

Shaleigh's shock was reflected in Teagan's response.

"Madam, are you sure?"

The woman chuckled, "Oh yes. If this child plans to prove that she is truly Master Cathal's reincarnation, let us see it play out in a match. I want to see how well this warrior can fight."

THE OVERLOOK

Shaleigh barely noticed Teagan take her from the throne room. They traveled down more hallways, but all of the gleaming wood and stained glass looked the same to her now. She had no interest in keeping track of where they were going. Her mind was stuck on Madam Cloom, the tiny woman in the enormous throne, and the words she had spoken that were now running through Shaleigh's mind.

Prepare her to compete.

Meryl had warned her that this could happen, but it wasn't right. She had won Madam Cloom over. At least, she thought she had. Did putting her into an arena to fight to the death in some bloody sport mean that she was considered the reincarnation or not? She had hoped that, one way or another, meeting with Madam Cloom would have put an end to her worries; instead she was just as confused as before, only now she knew just what kind of dragon she was up against.

"Here we are," Teagan said, breaking the uncomfortable silence.

Shaleigh blinked. This was a different bedroom than the one she had been in earlier. The drapes were drawn against the dwindling daylight, showing off a large bed with plenty of big, green pillows that took up only a small portion of the room. There was also a large sitting area and even a fireplace. Shaleigh stared at it, letting her eyes focus on the crackling wood and the lapping of the flames. There was something undeniably tangible about it. It forced her to remain grounded and not get lost in her confusion and unanswered questions. Teagan stood in the center of the room, his gloved hands clasped together and a troubled expression on his face.

"Why are we here?" she asked, not quite sure what to do next.

"This is to be your bedroom now. Does any of it...seem familiar?"

She stared at him. The crackling of the fireplace filled the momentary silence. It dawned on her that if she was the reincarnation of Master Cathal, she ought to be familiar with the place. Of course, Teagan knew the truth, didn't he? He knew that she was a fraud. He was possibly the only person in the entire building that would be able to know the truth. He meant well, of course, but she didn't know if he was trustworthy and she had to prevent Madam Cloom from finding her out.

Shaleigh sighed, turning to make sure the door to the room was closed.

"We're the only ones here," his voice was softer. "You can be plain with me."

She gave an apologetic smile. "Not a damn thing in here looks familiar. I guess it should though, right? I should have come in here and been like, 'Oh that's my favorite pillow!' or something."

He chuckled. "Something like that. Master Cathal didn't have a favorite pillow." He gestured to the throw at the base of the bed. "This was his though. Come, take a closer look." He picked up a candelabra from the nightstand and the wicks of the candles flickered to life. He brought the light over to the edge of the bed so she could see. Even then she had to lean down close to make out the detail.

The backdrop of the throw was a bright blue sky and row after row of tiny triangular trees, all stitched by hand. Little round, wooden houses bobbed between the rows with threaded smoke clouds trailing from their chimneys. She dragged her fingers across it, marveling at all the strands that had gone into making it. "This is beautiful. It ought to be framed."

"Probably," Teagan said quietly. "But he always insisted on using his favorite things instead of hiding them on a wall behind glass."

It made her think of her dad and his walls of pictures. Everything in his collection was framed or put on a pedestal, usually out of reach. She dragged her hand along the throw, noticing every little ridge of trees, every little puff of chimney smoke. "It takes away the feel of it," she said in understanding. "How can you appreciate something if you only look at it from afar?"

Teagan was quiet, and as the seconds dragged on, she

looked up at him. His eyes were studying her closely as the flickering candles cast shadows across his face.

She arched an eyebrow. "What?"

"I'm sorry, you just..." He turned away to put the candelabra back on the nightstand. "Your words sound very much like his."

"Come on, Teagan, we both know I'm no reincarnation." She folded her arms across her bare midriff.

"You lied to her then?" His voice was stern.

She shifted. "Uh. Not exactly."

He gave a mischievous smile. "You do know it is dangerous to lie to her, don't you?"

She rolled her eyes. "Oh, don't give me that. What choice did I have? If I didn't, she would have killed me. She looked like she wanted to."

"Yes...yes, I suppose she did."

"Not that it did me much good. I'm still going to be competing. What did she mean by that, Teagan? I'm no warrior."

He stood a bit straighter and clasped his hands together. She was beginning to think that was a nervous habit of his. "We will be putting on a performance two days from now. She'll want you to prove yourself in battle."

"I can't do that. I've never fought anything in my life!"

"I'm sorry, Shaleigh. I will do my best to help you. In the meantime, I will send in some food for you."

She shook her head. "I just want to sleep. I'm not even hungry."

He bowed low before her, and somehow the thought

of him leaving her alone to her thoughts made her panic more than the prospect of doing battle.

"What's going to happen to me?"

He stared at her for a long moment. "I'm afraid I haven't a clue. What I can promise you though is that I will do all I can to assist you, however limited it may be."

AFTER TEAGAN LEFT, Shaleigh stood for a while in the dark bedroom, listening to the fire pop and crackle in the hearth. She wanted to change, but she didn't see a wardrobe or a dresser anywhere. She doubted a pair of pajamas would be hung up in the closet but checked anyway. The closet was like a small room of its own with chairs and even a small circular window. Plain gowns, ruffled blouses, and simple skirts lined the walls. She walked inside and let her fingers graze the fabric. Cotton, knit, these were nothing like the outfits she had seen in the other room. Those had all been in vibrant colors and dramatic cuts, made to catch the eye. Soon weariness took hold, and she walked listlessly from the closet back to the bed with a yawn.

Part of her knew better than to sleep in a leather shirt and skirt, but she didn't care. She pulled back the covers and climbed into bed, surprised at how lumpy it felt. A feather flew up into the air as she got comfortable; the mattress or pillows must have been stuffed with them. She let her head fall against the pillow and stared up at the wooden beams of the ceiling. She was so very tired, but she was having trouble relaxing. Of course, that wasn't that much of a surprise considering she was a captive. It didn't matter how nice a room they gave her—she would still be a captive until she either proved herself or was killed.

Her fingers felt the mark at the small of her back, and the phantom feeling of Madam Cloom's rough fingertips returned. She reached down for the blue throw covered in trees. She pulled it to her face and breathed in the scent, smiling at the smell of honeysuckle. The scent helped to calm her hectic thoughts, her rattled nerves, and her sore back.

She fell into a heavy, dreamless sleep.

WHEN SHALEIGH AWOKE the next morning, Teagan was standing over her with a tight expression. The curtains were drawn back as she struggled to pull herself out from the heaviness of sleep. The warmth that Teagan had shown her the day before seemed to have drained out overnight.

"Come now, get up. Your bath is already drawn and Madam Cloom will be expecting you soon."

She nodded with a yawn and crawled out of bed, moaning as she realized how pinched she felt all over.

He sighed. "Goodness, you slept in that?"

She looked down at the faux leather armor which had covered her body in painful lines. She gave a sheepish grin. "I was tired."

He didn't find it even slightly amusing. Her smile faded as she stumbled into the bathroom. A small man about the size of Meryl with a grizzled beard came out and gave her a short glance.

"Hi," Shaleigh said, squinting, but he didn't respond. It was as if everybody was mad at her for some reason. The short man closed the bathroom door behind her as Shaleigh peeled off the outfit and slipped into the warm tub. She let her head rest against the edge and closed her eyes.

"Shaleigh?" Teagan's voice through the door made her jump. "Don't take too long now, we have an early appointment and a full day ahead."

"Okay," she mumbled and began to bathe herself. It was odd to be woken up by someone in the morning. For as long as Shaleigh could remember, she had been responsible for getting herself up and ready without the help of an adult to keep her on track. If she slept in, she had to deal with the consequences: either pay the bus fare to get to school, or sometimes walk. Either way, she would have to deal with falling behind in classes.

She learned at a young age that she had to be the responsible one in the household. Her father wasn't the type to nag her about not going to bed early enough or getting up too late. He had chuckled at the few notices she had brought home, and merely wanted to know where to sign. At first, she had thought his indifference was a blessing. None of the other kids at school had fathers who couldn't care less about the notices teachers sent home. They all had horror stories to tell. It was when she started getting into junior high that his care-free attitude had begun to lose its glamour. One of her classmates had asked if she even had a father. She had been forced to show his photo from the university website.

Shaleigh finished bathing and dried off before wrapping the towel around herself and heading into the bedroom. The short-bearded man was gone, and Teagan was pacing back and forth. She was beginning to think the kind, warm Teagan she had met yesterday was just as elusive as her father had been.

"There you are. Here, put this on, and come back in as soon as you're finished. I'll fix your hair, and then we can head out."

She put a hand through her wet hair, wondering if he understood how long it usually took her to get it ready. That wasn't a last-minute decision; it could take a full day of work unless he wanted to just tie it back again. She did as he asked, though, and slipped on the faded yellow gown that was far more modest than the skirt and top from yesterday. White lace embroidery detailed a V shape on her chest and the skirt had at least two layers to it, which made it more difficult to pull on at first. The sleeves came down just above her elbow and ended in thin lace ruffles that matched the waist of the skirt that fell to her mid-calf. She got the impression it was supposed to be longer, but she was rather tall.

When she stepped out, Teagan gave the first smile she had seen all morning. "Excellent! The color really brings out your eyes."

"Thanks." She had to take his word for it because she hadn't gotten a chance to see in the mirror yet.

"Have a seat." He motioned to a chair he had pulled over from the fireplace. "And I'll finish you up."

She did as he asked, wondering what he thought he could do. He put a hand to his chin and began walking around her slowly, as though she was an unusual sculpture and he wanted to find the best way to capture her on camera.

"You know this is probably going to take longer than a few minutes, right?"

"Nonsense! Why would you say that?"

She shifted uncomfortably. "I'm black," she said, hoping that would answer everything.

He was quiet a moment, then said, "I'm quite aware of the different skin tones of humans, Shaleigh, and of their different hair types. Please do not insult me."

Shaleigh bit her lip. "I mean, it takes a long time to get my hair done. Those twists Meryl took out yesterday took like four hours."

He arched his eyebrows and looked at her with a faint smirk. "Twists? Is that what you call them?"

She nodded. "Maybe we should just pull it back like we did yesterday?"

Teagan gave a low chuckle. "No, I liked your twists. I think I'll do that instead. Hold still now."

He stood up straighter and splayed his fingers out in front of her. Suddenly it felt like every strand of hair on her head was pulled outward at the same time, like her head was at the center of a plasma globe. It wasn't painful, but it was close enough to make her gasp. She glanced over to the mirror and got a glimpse of what was happening. Tiny amounts of her hair had been pulled out straight as though there were a hundred hands around her head, and slowly each strand was twisting on their own. Then, all at once, the twists fell against her neck again and Shaleigh sat there in shock. The work that had taken a professional hairdresser hours to complete, Teagan had finished in maybe two minutes.

"Go take a look," he grinned.

She eyed the twists in the mirror. Teagan hadn't done a perfect job, the twists weren't quite random enough, and she could see blotches of her scalp peeking through, but she could hardly complain. She shook her head around, smiling a little, happy to see how her twists bounced around with her. Behind her, Teagan laughed.

"Goodness, if I had known all it took to make you happy was to fix your hair, I would have done it yesterday."

"I'm sorry," she said, turning away from the mirror. "You just have no idea how much time that saved us."

"I can imagine. Magic is quite a useful tool, as you know." He set down a pair of pale yellow flats and Shaleigh slipped her feet inside them. They fit her perfectly, and she wondered if Teagan had used magic again to size them.

"Come now," he said as he headed to the door. "I believe if we hurry, we should arrive on schedule."

She followed Teagan through the halls, noticing that it was much busier than it had been yesterday. There was also an increase of soldiers.

"Is something going on?" she asked.

Teagan didn't respond right away but eventually admitted, "Nothing that you should worry yourself over." She couldn't see his face, but there was no missing the tension in his voice. She thought of Captain Briar the day before and the talks about the wolf attacks. For all she knew, battles could have broken out around the castle and wolves could be surrounding them, but she wouldn't have noticed behind these insulated walls. She tried to peek out through the stained glass as they passed, but she couldn't make out anything below that would indicate a war had started. Still, she felt rather silly getting caught up in her hairdo when something was obviously going on. They passed the steps that led up to Madam Cloom's throne room, but the hall continued upward, steeper than before.

By the time they reached another flight of stairs, Shaleigh was breathing hard. Teagan started up the next flight without even a backward glance. Shaleigh sighed and held up her skirt so that she could follow. Going to visit Madam Cloom tested her fitness far more than her explorations ever did back home. At the top of the steps, she could see daylight. Clear daylight, not filtered like it had been through the stained glass. Birds were chirping and she felt a slight breeze. When she finally could look out past the top of the stairs, Shaleigh was awestruck.

"WELCOME TO THE OVERLOOK." Teagan held out an arm before her. She was supposed to take it, but her feet didn't want to move. It was as though she was rooted to the spot by the sheer beauty before her. It reminded her of a flat footbridge, only it didn't connect to anything on the opposite end. It was simply an elaborate patio with a roof held up by pale columns against the robin's egg blue of the sky. Unlike most of the castle, this area was made of white stone that might have been marble. It gleamed in the morning sunlight and reminded her of the City of Aife, only here you felt as though you could touch the sky.

Vegetation grew over everything; every column was covered in it. A few pale statues stood in various areas, but the plants had been neatly trimmed to expose their colorless eyes and thin smiles. A rectangular table stood in the center and at its head sat Madam Cloom, whose eyes were fixed on her.

Shaleigh felt her body tighten. She knew magic was wonderful and all that, but her instincts were screaming at her not to enter this place. She had explored all sorts of decaying buildings back home, many places which had partially collapsed from decay. While she might not be able to describe it, she knew what solid structural support looked like, and this place didn't have it. With Madam Cloom sitting like a sated toad at the head of the table and Teagan's coarse attitude all morning, Shaleigh didn't know if she trusted either of them enough to step forward. Vines had crept into the dark alcove where Shaleigh stood frozen, inviting and urgent. It was too beautiful. She felt dizzy and put a hand on the wall to steady herself; suddenly Teagan was crouched at her side.

"Is something wrong?" His concerned expression shook the fear that gripped her. She glanced up to see Madam Cloom's smile broaden.

"It feels..." She closed her eyes and drew a deep breath. "It feels like a trap."

He was silent, and she could feel him studying her. "I assure you it's safe. I don't think you understand the power of the magic I wield. I built all of this by hand." He turned and glanced back to Madam Cloom. "Besides, do you think she would be sitting out there herself if she was at all in danger?"

Teagan made a good point. Madam Cloom may want her dead, but she wasn't about to risk her own neck in the process. He put a hand around her arm, and reluctantly Shaleigh allowed him to help her up the remaining stairs and approach the table. The breeze was cold but felt good against her trembling legs. She just needed to not think about how high up they were, or about how far the fall might be. Looking back at the entrance, she realized they must be at the topmost point of the castle. She pushed against the urge to dart back to the staircase and instead focused her attention on Madam Cloom.

The squat woman gave a thick laugh. "Oh dear, don't tell me you have a fear of heights..."

"No," Shaleigh said in a flat tone. "This place just didn't look..." She pushed away thoughts of the floor breaking away from the wall and tumbling to the ground far below. "It didn't look secure."

"Indeed." Madam Cloom was grinning ear to ear. "That's very good to hear. I would have a hard time convincing the people that you were a true reincarnation if you had a fear of heights. Master Cathal loved them! He's the one who had the Overlook built originally, wasn't he?" She glanced to Teagan, who nodded.

"He came here often to retreat from his daily chores," Teagan said. He was still holding Shaleigh's arm, which she appreciated because she wasn't sure if she could rely on her own two legs yet. He brought her over to the chair at the opposite end of the table and pushed her into it, then pulled out a flute and played an inaudible tune. He went around and stood just behind Madam Cloom with his hands behind him. Shaleigh wasn't sure she liked him leaving her side, but then again, this wasn't her game.

"I didn't bring you up here merely to test you, child," Madam Cloom said. "I brought you here to show you the land that makes up the Garden. If you are his reincarnation," she gave a small smirk. "Then you'll need to understand the Garden and its people."

A dark-haired man who was about Meryl's height came out with a tray of tall pink smoothies filled with something that looked like melon. He placed down a glass for both Shaleigh and Madam Cloom. At least Dean Hammond's parties had taught her about table manners. Since the rules here were different from the ones back home, she waited to see Madam Cloom's response, and upon seeing the squat woman tuck into her smoothie, Shaleigh did the same.

"You are already aware of the Slumbering Forest, I take it." With Teagan's aid, Madam Cloom stood and walked all the way to the edge of the Overlook. It must have been even windier at the edges because her wavy, gray hair flew back in the breeze. She turned back and smiled. "Come, girl, if you can't handle a bit of wind, how in the world do you plan to handle a kingdom?"

Those words were painfully true. Shaleigh had always prided herself on her courage, on her disregard for danger; yet here she was cowering away from a challenge that was all in her head. She clenched her fists and walked over. There was a brief expression on Madam Cloom's face, a wide-eyed glimpse of surprise perhaps, but it was gone in a flash and she turned back to point out toward the direction of the forest.

Walking through the Slumbering Forest had been terrifying. The shift from day to night to day again played tricks with her brain and with her sense of direction, without even considering the danger of the wolf pack and the creepy, coiled tendrils that trapped the Pello Pines. At this height though, the forest stood just beyond the edge of the city. Across the bridge, the trees looked normal for maybe a mile before the world went black. A black sheath with dots of starlight covered over the sick part of the forest like an unwanted blanket. It didn't belong; it felt as though someone had taken a paintbrush and blotched out a part of the world to keep it from being seen. Daylight didn't penetrate it and seeing how far it went down along the cut of the river gave her goosebumps. She thought of the city of Aife and bit her lip at the thought of Mawr living near that for so long.

"It's hideous," Shaleigh said, without thinking.

"Really?" The woman seemed genuinely surprised. "It was his crowning achievement. Those blood-thirsty trees couldn't kill any longer, and yet they weren't destroyed either. It was an act of both swift action and mercy."

Those words didn't sit well with her, especially the mercy part, and she didn't want to look at that darkness anymore. Shaleigh folded her arms around her middle and turned to notice that there was a very different scene at the opposite end of the Overlook. "You have farmland."

"Oh yes, the Pasture. It was once a wealthy kingdom, you know, but the rulers grew complacent. They forgot they had enemies." She shrugged. "The kingdom that was destroyed in a day, they say. Now it belongs to the Garden and it provides more than enough food for our people." Madam Cloom led her to the edge and Shaleigh followed slowly. Looking down at the tiny ants that were people tending to the fields, she couldn't help but think of what Meryl had told her. If she failed, she could be down there, harvesting vegetables for the rest of her days while her father searched fruitlessly for her back home. She looked up to see Madam Cloom climbing a set of stone steps that led to an upper level of the Overlook. Shaleigh closed her eyes for a minute and imagined what she would do if Kaeja was with her. Having Kaeja near always gave her a reason to be strong. If she ever wanted to see her friend again, she couldn't lose this game, no matter what she was put up against. With a deep breath, she climbed the steps, resisting the urge to look down at the ground far below.

The wind was so strong at this level that she gripped the railing as she squinted into the distance. Madam Cloom's gray hair flowed behind her and she laughed as Shaleigh took the final step up. "You sure this isn't too much for you?" Her voice sounded distant despite how close they stood. She held a hand out to the colorful streets and buildings in the distance. "That is the Marketplace, the gears that keep the Garden moving."

There was a wide main road that Shaleigh had seen earlier from indoors, but it extended into the horizon along the length of the river. Despite the early hour, the streets were quite busy. Carts of goods were pulled sometimes by two minotaurs at a time. One woman was hanging up dresses outside of her shop. A short woman was wiping down the windows of her storefront. In the distance, closer to the river, she could see the tops of ships and the dark spots of birds against the morning sky. The High Castle was more like a watchtower, she realized. The Marketplace was the real heart of the city.

She glanced over to the Slumbering Forest and wondered if any of the people below had ever seen the black sheath from this angle. Would they be as thankful for it if they saw what it looked like at this distance? Would they care? There was something eye-opening about seeing the land splayed out around her on all sides: the bustling Marketplace, the expansive Pasture, and the ominous Slumbering Forest. Then she realized there was an enormous field of rolling hills and valleys situated downstream along the river. It seemed to run up directly to the High Castle, but she could see the occasional flag standing along its path as though it was marked out for a race.

"What is that?" she said, with a hand down over her twists to keep them from getting in her eyes.

Madam Cloom gave a breathy laugh. "You'll find out soon enough, child." The woman patted Shaleigh's hand and every fiber within her tensed. "Surely you're not in that much of a hurry to reach your end."

SHE HAD to admit that she was glad to be climbing down the ladder from the Overlook. But Teagan seemed frustrated. For the rest of breakfast, Shaleigh had tried to keep up with the list of things that he and Madam Cloom had discussed, but much of it was over her head and neither seemed keen to explain it. Supplies needed to be ordered, decorations were being put in place, landscaping for paths needed to be done, and balloons needed to be prepared. One thing that she had heard mentioned was that Teagan would be giving her a tour of both the Pasture and the Marketplace; this seemed to annoy him.

"I'm far too busy to be doing this," he sighed as he walked briskly down the hall. Shaleigh had to break into a light jog to keep up with him. "I'll have to divide my work before we can head out, and some things only I can do." He frowned as though distracted.

"Perhaps I can go with you?"

"I'm afraid not." He gave a small smile. "We can't have you knowing all the secrets of High Castle." He lowered his voice, "We aren't yet sure if you are the true reincarnation after all."

"I can find my way around if you—"

Teagan laughed. "No, I can't have you wandering the halls alone either. You getting lost should be the least of my worries."

"What do you mean?"

"You are an honored guest," he said with pursed lips. "If you were allowed to wander on your own, there's no telling where you might end up. We can't have that."

He didn't want her trying to escape, she realized. Of course that was it. Her morning had been so busy, and her thoughts so filled with the enormity of the Overlook that she hadn't even considered escaping. How foolish would she have been not to try once had Teagan left her alone?

"You'll wait in the Memorial Chamber." His smile

turned mischievous. "I'll see who I can find to watch you." He pulled out his flute and did another inaudible tune.

She didn't like the sound of that. They came to a pair of double doors set into a stone archway. Over the arch were the carved words *Memorial Chamber* and additional symbols which she didn't recognize. Teagan took the large handles and pushed the doors open. He gestured for her to enter first.

She considered the dark room then looked back at him. "Are you sure you're not trying to ditch me?"

He smirked, "I don't think I would be permitted to ditch you, even if I wanted to." He reached an arm inside the room, snapped his fingers, and a spark of fire near the door made her jump. The flames traveled from the doorway along the wall in a little gutter, filling the chamber with light. He snapped his fingers again and the chandelier above burst into light. Shaleigh had to blink so her eyes could adjust.

"Please," Teagan said in a softer tone. "This shouldn't take me long to sort out."

She sighed and stepped cautiously inside. She had only gone a few steps when she heard a familiar voice behind her.

"You called me, sir?"

"Colin, yes. I want you to stay with Shaleigh here. Keep her in the Chamber until I return. I have some business to attend to."

Colin's tail swished back and forth anxiously as he stared at Shaleigh. The way he looked would have made anyone think she had been the kidnapper. "Are you sure, sir? I could see if Lieutenant Varg is around, I'm sure he wouldn't—"

"Don't question me," Teagan said, his voice hard. "Get in there and quit complaining. I'm sure she's far more frightened of you than you are of her."

"Somehow I doubt that..." Colin mumbled. He stepped inside with a sheepish grin. Behind him, Teagan closed the door and they both heard the click as the lock turned into place.

COLIN WAS WATCHING HER, knocking his hand against his leg nervously. "So, I guess Madam Cloom likes you then."

She folded her arms, "I don't know if that's the best way to put it. She puts up with me, sure, but she definitely doesn't like me."

He leaned against the wall, "I don't get the impression she likes anybody, except maybe the Captain, and that's stretching it."

Shaleigh nodded. Perhaps gaining a better under-standing about the people Madam Cloom kept close to her was the key to beating this gauntlet that had been laid at her feet. There was Teagan, who seemed to be at her side by force, though with the powers that Teagan had, she wasn't sure how Madam Cloom was keeping him there. And now there was Captain Briar as her ally. Shaleigh shuddered as she remembered the Captain with her sword at Talek's throat at the gates. That was one person she would rather not have as an enemy. Did Madam Cloom hold something over her head too, or was there something else that kept her close? It was difficult to imagine anyone supporting the woman out of choice. Shaleigh crossed her arms and asked, "Why do you think the Captain supports her?"

He shrugged, "Her family has always supported the High Castle, regardless of who sat there."

"What about you? You don't seem like a big fan to me."

Colin snorted and gave a thin smile. "I think she's the best leader the Garden's ever had. She's so classy and charming, who could possibly resist her?" He made a dramatic bow and his black tipped tail whipped into the air. "Oh, your majesty! Your shoes look a bit dirty, perhaps I should kiss them clean." There was a bang out in the hallway and Colin jumped a few feet into the air. Shaleigh gasped and they both froze, their eyes on the door. Out in the hall they heard a vague curse, as of an old man talking to himself, and a squeaky wheel indicated something was being wheeled down the hall again.

Colin gave a nervous chuckle and said in a trembling voice, "Maybe I was overdoing it...a little."

Shaleigh let out the breath she had been holding and laughed, shaking her arms to get rid of the tension. "You're an idiot. Don't talk like that. I've only been here a day and I know better." She already had her nerves rattled once that morning, she didn't need Colin's help.

"You should have seen yourself," his voice cracked. "You were scared stiff!"

"You're the one that jumped."

They stood there for a moment in the awkward silence. The stone floor and the size of the room meant their voices echoed. No one could hide inside the room without being seen, but if they were being spied on, they wouldn't be difficult to hear. Despite the fire that ran along the edge of the room, Shaleigh felt cold suddenly, vulnerable in this empty place.

Colin cleared his throat and said, "You're not still mad about me kidnapping you, are you?"

"Are you serious?"

He gave her an awkward smile, as though that was supposed to make up for everything.

"No. You kidnapped me, Colin, there is no 'good' after that."

"Ever?" He gave a heavy sigh. "I mean, I didn't have much of a choice. Madam Cloom is looking for the next reincarnation, it's not my fault you have his mark."

"So that's how you excuse it? I guess whatever it takes to keep from feeling guilty." She snapped, "Just point the finger at somebody else. That's probably easier for you."

He gave her a confused look, as though he hadn't considered it from her perspective before, as though the thought of her being angry was almost an insult. "I mean, what am I supposed to do? Feel bad about it? Look I'm sorry I took you away from your friend. You looked like you were having a good time in that house."

Shaleigh couldn't figure out if he was really that dense or that much in denial. "Normal people don't going around kidnapping people. They certainly don't expect to be friends afterwards."

He knocked his arm against his leg and stared at her for a long, uncomfortable minute. "Well I'm sorry, okay? I'm sorry I was forced to kidnap you."

She couldn't hide her disgust any longer. "Listen to

yourself, you don't even acknowledge that you did anything wrong."

"I didn't!"

She couldn't believe how difficult this was. It was like arguing with a child. "You took me away from my friends and my father. I don't know what's happened to them since then." She turned away to stare at the fire in the alcove before she said anything else. She wasn't sure how old Colin was, but she doubted he was older than thirteen. Maybe his kind was just slow to understand things, like Mawr not wanting to leave Aife. Maybe to him, kidnapping people was all just a sick game. "Maybe you're too young to understand. Maybe you've never had to lose someone in your life before, but it does things to people. Especially people who aren't strong enough to handle it."

"You're wrong about that." Colin was suddenly at her side and Shaleigh doubled back, a hand clutched to her chest in fright. She hadn't realized how quietly he could move. She wanted to yell, to tell him to back off, but his hands were trembling as he faced her. "I may just be a kid, but I've lost friends, family, people I cared about."

Shaleigh wasn't sure what to say.

"I lost my mother ages ago. I wasn't even old enough to know how she died. I would've joined her if Finn hadn't watched over me, but he's gone now too." His breathing was heavy and his tail jerked unevenly behind him. "You do see that I'm not normal, right? That I'm not like other people?"

"Yes." Shaleigh had to swallow. Her mouth had gone dry and she couldn't find words. "I—I thought you were part Faerie or something."

"I used to be human. I was born in this land, not in your world. Do you know what it's like growing up on the streets as a human here? No, you don't." He stiffened. "We're not even fit for pulling carriages."

She remembered looking out over the Pasture, looking out at all the ant-sized people working the fields. Why did she want to apologize? She wasn't in the wrong, he was. He was the kidnapper, she was the victim. Why was this suddenly so confusing?

"That's not true, that can't be true," she blurted out. "Captain Briar is human."

He laughed, "Sure, but she has that special Briar blood. Royal blood. She's a soldier from a family of soldiers. She's the exception." Colin dragged a hand through his brown hair and sighed. "Before I was trained as a Seeker, I lived on the streets. I stole just about anything to survive. I would steal a slice of apple out of a baby's hands if I was hungry enough." There was disgust in his eyes. "Have you ever been that hungry? Have you ever had to fight to survive?"

Shaleigh shook her head.

He jabbed a thumb to his chest. "I may do the dirty work around here, the ugly stuff that nobody approves of, but at least I don't have to be sorting through trash anymore. At least I don't have to sleep shivering in the rain and hoping that those damned wolves don't break through the gates knowing that I would be one of the first to get eaten." He turned and put a hand against the wall. "Sure, you're stuck here, but you have to admit you've got a pretty sweet deal. You get fed, you have a bed to sleep in —heck, you've even got Teagan taking you everywhere.

He barely has time for me, and he's the one that turned me into a stoatling to begin with."

Shaleigh blinked, trying to figure out what to say, what she could say. She didn't understand him and now that she knew more about him, she was even more perplexed. "I can't help the mark on my back, and you can't help being sent to fetch me. We're both from very different worlds, and I understand that." She paused. "So, you used to be a thief? Well now you're a kidnapper too. I'm sorry if you don't like that word, but it's true."

He gave a grimace and tried to avoid looking at her now. "It's not that simple. I didn't want to do it. I never wanted to hurt anybody."

She took a deep breath. "Well, you did. What I don't understand is why you put on this act. What exactly do you want from me?"

Colin put his head down and pulled his arms in close to wrap around himself. "I don't know. I guess, just not to be hated. When I lived on the streets, people didn't like me, they didn't want to be around me, but they never hated me." He looked up at her and there were tears in his eyes. "You're the first person to really do that."

Shaleigh debated what to say. "I don't hate you, Colin. Not exactly."

He gave a weak smile. "I guess that's something."

"Would it help more if I said I like you more than Madam Cloom?"

"Yeah, but that doesn't help much. I guess I have to work harder on that."

"Normal friendships don't start with kidnappings, you know." Shaleigh wished she hadn't said it as soon as the words came out. She could see that it hurt him, see the way he winced and the way his body closed in on itself, but she couldn't help it. The insult, the anger, the outrage, the pain: it was all still there even if it did hurt him. He might not be anything more than a pawn in this elaborate web, but he still followed his orders without question. That didn't exonerate him from blame despite how many sob stories he told her. Despite that, some part of her felt guilty for her words. Some part of her didn't like to see him in pain every time she brought it up.

COLIN CHANGED the subject after a few minutes of strained silence. "Have you ever been in here before?"

"This room? No."

"Here, you might like this." Without any further explanation he slipped a black-clawed hand into hers and pulled her further into the room. He must have felt her tense, because when he paused his expression was pleading and serious. "Come on, let me try and make it up to you."

She nodded, but something cold inside told her there was no way he could. He might be the kindest, most generous person in the world, but it wouldn't take the pain away. Despite that, she let Colin lead her further into the chamber. That was when she noticed six statues standing, flickering in the firelight, against the walls. The bodies of the statues were all black metal, each draped in a shimmering, colored crystal.

"Most of these were built in honor of the magicians

who helped create The Garden," Colin explained, as he pulled her toward one of the tallest statues in the room. "There was a bet on who could scratch out a land and tame it. They were to turn an unwanted, unlivable place into a land everyone would want to live in. Most of them were killed. Cathal was one of the few who survived and went on to found the city."

Shaleigh stared at the tall man who stood before them. "That's Master Cathal?"

Colin nodded. "He's a little intimidating, isn't he?"

That wasn't quite the word for it. The man towered over her and Colin, and in fact was taller than any of the other statues in the room. He stood with his feet apart and gripped a large sword with both hands. He looked like he was preparing to rush into battle. She moved closer to see if she could see his face, but the black metal of his body was faceless and cold. What she had thought at first was a dark halo around him, was actually black crystal, twisted into the shape of limbs, like dried up trees. They reached toward him with long, finger-like branches. Shaleigh thought of the Pello Pines and the dark shadow that hung over the forest to the west. This had to be the battle that ended in them all being put to sleep, trapped inside those black vines that had ensnared everything. As dark as the limbs were though, Cathal shone with his own light. His metal body was drenched with a vibrant, orange crystal robe that gave off a warm, amber light that flickered in the firelight lining the wall. The sword he gripped was made of two crystals, orange at its hilt and a clear white for its blade.

"He looks terrifying."

Colin chuckled, "I never met the guy myself, but Teagan says the statue is a disgrace to his memory." He shrugged. "Doesn't matter much to me. He's dead, I don't know why people obsess over statues so much."

"I do." Shaleigh put a hand out to feel the smooth crystal of the blade. "This is what people expect him to be. When anybody talks about Master Cathal, this is what they want, not some scrawny black girl." There was no way she was going to fit the look that he had, or ever match up to his memory. The portrait she had seen before didn't do him justice. In that small frame he looked like he was in a different time, a different place, a different world. Here, standing at his feet, watching as he was about to dive fearlessly into a tangle of trees that brought death, she understood how difficult this task would be. He looked like he was a warrior.

"You said he was a magician?"

"Absolutely. One of the best, supposedly." Colin pointed to a placard which read: The Great Magician Master Cathal. "All of these statues were magicians. All except hers, of course." He thumbed behind him.

"Who?"

He gave a knowing smile. "Madam Cloom, of course. Want to take a peek?"

"She has one too?"

Colin led the way. "Now do you really think she would leave herself out of the Memorial Chamber? This is where all of the greatest and most powerful leaders leave their mark." He led her to a statue that looked like it had been shoehorned in. It wasn't evenly spaced like the other five against the wall of the chamber. Now that she noticed it, she was surprised she hadn't seen it earlier. She thought of Teagan mentioning that he had put the Overlook together upstairs, how he seemed to imply that he had put together the entire High Castle. If that were true, how had he gotten away with making Madam Cloom's statue look so misplaced?

Madam Cloom sat atop a black metal throne with red crystal flowers blooming all over it. She was dressed in a crimson crystal gown and her hair, which was made of white crystal, flowed down her back to pool around her feet. She held a blue scepter cradled in her hands and a large white crystal glinted at its head. If Shaleigh had been asked to point out Madam Cloom's statue in this room, she never would have chosen this one. The only part of it that seemed like it might belong to her were the red flower crystals...but that was it. She looked like she was lounging in repose, with neither the fierceness that Shaleigh had seen, nor her frightening determination and callousness. She walked around it to look at the placard nestled beneath her feet: G. Cloom, Steward and Caretaker of the Garden.

Shaleigh blinked. "Steward and Caretaker?"

"Those are her official titles." Colin crossed his arms and looked up into the statue's empty eyes. "Despite the fact that she makes everybody call her 'Madam.' I guess when you're in the big seat, you can make any demand."

"So, she's not a Madam."

"Nope. She's not the real ruler, if that's what you're asking. She's calling herself the Madam of the Garden, but really, that ought to be your title. Once you prove yourself of course."

It was silly really, how excited it made her to look at that little plaque beneath Madam Cloom's statue. It didn't give her any more leverage than she already had, it didn't give her any information that wasn't already known by the general public, and it didn't get her any closer to claiming the throne. It did, however, give her hope that she might somehow have a chance. Even if Madam Cloom did find a way to get rid of her and Shaleigh was stuck as a laborer for the rest of her days, Madam Cloom was not a real ruler of anything. She was a poser, just like Shaleigh was, and that put them on equal footing.

THE TOUR

Shaleigh and Colin both turned as the bolt drew back on the door and Teagan entered the room. He had changed out of his black suit into a tan one with white accents. The change of color only made his red hair more vibrant. He smiled when he laid eyes upon them, as though relieved to see that they hadn't disappeared in his absence.

"Excellent work, Colin," he said in a silky voice.

Colin gave an enthusiastic half-bow. "Anytime you need me, sir, I'm here."

For a brief moment, Teagan's smile faded and he wore a strange expression, one that seemed to imply he knew the weight of such a responsibility. Shaleigh wondered how much pressure must be on his shoulders. As the High Faerie, he oversaw the High Castle of course, but that seemed to go much farther than simply ordering servants around. He had to handle the flower arrangements in the throne room, prevent the careful precipice of the Over-look from collapsing, and tiptoe through a minefield of arguments with Captain Briar. She wondered if Colin's mere presence, knowing now that Teagan had had a hand in transforming the boy from a meager thief into a stoatling kidnapper, made him uncomfortable. The brief glimpse of weakness Teagan had shown was gone, and his face became the normal mask that she had grown accustomed to.

"Are you ready for a tour of the land, Shaleigh?"

She pursed her lips, not quite sure if she understood. "Outside of the castle?"

"Certainly, unless you have some aversion to the outdoors..."

"No, no, that sounds good to me. Great, I mean!" There was a glint of mischief in Teagan's eye that made her quicken her pace to the door before he changed his mind.

"Can I come too, sir?" Colin asked in a timid voice stopping them both at the door.

"Come now, Colin. You already know all about the lands. Unless you're feeling homesick."

Colin shrugged, his eyes darting to Shaleigh. "I won't get in the way, promise. I just want to tag along."

Teagan turned his gaze to her. "Will it be a problem for your kidnapper to join us? I'm not keen on you two getting into a scuffle, certainly not outside the castle walls."

At the mention of him being a kidnapper, Colin flinched and dropped his eyes. Shaleigh sighed and weighed her options. She could say no and break this truce off now—part of her wanted to. She couldn't deny the vengeful streak within that wanted to continue to see the boy hurt for stealing her away. Then again, Colin was one of the more straightforward people she had met in the High Castle. He didn't hide behind masks or speak in riddles, and she found that she understood him possibly better than he understood himself. Compared to the rest of the political games she was falling into, it was rather refreshing to have someone relatable around. Not only that, but she was starting to like him, which made it difficult to continue being angry with him. "I don't mind. He can come."

Colin's face lit up and he bounded toward them, crossing the chamber in only a few leaps. Teagan held up a hand and Colin slid to a halt. "However, you must stay by our side and you are not allowed to wander off alone without permission."

"Will do, sir." His words were steady but his tail swished back and forth behind him in excitement. Teagan lowered his hand and Colin left the chamber in a flash.

"Help me keep an eye on him, won't you?" Teagan asked. "He's nearly impossible to control at times. Especially when he's so excitable."

She blinked. "Sure."

As Teagan led the two of them down the hall, Shaleigh couldn't believe what she'd gotten herself into. Somehow in the space of an hour she had not only grown sympathetic to her kidnapper but allowed herself to be his chaperone. She hoped she had made the right decision.

As SOON AS they stepped outside of the castle, guards were at their sides. There were four of them total, all holding pikes taller than themselves. This was an entrance of the castle that Shaleigh hadn't seen before. It wasn't as busy and looked more like an official entrance than the one she had come through. Beautiful roses grew around the iron fence on either side of the walkway, giving a small amount of privacy even though she could hear the bustle of people not far off. A carriage stood waiting for them with a brutish minotaur leaning against the front of it, talking with others of his kind. A thick leather harness wrapped up around his chest. He had humanoid hands but his legs were the hooves of a bull. Dark brown fur, course and stiff like a cow's, covered his body and a large ring fell from his nose piercing.

Teagan stepped up to the carriage and said in a booming voice, "I hope you aren't too terribly busy, Graddic, to take us to the Pasture?" The minotaur jumped and his comrades quickly grew scarce.

"Of course, sir!" Graddic grunted in a voice that didn't seem accustomed to speaking. He hurried around the side of the carriage to hold the door for them. "Many apologies!"

"I have quite a full schedule today, so it would be problematic to request a different carrier." Teagan gave a loud huff as Colin crawled in first, looking like he knew exactly what it felt like to be in Graddic's shoes. "I hope to have no more delays, Graddic. Can you promise that will not happen?"

The minotaur stamped his hooves nervously into the dirt as Shaleigh climbed in. "No more delays, sir. Promise!"

"Good. Let's be quick." Teagan climbed inside and slammed the door closed behind them.

Shaleigh sat with her hands clasped between her knees, not quite sure what to say or do. She glanced to Colin, who gave her a wide-eyed expression. Teagan sighed, "If you two have something to say, please say it so we can end this silly silence."

Shaleigh looked down at her feet and Colin cleared his throat. "I just didn't realize we were in that much of a hurry, sir."

Teagan shifted in his seat, switching his crossed legs, and that was when Shaleigh realized what he was doing. She had seen her father do it before when he was taken off guard by a question about his wife while in the middle of a completely different conversation. He didn't do it so much these days, but when she was younger and his delusion wasn't so firmly rooted, it was a common scene. Teagan was not only trying to figure out what to say, he was stalling so he could come up with an excuse.

"We are," Teagan said, his expression carefully chosen so as not to give the slightest indication of doubt. "As I said, we have a very full schedule and we don't have time for our carriers to be chit-chatting on the job. When I require their services, I expect them to be punctual."

Shaleigh pursed her lips to keep from saying something she might regret.

~

THE CARRIAGE ROLLED beneath a great covered bridge, only it wasn't covered with wood or stone like the ones

Shaleigh knew back home. Instead this bridge was made almost entirely of roses. Bright yellow and pale orange roses that greeted them as they went into the bridge, and then the carriage's interior became quite dark as though it had become twilight outside.

"Oh, this is my favorite part!" Colin whispered, as though afraid to break the spell.

Normally Shaleigh might have been frightened, since it was reminiscent of the day-to-night transformation that had happened in the Slumbering Forest, but this was different. As the carriage grew darker, Shaleigh could barely see Colin and Teagan, who were sitting right next to her. The cabin filled with the mingled perfume of the roses. It shifted as they moved through the bridge from the dainty sweet scent of a lady's perfume, to a heavy sweetness that clung to the back of her throat, to the rain-kissed petals of moonlight that tickled her nose. As light slowly crept back into the carriage cabin again, the scent fled with the shadows, and Shaleigh found the normal air plain and boring compared to the scents they had left behind.

"That was wonderful!" Shaleigh turned in her seat, trying to look behind them, but the carriage had no way of looking backwards except to open the doors.

Teagan smirked. "We should be getting close." He banged on the side of the carriage and yelled out, "Take it slow once we reach the fields, Graddic!"

The minotaur gave a muffled response, but Shaleigh was too spellbound to hear what was said. "I've never seen so many roses together before. They're all in full bloom too, can they even do that?"

Teagan closed his eyes and said, "Master Cathal's first request was that the Garden always be frozen in springtime, but without the problems that it could bring. He wanted the plants to bloom as though filled with the vibrancy of heavy rains and chilled with the night wind." He opened his eyes, his mouth curving into a frown. "He wanted it to be a cheerful land, one that brought happiness to even the hardest heart. He wanted it to be filled with love and hope and cheerfulness always."

Colin whistled. "He kind of shot for the moon, didn't he?"

"No magician got anywhere without believing in the impossible."

"Yeah, but all the magic in the world can't make a place like that. No offense, but he sounds kind of naïve," Colin pointed out.

Teagan didn't respond and turned towards the window. Outside they passed by an enormous orchard. The trees were planted equally far apart so that as they passed; it reminded her of soldiers standing in rows.

"Where is everybody?" she asked.

"Probably farther in," Colin said, gripping his seat. "It may be spring all the time, but that doesn't mean the harvest comes in all at once."

"The Pasture is divided up into sections," Teagan explained further, "These are the fruit orchards, but we'll reach the vegetable fields soon. We have an herb house and a chicken coop as well."

"Only chickens then? You don't raise cattle?"

Teagan arched his eyebrows at her as though the idea was abhorrent.

"I mean, we eat cows back home where I—"

Teagan glanced up to the front of the carriage. "No, we don't do anything so barbaric here. I wouldn't even entertain the notion to be frank with you." He must have seen Shaleigh's expression because he added with a smirk, "No offense, but humans from your world are brutal creatures."

Shaleigh wasn't sure what the problem was. How was eating chickens any different than eating cows or fish for that matter? She opened her mouth to ask, but Colin began shaking his head urgently and aimed a thumb at the front of the carriage. "He—can—hear—you!" He mouthed.

It was then that Shaleigh realized that Graddic, like every other minotaur in the Garden, was part cow, and that eating cattle was probably seen as cannibalism. "So, wait a minute, you're telling me that his parents were..."

"Two minotaurs," Teagan said, a smirk still playing on his lips.

"So...how do cows...?" she asked, not quite sure what she was trying to ask.

"Minotaurs come about when magic goes wrong," Colin said with a frown, "Well, not wrong exactly, but when it's used in an unnatural way. It's what Teagan used to transform me into a stoatling. Nobody's really sure when the first minotaur came about. Probably somebody pissed off a magician somewhere along the way, and they transformed someone." He turned to Teagan. "I mean, you know I'm grateful to you for changing me, sir, but I don't think that first minotaur was very happy."

"Uh...how did they become an entire race of creatures?" Shaleigh grimaced after she asked that aloud.

"They had children with humans," Teagan said, keeping his gaze trained on the window outside. "The curse or the charm, however you want to look at it, was passed on to each new generation."

The carriage began to slow. "Here we are," Teagan said. "These are the vegetable fields, and where most of the workers are now. We'll step out and greet them in a few minutes."

The rows of trees had ended and long flat fields stretched out on either side of the road—rows and rows of plants as far as you could see in any direction. The carriage slowed to a crawl and Shaleigh could see people working the fields. Several women were pulling up heads of lettuce, a line of men was pushing wheelbarrows alongside the road, and even a few children ran barefoot beside them—not playing, but rather picking up any of the lettuce heads that rolled free.

One thing was clear to Shaleigh. These people were treated quite differently from those who had the privilege of living in or around the High Castle. There, even the workers who pushed the flower carts were dressed in polished shoes and unwrinkled shirts, but these people were dressed in old, patched clothes. Their bodies were lean with work and their faces hallow from fatigue. Even though the carriage bore the mark of the High Castle on its flanks, not a single person raised their eyes to them. It reminded Shaleigh of the plantation owners in the South traveling through their fields of slaves, slaves forced to work to survive. One woman who must have been in her sixties stood up with a hand on her lower back and shielded her face from the sun; her eyes met Shaleigh's and she frowned. Shaleigh moved away from the side window as her stomach dropped and she clutched the edges of the seat.

Teagan banged once again on the wall of the carriage. "Stop at the Rest House, Graddic. We'll take a short walk."

Shaleigh suddenly didn't know if she could stand touring the Pasture. If that old woman she had seen was any indication, she didn't think they would be very interested in seeing her. The carriage came to a long building that looked as though it was barely standing. The walls were made of wooden planks, but they were so sun-bleached and warped that it looked like one strong wind might knock the entire building to the ground. This looked like the place where the wheelbarrow pushers were bringing their produce, but it also appeared to be where the workers came to rest as well. Several men and women sat on the ground outside in the shade of the building, sipping from metal cups. As the carriage rolled to a stop, several weary faces looked in their direction. Shaleigh felt her heart leap into her throat.

Graddic came around to the side of the carriage and pulled the door open. A blast of warm, earthy air swirled into the cabin. Shaleigh focused her gaze on her feet. She didn't want to be the target of so many eyes. Not only did it remind her of her father's annoying parties, but somehow, she felt like she was enacting treason against her own people. Hadn't her father been distantly related to a freed slave? By agreeing to take on this role, was she no better than a slave owner?

She felt Teagan lean close, his voice silky and calm.

"Getting cold feet?" He did sound concerned, but there

was also that unmistakable glimmer of amusement at her discomfort. Perhaps it was in his Fae nature to take glee in the suffering of others. Shaleigh glared at him.

"You can't ask me to do this. I..."

He arched an eyebrow in complete confusion. He had no idea what her problem was. He had no clue about the Civil War. Teagan might consider her barbaric for eating beef, but in that moment Shaleigh saw their entire civilization as monstrous. She tried her best to find a way to explain it so that he could understand.

"I'm descended from a family of slaves. They were forced to...work fields like this."

"Ahh, I see." Teagan sat back, considering this for a moment. He smiled back at her. "These people are not slaves. They're refugees." Seeing how little that helped her, he sighed. "Colin, escort her, would you?"

"You're not coming with us, sir?"

"No, I fear my presence will taint the experience."

Colin rolled his eyes. "So you're trying to make Shaleigh go out there, but you're not doing it?"

Teagan narrowed his eyes. "Are you trying to annoy me?"

"Absolutely." Colin grinned and looped an arm around Shaleigh's. "Come on, we'll show him there's nothing to be frightened of." He laughed at Teagan's glare, quickly dragging Shaleigh with him as they stepped out of the carriage.

Shaleigh had expected awkward stares, uncomfortable looks, accusing words...instead she heard applause. Colin walked her a few paces out from the carriage, then slipped his arm free and held out his arms. "Ladies and gentlemen, may I present the future Madam of the Garden."

Despite her trepidation, Shaleigh couldn't refrain from smiling. The applause wasn't letting up, and unsure of what she was supposed to do, she nodded in various directions.

It was as the applause died down and a strong breeze blew by that she heard the words that made her limbs go cold. "I doubt this one will last a week."

Colin's smile faltered only a little and he looped his arm around Shaleigh's again to half-pull, half-escort her toward the crowd. They approached a group of three woman, two with their gray hair done up in a braid or a bun, and another with only a few flecks of silver showing in the front. "Greetings, my lady," they curtsied, but their faces showed very little kindness.

"Er, perhaps you didn't hear me," Colin urged, "This is Shaleigh of the Human World, and she'll soon be the Madam of the Garden."

"We heard," the woman with the braid said with a sour expression. "Goodness, child, do you really expect to lead the Garden?"

"Yes," Shaleigh said with a shaky voice. "I think I can do a better job than—"

The woman snickered, "You barely know how to step out of a carriage properly. You'll find our lands a tad more complex." The three women broke into peals of laughter and Shaleigh felt the heat rising to her cheeks. Her pulse was pounding in her ears as she watched the three women laughing at her, and she couldn't figure out what in the world to say. The determination she had shown before

Madam Cloom seemed to crack and fall to pieces at the woman's blunt words. She wanted to run back to the carriage, leap inside, and hide away from these people and everything they represented, but Colin held her fast.

"My word," a silky voice lilted behind her. "I hadn't realized how devoted the workers of the Pasture were to Madam Cloom." Teagan had emerged from the carriage. Shaleigh watched as not only the three women, but every worker she could see backed away from him.

Teagan approached. He didn't look upset though, he looked entertained. "It was my assumption that the people of the Garden were keen to have their reincarnated ruler back upon the throne. However," he said to the woman with the braid. "Perhaps you are content with your place here."

The woman's lip trembled and her eyes went wide; it was clear she wasn't sure how to respond.

"You are content here, are you not?" Teagan pressed.

"Yes, sir, most content."

"You would scoff at a new leader on the throne, would you?"

She paused. "No sir, I would welcome them."

Teagan smiled. "So you would see Madam Cloom dethroned? That sounds rather treasonous."

"No, sir!" she blurted, her hands trembling as she collapsed to her knees. "Please, sir, I don't mean any harm. I would welcome whoever you see fit to place upon the throne."

Teagan chuckled and Shaleigh realized that a strange hush had fallen over the crowd. He crouched down beside her and said, "Perhaps you should learn to watch your tongue more. If it flaps too much, it might just fly away from you."

Fat tears were welling up in the woman's eyes as she muttered apologies, trying hard not to break into sobs.

"Would you like to see what I mean?"

The woman shook her head, but Teagan grinned as he leaned closer.

"Don't," Shaleigh said in a small voice.

Teagan glanced back at her and his disturbing smile vanished. "Are you certain? This might be an ideal time to dispense manners."

Shaleigh swallowed despite her dry mouth. "Don't do it, Teagan. She's allowed to say what she thinks, even if I don't agree with it."

Teagan shrugged and got to his feet. "As you wish, though I don't think it's very wise to show compassion in front of them. Some people deserve punishment. Madam Cloom is a proponent of punishment more than kindness."

"She isn't here though, is she?" Shaleigh retorted. She turned to the woman who was now sobbing on the ground. The other gray-haired woman was crouched with her, rubbing her back, but the third woman was staring back at her.

"Thank you," she whispered.

Shaleigh gave a small smile and turned away. "I think I've seen enough of the Pasture today, Teagan, and I'm sure they've seen more than enough of the both of us."

"Very well then." Teagan gave a low bow. "Colin, if you would escort the lady back to the carriage." He turned his back on the three women without a second glance and approached Graddic with plans to leave.

As she was stepping up into the carriage, another woman rushed forward. She was much younger than the trio had been. Her skin was darker than Shaleigh's but she had large white splotches—much like Shaleigh's own mark—only they had crept up her throat and along her cheeks. She wore a desperate grin and shook Shaleigh's hand with both of hers.

"Good luck," she whispered. "Whatever you do, don't let anyone stop you."

It felt like the woman was shaking her arm off, and Shaleigh wasn't sure what to say. She glanced to Colin, but he looked shocked.

"She'll try to claim you're a fraud, a fool, anything to keep you from winning. Don't let her."

Teagan approached the woman from behind and put his hands on her shoulders. "That's enough, Lauren. Leave her be."

"Teagan?" Lauren's face seemed to light up at the sight of him. She turned and wrapped her arms around Teagan's waist in a tight hug. His eyes went wide, and he glanced back at the other workers who were still watching from the Rest House with concern.

Shaleigh reached down and pried Lauren off him. "So...you were another reincarnation?"

She nodded, "I was, but I wasn't very good. Not nearly as good as you are." She beamed, "I know you'll win. You have to!"

Teagan whispered something to Colin before moving around them and climbing into the carriage. Colin gave a quick nod and looped an arm around Lauren's. "Come, miss. Better step back. We've got a busy schedule today."

Shaleigh pursed her lips and watched as Colin pulled the girl away. She spotted a scar on the back of Lauren's head where her hair hadn't quite grown back as she walked away. Shuddering, Shaleigh climbed aboard the carriage.

~

IT TOOK a few minutes for Graddic to turn the carriage around completely, but that was plenty of time for Colin to bid farewell to Lauren. Then, in a few four-legged bounds, he lunged at the carriage and latched onto its door. The carriage rocked sideways, standing on two of the four wheels before it adjusted to Colin's weight.

"Watch it, you damn weasel!" Graddic called from the front of the carriage. "You topple it, and I'll topple you!"

Colin gave a bashful grin and slid inside, sweeping his black-tipped tail around and nearly hitting Shaleigh in the eye.

"Sorry," Colin dropped down in his seat with a bashful grin. "Lauren certainly was insistent. I didn't think she was going to let you leave, sir." Colin laughed, but Teagan didn't respond. Instead, he stared through the window as the crowd of workers grew smaller in the distance and rows of vegetables passed by. His expression was very different from the one he'd worn before with those three women; it was softer somehow, more like how he had been the night before. He was less like some high and mighty Faerie and more like a friend. She much preferred this Teagan to the one she had seen just a few moments ago.

"You knew Lauren well, didn't you?" Shaleigh looked for any change in his expression, but Teagan was persistent in keeping his mask in place. "I don't think I've seen anyone hug you before."

Teagan gave a heavy sigh and turned to them. He couldn't quite meet Shaleigh's eyes. "Lauren was another kidnapped human. For a time, we thought she could be Master Cathal's reincarnation, but that didn't last long. She was only eight when we found her, and the people didn't take to her. It's difficult to ask a populace to follow the orders of a child, or even to respect one for that matter. On top of that, she was..." A pained expression came over him. "She was too naïve for this work."

Naïve. In a way Shaleigh could understand the temptation to just allow yourself to go along with whatever Madam Cloom or the populace decided, but that wasn't what she wanted to do. She didn't want to put her future into the hands of so many violent people. No, if she wanted to do this, she needed to do it herself, by her rules, regardless of the consequences. Sure, she might make rash decisions or say the wrong things, but even if she did fail, at least she would know that she had done everything in her power to get home. At least she would know that she tried her best.

Colin whistled. "Wow, so Lauren was eight when you saw her last? That must have been over ten years ago." Colin's attempt to keep the mood light was like trying to shine a light into a deep well. "I bet you didn't have a single Seeker at the time. Who brought her over?"

"Seekers were several years off. I was reluctant to train anyone in the ways of kidnapping, even if it was for the good of the Garden. In the end though, Madam Cloom was right—even I cannot be everywhere at one time." He turned to Shaleigh with a small smile. "Please don't take offense. I'd kidnapped many others before Colin retrieved you."

"Are they always young?" Shaleigh asked. "I mean, I'm sixteen, Lauren was eight, that's a pretty wide gap."

"Typically, if the scar shows up, it appears at a young age. I believe the oldest contestant we had was a few months shy of twenty."

There was something very odd about him referring to the kidnapped humans as contestants, as though they were getting put into a raffle. Though she supposed if she was forced to kidnap so many people, she would need some way to alleviate the guilt. She thought of Colin back in the Memorial Room. He didn't even like to refer to it as a kidnapping.

"She had a scar..." Shaleigh tapped on the back of her skull, right above the nape of her neck. "How did she get that?"

Teagan pursed his lips. "I didn't cause the blow if that's what you're asking. She received that wound during the Games. Her opponent was a seasoned warrior. She was unconscious for nearly a week afterwards." He dropped his eyes. "As I said, she was only a child at the time."

If someone did that to a child during the Games, Shaleigh thought, what chance did she have? There would be no appealing to her opponent. And if she couldn't cut it in a fight? Well, hopefully she would be as lucky as Lauren was to keep her head, and to have an opponent who would perhaps take enough pity on her not to kill her when given the chance. As the shadows from the orchard began to fall over them, Shaleigh realized just how much she was out of her league here.

Teagan shifted uncomfortably. He must have seen her panic because he started floundering. If there was one thing she had learned so far, it was that Teagan very rarely floundered. "Madam Cloom can make some rather extreme, rather unpleasant, rather *unpopular* decisions. The attitude you saw back there was but a taste of the disgust most of the Garden has for her." He forced a strained smile. "But that is why you're here, right?"

Shaleigh didn't respond and stared out at the criss-crossing trees. The more she thought about it, the more such a ruthless decision seemed right in line with what she knew about Madam Cloom. It was cruel, heartless even, but it showed what lengths the woman would go to in order keep her position of power. Teagan, in many ways, was even more of a pawn than Shaleigh was, and had been so for a long time. She thought back to the Rest House in the Pasture and to those three women. Teagan's actions seemed almost in direct conflict with how he seemed to feel, but she was beginning to understand why. She was beginning to understand where he was coming from, or at least she hoped she was.

"What you said earlier to those women," she started. "You were very careful to make me look like a savior."

"Oh?"

"That whole bit with the old woman. You weren't really going to get rid of her tongue, were you?"

Colin blinked curiously at him as well, and Shaleigh realized for the first time that he might never have considered that Teagan was putting on an act. Had he seriously thought Teagan meant to have the old woman's tongue fly off into the trees? Perhaps he was just as naïve as Lauren.

"That's what you meant right? You want the people to think I'm rescuing them from you and Madam Cloom."

Teagan gave a weak chuckle. "Dear me, I hadn't realized I had become so transparent. I must be losing my touch."

"I'm not dense. I've had to deal with complicated people before, you know. I grew up with my dad, complicated is my middle name."

"Wait," Colin said. "So…you weren't going to make her tongue fly off?"

"Don't tell me you're disappointed," Teagan chuckled.

"I mean, a little." Colin glanced to Shaleigh and quickly backtracked at her glare. "Not that I didn't feel sorry for her! I mean, the poor lady was in tears, and all she did was say what everybody else there was probably thinking." He groaned, "I mean, it's a good thing you spoke up, Shaleigh."

"Come now," Teagan said. "I didn't doubt her for a moment."

"Wait," Shaleigh said, turning to Teagan. "I gave you an order back there, didn't I?"

He blinked, "Excuse me?"

"I mean, I said not to punish the lady and you had to back off, didn't you? You have to do as I ask out here."

Teagan's eyes narrowed. "It's hardly that simple. You

do have some say over what I can and cannot do, but only to a certain extent. If you were to ask me to take you home, for example, that would be out of the question. If your request is in line with my duties, then yes, I can accommodate you to some extent."

"Pretty much, yes and no," Colin clarified, shaking his head. "You are slick with words, Master Teagan."

Teagan gave a wide smile. "Thank you, Colin."

"Look," Shaleigh sighed. "Regardless of what limits I have, whatever happens, just don't make people cry, okay? I don't like it."

He smirked, "That's a very quaint opinion, but I'm afraid such tactics are necessary. Yes, I am charged with giving you a tour of the lands, but you are also being introduced to the people. Think of it as a show. The populace has seen many contestants brought in before you, like Lauren, and none of them have succeeded. Therefore, we need to build a strong memory of you, and we need them to trust you."

"You mean, more than they trust you and Madam Cloom," Shaleigh corrected.

He paused for a moment, trying to find the right words. "I am merely enacting the will of Madam Cloom."

"Not entirely though, or else you wouldn't be working so hard to make me the new leader."

"Nonsense," he gave a nervous laugh. "It is my station to serve the Garden, regardless of who sits upon its throne."

The carriage suddenly went dark and their conversation was cut short. They were inside the tunnel of roses again, and just as Shaleigh realized it, the mixture of scents flowed over her. She breathed in deep, able to appreciate all of the flowers' nuances. When she took the time to notice, she fancied she could almost smell every single one.

~

AFTER THEIR RIDE OUT to the Pasture, they stopped at the High Castle for a quick lunch. They ate through a basket of sandwiches and apples, camping out among the flowers of the gazebo while Teagan attended to business. Colin was a bundle of nerves. For someone who had grown up on the streets, stealing for a living, there was a nervous excitement in his voice now when they were about to tour the Marketplace, and he would see those same streets again.

"I guess you've never been back?" Shaleigh asked as she bit into an apple.

"No, I guess I was afraid of seeing those same shop-keepers again." He chuckled, "You know—the ones who used to shoo me out of doorways when it rained or who would chase me down the street when I stole something. I only left five years ago. I'm sure they're all still down there."

"You don't have to go back if you don't want to. You could stay here."

Colin's expression was distant and she realized he wasn't really listening to her anymore. "Mostly I'm afraid of not having Finn there when I go back."

Finn was Colin's lost friend; he had mentioned him when they spoke in the Memorial Chamber. Shaleigh wasn't sure if 'lost' meant he had died or if he just left, and decided not to ask. It was obviously a sensitive topic. Colin looked like he was trying to build up the courage to say more, so Shaleigh was patient and waited for him to continue.

"When I was younger, and the first calls for volunteer Seekers came out from the High Castle, I thought I was going to be great. I thought I would be the best, but I was a pretty arrogant kid. I mean, just because you're fast on the streets and you can palm a loaf of bread on occasion doesn't make you an expert thief. It takes more than just skill, it takes a lot of preparation, more than I realized at first." Colin dipped his fingers into his water cup and rubbed his hands together vigorously like a raccoon to clean his fur. "Finn knew though. He knew as soon as I signed up that I wouldn't be any good."

"No offense, but that sounds kind of rude to me."

"Oh no, he wasn't like that. He just knew it was going to be a waste of time." Colin pulled his tail forward and began cleaning it as well. "I wanted to become a Seeker 'cause I thought I was tough. I thought I could do anything. Finn told me I would fail, but I didn't want to listen. I thought he was jealous."

"But you're a Seeker now, so I guess he was wrong in the end, right?"

Colin gave a small smile. "Each year I barely made the cut. Mostly, I think Master Teagan appreciated my sense of humor. It took away the burden of the training, the tests, the endurance challenges. I really didn't know what I was getting into. Finn was so angry. I would write him regularly during those years, and he would write me back when he could. While I worked my butt off to be a Seeker, the treatment of humans in the city grew worse. Finn stopped writing as often; I'm sure it became difficult to find paper and ink to write with. The last letter I got from him said he was going to take his chances in the Slumbering Forest."

"Mawr and I barely escaped from there!"

"Yeah, those wolves have that land claimed. Even Madam Cloom isn't foolish enough to send her troops in there very often. If you two hadn't had a Faerie with you, I doubt you would have survived."

Shaleigh felt a lump form in her throat. With how busy Madam Cloom had kept her, she had almost forgotten about Talek. He had saved their lives in those woods. The thought of him having to live out there all alone made her anxious.

Colin continued, "Anyway, it's not supposed to be so bad on the edges of the woods, but you have to keep your wits at night. Those wolves can move quickly in a pack, and they'll attack the gates of the High Castle if they're in the mood. If it's a full moon, they'll kill anything in their path."

"Is that what happened to Finn?"

Colin nodded, biting his lip to hold back tears. "I got word that a regime had been sent into the Slumbering Forest to kill off a rowdy bunch of wolves. They attacked the gates three times in three nights, and merchants were afraid to head out on the north road. At the wolves' camp, they found my letters I had written to Finn. A few of them hadn't been torn apart. I was the only person they knew to notify about his death."

She reached over and rubbed Colin's back. He curled his knees in tight and his ears drooped slightly. "I'm sorry, Colin."

"I know it sounds crazy, but I think Finn was still watching over me in a way. I was going to leave the Seeker training after I got word about what happened. I went to visit Master Teagan here at the gazebo to inform him, but when I told him why I was leaving he took pity on me. That night he turned me into a stoatling, and now I think I've become one of his favorite Seekers."

Shaleigh couldn't bring herself to say anything. That seemed a rather disturbing way to think about a friend's death, but it seemed to help Colin. Just mentioning it brightened his mood as he gathered the remains of their picnic. She couldn't help but think of her dad and his strange way of dealing with her mother's disappearance. It seemed necessary to find a way to rationalize the death of a loved one, even if it might be unhealthy.

AFTER BEING in the Marketplace for only an hour, Shaleigh was already exhausted. There were shops upon shops, street vendors hawking their goods at every corner, and every inch of road was filled with carriages, wagons, and a bizarre variety of people. Minotaurs towered over most, but they could be obscured by wagons filled to the brim with goods. Even within the carriage, the noise was loud enough to make talking with Colin and Teagan difficult. To them, this seemed to be a typical day in the Marketplace.

She hadn't really understood what Colin meant about the treatment of people here, but it didn't take long to figure it out. Every person on the street who wasn't a minotaur had some distinction that made them appear not fully human—whether it was a set of golden eyes, a pair of ears that poked out through their hair, or a strange gleam of color on their skin. On closer inspection, none of them were fully human. The only ones she could guarantee were human were the people she glimpsed in the alleyways sleeping, or dressed in rags, or sitting forlorn on a bench. That was the existence Colin had escaped when he became a Seeker. In many ways, that was the future she was trying to resist.

There was one group that puzzled her though. She began identifying them by their long robes, which were fastened around the waist by a thick belt—a very different fashion from most in the streets—and usually accompanied by a piercing, unnerving gaze. The first she saw was a woman with light pink skin wrapped up in a dark robe. She had a pipe clutched in her teeth as she leaned against the wall of an apothecary. Her eyes met Shaleigh's for only an instant.

"Does she own the apothecary?" Shaleigh asked in a voice loud enough that Teagan could hear. He leaned over her shoulder to look for himself.

"No, I doubt it at least. She's likely a supplier, a magician from the north, more than likely from the Sanctuary. Those robes are typical of any magician from there."

Shaleigh turned to him. "A magician, like Master Cathal?"

"Yes, though you can never tell the skill of one unless

you test them, and I'd discourage trusting them at their word. They're rather renowned for their boasting. Some have the skill to call upon the powers of nature itself, to twist space around them, but others are better suited for changing the color of a tunic. It all depends upon the magician. That one is likely more of a traveler, someone who picks up valuables and brings them here to be turned into tonics or potions."

"Master Teagan?" Colin had been staring out the other side of the carriage at a pastry shop. "I'd like to get out here if I could. Have some catching up to do."

"Very well. Find us within the hour." Teagan glanced up the road at the long line of unmoving carriages. "Perhaps we should walk the rest of the way. The dress shop isn't far, but I would like you to meet Vivian. She'll need to take your measurements."

Colin hopped out of the carriage, and Shaleigh saw a few faces look up at him in surprise. Even here, a stoatling was an unusual sight. Then they glanced up to the carriage, likely at the royal symbol on its flank, and cast their eyes aside. In a moment Colin had slipped into the crowd. Despite his long tail and unusual appearance, his short stature was an advantage here.

"Will he be able to find us?" Shaleigh asked, worried.

"He should be. He is a Seeker after all," Teagan said as he opened the door on the opposite side of the carriage. "Come, there's no point waiting here." If she thought Colin had gotten a few stares earlier, they were nothing compared to the reaction she and Teagan received. One woman, carrying a basket on her head, stopped in her tracks and just stared at them, her mouth gaping open. Slowly the shocked expressions turned to excitement.

"Is that Master Teagan?"

"From High Castle?"

"He's just a myth, isn't he?"

"Who's the girl?"

Teagan chuckled and took Shaleigh's hand in his, walking straight into the crowd, which parted aside for him. One old man reached out to a boy, who was frozen and confused in Teagan's path and pulled him hard to the side. "Be still!" he cried at the boy's complaints, "That's the High Faerie from the castle. And take that hat off!"

It was uncomfortable to have so many eyes on them, but after the visit to the Pasture, Shaleigh understood their desire to please. She doubted the older woman was the first Teagan had driven to tears for the sake of public appeal. They passed by a bearded man in magician's robes, who only begrudgingly moved to the side with a displeased grunt.

Teagan paused beside him with a warm smile. "Come now, sir, would it hurt you to smile more?" That was when Shaleigh realized that Teagan was eating this up. The bearded man only glared, but as if on command, all of the people who had heard Teagan's words broke out into desperate smiles. Teagan was brimming over with cheer and after two blocks, Shaleigh was grateful to finally reach the dress shop and be done with the charade.

"Why do you let them do that?"

Teagan pulled off his gloves. "What do you mean?"

She lowered her voice, "They practically worship you. It's disgusting."

His smile faltered a little, and he tucked a black ribbon that had fallen down his wrist back up into his sleeve. "They fear me, which can look very much like worship. They fear me because they fear Madam Cloom. As I said, I am her reach here. I do as she asks."

Shaleigh frowned. "But you're not her. That was all you back there."

He sighed and his smile faded. "I'm sorry that you disapprove, but my orders stand. I have been requested to remind them of their place. It is my understanding that their place, more or less, is far beneath Madam and therefore far beneath me. I treat them as such." Teagan lowered his voice, but his tone was no less snarky. "Again, if you wish me to act differently, then perhaps you need to work harder to make your way to the throne."

Shaleigh shook her head. His excuse was always the same, just worded differently.

"I'm going to step inside and see if Vivian is available to see you for a few minutes. Stay put."

She nodded. Honestly, she wasn't sure where she would even go if she ran. Running home was not exactly an option.

THE MINUTES PASSED and Shaleigh waited, leaning against the wall of the dress shop. In the carriage, she was at a height where she could at least see where they were going. On the street, the road felt even more crowded. The space that people had given Teagan, merely because he was the High Faerie, was quickly overtaken by foot traffic. A light breeze was all that made the confining space more bearable. One man, carrying a ladder, asked her to step aside. A little boy ran past, giggling to himself as a trio of piglets kept close at his heels. Shaleigh had to dip into an alleyway to keep from getting run over completely.

Where the road itself was packed with people, the alleys were almost deserted. They had passed by several that had a few poor humans scratching out an existence, but this one looked empty. She positioned herself so that she could see Teagan when he came out of the shop, and waited, watching the crowds pass by. She was doing another idle scan of the area when she noticed someone staring at her. On the opposite side of the street, a man was standing in the adjacent alleyway dressed in what looked like a poncho made of a thick cloth and a wide-brimmed hat that shaded his face in the afternoon light. She looked away quickly, fixing her eyes on the door of the dress shop and wishing that Colin was still around. She thought of what he'd said to her, about how humans were treated in the Marketplace, and stepped a bit closer to the door. Teagan was taking his time.

The man in the hat stepped into the throng of people and started heading her way, his eyes focused on her. She folded her arms. Street harassers were apparently not unique to her world. The man stepped over to her. He was hunched forward and invaded her space more than he needed to. When he spoke, his voice creaked. "I've got some fresh, stuffed lizard tails if you're interested, ma'am."

Shaleigh avoided his gaze. She wasn't sure if that was supposed to be a metaphor for something else or if he really did have lizard tails. "No thanks," she muttered.

"Are you sure?" He produced a rectangular plate where eight or so tails were skewered, propped up like appetizers. Each plump, dark brown tail was about as long as her hand and had weird yellow liquid dripping beneath them. The smell wasn't terrible, but it wasn't exactly appetizing either. "They're fresh, straight from the Slumbering Forest! Just picked them up the other day, in fact."

"No thank you, I'm not interested."

"Perhaps I saw you there?" His voice lost its squeaky edge and Shaleigh recognized it immediately. She peered at the man's face and realized that his white hair could easily be quite long if it wasn't done up with twigs and ribbon.

"Talek?" she gasped. He put a finger to his lips and walked down the empty alleyway. Shaleigh gave a quick glance at the door of the dress shop before following. "How did you get in? You must be crazy to—"

"Didn't I say I would try to help you if I could?"

"Yes, but I didn't think you would actually get inside." She glanced over her shoulder, expecting Teagan to appear.

"Don't worry about him right now. I need to know." Talek took her hand and Shaleigh blushed. "There are rumors that there will be a competition tomorrow."

Shaleigh gasped, "Wait, that's tomorrow?"

Talek's conspiratorial smile faded. "So you are involved then."

"Yes, unfortunately. I'm supposed to compete against a warrior," she scoffed but the terror welled up inside her. "And here we've been touring around in a carriage all day."

"I am sorry, Shaleigh." he sighed in sympathy. "The

competition is all a farce, you know. Any excuse to turn up your corpse." He cocked his head to the side. "But it does look like you got Madam Cloom's attention at least."

She sighed. "I don't know what good that does me. If I'm going to die tomorrow, I'd rather be preparing for that than waiting in the streets here for a dress fitting."

"But you've seen it, haven't you?" He gestured to the crowds of people filing through the street behind them. "You've seen the dissent in their eyes. They fear her and everything she touches. This place is more a disease than a kingdom."

From behind them, she heard Teagan calling for her. For all the power he had and all the magic at his fingertips, it was kind of silly that he resorted to calling her name when she wasn't in sight.

"I've got to go." She turned to leave, but Talek was still holding her hand and wouldn't release his grip.

"Don't fret," he whispered to her, though his gaze was fixed at the end of the street. "I'm working on a plan to set you free." He gave her hand a squeeze, then turned to hurry to the other end of the alleyway. Shaleigh walked back to the entrance of the dress shop where Teagan and Colin were waiting for her.

"There you are," Teagan snapped, "Didn't I ask you to stand right here and wait?" Colin stood silently at his side with an amused grin.

"I tried, but there are too many—"

Teagan was in no mood to hear her reasons and held the door until she stepped inside. He slipped something out of her hand before Shaleigh could even notice. "You will not be needing this in here." He handed the item to Colin who beamed.

"Oh my gosh, lizard's tail! Do you mind—?" He held it up by the end so that the yellow liquid dripped out onto the floor. Shaleigh tried to look at him, not the tail.

"Go for it," she said, hiding a grimace.

Colin devoured it in two bites.

THE REST of the day was spent getting measurements, which Teagan assured her were very important. It didn't make much sense to Shaleigh. If Teagan could resize anything to fit her, why even go to a professional tailor? But getting fitted for your last battle was almost a rite of passage, and magic alone couldn't possibly compete with tradition, he insisted. Vivian was more than ready for the task, promising to work overnight to make sure her outfit would be ready come morning, and triple-checked each measurement before she was satisfied.

The sky outside was nearly dark by the time they finished. The streets had turned from flocks of busy workers to flocks of happy party-goers, and every over-heard conversation was about the Games tomorrow. Shaleigh felt exhausted.

All the way to the castle, Colin and Teagan spoke of nothing but the Games: the plays that would be performed, the dancers who would be there, and the clothes of every shape and fabric that would be on display. Teagan regretted that Shaleigh had to fight at all since it would be the perfect time for her to wear a lovely gown. That was honestly the least of Shaleigh's concerns.

The more she heard about the Games, the more she wanted to curl up under her bed and hide until it was all done with. She was pretty sure that she would die tomorrow, likely at the hands of a skilled warrior who had been in more battles than she had fingers. If she was lucky, she would turn out like Lauren: doing hard labor for the rest of her miserable existence. In retrospect, maybe dying was the kinder option.

She was more than happy to be allowed to return to her room when they returned to the High Castle and had to practically twist Teagan's arm for him to allow her to have dinner alone. It was only when he learned that Madam Cloom was retiring early in preparation for the Games tomorrow that he obliged, and even then, he offered to check up on her later. It was odd the way he shifted so easily; one minute he was a callous, fearmongering tool of Madam Cloom, the next he was a caring, considerate friend and guide. She wasn't sure which one was the real Teagan, but had to admit that she felt a little guilty at his crestfallen expression when she declined his offer. He probably didn't even realize he was so confusing.

Shaleigh closed her bedroom door behind her and flung herself onto the bed. She lay there for a long time just listening to the crickets outside. When a servant came with food, she asked them to leave it on her nightstand without even bothering to get to her feet. She didn't care about the concerned looks or being asked at least three times if she was alright. She simply wanted to be left alone.

She ate her dinner in silence and considered tossing grapes at the portrait of Master Cathal on the wall. It was his fault, after all, for putting her through this mess. If he had decided to die quietly without any grand predictions about coming back in the future, her life would never have been mixed up with this place. She never would have had to deal with the Games or be killed for the entertainment of strangers.

After her meal, she changed and pulled out her camera as she stretched out on the bed. It felt good to have the instrument in her hands again and even with the weight of the Games on her shoulders, merely holding it gave her a sense of control and—tenuous as it was—a sense of hope too. She turned the camera around in her hands. She hadn't had time to examine it since Talek retrieved it in the Slumbering Forest. It had several scuff marks on it, and the strap was held together by mere threads. Despite what it had been through, she could still scroll through and look at the different photos it had taken. She saw several of the Slumbering Forest, lit up with the flat, white light of the flash, glimpses of the wolves occasionally visible in the distance or in odd corners of the pictures. Even as lopsided as the pictures were, they still gave her the creeps. She crawled under the covers as she scrolled farther back in time.

It took her a minute to recognize the old bed and leaf-strewn rocking chair in the next photo. The Tree House felt like it had been a lifetime ago, and she was shocked to find, after flipping through each of the photos, that she hadn't taken a single picture of Kaeja. She went back further, back to the photos she had taken in Dean Hammond's backyard, but there were only more landscapes: gorgeous fountains, manicured shrubberies, and the house lit up for the party. She had to squint at that one, hoping that maybe she could spot her father through the distant windows, but it was fruitless. She reached the long, dark halls of Ferris Factory and felt disgusted with herself.

She had been an avid photographer for years, taking pictures of buildings falling apart and beautiful landscapes, but now she didn't have a single photo of what mattered most: her family and her best friend. Tears overwhelmed her and she resisted the urge to push the camera over the edge of the bed. Instead she propped it up on the nightstand and blew out the candles. Her heart ached. She wanted to see her father, to say goodbye; but in her foolishness, she couldn't even do that. All she could say goodbye to were forgotten passageways and an ugly fountain statue.

Shaleigh buried her face in her pillow and let the tears fall free, cocooning herself in blankets. She couldn't get warm despite the blazing fire in the fireplace and the three layers of blankets. Even if she did survive tomorrow, she might never see her father again, and she didn't even have a picture of him to ease her pain.

A PARTY IN THE CLOUDS

*M*orning came with a bustle of activity. Teagan's light rap on the door was the only warning she had before he came in with one assistant carrying a garment wrapped in silk, and another carrying her breakfast tray. He held a scroll in his hands, clutching three more under his arm, and barely looked up as he spoke.

"Good morning, Shaleigh. Apologies that we must wake you so early, but your outfit has arrived and your breakfast is ready. I want to get you dressed first before you even take a bite because we need to make sure everything fits as expected. Vivian is grabbing a bite and should be with us shortly."

Shaleigh opened her eyes blearily.

"Come now," he said when she didn't move, but when he finally looked at her, his features softened. "Did you sleep well?"

She shook her head, positive that the puffiness of her eyes and cheeks spoke of her long night. He studied her a moment before ordering the others out then sat down on the edge of the bed. "You can have breakfast first if you prefer. I hadn't considered..."

She yawned. "It's alright, you're just following orders, right?" It came out harsher than she'd intended, but she wasn't in a mood to take it back or play nice.

Teagan pursed his lips. "This is the challenge she has chosen for you. I wish I could say that you need not attend, but we both know she would find a way to force you."

"I guess that's true. Even if she told you to drag me out, you would do it, wouldn't you?" She gave him a half-hearted smile, but Teagan didn't return it.

"She wouldn't make me drag you." Teagan paused, searching for the right words. He clasped his hands on his legs and stared at the floor. "I don't think you understand what the Games are for, from her perspective. This isn't just a show for her pleasure, this is a display of power. This is where she shows the people of the Garden what the kingdom is capable of, or more precisely, what *her* kingdom is capable of."

"Okay, I get it." Shaleigh said, rubbing at her eyes. "The Games are her time to show off, and if I was a no-show, she'd be pissed."

Teagan shook his head. "That is a bit of an understatement," he said shortly. "You're the main event. You're the reason people are filling the seats right now, before dawn, hours before the Games begin. If you didn't show, or if there was any kind of flaw in her program, she would likely ask me to kill you."

Shaleigh stared at him with wide eyes. It was the

casual way he said it, as though it was small talk over tea and cakes, that sent shivers through her. She understood how the old woman had felt in the Pasture yesterday morning. At the time, Shaleigh had seen Teagan's methods as disgusting and vile. Now, she could see the monster—the killer—Teagan could so easily become. It was no wonder that Madam Cloom was determined to keep her throne. With a servant like Teagan at her side, who would challenge her?

"And to be honest, Shaleigh, I rather like you." Teagan furrowed his brows. "I really wouldn't want to have to do that to you, you do understand that, right?"

Shaleigh swallowed down the lump of fear that had formed in her throat and nodded.

Teagan watched her closely, and a frown formed on his lips. "Do you think me...barbaric?"

She blinked at him. "What?"

"You do, don't you? I recognize that look. It's different from the fear I see on the faces of those in the streets of the Marketplace and in the fields of the Pasture." His voice became a whisper. "You're disgusted with me, aren't you?" He sounded genuinely hurt.

Most people would have lied. They would have lied and given the biggest grin they could, apologies and reassurances spilling from their trembling lips. Most people would not want to alienate a self-admitted assassin, the one person who could potentially persuade Madam Cloom not to kill her, and the man who had stood up for her these past few days. Perhaps it was because Shaleigh felt her own death hovering over her head and weighing down her spirit. Or perhaps it was her own self-loathing being projected onto her captor. Either way, the words came out regardless.

"Yes, I am disgusted with you."

Teagan looked like a child who had just watched their favorite toy get shredded to pieces. He kept opening his mouth, as though words refused to obey him. "But...but why?"

"You have a disgusting deal with a disgusting person that makes you do all her disgusting dirty work," Shaleigh stated, feeling ruthless. "Isn't that reason enough?"

"Yes, but..." He got to his feet and walked to the hearth. The fire had died down to a few smoldering embers; Teagan had urged the servants to leave before they had a chance to rekindle it. He put his hands on his hips and hung his head low. It was odd to see this reaction from him. He had never really seemed human until now, even though he was clearly still a Faerie. Part of her wondered if that was the problem. Perhaps Faeries weren't supposed to ever be disgusting. She considered apologizing, but that felt wrong too. She needed to be honest. It was that same burning need she had when her father went into one of his delusions. Honesty was what kept her grounded, kept her sane.

"You can't possibly be surprised," she said.

She climbed out of bed and walked over to him, but he avoided her gaze.

"Oh, come off it! We went on a whole tour of the lands yesterday, just so you could show off what a frightening Faerie you were, and you're surprised that I'm disgusted by you?"

He folded his arms and gave a heavy sigh. "That was to let the people see your face. It had nothing to do with me."

"Please, you didn't make that woman cry just so she would know who I was. You did it for yourself."

His words came out clipped as he stood straighter, "That was a strategic measure."

"Whatever. I don't believe you."

"They needed to see you as the compassionate one, the kind-hearted one, the one who would help them. I told you this yesterday!"

She sat down on the edge of the bed and nibbled on her breakfast, letting him stew in silence for as long as his ego would let him.

"I will not stand here and be insulted!" he snapped after a few seconds. "You have one hour to bathe, eat, and dress. Do you think you can manage that on your own?"

"Yes," she managed through a bit of toast.

"Don't answer me while you're eating. Habits like that will never win Madam Cloom's favor." He stormed for the exit, swung open the door, and stood there for a moment as though he wasn't sure if he really ought to leave. "The armor is tricky. I'll check on you in a half hour. If you haven't figured it out, I will assist you." With that he slammed the door and Shaleigh nearly dropped her plate, and soon bowed her head.

AFTER TEAGAN LEFT, Shaleigh began to realize the reality of what she had done. She had turned the only powerful person in the castle who she could call an ally into an enemy. It was truly a screw-up of monumental proportions, one that her father could probably write a whole case study on. Teagan did disgust her, there was no doubt about that. Oddly enough, it wasn't his personality that did it. She had actually grown fond of him before seeing him out in the Garden yesterday. She never should have said it to his face, though. That was foolish. She had to figure out how to gain his trust again, if she could.

Shaleigh ate quickly and dealt with a cold sponge bath since she didn't know how to warm the water. She tied her twists up and pulled on the undergarments one of the servants had laid out for her. She was rather proud of herself for making such good time. In fact, she was certain she would be ready by the time Teagan returned, until she eyed the armor. When he had mentioned it would be difficult to put on, she had imagined a complicated wrapping process or that it would have ties in the back. She hadn't imagined there would be almost ten pieces to it, each one with buckles and straps to make it more confusing.

She had almost gotten her left arm on when there was a knock and Teagan breezed in, a smile on his lips when he saw her state of readiness. "I warned you it was tricky."

"No kidding," Shaleigh muttered as she tried to buckle the leather arm piece over her left bicep, her arm held up above her head. She was about to use her teeth when Teagan came to her side and assisted. He avoided her gaze though, which meant they were probably still arguing.

After getting her arms ready, Teagan began pulling on the front and back parts of the chest piece which tied along her sides in a complicated lacing.

"I don't have a clue how I would have managed that," she confessed.

Teagan chuckled, "You wouldn't have. This is practically impossible to put on without assistance."

She clenched her teeth. She wanted to ask him why he had expected her to put it on herself in the first place, but perhaps that was the point. Just like she couldn't dress herself for battle on her own, she couldn't plan to succeed on her own either. She needed Teagan's help, which he knew. Shaleigh sat down on the edge of the bed and lifted her legs so Teagan could tie on the pieces for her calves and thighs. He had finished up one leg and was moving onto the next when she mustered up the courage to talk.

"I'm sorry I snapped at you earlier."

He closed his eyes briefly. "You're worried about the impending battle. It's natural to be uneasy." He turned to her with a smirk. "However I don't think I've ever been insulted quite like that by a human."

Okay, so a simple apology wasn't going to cut it. Teagan expected more. "I shouldn't have said it, even if it is true."

His smirk cooled as he got to his feet, her leg forgotten in his budding anger. "You still insist on it then?"

"I don't want to be your enemy, Teagan. I just want to survive today. I'm sorry you find my opinions insulting, but I can't help what I feel. Maybe your acting was so good yesterday it fooled me too."

His expression softened as he knelt back down to armor the other leg. "Perhaps that is true. I forget that humans have a difficult time seeing intents and purpose behind words."

"I never thought about it like that, but I guess that's true. My father back home, he suffers from...delusions. His colleagues at work call him crazy, but hardly anyone ever asks why he suffers from them. They just want to slap a label on him."

Teagan helped her to her feet, then gave her a short bow. "I hope that you'll refrain from slapping labels on me then, Shaleigh."

She smiled, mostly because Teagan bowing to her just seemed so ridiculous after seeing everyone else grovel before him. "I can do that."

He pulled out the next piece and wrapped it around her waist. It was like a cross between a waist apron and a skirt; she grunted at the weight of it. "This feels way too heavy for me. It'll slow me down."

"It's to provide extra protection from here down." He held a hand out at her navel. "For women, it's seen as necessary."

"Necessary to weigh me to the ground," she said, already wondering if she would even make it to the Games. Teagan wrapped something else around her waist and began buckling it in front. She looked down to see a scabbard hanging at her side. The sight of it made the breath catch in her throat. She knew that she would be in battle, but she only had a vague notion of what that meant. It was going to be a one-on-one fight at least, so nothing like what she had seen in movies, but seeing the length of the scabbard as it hung against her heavy skirt made it all real. She understood the idea of dying last night when she was crying in bed with her camera, but now she understood that she might have to kill someone, or try to, at least.

Teagan went over to the breakfast that Shaleigh had rushed through and picked up the long, silk-wrapped package that had also been left on the table. She had been so angry with Teagan, she hadn't even noticed it sitting there. He held it with great respect and unwrapped it carefully, pulling back the layers of red silk, revealing the gleaming sword underneath.

"It has been forged specifically to match your height and strength." He held the blade out and Shaleigh wrapped a shaky hand around the hilt. It was much lighter than she expected. She swished it about in the air, excitement and terror mingling in her gut. She held it up and let the light dance off the blade. She was in no way an expert, but it looked very sharp. She would certainly not want to be on the opposite end of it. The warrior would be wielding a blade that had seen many bloody battles, a blade that had kept them safe for years and been relied upon for survival. And here she was with her newly minted sword, swinging it around a bedroom.

She lowered it to the ground and turned to Teagan. "I don't know if I can go through with this," she whispered. "I don't know if I could cut someone, even if I wanted to."

Teagan assisted her in sheathing it. "You will because you have no choice. There is no alternative, at least not one you ought to consider." There was concern in his eyes and he put a hand on her shoulder. "If you need inspiration, think of Lauren in the Pasture. You see the state she is in, the life that she lives. I don't enjoy kidnapping children and forcing them to fight, but if you fail to prove yourself today, I'll have to find another. It might not be for a couple of years, or it might be just a few months from now, but it is the rule of the Garden that we should search for Master Cathal's reincarnation." He bit his lip, as though trying to decide if he should say more. Shaleigh wondered then how different it might have been to meet Teagan outside of being bound to the Garden and to Madam Cloom. She knew very little about him personally, and there was something unfortunate about that, especially knowing how little time she had left.

"I think you have a good chance today. Remember, you don't have to kill your opponent, you need to look competent in combat."

She smirked. "You make that sound easy."

"I know it sounds impossible right now, but remember this is as much as test as it is a battle. Even if you take a terrible wound out there, if you can survive and outmaneuver your opponent, you will be seen as a strong leader. That is what Madam Cloom needs to see, what the people *want* to see. You must be strong. If you show any hesitancy, any weakness, she could use it against you. Do you understand?"

Shaleigh nodded and pushed down the butterflies that were forming in her stomach. "Yes, but it doesn't help my nerves at all."

He smiled and squeezed her shoulder. "You are stronger than many that have come here, and I have no reason to lie to you. Just remember my council and stay alive."

She took a deep breath as Teagan led her out of the bedroom. The sword on her hip felt heavy, despite how lightweight it felt in her hands. She could remember his words, that certainly wasn't the problem. But staying alive, oh yes, that was the tricky part.

~

THEY WENT to the main entrance, where a small group of guards stood waiting. Captain Briar stood in front, but there was no sign of Lieutenant Varg. The group saluted Teagan as they approached. The Captain smiled as she looked Shaleigh up and down. "The armor looks good on you."

"Thanks," Shaleigh said. She certainly didn't feel very powerful in it, but at least the layers made it a bit more difficult to see her trembling.

"If you would escort her to the carriage," Teagan said before turning to Shaleigh. "I need to pay a visit to Madam Cloom, but I'll catch up shortly."

Shaleigh didn't even have the chance to ask why before he turned on his heel and headed down a separate hallway. She turned to the Captain. "I don't understand. Why do I need guards? I didn't need them yesterday."

"People do crazy things when the Games begin," she said with a sigh. "It's merely a precaution since Teagan won't be with you. Ready then?"

Shaleigh nodded. She looked at the different guards around her, but none of them looked familiar. She suddenly wondered if one of these soldiers would be her opponent, perhaps Captain Briar herself. She definitely wouldn't survive then. As they went out the front gate, she looked around for any sign of Colin, Mawr, or Lieutenant Varg, but there was no one. The streets were dead, other than a long line of carriages lined up along the main road in front of the castle and a group of minotaurs huddled together laughing and chatting.

"Oh great," the Captain muttered and clenched her hands into fists. "Graddic! Am I correct in assuming you assisted with the tour yesterday?"

Graddic raised his large head, his eyes wide and his nose piercing swinging. "Yes ma'am! I sure did."

"Did the High Faerie really trust you of all creatures to pull his carriage? He must have been in a hurry."

He seemed to take some offense at her words but shrugged. "Master Teagan relies on me often for his travels, especially when he's in a hurry."

She turned to Shaleigh. "Get in, child. Don't take too long getting to the Games. Madam will be expecting you to arrive early."

Some part of her bristled at being called 'child,' but Captain Briar's authoritative tone left little room for complaints. The soldiers helped her climb into the empty carriage, but she could still hear the Captain outside and moved to peer out the window.

"No fights, no arguments, and no delays, you hear me, Graddic?"

"Yes, ma'am. She'll get there with time to spare, I promise."

"Good. She better." The Captain left behind two soldiers to guard the carriage, taking the rest back inside with her. Graddic watched her go and then turned to the soldiers.

"You two really plan to walk the entire way?"

The man and woman exchanged a glance, but the man spoke first. "Our orders are to watch the girl."

"Aye," Graddic chuckled. "You can watch her from the foot trail. I don't want you two slowing me down once we hit the road. It's a steep, difficult climb, and I don't think the Captain wants you two catching a ride along the way."

"But we must assist if there's an attack," the woman argued.

"Aye, assist! She'll have me with her, won't she? And she's the embodiment of Cathal, right? Don't you think it's a little insulting to think she needs a babysitter all the time?"

"I suppose," she started. "But—"

"Take the foot trail if you want, but if I see you approach the road, there better be a damn good reason for it."

"Yes...alright," the man said and started off for the trail. The woman was reluctant, but Graddic folded his muscular arms over his wide chest, and that seemed to motivate her to move. As the pair scrambled off, shooting worried glances back at the carriage, Graddic broke into a laugh.

"Silly stints," he said to Shaleigh. "That's a pair of new recruits if ever I saw them." He went around to the front of the carriage again. Shaleigh leaned back in her seat, wishing that she knew someone here. The only guards she had to rely on had just been chased off, and although Graddic had seemed fine the day before during the tour, she was beginning to wonder if that was only because Teagan had been at her side. Apparently traveling without the High Faerie was a very different experience.

The minutes ticked by, but still they weren't moving. The night sky was lightening and soon enough the sun would be peeking over the tree line. She could hear the minotaurs' raucous laughter from the front of the carriage. They certainly weren't in a hurry, and yet Captain Briar had indicated that Madam Cloom expected her there early. Hadn't Teagan mentioned that the Games began at dawn? She felt the hilt of the blade on her hip and reached for it. The feel of the cold metal in her grip, the ridges along the hilt, gave her confidence. Even if the odds were impossible, she at least wanted the chance to prove herself. She wanted the chance to win.

Shaleigh pushed open the carriage door. "Graddic, we need to get moving. The Games will be starting soon."

"What's that?" he asked. She could hear his hooves scrape across the gravel road as he made his way around the carriage. He was a giant of a creature, far taller than the carriage itself. The harness he wore around his bare chest was made of thick leather straps and buckles that he hooked up to pull the carriage along, but years of service made him quite strong. The horns atop his head looked deadly. They curved upwards into sharp points, far more accustomed to battles than the blade she wore on her hip.

Shaleigh tried to sound authoritative. "We need to go! Are we waiting on something?"

"Calm down," he snorted steam through his nostrils. "Are we in a hurry this morning?"

She blinked. "You heard what Captain Briar said, she expected both of us to hurry."

He chuckled as he drew nearer to the door, placing one of his massive hands on the roof of the carriage and leaning forward just enough so that Shaleigh had to back away or else get one of the horns in her face. "It's cute that you think you can give me orders, being the tiny human that you are."

Shaleigh tried to calm her breathing. She was pretty sure Graddic could maul her with those horns if he wanted to. Sure, he might get into trouble for it, but judging from the way Captain Briar spoke about him, it wouldn't be entirely unexpected. She had to admit, he was intimidating, and it was no wonder Teagan relied on him so much. Compared to the other minotaurs, he was a regular beast. If he could be persuaded to work with her instead of against her though, he might be a powerful ally. She just had to find the right words.

"You told those guards it was a difficult climb. Too difficult for you too? Is that the reason for the delay?"

He growled and lunged his horns forward. Shaleigh backed away until she was against the opposite door of the carriage. "You've got a nasty tongue there, child."

She put her hand on the hilt of her blade, wishing she had drawn it earlier. Graddic had crowded her into the carriage to the point where she didn't have room now. "I need your services, Graddic. I don't need them in an hour or a day, I need them now."

He backed off a little and pulled his horns up so they were out of her face. She took a deep breath to calm her fluttering heart.

"Ah, so this is a business discussion. I like the sound of that." He gave a pointed look to her hand on the hilt of her blade and she removed it reluctantly.

"Yes. Just business."

He snorted hot breath into her face. It smelled of wet hay and oats. "Go ahead then. What are you going to offer me for being in a hurry?" He laughed and his brown fur rippled. "Money? I'm sure you have loads of that, being a prisoner and all. What in the world does a child of the human lands possibly have at her disposal? I'm not interested in frilly dresses."

She thought for a moment. He had a good point of course. She didn't like to think of herself as a prisoner, but it was absolutely true. She had little to offer because she had little that she actually owned here. Graddic, to his credit, gave her plenty of time to answer, but Shaleigh's mind was a blank. The only thing she could think of was the sword, and she couldn't possibly give that away.

Graddic snorted with laughter. "I thought not, silly child." He turned to climb out of the carriage.

"Wait!" Shaleigh cried, leaning forward. Graddic turned with a groan. "The next time Teagan needs your services to go to the Marketplace, I'll make sure he...accommodates you."

That seemed to get his attention. "You mean, he'll buy me dinner?"

She nodded.

"And ale too?" He held up a pair of beefy fingers. "It's not a proper dinner without at least two."

"Sure. I mean...yes, he will."

Graddic gave a hearty laugh. Shaleigh wondered at first if he was mocking her, but then he put his hand out and Shaleigh shook it, trying hard not to notice how tiny her hand was compared to his.

"You have yourself a deal, child!"

"Shaleigh." she corrected, "My name is Shaleigh."

He lowered his head. "Sorry about that. Shaleigh, then."

As he closed the carriage door and headed up to the front, Shaleigh felt herself slowly deflate. She slumped in her chair until her knees rested against the seat across from her. In a moment the carriage was moving and she closed her eyes. She had no clue if she could even offer the things she promised, but she was desperate. Graddic's job might be on the line, but her life was too. She really didn't have a choice. She felt the hilt of her sword and felt rather proud of herself for getting out of that mess without having to draw it. That luxury probably wouldn't last very long.

They passed through the gates of the High Castle, on the opposite end from the road that led to the Market-place. Through the gates she could see a wide grassy field, the road carving through it and sloping steadily upwards. A heavy fog must have rolled in overnight and still hung over the field. The night sky brightened, but the fog seemed reluctant to let any light through. It made her uneasy for some reason, probably more due to her nerves than anything else. That was when she realized the carriage had stopped.

"Not again," she sighed. Was she really going to have to make an arrangement for every leg of this journey? There were voices out front, but they were harder to hear than earlier. It was like Graddic was attempting to be quiet. But she recognized his deep belly laugh and was about to open the carriage door to remind him of their arrange-ment, when the door opened on its own.

~

SHALEIGH GASPED. There stood Teagan in in the misty light. His red hair looked bright and otherworldly in the twilight and she almost didn't recognize him at first because of it. He smirked and climbed inside. "My apologies for the delay," he said as he knocked twice on the carriage wall and Graddic began pulling them again. "Madam Cloom had quite a list for me, I'm afraid. How did things go for you?"

"Terribly," she said and described to him all the problems she had run into, from her annoyance at his sudden departure to Graddic sending away the guards to the minotaur's absolute refusal to take her without some kind of arrangement.

Teagan listened to her woes patiently, looking quite displeased by the time she finished.

"So…you'll talk with him then?" She asked.

"Graddic? Oh no, he did just fine. It's you I'm disappointed with."

"Me? What did I do?"

He steepled his fingers and leaned back into his seat. "To be frank, it's more what you didn't do that has me a bit concerned. I set up this entire scenario just for you, but you still didn't rise to the bait."

"What are you talking about?"

"I was hoping you would react quite differently bearing a blade at your side. You were supposed to threaten him, to intimidate him, to make an example out of him." He exhaled through his nose. "Instead you maneuvered him. I suppose I can't complain, the results were the same, but I was hoping you would be more dramatic in your methods. Cause a stir among the other minotaurs perhaps. Make them shy away from you when you approach, drop their eyes when you look at them, possibly even spread whispers about how dangerous you are. That would have been far more preferable."

"Wait, so you set all of that up with Graddic? Even when he was threatening me in the carriage?"

"Oh yes," he chuckled. "Though that was rather kind of him to try to push your hand. I'm surprised you resisted a fight. Captain Briar was in on it too, of course. Those other guards are nowhere near us now. Likely they reported back to the Captain to prepare for the Games."

Shaleigh couldn't believe her ears. "Why would you do that?"

He leveled her with a stony gaze. "You have no reputation here, no pull with the people. You need to tap into something that makes you angry, something that fuels your rage to do what must be done. The people need to fear you if you ever wish to gain their respect."

She narrowed her eyes, "You mean like you do. Make them afraid and leave them crying in the street?"

"That's a bit melodramatic," he sneered. "But yes, more or less, that's the goal."

She crossed her arms and looked out the window at the field. The blades of grass stood motionless as they passed; the fog stayed low to the ground, blocking out most of the view. They were moving up an incline now. She thought of the magician Teagan had spoken to in the Marketplace, and the look of disgust on his face. "If I do find a way to survive this day, I don't want to rule like you and Madam Cloom do. I don't want to rule out of fear."

Teagan gave a bitter laugh. "I'm afraid it is necessary."

She glanced to him, "I don't want people to be afraid of me though. I don't like it, and I don't see how you can stand the looks you get because of it."

His smile faded. "I assure you, it is the only effective means of keeping a population under control."

"What about Master Cathal? Did he rule like that?"

Teagan was taken aback and it took him a moment to find his voice again. "Master Cathal was renowned for his powers, especially after he formed a bond with me. Of course he was feared."

"But I bet he didn't have to make his people cry like you do, did he?"

Teagan was silent.

"That's the difference. That's respect, not fear. If I must do this, that's how I want to run things."

The two of them sat in silence until the carriage came to a stop.

"Come," Teagan said as he opened the carriage door. "It's a short climb to the ridge."

THE AIR WAS brisk as she stepped out of the carriage and onto the dirt path. She looked ahead and saw Graddic unbuckling himself from the front of the carriage. The hill ahead was quite steep, but she could see the edge. The fog ended at the ridge, where beams of morning sunlight broke through. Shaleigh gasped. Was it morning already?

They couldn't be the only people here. Teagan said people were grabbing seats last night.

"Are we late?" she asked.

"Not at all," Teagan replied. "We're right on time."

She felt something heavy fall on her shoulder and had to adjust her footing to keep from falling.

"I hope that lovely piece of acting didn't ruffle you up too much." Graddic loomed over her and grinned. "But when Master Teagan asks me to do something, I like to do it right, if you understand my meaning."

Shaleigh forced a smile. "Sure, it's no big deal."

"Ha-ha!" He squeezed her shoulder and gave her what he probably thought was a light shake. Shaleigh grabbed onto Teagan's arm to keep from getting knocked to the ground. "I knew you wouldn't take it to heart! To be honest, I'm looking forward to your blade work. I was afraid if you got angry, you might slice me up!" He pulled her in close with an awkward, one-armed hug. "I should have known that Cathal's reincarnation wouldn't have to resort to such a level."

Shaleigh kept a death grip on Teagan's arm, hoping that he would get her out of the awkward situation, but Teagan ignored her wordless pleas for help.

"Thanks, Graddic," she managed, her voice muffled through his hairy arm.

"I hope you'll still treat us with a good show all the same now. I don't think anybody wants to see you chat in the arena, you know?"

Teagan pulled away from her and moved up the hill-side. For a moment, Shaleigh felt light-headed. Graddic wasn't the only one with high expectations. She would need to fight. She would need to use her sword and really try to kill someone. Teagan knew it too. Perhaps that was why he couldn't look at her now; he was dreading having to pick up her corpse later. Her hands trembled at the thought of it. "I'll see what I can do," she managed and pulled free from Graddic.

"Watch your step up there, that grass is slippery!"

She nodded and picked her way up the hill toward Teagan. He stood waiting for her a few steps from the edge of the ridge, that annoying smile back on his lips. "Graddic seems to have taken a liking to you."

"Yeah well," she forced a smile. "I did promise that you would buy him ale later."

Teagan broke into a laugh. "Oh yes, that's right. I'll be curious to see how you convince me to do that."

"I guess I don't have long to do that, do I?"

His smile faded and he gave her a pained look. He wanted to say more, she could read it on his face, but instead he held out his arm to her. She considered refusing it. Would having Teagan's help make her look weak? She certainly felt like she would fall into a thousand pieces at any minute from nerves alone.

Teagan could tell she was hesitating. "It's alright, trust me."

That was all the motivation she needed. She looped her arm around his

"You're trembling."

She gave a quick nod. "I know, sorry."

He pursed his lips and gripped her arm tighter. "You'll do fine. Don't be so nervous."

Shaleigh figured they both knew he was lying. There

was no way he could possibly still have faith in her. She wondered how many others he had said the same words to, how many others he was forced to walk up this hill and to their death.

~

WHEN THEY REACHED THE TOP, Shaleigh was blinded. The sun was directly opposite them, and she had to shield her eyes to be able to squint. She had expected maybe a stadium, maybe something like an outdoor theater, perhaps even a building. She hadn't expected anything close to this.

The sky was filled with enormous hot air balloons of every color imaginable. One was bright yellow with green stripes, another was red with bright blue polka dots that matched the robin's egg blue of the sky, and another was a rainbow of colors. There were dozens of them hovering over the deep gully that sloped below. In the center of the ring was an enormous pillar of stone and wood. Atop was a wide platform that must be where the stage stood. Crowds of people sat along the edges of the ring, but she could barely see their faces.

Standing at the peak of the hill in the chill morning air, she shivered and felt tears well in her eyes. She couldn't tell if it was from the cold, from fear of the upcoming battle, or from how overwhelmingly beautiful it was. She wished she had brought her camera with her. Teagan would never have allowed her to bring it, but she had the despairing thought that she might never again see anything as beautiful as this. She felt grateful even to be given the chance to see such colors. A strange calm came over her, the sight bringing a comfort to her soul that she hadn't even realized she was seeking. If she had to die today, this was the place to do it. Not in the grimy, dirty streets of her world, not in the forgotten hallways of decaying factories, but here amid beauty beyond anything she could have imagined.

She felt Teagan tap her arm questioningly. He was concerned for her but displayed it in a deft move that wouldn't be seen from a distance. This was a test, she reminded herself. There were hundreds of eyes upon her and she had a performance to play. Shaleigh took a deep breath and smiled at Teagan who lifted his chin in pride.

"So where do I need to be?" she asked.

"We shall be boarding the balloons. Here, come with me."

A PERFORMANCE TO PLAY

At first Shaleigh thought Teagan was joking. She looked all over the gully but didn't see a see a single balloon on the ground. All of them were in the sky, hovering like enormous, plump bumblebees with vibrant colors.

"How are we supposed to do that?"

"There are bridges," he stated simply.

Propped against the edge of the gully was what she had first thought was an anchor for a balloon, but now she saw that it was the end of a rope bridge. Planks of wood ran along its base with thick ropes as handrails. It looked like it was fastened deep into the ground, but the bridge swayed back and forth with the strong wind. The other end was attached to the entrance of a hot air balloon.

"It doesn't look very safe," Shaleigh whispered.

Teagan chuckled, "I don't see why you're so concerned. Didn't you just say that you didn't expect to have long to live today?"

Shaleigh bit her lip. It was one thing to die in combat, it was another to fall such a great distance from trying to board a hot air balloon. Teagan stepped confidently onto the bridge, his arm still wrapped around Shaleigh's. She put a foot out and felt the wood bend beneath her. She shook her head and grabbed hold of the wooden pole that fixed the bridge to the ground.

"I'm not getting on that."

Teagan froze and blinked in confusion. "I assure you it's safe."

The small amount of swaying from a distance seemed far stronger now that she was close. The center of the bridge swayed so much she was certain she would either pass out or vomit part of the way there. It wasn't the height that bothered her, it was that the bridge was so structurally unsound. The ropes were fraying in places, she could see tendrils blowing in the wind. Some of the wood looked rotted and at least twenty percent of the boards were missing. If it looked structurally sound, Shaleigh could jump around on it all day without worry. This was different though. It didn't look like it was held up by magic, like Madam Cloom's Overlook, nor did it possess the color and cleanliness that indicated it was one of Teagan's creations. It looked like a poorly-made rope bridge that was hardly ever used.

"Teagan..." she whispered, trying to find the words to explain her unease.

"Come now, have I asked you to do anything before that would put your life in danger?"

She glared at him. "You asked me to come here, didn't you?"

He frowned. "Besides that, of course."

She took a deep breath and tried to ease the butterflies in her stomach. "You're not helping."

He leaned in so close that she could feel the warmth of his breath on her ear. "Remember what I said about showing weakness here. They want you to fail. Don't let them intimidate you. Why do you suppose Madam Cloom insists that the Chosen be brought to the Games in this way?"

She gave a weak nod. He spoke the truth, but that didn't prevent her from shaking.

"Madam Cloom was able to walk up these bridges earlier this morning without a moment's hesitation."

She looked at him. "Really? You're not just telling me that to make me walk, are you?"

He gave a sly grin. "Of course not."

Shaleigh rolled her eyes. Teagan was the worst motivational speaker. Even Mawr would have given her more confidence. "Alright, just don't let go of me, okay?"

"I wouldn't dream of it."

It took a few more seconds of deep breathing before she could convince her feet to shuffle forward. She hadn't intended to clutch Teagan's arm as hard as she did, but he didn't complain. Her other hand gripped the rope to the point she thought she might give herself rope burn. Around the middle section of the bridge a large wind gust struck them and they both stopped. The ropes squeaked and groaned as they drifted to the side. The balloon in the distance seemed to lurch. She wrapped her forearm around the rope and looked up at Teagan. He braced himself but didn't look nervous. She wondered if Teagan had no concept of how gravity worked. Thinking back to the Overlook, it seemed possible.

They drifted further to the side and she leaned against him as the bridge moved sideways. The balloon ahead looked like it was at a forty-five-degree angle.

"Teagan," she whimpered.

"Don't be frightened," he chuckled. "If there really was anything to fear up here, do you think I would be so calm?"

"I don't know. You seem pretty invested in this High Faerie role of yours."

He broke out into deep laugh as the wind blew even harder and they drifted to the side again. It whistled in her ears to the point where she could barely hear. The hot air balloon hovered calmly in the distance. What bothered her was that the balloon looked almost completely sideways. This brought on a vertigo spell and she wondered what would happen if she fainted. They would probably wake her just in time to fight.

"Goodness," Teagan called over the wind. "Perhaps I should have extended it out a bit more. I hadn't realized it was so windy today."

Shaleigh could only nod. The wind stole the air from her lungs. She bent her legs and would have crouched had Teagan let her. The bridge swung to the left, then to the right, then to the left again as it slowly found its center. The wind finally died down, but Shaleigh's stomach was still moving. Teagan tried to move forward, but Shaleigh couldn't move. Her body wouldn't let her; the dizziness and nausea made her afraid.

"Are you alright?" Teagan asked.

"Give me a minute," she muttered, forcing herself to take deep breaths. Slowly the nausea faded. The light-headedness was still there but she could move her legs again. "I'm just going to keep my eyes closed, if that's okay with you."

"Of course," he said in an amused tone. "Don't let go of me or the rope though. If you do faint, I want to be able to catch you at least."

Slowly they made their way along the bridge. She was probably playing right into Madam Cloom's expectations. The silly teenager from the Human World who couldn't even handle a simple rope bridge without passing out. At least she had kept her stomach in check though, and Teagan wasn't having to carry her. She thought of Lauren having to make this trip at only eight years old. She probably did pass out. She probably had to be carried. During the fight she had probably been bawling her eyes out.

Shaleigh set her jaw and forced herself to stand taller. She couldn't let herself be intimidated. That was all this was, a game of intimidation. She had to be more than that. She had to prove herself, not just so she could get back to her father, she realized, but also for all the Laurens who had come before her, for the others who had not been strong enough to stand this terrible test.

As they approached the balloon, Shaleigh broke into a quick walk and stumbled onto the platform without Teagan's aid. She took hold of the metal handrail along the edge of the wooden basket and leaned heavily against it. She had to keep breathing. The wind here was practically nonexistent, she realized, and she understood then what Teagan had meant. He must have some kind of barrier up to keep the balloons from flying away, though it was rather convenient that he forgot to extend it all the way along the rope bridge. There was no way Madam Cloom had come this way without protection.

"Can I help you, ma'am?" There had been someone waiting in the basket, someone dressed in bright colors, but Shaleigh couldn't acknowledge anything right now. She needed to gather her composure first.

"Yes, we need a connection, please," Teagan said in his silky voice stepping into the basket. Thank goodness he was there to help.

She took in a deep breath and forced herself to stand a bit taller. "Yes," she said as she turned around to greet the balloon attendant. "We need a connection."

The man had reddish-brown skin with light blue lines along his cheeks that matched his eyes. Another being that must have been part human and part something else. He wore a floppy yellow hat with orange polka dots and a matching shirt and pants that looked rather ridiculous. Then she realized it was the same color as the hot air balloon above them.

"What balloon do you need?"

"Excuse me?" She looked out at the wide array of balloons around them. Was she supposed to tell him a color? How was she supposed to know that?

The man gave a thin-lipped smile with a brief glance to Teagan. "Who are you trying to reach, ma'am?"

"Madam Cloom," she said.

"Ah, very good then." He turned around to a wooden ship's wheel, only the arms were swathed in different fabric swatches. He pulled down a piece of wood that was wrapped in purple fabric with black stripes.

"That would be the purple and black lines." He went over to unlatch the opposite entrance of the wooden basket. The door lowered down like a tiny drawbridge, and Shaleigh looked to see another rope bridge unraveling itself in their direction. "You'll need to be connected to the green and blue vertical lines first. Then you can head straight there."

"Excellent, thank you," Shaleigh tried to give a warm smile, despite the dread that filled her at having to walk across two more precarious bridges.

The man crouched down and hooked the bridge up to his exit. This bridge was on an incline, though it didn't sway at all in the wind.

"Tell me again, why balloons?" she whispered to Teagan as the man tied the bridge onto the balloon, pushing back his floppy hat that kept falling into his eyes.

"They offer the best view of the performances." He nodded over to the precipice in the center of the gully. All the balloons hovered in place around it. They were easier to see at this range, and she could even pick out their formational pattern. They floated in concentric rings around the precipice, but also at various levels of height, giving multiple layers probably for the wealthier or more influential members of the Garden. "Not only that," Teagan added, "but it's also the safest location."

Shaleigh laughed at that, garnering a curious glance from the balloon attendant. "Safer? Really? What kind of crazy person thinks this is safe?"

Teagan frowned. "I did."

Her laughter broke off. "Do Faeries normally use balloons like these?"

"Of course not! We sit in the trees, but that idea rather unsettled Madam Cloom. She thought it would be too reminiscent of when Faeries ruled to be...*appreciated* here."

"Isn't that what keeps the Garden running though, your magic?"

"Ah, not quite. It is my magic, but it is bolstered by the pact put together by Master Cathal. So, to be precise, it is Faerie magic mingled with that of a powerful magician."

"There you go," the man announced as he stood up brushing his hands against his pants. "All set."

"Excellent," Teagan said as Shaleigh gave a heavy sigh. Together they stepped onto the next bridge. This time Shaleigh was determined to keep her eyes open the whole time.

THE NEXT TWO bridges were nothing like the first one they had climbed. Without the wind she could even enjoy them, and Shaleigh had no problem walking across the next bridge. By the time they reached the third bridge, she was actually looking forward to it, and insisted she didn't need Teagan to escort her.

"If you insist," he smiled. "Though Madam Cloom might find it reckless."

"Good," she said with a grin. "Didn't you say I couldn't show any weakness?"

Teagan chuckled.

Madam Cloom sat on the largest balloon in the air,

which wasn't entirely surprising since she enjoyed taunting others with the amount of power she had at her fingertips. Shaleigh wouldn't be surprised if Teagan had been called in simply to make certain the balloon was of an appropriately arrogant size. The basket beneath it was equally grand. She noticed that most of the connection balloons they had traveled through had uncomfortable wooden chairs to sit on, but Madam Cloom had a set of plush couches. That also wasn't surprising. The sides of her basket were made of wrought iron to give the clearest view of the stage, which must have been quite heavy for the balloon. Shaleigh frowned. It was another example of impossible physics only made possible by Teagan's magic. Again, she had to remind herself that if Madam Cloom could sit there without worry, then it should be safe for her as well.

Madam Cloom gave a dry laugh as Shaleigh approached without Teagan's escort.

"Excellent," she cooed with a forced smile. "I'm so glad to see you made it."

"Good morning, Madam." It was a struggle to make her voice calm.

Madam Cloom looked up to Teagan and gave a genuine smile. "It seems you were deemed unnecessary this morning, Teagan."

He gave a brisk bow. "Indeed, she insisted on greeting you directly."

She narrowed her eyes a bit. "Oh yes? How lovely."

Shaleigh stood there for a moment, not quite sure what she was supposed to do, but not daring to ask. Teagan stepped forward and indicated a smaller couch at

Madam Cloom's side. Once she was sitting down, she realized that despite Madam Cloom's short stature, her chair had her sitting higher than anyone else. Even the nearby balloons had to hover at a lower level from her. The only person above her was Teagan.

"So, what are these Games like?"

Madam Cloom laughed, "Oh they are unlike anything you've probably seen in your simple world, child."

Shaleigh was taken aback by the demeaning comment, but held her tongue. This was a challenge, she reminded herself once again, one that would test her limits to control her temper. She needed to keep herself in check despite the urge to lash out.

"Oh excellent! The first one looks to be a performance. A drama of some kind. These are always entertaining." Madam Cloom leaned forward eagerly. "What a wonderful way to begin the occasion! Was this your idea, Teagan?"

Teagan stood on Madam Cloom's opposite side with a grim expression and didn't respond.

Below them on the precipice, actors emerged from stairways on either side of the wooden structure. They were dressed in long brown robes with bits of ivy strewn about their heads. Madam Cloom's balloon was quite close to the show, but it was surprising how clear their voices were from this distance. Either the actors' voices had some type of spell on them, she decided, or the balloons themselves were enchanted.

The play opened with a young blond woman pining over a married man with children. The blond donned the look of an old woman, and soon befriended him and his family. Shaleigh could guess where it was headed. She had seen plenty of movies with a similar plot: it would either turn into a romance or a comedy. When one of the man's children realized the blond woman's disguise, she expected it to be funny.

The blond woman was put on trial and found guilty of misleading the family, which apparently meant she would be put to death. That seemed quite extreme to Shaleigh, and she was happy to see the man protest against it. As he fought to tear her away from the guards, he himself was cut through. It wasn't an act either: Shaleigh saw the sword go through the man's belly and out the other side. Blood spouted everywhere as he cried out in pain. Shaleigh squirmed in her seat as the man fell to his knees, clutching at his stomach and sobbing. Madam Cloom gave a low laugh as the blood poured out beneath them. Shaleigh looked to Teagan, hoping that the blade was somehow enchanted, but his look said otherwise. She took a deep breath and watched in mute horror as the man was dragged sobbing from the stage.

The next scene was to be the young blond woman's execution, only this time it was a different actress. The woman was older than the young actress had been, and her blond, frizzy hair hung in loose curls around her head. Tears were streaming down her cheeks as she was led bound to the center of the stage. Her head was soon tied down to a stone block, an executioner's block.

"Surely they won't..." Shaleigh whispered. Her mouth was dry and her fingers gripped the arms of the couch.

Madam Cloom hummed an assent and leaned over to

speak in a low voice. "It is rather gruesome, isn't it?" She drawled as a man in a black hood stepped onto the stage.

A drumbeat began. Shaleigh didn't want to watch and yet couldn't bring herself to look away. She swallowed down the lump in her throat. She couldn't show weakness before Madam Cloom, but she couldn't sit here mute either.

"They aren't really going to kill her, are they?"

"Fake wounds aren't permitted on this stage," her voice lilted with enthusiasm. "The audience demands realism, and realism must be delivered."

"They're really killed?"

Teagan stepped around behind Madam Cloom and crouched down between them. "The actors are not killed, merely the prisoners."

Shaleigh felt nausea creeping up as the executioner lifted his axe high to the cheers of the audience. "But that man earlier..."

"He will recover, I promise you," Teagan assured.

As the executioner brought the axe down, Shaleigh had to turn away. The woman's scream was cut short, and the crowd went wild for it. Cheers erupted from every balloon in sight, whistles and screams arching over the din of noise. Shaleigh thought she might be sick and forced herself not to look at the stage.

Madam Cloom sat back in her seat and motioned for Teagan, who was almost instantly at her side. "I want to make an announcement," she said.

"Of course." Teagan pulled off his glove and put his hand to Madam Cloom's throat. It was a strange sight after knowing the woman below had been beheaded. He held his hand there for a moment, eyes narrowed, humming notes under his breath. A thin black ribbon slid down his wrist from beneath his cuff, tied into a knot. Shaleigh had seen it briefly before at the Marketplace. At this angle Shaleigh was sure she had seen some silver inscription on it, but it was too small for her to read.

He pulled his hand away and gave a quick nod before replacing his glove, careful to push the ribbon back into his sleeve. Madam Cloom stood and went to the edge of the basket to grip hold of the gate. Teagan gave Shaleigh a concerned look, and it was then that she understood why Madam Cloom had waited until then to make an announcement. She took a deep breath and sat up straight.

"Attention everyone! Please lend me your eyes and ears for a few moments." Her voice boomed over the gully, even louder than the voices of the actors. All eyes turned to them, from each colorful balloon to the masses of people crowded beneath them. Shaleigh closed her eyes and took another breath, trying to ignore the bloody mess that was being mopped off the stage by a handful of assistants.

"In honor of the talented drama we just witnessed, I would like to introduce someone who has already made something of a name for herself. Please welcome Shaleigh, the girl from the Human World who we believe may be the reincarnation of the great Master Cathal."

Shaleigh should have seen this coming. It was the perfect chance to throw her off guard, to undermine her before the entire population of the Garden, and to show how weak and frail she was. She had to admit it was quite clever. Despite Teagan's reassurances earlier, she wasn't at all prepared for this. Nothing could have prepared her for that gruesome scene on stage.

Excitement darted among the crowd. Several got to their feet and donned glasses to get a better look at her. Shaleigh forced her lips into a grin.

"She might not look it, but she bears perhaps the closest mark we've seen, despite the obvious physical differences." Madam Cloom gave a short laugh at the end, which pulled more laughter from the audience. Shaleigh drew back into the cushions of her chair, wishing she could hide behind it.

"I'm sure many of you have seen her, roaming about the Pasture or the Marketplace, as clueless as a lost puppy." More laughter. Shaleigh felt like she was back in high school, only being the butt of a joke in a classroom was entirely different from having an entire city laughing at you. This made Dean Hammond's party look like a picnic.

She felt Teagan's warm hand on her shoulder and took a shaky breath. He squeezed, and Shaleigh knew what he was trying to say: be strong, be confident, don't doubt yourself. Really it was what he had been telling her all morning; she simply hadn't understood how important it was until now.

"Despite her adjustment problems, my brilliant servants have shown her the highest hospitality and comforts. We shall groom her to be a leader that the Garden can be proud to claim. Her name and great deeds will reverberate throughout history, the same as mine, and the same as Master Cathal's." She held out a hand and turned back to Shaleigh, "I give you Shaleigh Mallett, our newest Chosen."

Shaleigh got to her feet with her heartbeat pounding in her ears. She felt like a ghost as she waved to the onlookers. There must have been hundreds of them. Instead of laughing, they were cheering, even applauding. She saw genuine excitement on their faces. Teagan put a warm hand to her throat, and she jerked to the side.

He blinked. "It's to amplify your voice," he stated simply and replaced his hand as he hummed the same tune as earlier.

"I don't need it," she said through a clenched smile.

He arched an eyebrow at her but continued his humming. She wished that her legs weren't trembling so much beneath her. She had seen Dean Hammond give plenty of speeches over the years, and although his were given in his home or out in his backyard, he always seemed so comfortable. Even her father could give speeches sometimes, even though he was the most socially awkward person she knew. Teagan stepped back and gave her a short nod and an encouraging smile.

She stepped forward to the edge of the basket, surprised that Madam Cloom stepped aside for her. She gripped the cold metal and tried to think of what to say. "Greetings, everyone." Her voice boomed over the gully, sounding almost unrecognizable. She broke out in a sweat despite the chill morning air. "I'm honored to be here, to be among you, and to be a Chosen... person." *Chosen person*, she thought, that's a great line. "I'll admit that I don't understand, or really agree with everything I've seen here so far, but I hope to be able to help."

She looked out at the confused faces, at couples whispering to each other, at the falling smiles. She was losing them. She had to think of something more to say, she couldn't leave them upset. Not when she probably would never get another chance. "I only hope that I can be as gracious, as patient, and as...well, as wise as Master Cathal was. I never met him, of course," a few weak, polite chuckles went through the crowd. "But if I can be even half as great a leader as he was, then I'm doing the right thing. Thank you."

She gave a quick curtsy, which surprisingly brought about applause. They're just being polite, Shaleigh thought to herself. She had completely bombed it. She could just imagine her English teacher back at school shaking her head. How in the world could she use the word 'thing' in a royal speech? She was hopeless at this. Even when her life depended upon it, she couldn't get it right. She turned around and tried not to look panicked as she somehow found her way back to her chair without toppling to the ground.

Teagan was at her side in an instant and she was grateful to feel his hand against her throat. She mouthed at him once he finished humming, "Is it off?" He gave a quick nod. Madam Cloom was back at the gate, and Shaleigh was surprised to hear the annoyance in her voice.

"I believe next up we have a pair of fabulous dancers. Let us continue with the Games, shall we?" The crowd erupted into applause. When Madam Cloom turned around, her smile was gone and she looked angry. Surely, she wasn't upset that Shaleigh had destroyed that impromptu speech? Teagan came to her and removed the charm as Madam Cloom sat back in her chair.

"Thank you, Teagan." She huffed, then gave a toothy grin to Shaleigh. "I swear, all you have to do is promise a bit of bloodshed, maybe a few deaths, and they go absolutely wild."

Shaleigh took a moment to make sure her voice wouldn't waver. "But you set up these Games, don't you?"

She sighed. "It's necessary to keep them in line. They are a difficult crowd to please, but perhaps one day you'll understand that yourself. Give them water and they want wine. Give them bread and they want mutton. Give them a historical play and they want it filled with the blood of their enemies." She chuckled under her breath and held her hand out. A servant appeared with a glass of red wine. Madam Cloom drank deep and said nothing more.

Out on stage two lovely ballerinas began a jerky dance together. Shaleigh eyed the other balloons instead, watching the men and women enjoying the show. She searched for any sign of that cruel glee that Madam Cloom spoke of. She spotted several who waited intently for the dance to turn dark, which Shaleigh guessed it probably would do. That seemed to be a theme in the Games so far. Most of them had that same queasy expression that Shaleigh felt. Most of them were just as horrified as she was, at least, of the ones she could see. She wondered if the crowds on the ground were any different, or if the reason that it was 'safer' to be in balloons was because the populace didn't entirely approve either.

"Speaking of bloodshed, isn't it time for her to be

going below? She's up next, isn't she?" Madam Cloom pointed her glass to Shaleigh.

"Indeed, Madam. It is about that time. If you will excuse us," he gave her a short bow. She waved him off.

"Go on then," she said with a tiny smirk. "Just don't take forever."

Shaleigh felt her stomach drop just when she had begun to get a handle on her nerves. It felt like the Games had only just begun, and already she would need to fight. She wondered how long it would take them to clean up her blood off the stage before the next performance.

Teagan came around and helped her to her feet, but they didn't head to the bridges.

"Where are we going?" Shaleigh asked, trying not to catch Madam Cloom's attention.

"You'll see," he said and slipped off his gloves. That same black ribbon fell around his wrist and the silver lettering caught her eye. Whatever was written on it wasn't in English. Teagan pursed his lips, slipped it deftly into his sleeve again, and gestured for her to come to him. They were standing at the edge of the basket behind the couches where Madam Cloom sat; there were no balloons on this side.

"But the stage is behind us," she whispered, stepping closer so that she was within arm's reach.

"The bridges take too long, and Madam Cloom requested haste." Teagan put an arm around her waist and Shaleigh felt the blood rush to her face. She put a hand on his arm with the intent to push him off, but Teagan was insistent.

"I'm a Faerie, remember?"

"Okay, what does that have anything to do with—" She gasped as he leaned down and looped his other arm around her knees, pulling her easily into his arms. "Hey!"

Teagan leapt onto the metal fencing of the basket. She had just enough time to gasp for air before he leapt and gravity took hold as they careened toward the ground.

WIND WHISTLED past her ears and the ground rushed up to meet them. Tears were whisked away before they even left her eyes. She gripped Teagan's arm so hard she thought she might break it. He had said he was a Faerie, but what the hell did that mean? Was it code for: it's time to kill you?

They were only a few seconds away from hitting the ground and Shaleigh held an arm up to protect her face against the impact. Then they slowed and soon they were hovering in the air like a pair of interlocked feathers. She looked up at Teagan, her cheeks wet and stinging.

"I told you," he said with a smirk. "I'm a Faerie. I thought it was understood that I could fly."

Shaleigh stared at him. Was this his sick idea of a joke? Was it somehow amusing to make her think she was going to fall to her death? Most of the time she tried to give him the benefit of the doubt, to not assume that he intentionally meant to be cruel even when he assaulted people, but this was entirely different.

When they finally touched down, Shaleigh couldn't push out of his grip fast enough. He let her go and she tumbled, weak-kneed, to the ground. The wet grass was cold on her palms, but she was just so happy to feel steady earth beneath her that she gripped her fingers into it.

Teagan squatted down in front of her, still wearing that stupid smirk. "I take it you didn't enjoy that."

"You're crazy," she gasped, still breathless.

He chuckled, but Shaleigh wasn't finished.

"Don't you ever come near me again!"

He blinked, "What? It was merely a jest, I meant you no real harm."

She was shaking from head to toe and couldn't tell if it was from the damp grass soaking through the gaps in her armor, from her terror from the fall, or if she was simply that furious. "How the hell was I supposed to know that, Teagan? You jumped off!" She glanced up to the balloon's basket hovering so far above them and shuddered. Teagan at least had the decency to be dumbstruck. "You just finished telling me this morning how you would hate to have to kill me, how much you wanted to help me because Madam Cloom could have me murdered at any time. How was I to know this wasn't her idea? How was I supposed to know you wouldn't let go?" Her voice cracked at the end and she turned away from him.

"I'm sorry," Teagan whispered. "I hadn't even considered that you would see it like that. I merely thought it would surprise you, and perhaps you might—"

"Might what? Enjoy falling to my death?" Her throat was constricting, but she fought back the tears that wanted to overwhelm her. She couldn't break. "Damn it, Teagan," she wiped at a tear that rolled down her cheek. "You're supposed to be supporting me here. You're supposed to be on my side."

Teagan clutched at his arms as though her words had truly wounded him. "I'm sorry. I am trying to support you. I suppose...I'm not very good at it."

Shaleigh tried to climb to her feet, but her legs were still too shaky. She couldn't bring herself to stand, and instead she fell on her rear again. "Damn it!" she clawed her fingers into the dirt.

Teagan crouched down beside her and put an arm around her shoulders. "Calm down, relax for a moment."

The absurdity made her break into laughter. "Calm down? I'm about to go fight to my death, and you want me to calm down?" She sniffled like a child who had skinned her knee. "Can they see us down here?"

"Who?"

"The people above us. The people in the balloons, Madam Cloom, all of them."

"No," Teagan said. His voice was different now compared to the cocky man who had gleefully leapt into thin air, dragging Shaleigh with him. He squeezed her shoulders and said in a whisper, "You don't need to always be strong, Shaleigh. You have every right to be angry. I've wronged you, and there's really no way I can make it up to you."

Shaleigh took a deep breath. "You get carried away, that's your problem. Just like in the Pasture. People aren't your playthings, you know."

There was a loud boom that shook the entire gully.

They both jumped, and Teagan leapt to his feet. "What in the world?" He turned around and searched the ground. The music that had been accompanying the dancers paused; evidently the noise was loud enough for the audience to hear it as well. Then Shaleigh spotted something enormous coming toward them through the grass, bounding in fluid leaps.

"Shaleigh!" Mawr called as he drew close, "Are you alright?"

Teagan stepped forward to try and intersect him. "Halt right there! I can assure you she's perfectly fine." His words were terribly ineffective. Mawr didn't even slow his pace and kept bounding forward like an adorable battering ram. The High Faerie was tossed aside as though he were nothing more than a shrub.

Shaleigh got to her feet and wrapped her arms around the lion's stone head in a hug. He felt coarse and cold, but she was so relieved to see him that she didn't care. His long whiskers scraped against her arms and caught in her armor like thin spears, and something on his face dug into her cheek, but she continued hugging him anyway. "Mawr," she whispered. "I'm so happy to see you!"

"I saw him jump off that balloon with you, and I was worried he might have killed you!" Mawr urged, his eyes rolling toward Teagan, who was getting to his feet. "I couldn't just stand there. Those minotaurs tried to hold me back, but I told them I needed to see if you were alright. So...I jumped."

Her eyes went wide and she pulled back so she could look him in the eye. Something was different about him, but she wasn't sure what. "You didn't hurt yourself, did you?"

"Oh no, I was alright. You're the one that's easy to break, Shaleigh." He nuzzled her hand and scraped her fingers a bit. That was when she noticed the golden chain around his neck.

"What is this?" she asked following it up and around back to his face. "Glasses! Mawr, you can read again!"

"Oh yes! They hadn't let me see you, so I couldn't show them to you. They won't let me anywhere near the castle." He turned around and used his massive body to block her from Teagan. "Who are you?" he demanded, "And why are you trying to kill my friend?"

Shaleigh stepped around Mawr's body so she could see Teagan's exasperation. His expression was priceless. "My apologies, Mawr." He gave a brisk bow. "My name is Teagan, and I had thought Shaleigh would enjoy it. I had no intention of harming her."

Her eyes narrowed. What was he playing at, not including his title? Every time she thought she had a handle on him, he threw her off guard. Perhaps he thought it was funny for a Living Statue to be so attached to her, or perhaps he was trying to prove that he too could be her friend, that he could command respect without relying on cheap intimidation tactics. At least, she hoped the latter was his angle.

"You obviously haven't been around many humans then," Mawr scoffed. "They're not as hardy as the rest of us. Their bones are very fragile and they lose blood easily." His voice grew soft as though he recalled every death he had seen in Aife.

"Mawr, it's alright. Teagan has promised not to do it again, haven't you?"

Teagan pursed his lips but nodded. At least he knew when he couldn't win an argument.

"I don't like him," Mawr rumbled in a whisper to her that was clearly audible to Teagan. "He looks too much like a Faerie."

"That's because he—"

"I don't think it's wise to stay down here," Teagan said, cutting Shaleigh off. "Those minotaurs will be looking for you, and it's not exactly difficult to spot you from a distance."

Mawr eyed him with some suspicion, but then turned fearful eyes up to the walls of the gully again. "Yes, you do make a good point, Mr. Teagan."

"Besides I've got to get Shaleigh ready. She has a show starting soon."

"A show?" Mawr asked looking worried. "I hope not like the one where that nice old lady died. She looked really upset! I couldn't watch it."

Teagan frowned, and a sadness tugged at him as though he had forgotten not to care.

"It's not going to be a show like that," Shaleigh said, reluctant to tell the truth. "I'm sure Teagan will make sure you're in a safe place, won't you?"

He nodded. "Stay here. I won't be but a moment."

Shaleigh waited as Teagan led Mawr away. Above her, music from the dancers' performance lilted down and echoed off the grass-covered walls of the gully. From down here, the crowds were distant, Madam Cloom was nowhere to be seen, and for the first time in days, Shaleigh was alone with her thoughts outside the confines of her room. She let the humid air fill her lungs.

"Try to stay alive," Shaleigh said to herself. "You can do

that. You've been doing it for days, right? Doing it with a sword shouldn't be that different."

"Shaleigh?" Teagan had moved so quietly she hadn't even heard him approach. "Are you ready?"

"I hope so."

~

TEAGAN LED her to the center of the gully, to a cylindrical pillar, on top of which stood the stage. She had thought it was a natural rock formation, but now she saw that the structure was made entirely of wood. It towered over her and through cutouts that looked like windows she could see the bustling of people inside.

Teagan stepped forward and pulled back the leather flap that hung over the entrance. Her eyes took a moment to adjust to the darkness. A center hallway led inward but tiny chambers, likely dressing rooms, broke off on either side of it. A few were closed off, but many were left open. At one table, a man put thick, colored makeup on his cheeks, and in another, a woman pulled on a long pink wig.

"After your battle, we're scheduled to have clowns enter the stage," Teagan explained.

"That makes sense," she said sarcastically. "I guess they'll need the humor after I bleed out."

Teagan gave a weak smile and urged her forward. They walked through slowly, mostly because people kept darting in front of them between the small chambers. Although Teagan's presence garnered respect here, these people didn't have time for pleasantries or bows. All they could manage was a quick nod on occasion.

"Shaleigh? Is that you?" She turned and spotted Lieutenant Varg in one of the rooms at his own table, dressed in a full suit of shiny, metal armor. She grinned and maneuvered around a pile of boxes to get into his room. He patted her shoulder, "I heard you would be here! Did I miss your speech?" His smile faded as he gave a curious look at her outfit.

"You're the last person I expected to see down here," Shaleigh said, her eyes drifting to an open locket on the desk. Inside she could just glimpse the smiles of a dark-haired woman and two young boys. "Are you on duty?"

"No, no, I was asked to be in some sort of combat," he shrugged and Shaleigh felt a cold pit form in her stomach. "Unfortunately, they won't tell me who it's against. Some novice, but that hardly counts as combat to me." He laughed, obviously expecting her to join in.

Shaleigh stared at him, wishing she had misheard him, wishing she hadn't spotted that locket, and wishing she could remember to breathe. "Oh god," she whispered. "No...it can't be you!"

His laughter faltered, "What do you mean?"

"You're the one?"

Teagan stepped in front of her and redirected her toward the door of the chamber. "It's not important, Lieutenant."

"What's she talking about? I'm the one what?"

"She's merely upset," Teagan soothed. "She's had a rather stressful day and will be needed up top shortly. Come, Shaleigh." He turned and Shaleigh followed him down the rest of the hall in mute shock. She couldn't fight Lieutenant Varg. He was perhaps the nicest soldier in the entire castle. She couldn't even imagine pretending to fight him, not after the kindness he had shown her.

They were alone by the time they reached some sort of elevator shaft and Shaleigh grabbed Teagan's arm. "Is it true?" she asked, her eyes searching his. "Is he my opponent?"

Teagan gave a short nod.

"You knew the whole time, didn't you?"

"I did not. Had I known, I would have given you some warning." He sighed. "I'd guess this was Madam Cloom's idea, or Captain Briar's."

"Oh, don't even start ragging on them."

"Honestly I'm as shocked about this as you are. Surely you believe me. I may be cruel at times, and I suppose sometimes even disgusting." Just saying the word made him shudder. "But I would never exploit your emotions like that. That is a blow only of Madam Cloom's caliber, I assure you. Either that, or the Captain simply chose him for his fighting finesse, since even he didn't know precisely what he would be doing."

A series of pulleys above their heads creaked and groaned, and a large crate landed in front of them. At least, judging by its walls, it looked like a large crate. Its floor was solid wood. Teagan wound a handle on the side to pull the door open. He turned to her, expecting her to step inside, but Shaleigh couldn't bring herself to move. Her body refused to obey her suddenly and she pursed her lips. He crouched down in front of her.

"You know I'll be rooting for you," he said, putting a

hand on her shoulder.

She gave a dry laugh. "I don't think the fight will last long enough for you to root for me."

He squeezed her shoulder and his mask fell. For the first time ever, he looked genuinely sad. "I'm sorry, Shaleigh. I wish I could have helped you more, prevented this from happening."

She swallowed down the lump in her throat. "You can't help it. In a way, you're a prisoner here too, aren't you?"

He blinked at her, taken aback, then looked to the ground. He took a deep breath. "If you are injured, know that I'll be the first one at your side."

"And if it's fatal?" she asked, her voice barely more than a whisper.

He put a hand to her cheek. "Our healing capabilities are the best, but if you are injured in a way that we cannot heal you, then I will make sure your suffering is brief."

It was so strange to think in five minutes she could be lying on the stage, dying, and the one person who understood her, the one person who would be compassionate to her suffering would be Teagan. Annoying Teagan who was so caught up in his ego trip that he forgot that not everybody worshiped him. Disgusting Teagan, making poor old ladies cry in the streets. In that moment though, he was the only person left and she didn't want to leave him. She jumped forward and wrapped her arms around his shoulders, squeezing tight, letting tears fall against his jacket. "I'm scared," she sobbed.

He rubbed her back. "I know. I'm scared for you too."

Her tears fell against the soft black fabric of his coat.

He smelled of flowers. As she cried, he held her, soothing her fear the only way he could. They stayed that way for a long time before she heard horns blare above and Teagan gently pried her off. His eyes were red, as though even he had shed a few tears. "You must go now. I'm afraid we haven't any more time."

She wiped her face with one hand and nodded.

"Good luck," Teagan whispered, rubbing her arm. "I hope you win."

She gave a mute nod, not trusting her voice any longer, as she stepped into the crate. He closed the door and pulled a lever on the side. Shaleigh stared into Teagan's gaze for as long as she could before the crate closed and she was in complete darkness. Above her head a counterweight shifted and slowly she began the climb to the top. As though anticipating how panic-inducing waiting in complete darkness would be, cuts had been made in the elevator shaft that let her see exactly how high the lift was climbing. Each time the darkness closed over her, she remembered Teagan, and tried to calm her nerves. When she spotted the balloons hovering in the air, she pulled out her sword. She wasn't sure what to expect when she got to the top, but she wanted to be prepared for anything.

The lift came to a halt at a set of stairs. At first, she wasn't sure how to open the door until she spotted a chain that hung against the inner wall. When she pulled on it, the door opened only a little, and it took her a few moments of tugging to get it to open all the way. She stepped out to the base of the short stairwell. Sunlight streamed down from up above and she could hear the roaring excitement of the crowd.

She took a deep breath before climbing the steps and entering into the sunlight.

~

"IT LOOKS like our newest Chosen has finally made it to the arena!" Madam Cloom's voice boomed over the roaring crowd.

Shaleigh turned to face her opponent, but she was alone on the stage. She could see all the many faces staring at her from their balloons. At eye level, along the grassy fields of the gully, the majority of the Garden's populace stared; she hadn't realized how many there were. Each of the four quadrants must have had several hundred people packed in, and they were all cheering—creating a roar of sound. She shook her arms and legs, letting the strong wind pull her from the fear-induced breakdown she had below.

"Our opponent seems to be running late." The annoyance in Madam Cloom's voice was clear. It took a moment for Shaleigh to spot her balloon amid all the others, even as grand as it was. Teagan was at her side, whispering into her ear. He must have had to hurry back. Perhaps Lieutenant Varg had dropped out when he knew who he was going up against. Perhaps they wouldn't make her go through with it.

Don't be silly, she told herself. *They would just find a replacement.* It really didn't matter if they put an amateur or an expert up here, there was no way Shaleigh could win this. She had to try though. She refused to just lay her weapon down and concede. Even if it might save her life, what kind of life would that be? No, even if she had the slightest chance, she had to try. Otherwise she would always regret it, and she was tired of regrets. She put a second hand on the hilt of her blade to keep it from visibly shaking. Then she heard the counterweight for the other elevator shift, and the gears vibrated the wooden floor beneath her.

Someone was coming up. Part of her wanted it to be Lieutenant Varg. He might go easy on her, give her a non-lethal blow at least, where a different soldier might not hold back at all. She glanced to Madam Cloom. Teagan must have removed her charm because they were deep in conversation now. She pointed to the ground and Teagan gave a brisk nod.

Scared, she heard the crank turn for the elevator door and turned her eyes to the second stairwell for the stage. Up came someone dressed in a full suit of scaled, leather armor, complete with a plumed helmet and face guard. All Shaleigh could see were his eyes, and they certainly didn't belong to Varg. He pulled out his own sword, a heavier blade than Shaleigh's, and probably well-used.

"What happened to the Lieutenant?" she asked.

The armored man shook his head.

"He's alright, isn't he?"

He stood straight and gave her a half-bow, his eyes never leaving hers. She glanced over at Madam Cloom, who hurried to get her megaphone vocal chords back. Shaleigh bowed as well. A small part of her hoped that Madam Cloom would call it all off.

"Let the Fight for the Garden begin!" The crowd burst into shrieks and cheers. Shaleigh had barely stood up before the armored man was rushing toward her. She attempted to block his strike, but she nearly fell over from the sheer force of it.

"Use both hands," the man instructed in a muffled voice. "And watch your footing." He gave her time to stand again and reset her stance, which was basically standing with her feet apart and keeping her sword up.

He rushed her again, and Shaleigh tried to block him with her blade. This time his attack wasn't nearly as strong and she was able to hold him off.

"What are you doing?"

"Keeping you alive," he said and Shaleigh looked up into his eyes. There was something familiar about them, but she wasn't sure where she had seen them before. She had seen so many people and been escorted by so many guards it was hard to keep them all straight. "Push me back and jab at me while I'm on the ground. Make it look good."

She gave a deft nod, then shoved back with her weight behind the blade. The armored man not only fell to the ground but tumbled as though she had really pushed him that hard. She heard gasps from the audience and then the entire gully went silent; all eyes were on her. Remembering his words, Shaleigh jabbed at him. Not only did he easily dodge that, but he swept his own blade around only a few inches away from her face. Shaleigh was pretty sure her heart stopped for an instant and she backed steadily away from him.

He sprang to his feet and she winced, surprised at how

fast he could move. Even Captain Briar would have trouble keeping up with him. He advanced again, his blade making quick swipes in the air. Shaleigh held her sword up helplessly, barely blocking each swing.

"Strike my hand, point your blade to my throat," he said.

"No, I—"

"Do it! We don't have much time."

Hoping she wasn't going to really hurt him, but still wanting to make a good show, she sliced at his bare fingers. He cried out in pain as his sword clattered to the floor. She bit her tongue but held the tip of her blade to the man's throat.

Cradling his injured hand against him, he lifted his other hand into the air. "I yield," he called out.

Cheers erupted from all around; the shrieks so loud Shaleigh could hear little else. She glanced down at his hand to see blood trailing through the cracks of his armor. What had she done to him? Surely, she hadn't cut too deep or worse yet...taken off a finger.

"You're a skilled fighter," Teagan's voice boomed over the noise. Slowly the cheering crowd grew quiet. "Yet I don't believe I've seen you before."

"I suppose my skills aren't always appreciated," the armored man replied with a muffled voice. The familiarity of it tugged at her again.

"Remove your helm, stranger," Teagan said with eerie calm.

The armored man sighed, "I would rather not, if it's all the same to you, sir."

There were gasps and suddenly Teagan landed on the

stage. He must have known this wasn't Lieutenant Varg.

"I've got this," she insisted, but Teagan didn't even look at her.

"I said take off your helm," his voice boomed across the gully. "I want to see who you really are."

"You just have to know, don't you?" the armored man chuckled. "Alright then, if you insist. Here I was trying to save you the trouble." He reached up and unhooked the helm from around his jaw. It took him a moment to pull it off with his good arm. White hair poured down his shoulders, and there stood Talek. Murmurs broke out all around them, but none seemed as shocked as Teagan.

Talek ran a hand through his hair and flashed a smile, "It's been a long time, Teagan. I've missed you."

TEAGAN LIFTED a hand to his throat and hummed a tune in quick time.

"Do you know each other?" Shaleigh asked.

"Oh yes," Talek grinned.

"What are you doing here?" Teagan growled, "Don't you know you could be killed?"

"Of course, but I couldn't abandon you..." He glanced at Shaleigh, "or her. You see, I don't do that to those I care about."

Teagan tensed.

"I couldn't stop worrying about you after you left. Especially knowing you were trapped here of all places," Talek stepped closer to Teagan. "Of course, it's difficult to get anywhere near you anymore. She keeps you like a caged bird in this ridiculous Garden." He took hold of Teagan's wrist, and to Shaleigh's surprise, Teagan didn't push him away. Instead he looked as though the very sight of Talek was tearing him apart.

"I have to say I'm flattered," Talek added with a sweet smile. "My life is still precious to you, isn't it? Even after all this time." He wound a hand around Teagan's arm and pulled him closer. "Why do you keep me away, Teagan? Didn't you miss me, even a little?"

"They'll kill you," Teagan whispered.

"Come now, I doubt it'll be as bad as all that. You're their High Faerie, aren't you? Surely you can pull some strings for me of all people." His eyes narrowed. "Or are you too brainwashed to be able to make decisions like that? I hope you haven't let this silly idea that you're some kind of grand magical being get to you. You're not that important." He looked around at the shocked audience, "And now, they all know your dirty little secret." He leaned in close and planted a kiss on Teagan's cheek. "They all know that you and I are lovers."

That snapped Teagan out of it. He pushed Talek back so hard he nearly fell to the ground. "We haven't been that in a very long time."

Talek's smile fell and Teagan walked over to kick his blade away from him. He replaced his voice enhancement and turned to the audience, his normal mask back in place. "I'm afraid the Games will have to be put on hold for a time, ladies and gentlemen. It seems we must first deal with an intruder." His voice was calm, but Shaleigh could see the cracks in his facade. Despite his attempts to remain in control, he was trembling.

PART III
MISSTEP

THE LURE OF POWER

On Teagan's orders, Shaleigh used the elevator to return to the ground floor. When she reached the bottom, Captain Briar and a handful of guards were waiting.

"You'll be coming with us. Teagan will deal his little friend," she said in disgust.

She followed them outside, noticing that all the small chambers were now empty. The guards had cleared everyone out. She passed by the desk that Lieutenant Varg had used earlier, but it too was empty. "Lieutenant Varg, is he alright?"

"He's fine, he just needs to learn to watch his surroundings better. He's lucky that stupid Faerie didn't take off his head instead of just knocking him out."

Shaleigh wanted to know more, but it was probably best to choose her words carefully. She could get the Lieutenant into more trouble if she wasn't careful. She eyed the five guards accompanying them with suspicion.

"Am I in any trouble?"

"I doubt it. It's not your fault the trespasser found a way in. Madam Cloom wants to make sure you're as far away from that creep as possible."

Getting out of the gully was far more difficult without Teagan's assistance. They climbed up a steep hill that snaked back and forth up the southern edge. Once they had gotten higher up, Shaleigh could make out the stage again, but neither Teagan nor Talek were there.

"Are they going to execute him?"

"Talek?" Captain Briar looked at the stage with a glare that could poison a snake. "If I had my way, he would be. One less Faerie in the world at least. They're cocky jerks, believing their opinions are the only opinions out there. I think that's pretty clear after today. Teagan's hardly an exception. Without that bond, he'd be as unruly as that white-haired creep."

"I got the impression they knew each other."

"Oh, I'm sure they do. Faeries get around, or so I'm told," she grimaced. "I don't know, there aren't really rules for how to deal with a situation like this. We've had Faeries try to raid our caravans occasionally or even try to sabotage places in the Marketplace, usually near the docks. But I've never seen one brazen enough to sneak their way into the Games, and certainly not attack the future Madam of the Garden."

It was flattering to hear the Captain talk about her in such a high regard. Most of the time Shaleigh got the impression she saw her as more of a nuisance than a leader. Instead, the Captain really believed she was Master Cathal's reincarnation. Shaleigh was still a fraud though, and she knew better than to tell the Captain the truth.

"You don't like them much, do you?"

"Who? The Faeries?"

Shaleigh nodded.

"You'll be hard-pressed to find a creature more two-faced. Or unpredictable." She shook her head. "I suppose Teagan didn't tell you about the Faerie Rebellion?"

"No, all I know is that he's bound to Madam Cloom somehow."

"Ages ago, before anyone dared bind a Faerie to themselves or to any patch of land, they served the courts of various kingdoms. They were preferable over magicians because the magicians demanded pay out of pocket and were reluctant to do all the stupid things that kings and queens demand. So out with the magicians, and in with Faeries. They didn't mind doing tasteless tasks as long as they could have a bit of fun in the process. They're simplistic creatures and will gleefully give out torture if there is any amusement to be had in it.

"What no one realized was that the Faeries had other plans. One night almost two centuries ago, a red moon rose into the night sky. My people knew it was a bad omen, but they didn't know how bad. The Garden was young then, only around a quarter of a century old."

"Your people?" Shaleigh asked.

"Yes, my great grandparents ruled the Briar Kingdom at the time. Oh, you can't find it on a map any longer, but it used to be where the Pasture is today. The night of the Blood Moon, the Faerie who was in my family's employment betrayed us.

"In the span of an hour, he set fire to the entire city. He used his magical speed to lock up every home before starting the flames. The night watchmen, he slaughtered like swine. The King and Queen woke in time to catch him locking up the doors of their children—my grandparents—about to set fire to the room. So no, I can't say I like Faeries at all. Personally, I think the entire land would be safer without them, but Madam Cloom forbids any sort of violence against them." The Captain clenched her teeth. "She fears their mad Queen, I suppose. If I were her, destroying their people would be my first choice. Just as they tried to destroy mine."

They had reached the crest of the gully, and Captain Briar pulled a soldier aside and berated him with questions about Talek's location. Shaleigh tried to overhear, but the other soldiers ushered her into a waiting carriage. Graddic wasn't her driver this time, and there was no sign of Lieutenant Varg or Teagan anywhere.

The ride back to High Castle was quiet, which left Shaleigh alone with her thoughts. On one hand, she understood the Captain's fear of the Faeries far better now than she had before. It also explained the fear that Mawr had shown when he found out that Talek was one of them. At the same time, Shaleigh had problems believing the story. The idea of someone locking the doors of every single home in the entire city was a little far-fetched; it was the type of story told to children to get them to desire vengeance, not one that held much water on its own, especially since the Captain failed to mention any motivation. Still, even if that was how it happened, it seemed strange to blame all Faeries for the actions of one.

Then there was Talek. Here she had thought his sole purpose in coming to the city was to help her, but thinking back on it, that was a rather selfish assumption. But he had never once mentioned his desire to see Teagan, and showing up on stage was plain ludicrous, especially now that she knew more about the bloody history of Faeries. At the very least he would be kept as a prisoner, but somehow that didn't seem likely. If Shaleigh had been the one to ruin Madam Cloom's Games, Teagan said she would be killed without a second thought. At this point, Teagan's favor might be the only thing keeping Talek alive.

She wasn't even sure if Teagan could kill him. If Madam Cloom ordered it, she doubted he would be able to. She had seen the shock that came over him on stage. It wasn't embarrassment that held him frozen for so long, it was affection and then horror. It was like he was going over all the different ways that Talek could be killed, each more terrible than the next. Despite whatever Teagan might have said to calm the waters, those two had a strong history together—so strong that he barely realized his fearsome reputation was collapsing all around him on that stage. Her dad used to do something similar when she was younger, when the pain from her mother's leaving was still fresh; he would come across a book, an item in the store, hear some song, and become utterly stricken. He would freeze just like Teagan had, as though caught in a playback loop of the past. Seeing that same reaction in Teagan, despite their different points of view, nearly broke her heart.

Damn it, she didn't want to get wrapped up in this. She

had her own troubles. She needed to stay focused on her dad and Kaeja. She turned sideways along the bench so she could bring her knees up to her chest. The wheels of the carriage hit a rough section and she wobbled back and forth. It reminded her of the Slumbering Forest and their escape. Talek had gotten her out of that mess too. No, that was putting it lightly. He saved their lives. Oh sure, Mawr might have survived if those wolves couldn't figure out how smash his body parts to pieces, but she hadn't stood a chance.

Her hand fell to the hilt of the blade on her hip and along the smooth sheath. That was twice, twice he had saved her life. It was a foolish move, getting on that stage and pretending to be Lieutenant Varg, but she owed him for it. He might have come to the city to catch Teagan's eye, but she was the reason he was behind bars now. If he was killed, it would be on her shoulders.

She leaned back and looked out the window as High Castle drew nearer. Perhaps she needed to put her own goals on the back-burner, at least for now. As much as she hated to think it, her dad would have to wait. He had waited this long. Besides, Kaeja wouldn't want her to abandon a friend who had risked so much for her. That was a strange feeling, to think of Talek as a friend when she hardly knew him. Captain Briar would make his life a living hell too. She needed to get him out of there, though she hadn't the foggiest idea how.

The carriage passed under the gates and Shaleigh sat up. Colin was waiting outside and a very Teagan-like smirk came upon her face. She had an idea, but it would take some convincing.

~

COLIN WAS OPENING the door before the carriage had even come to a complete stop. "Are you okay? Sorry I couldn't catch up sooner. They had me looking for more Faeries that could be sneaking around."

Shaleigh eyed the entrance. There were no guards that she could see, but that didn't mean it was safe to talk around the minotaur. There would be more carriages arriving from the Games soon, so it was best if they got inside quickly.

"I'm...actually feeling tired. Could you help me find my way back to my room?"

He shrugged. "Sure, I guess. Teagan told me to keep an eye on you anyway."

There weren't any guards posted inside the entrance. Perhaps they were still looking for suspicious people at the Games or with Talek. If anyone confessed to letting him in, or recognized him from the Marketplace, there would be hell to pay.

They walked in silence, and despite her request to have help finding her way back, Shaleigh didn't need Colin's help at all. He knew it too after she made the first three turns and gave her a confused look. When they finally reached her room, she pulled him inside, and closed the door behind them.

"Hang on, what are you doing?" Colin asked as she bolted the door.

She turned around in all seriousness. "I need a favor."

"Oh crap."

"You don't even know what I'm going to ask."

Colin sighed and sat down in one of the chairs by the hearth. "I knew this was coming. I just didn't know it would be so soon." He picked up his tail and rubbed the end nervously. A thought occurred to him and he froze, looking up at her with wide eyes. "You don't want someone killed, do you?"

She rolled her eyes. "No, don't be ridiculous." She sat down opposite him. "You're a thief, right? Or at least you were before you became a Seeker."

"Yeah," Colin said slowly with a dubious expression.

"Did you ever get locked up?"

He sputtered at her, speechless. His tail twitched in agitation in his hands. "...what?"

"Did you ever get caught?" She sat back in her chair. "I guess what I'm asking is: do you think you could sneak us to the cells without getting caught?"

Colin gave a slow grin. "You want to go see that Faerie, don't you?"

She nodded. "He saved my life in the Slumbering Forest, then again this morning. I can't let them kill him, Colin. You know they will."

He scratched at the dark fur on his forearm. "Probably. Faeries freak people out. I mean, they're kind of scary. You've seen how Master Teagan gets when he's angry. I don't think this place is big enough to handle two."

"Oh, trust me, I think Teagan's going to want to get him out of here too."

Colin laughed. "No, Teagan will want to hold the axe. I mean, he's the only one that could, really. I've heard about some crazy things that happened to folks who tried to kill a Faerie. One guy got cursed so bad, he started losing—"

"You couldn't hear them on stage, could you?" Shaleigh stared at him. "You couldn't hear what they said."

"Nobody could. It looked like he put some kind of spell on Master Teagan though. It was like he was frozen for a minute." He shuddered. "Faeries just look at a person and they can control them."

"His name is Talek, and he's Teagan's ex."

"His hex?" Colin asked, dumfounded.

"No, his ex. They used to be lovers."

Colin's eyes went wide. "Wow, really? I can't imagine anyone having sex with Master Teagan." He clamped his mouth shut. "Don't tell him I said that, okay?"

Shaleigh sighed. "Look, are you going to help me or not? You owe me."

He sighed and his tail twitched.

"Come on, Colin. You're the only one who can help me."

"You must be pretty desperate if that's the case."

THE STAIRWELL LEADING down to the prison, located at the base of the castle, was near the Memorial Chamber. So that was where Colin opted to start their journey. He said it wasn't frequented very often since the prison had multiple entrances, so it should be easy to slip in one door and out another without anyone taking notice. The hallways were surprisingly empty as they made their way to the Memorial Chamber. Shaleigh wasn't sure if most of the workers were down at the Games still, if there had been orders given to stay out of the halls, or if most were cowering in their homes at the knowledge that Faeries were sneaking into the city.

A few armored guards passed by, giving Colin a nod. Apparently, it was normal for him to be moving about the castle, probably they assumed he was on some errand for Teagan or Madam Cloom. They slipped into the Memorial Chamber without any trouble.

"Okay, so this is going to sound weird," Colin said as he pushed the door closed. "But we'll make less noise if I'm carrying you."

"What?"

He pointed down to his own black fur-clad feet. "I'm built to not make a sound, remember? Even if we left your shoes here, you would still make more noise walking than I would. I'd rather we not leave behind a scrap of evidence to show we were down there. If anyone found out I did this, I could be in some serious trouble." He glanced to each set of doors, as though expecting Teagan to burst through at any moment.

"If you say so."

"Don't worry, I won't drop you." He smiled. "I carried you a lot when I kidnapped you."

She stared at him. "Is that supposed to make me feel better about this?"

He shrugged and crouched down. "At least you know I can do it. Here, put your arms around me, that way I can use my hands."

With reluctance, she climbed onto his back, though it was difficult with his tail in the way. He stood up easily, and Shaleigh had to admit she was shocked. He didn't have the typical build to be capable of lifting her, but then again, he was the only stoatling she knew.

After a few steps, she understood better what he meant about her footsteps making noise. Colin didn't make a sound. It was like his feet were wrapped in layers of cotton. He picked up a chain around his neck that had fallen beneath his shirt. It was a tiny, silver flute with only three holes drilled into it. It reminded her of Teagan's flute. He gave a quick trill of notes that could have been wind chimes from another room, and then the room grew brighter.

"This lets me move with the shadows," he whispered. "We can talk in a low voice like this, but if you scream, anybody can hear it."

"So…it turned us invisible?"

"No, it just makes us less noticeable. If we're in a pool of shadows, we blend in with them. If I'm standing in front of a sunny window though, I'll look like some creepy black shadow. Don't talk above a whisper and don't fall off."

"Okay." She wrapped her arms tighter around his neck.

"Ack, and don't choke me!"

"Sorry," she muttered loosening her grip. "I'm just nervous."

"Me too. I've never broken into our prison before. I really hope it works." He padded across the room and pushed open the opposite door. Only he did it so freaking slowly that Shaleigh was tempted to reach out and shove it, but she pushed down the urge. Sneaking around was Colin's area of expertise, not hers. If he decided it took five minutes to open a door, then that's what it took.

They exited the chamber and moved down the hall, slinking from shadow to shadow like a scurrying mouse. They reached a metal door, one that Shaleigh didn't remember seeing before, and again Colin started pushing it open slowly. He had it open only an inch or two when he froze and darted to the side, crouching down on the ground with his hands at his sides. Now that she was listening, she could hear footsteps coming up the stairs. Two guards exited, talking about their lunch plans. Colin didn't just wait until they passed, he waited until they had left the hall completely. Then he went back to the door. The guards had left it slightly ajar and he started opening it again. Shaleigh bit back a sigh, knowing this was going to be a slow process.

Once they were in the stairwell and Colin had put the door back the way he found it, he moved to all fours and began bounding down the steps three and four at a time. Shaleigh had to loop her legs around his waist to keep from falling off. It had to be uncomfortable for him, but Colin didn't say a word. Footsteps echoed up from below and Colin leapt to the ceiling, clinging to the cracks in the stone with his fingers.

Shaleigh gasped. Colin's feet dangled below and even though she had her arms and legs wrapped around him, she wasn't sure how he was going to get out of sight in time. She already saw the head of a guard coming around the last set of spiral steps. Colin reached a foot out and dug the claws of his toes into the wall. He used the leverage to turn himself around so that his stomach faced the floor and Shaleigh's back was against the ceiling's edge. Shaleigh gave a sigh of relief and Colin turned his head to the side with a smile.

"What? I can be pretty flexible when I want to be."

She leaned her forehead against her arm. "Could you warn me next time?"

"Where else am I supposed to go? Every alcove has a torch in it. I can't hide in there. Nobody ever remembers to light the ceiling ones in these places, thank goodness. Otherwise I wouldn't have anywhere to go."

It was just one guard this time, moving quick to catch up with her comrades. She stopped for a moment and leaned into one of the alcoves. Shaleigh caught Colin's eye, but he was concentrating to stay aloft. His tail betrayed his nerves. Despite how much he boasted, it couldn't be easy to stay quiet when his claws were clinging to stone walls. The guard gave a loud sneeze and they both jumped.

"Whew!" she said as she took a few more steps up, then paused for another big sneeze. "Don't know what's wrong with me..." Colin didn't budge until they heard the door close at the top of the stairs.

He fell from the walls, twisted around, and landed noiselessly on his feet, straddling several steps. "How's that?"

It took her a minute to get her bearings and her foot slipped to the ground for just a moment. Colin took hold of her arms and hoisted her up again in a flash. "Watch yourself, please," he muttered. "If Teagan is down here, I don't want to give him any indication we're coming."

"Sorry."

He eyed her for a moment. "You still want to do this? If you want to back out, this is the time to do it."

"I'm good." She tightened her grip around his neck. "Let's keep going."

They went down three landings before they could make out voices; it sounded like only two guards. Colin slowed his pace and arched his upper body forward. He crouched down at the last bend so they could see into the room beyond. There were two men chatting: a short man with bushy eyebrows and a lanky man with a scrunched face. They sat at a wooden table playing cards, but there was another guard as well, a woman who was standing near the far wall. It took Shaleigh a moment to recognize the Captain. The headgear that she had worn in the arena sat on the side table along with the sheath of her curved blade. Her dark dreadlocks hung around her face, giving her a hawkish appearance. She had a cloth in one hand and was wiping down her blade. From what Shaleigh could see, the Captain was standing in the only pool of shadow that Colin might have been able to use between here and the hallway on the far end.

"Can you make it?" she whispered. Colin gave her the barest nod.

"We won't be able to use the floor though." He glanced up to the simple chandelier above their heads, "Or the ceiling for that matter."

"How then?"

He sighed. "I hope you brought a spare change of clothes, cause you may need them." He turned and dug his clawed fingers into the wall of the stairwell and slowly climbed up with his back legs too. Then he started to turn sideways along the wall like a gecko.

Shaleigh was having trouble hanging on without choking him though. "Colin, stop. I can't hold on."

"Move down."

"Excuse me?"

"Put your arms under mine. I need to use my arms more anyway."

Shaleigh stared at him. If she moved down, she would be saddled just above his tail. It seemed far too crude.

"Hey, this was your idea," he muttered. "If you want to get through that room, then we need to move together. We don't have time to be polite. If you have a better plan for how to get over there, I'd love to hear it."

He was right, but that didn't make it any easier. Grudgingly she wiggled down his torso so that her legs were wrapped around his waist and she was grabbing under his arms. Then they began to make their way across the room. Moving one limb at a time, it was a slow pace.

"You sure you won't join us, Captain?" the man with the bushy eyebrows asked, "I promise you it's all in good fun."

"No," Captain Briar said with a sigh. "We're down here to keep the prisoner in his place, not to play games."

"Aw, come on, sir." the lanky man said in a hoarse voice, "He's got those cuffs on. Those are Faerie-proof, you know that. Not even Master Teagan himself could break out of those."

"Don't give her any ideas," his friend chuckled. "I'm sure the good Captain wouldn't mind if every Faerie in the Garden was given the boot. Am I right, sir?"

Captain Briar gave a grunt but didn't look up from her blade.

"Isn't he supposed to be coming soon?" the lanky man asked.

"He'll come when he's ready. Meanwhile I'm going to pretend that you two are enjoying your game, what little of it I'm allowing you to play, and not starting ridiculous gossip."

The lanky man went a bit paler. "Yes, sir."

They turned back to their cards but gave the Captain a worried expression every few minutes. Shaleigh had been hoping they would be more of a distraction, but now the room was completely silent in light of the awkward conversation. She and Colin were about to move along the wall behind the Captain.

Colin took a deep breath. His hands were shaking with each reach outward. Of all the people who had to be standing watch in these dungeons, why did it have to be Captain Briar? Arm over arm, leg over leg, Colin moved them carefully behind her, until Shaleigh could have put her hand out and tugged on one of the Captain's dreadlocks.

The Captain turned suddenly and held her blade up to examine it. "Excellent," she whispered, then turned to look at where Shaleigh was hiding. She squinted hard at the wall. Shaleigh held her breath. Then with surprising speed, she extended the blade and held it perpendicular to the wall. Colin jerked his head down just in time to keep his ear from getting skewered. Shaleigh only hoped her panicked breaths were quiet enough. Captain Briar angled the blade to the left and right. Then she flipped the blade around and slipped it into the sheath on her belt.

"Alright, deal me in for one game," the Captain said, pulling her chair over to the table.

Colin was frozen against the wall, trembling from head to toe, and breathing so hard that Shaleigh kept having to readjust her arms around him so she wouldn't fall off. They only had a few more steps to go until they could reach the hallway. She was about to motion to him that maybe they should get back on the floor when she felt a weight on her hip shift. Her own blade shifted slightly from its sheath, and although it didn't fall out, the noise was unmistakable in the tiny room.

Captain Briar spun around with wide eyes, studying the wall where she and Colin were stuck. Shaleigh squeezed Colin's shoulder, but Colin was petrified. He was shaking so bad that Shaleigh wasn't sure how long his claws would hold them both against the wall.

"Did you hear that?" the Captain asked, looking suspicious.

"No, sir," the man with the bushy eyebrows said. All the same he got to his feet and put his hand on the hilt of his blade. "Where did it come from?"

"That wall," she pointed right at them.

Shaleigh leaned down close to Colin's ear and whispered as quietly as she could. "We have to move."

Colin shook his head.

"Please," she urged as the Captain approached. "I know you can do it."

Trembling, Colin put out a hand and began to move at an even slower pace than normal. At first, she didn't understand why, but then she realized that it was entirely possible that Captain Briar knew about Colin's abilities; worse yet, she might be expecting him to try something.

"Did it sound like metal scraping on metal?" the lanky man asked, still seated at the table with a handful of cards. "I've heard that plenty of times down here. It's the spooks. They get all antsy when there's bloodshed about. Probably that killing at the Games got them stirred up."

His friend relaxed a bit, but the Captain didn't look certain. She stepped to the wall. Even though Colin had mostly moved out of the way, his tail was still back there. Between trying to balance against the wall and his nerves, it was flicking in all sorts of directions. The Captain reached out for the wall, only inches away from Colin's tail.

Colin whimpered. Shaleigh reached down with her leg, grabbed his tail, and pulled it to the side just in time to avoid the Captain's hand landing right on it. Colin tensed and wiggled for a moment, trying to regain his balance without his tail as a counterweight, but it was impossible. He leapt off the wall, twisted in mid-air, and landed soundlessly on all fours. He moved through the lighted areas of the room for only a few seconds before melting into shadows in the doorway.

Shaleigh glanced behind them to see the Captain dragging her hand along the stone wall. She wasn't one to discredit her senses, but the two guards at the table had fortunately returned to their game. Although Shaleigh and Colin were out of immediate danger, getting to Talek was only half the problem. Even if they could free him, they would still have to find a way out afterwards. Somehow, she didn't think the Captain would fall for that trick twice.

~

THE HALLWAY that led down through the prison cells was far darker than the guard room, which made it easier for Colin to move. Still, he didn't stop until they reached the stone wall at the far end.

"That was way too close," he chuckled weakly, putting a hand against the wall. "I can't stop shaking! It's a good thing you were able to grab my tail like that."

Shaleigh grinned, her heart still pounding in her chest. She was about to thank him when she heard a man's voice.

"Now who is there? Who comes to visit me wrapped in a blanket of shadow?"

She turned to see Talek staring at them through iron bars. He sat cross-legged on the stone floor, his hands and legs clasped in heavy metal manacles. The thick leather armor he wore on stage had been stripped from him, leaving him donned in crimson, the same as when she had met him in the Slumbering Forest. His white hair hung like a tangled mess around his face, his eyes dark and keen.

"There's no need to hide," he cocked his head to the side and gave a sly smile. "I promise I'm in no position to fight you."

Colin backed away until Shaleigh could feel the wall behind her. "Take this glamour off," she said.

"Are you sure?" Colin asked, gazing at Talek with trepidation. "He'll know we're here then."

Shaleigh sighed and dropped down to the ground. "If you're so bothered, just take it off me. Leave yourself hidden."

Colin fumbled with his silver flute.

"I hear your voices," Talek whispered. "Much like the moaning of spirits or the howling of distant wolves. Here with me, but not."

Colin blew the almost inaudible notes on his flute, but Talek didn't seem to hear them. Once the last note finished, she felt the heavy shadows lift from her shoulders like a cloak. Talek's entire demeanor changed and his eyes went wide.

"Shaleigh? How in the world did you get in here?"

"I've got good friends." She stepped up to the cage and sat down close to Talek. "Did you think I wouldn't help you?"

"To be honest, no. This is a dangerous place for a young human to be, don't you think? I don't want you to get hurt, not after I worked so hard to save you."

"But that's why I'm here. You saved me, now it's my turn."

He gave her a warm smile. "You're quite kind to me, Shaleigh. In this part of the world, I'm not used to such civility. I'm afraid, though, that the only person who can help me now is Teagan. He's the only person with real power in this place, and it's not even his to control. Such a pity."

"What do you mean?"

Talek held up his chained wrists. "These are magically sealed, my dear. Only magic can open them, and any magic within them is cut off. I don't exactly have much magic, but still."

"Maybe I can talk with him," she said, thinking out loud. "I don't think he wants to hurt you. If anything, I think he'll want to help you."

Talek sighed and shifted his legs. The long chains dragged and clinked across the stone floor, echoing along the walls. "He's not going to listen to you, I'm afraid. I was hoping he would listen to me at least. He used to listen to me, but..."

"Talek," Shaleigh whispered, afraid to ask the question that bore down on her. It felt too conceited to mention it here with him locked in a jail cell. She ought to be thinking about how she could help him, not herself.

He smiled at her. "Go ahead, ask me. You obviously have something on your mind. You risked a lot to see me, and..." his voice broke a bit. "I may not be around much longer. You had best ask while you can."

Shaleigh felt her throat constrict as she forced the words out. "You've saved me twice, but I barely know you. Why did you do it?"

Talek was quiet for a long time before he spoke. "There's something about you, something that feels different. I don't know if you really are the reincarnation of Master Cathal, but ever since that camera fell out of the sky in the woods, I felt that we were connected somehow. It was a fluke that I found you and could help you and your stone friend. Then seeing those guards drag you off, it gave me the courage to sneak into the Marketplace. I had wanted to do it for so long, but seeing you, well..." he shrugged, offering a small smile, "I guess you could say you inspired me. I know what happens to a Chosen if they don't meet the requirements. You may not get tossed to the wolves, but it's close enough. I didn't want that to happen to you." His gaze fell to the floor. "Then there's Teagan, trapped and alone; his bond with the Garden is destroying him from the inside out."

Shaleigh nodded. "He frightens me sometimes. He made a woman in the Pasture bawl her eyes out. And last night he threatened to kill me if I didn't show for the Games."

A tear fell from Talek's cheek and splattered onto the stone floor. "I was a fool to think I could save the both of you. I thought that I could send you back to your homeland, and then bring Teagan home with me. Somehow I thought I could fix everything." He looked up at her with a smile despite the tears in his eyes. "It hasn't quite worked out the way I planned."

"You didn't think they would unmask you on stage, did you?"

He shrugged. "It sounds ridiculous now, but it never really occurred to me. I've been told I can be rather rash at times. I suppose I don't always think things through very well." He wiped at his cheek, dragging the chain across the ground. "I'm sorry. You shouldn't waste your time with me. I put myself here; you never had a choice."

She reached through the bars and took his hand. His fingers felt as cold as the iron around his wrists. "You've saved my life twice, and I won't forget that. I'm going to get you out of here, one way or another."

"I don't know how, but I would be grateful if you tried."

She felt a nervous tap on her shoulder. "Shaleigh, I've got to charm you again. The guards are coming."

"I'll be back, I promise," she said to Talek as she backed away towards Colin.

"Thank you," he whispered, but Talek was no longer looking at her. He was focused on the voices down the hall. It was the same as that day he had pulled her into the alleyway in the Marketplace. She knew exactly who was coming.

"Hurry," she whispered to Colin. She couldn't see him in the shadows on the opposite wall, but she knew he was there. Down the hall, she heard footsteps approaching and flattened herself against the wall as she waited for Colin to hide her again. It was unnerving. She couldn't see Colin, nor could she hear his flute, but just as she started to make out the bright red hair in the distance, the world grew a bit brighter. Colin was crouched down in front of her and quickly she climbed on his back. Colin didn't give instruction or say anything. Instead he climbed up along the wall and onto a ledge. The opening must have once housed a great arched window, but it had been boarded up. It felt very out of place compared to the care with which Teagan had built the rest of the castle. Through the wooden slats, afternoon light beamed through, but Colin didn't seem to have a problem with it. Shaleigh watched with nervous breaths.

Down below them, Captain Briar was walking with Teagan, a loop of keys in her hands.

"Are you sure it's a good idea to talk to him alone?" she asked with suspicion. "I think almost the whole city is aware that you two have a history."

Teagan gave her a glare. "I would appreciate it if you didn't question me, Captain."

She put a hand on her hip. "Then who will, sir?" She smirked. "Unless of course you've gotten approval from Madam Cloom to be down here with him."

"Of course she knows," Teagan said. "Now if you'll excuse us."

The Captain didn't leave. "Why are we delaying? We ought to kill him immediately. The longer he's here, the more dangerous it could be."

Teagan sighed, but Shaleigh could see the panic in his eyes.

"Or," the Captain started, "we could banish him from the city. Though I don't think that would work, would it? He got in before, he could do it again. He doesn't seem very fond of rules, though none of your kind do."

Teagan gave her a thin-lipped smile. "Thank you for your assistance, Captain. I think I can handle it from here." He eyed the keyring in her hands. With a glare she handed them over and headed back to the guard room.

Shaleigh started to ask Colin if they should stay and watch the conversation, but Colin put a finger on his lips and shook his head. Then he indicated for her to crawl off his back and sit down to get comfortable. The only way out at this point, she realized, was down the hallway. That was when it occurred to her that Teagan might be able to still see them in this transformed state. They were stuck here regardless until Teagan left.

~

TEAGAN GAVE a heavy sigh and picked up a chair that was sitting against the wall. He went to Talek's cell, opened the door, and stepped inside. Without saying a word, he put the chair down and sat, his gaze never leaving Talek.

"It has certainly been a while since I've seen you," Teagan said after a moment.

"Yes, it has." Talek pulled his legs up to his chest. "I've been trying to figure out why you're so keen on avoiding me."

Teagan indicated his own chair. "Would you like to have a seat? I'm sure it would be more comfortable than stone. There's no point in you being treated like an animal here."

"No, that's alright." Talek cocked his head to the side. "So, you don't deny avoiding me?"

Teagan sat back in his chair and the wood squeaked beneath him. "You're imprisoned because of your own foolishness. That's hardly due to me avoiding you."

Talek made to protest, but Teagan interrupted him.

"Look, you've put me in a terrible position by coming here, especially in the fashion you chose. Madam Cloom is livid. She's asked me to have you put to death."

Talek's gaze was intense as he stared at Teagan with his arms wrapped around his legs. It was a strange expression, one that Shaleigh hadn't seen on him before. There was something dangerous about it, and it made her feel uneasy. "Must you always do what the old bat says? You do know that she doesn't have your interests in mind, right?"

Teagan sighed. "Now you know I don't have much of a

choice in the matter. What you should be concerned with—"

"There's always a choice, love. You know that."

Teagan put a hand to his temple. "Let's not get into this."

"You choose to stay here and be this woman's pet. If she asks you to dole out death, you do it. If she asks you to kidnap children, you don't delay. Tell me, is there any atrocity that could be asked of you that you would find abhorrent? Because I don't think you've ever refused a single command."

Teagan balled his hands into fists and leaned forward in his chair. "I chose this. I know you don't like it, but that won't change anything. I wish you would be honest with yourself. I left, and I have no intention of ever going back."

Talek gave a short snarl. "You don't mean that. You're merely a glutton. You soak up the admiration and the power here as though it's really yours, but it's not. It's all a charade. You don't have any real power, you're just a pawn to that horrible woman. You're a very small piece in a rather disgusting chess match, and it's twisting you, tearing you apart." A tear fell down Talek's cheek. "By the time you finally understand, there'll be nothing left of you. The man I fell in love with will be decimated."

"You're obsessed, Talek. You need help. Goodness, how long have you been trying to sneak in? Captain Briar said she turned you away from the gates the day they brought Shaleigh in, and it wasn't the first time either. How long have you been skulking around my city?"

Talek smiled wolfishly and got to his feet. It took an

effort with the weight of his chains. "Ah, so there's the real reason you came to speak with me. You're trying to figure out if I have others with me, other Faeries trying to sneak in and destroy the beautiful Garden. *Her* beautiful Garden." Teagan's shoulders tensed. Talek leaned his back against the bars of his cell, wrapping his fingers around them. "Your old flame shows up, and she wants me out of the way as quickly as possible. Even I am not enough to convince you because your loyalty to her is that strong, stronger than any love we had."

Teagan looked away, speechless.

"Please tell me she hasn't forced you to sleep with her yet."

Teagan was on his feet in an instant. "I can't believe you would even imply such a thing," he snapped. "Of course she's concerned. Our Captain is calling for your head. Our people demand answers. They deserve answers."

Talek stepped toward him. "Calm down, there's nothing to be embarrassed about. We all know Cathal seduced you to begin with. I just wish you would have brought me with you, or at least told me what you were going to do. One night you're there, curled up beside me, and the next morning you're gone." He gave a weak laugh. "It's alright though. I've forgiven you. You have a sickness, a compulsion, and its name is power. I just have to break you of it."

Teagan turned away. "I wish you would quit playing these idiotic games. You could be killed here, and all you can think about is the past."

"No," Talek whispered and put a hand on Teagan's arm.

"I'm trying to see the future. You're the most powerful being in this stupid city. You could disobey her, set me loose, and we could leave together. Once we got to the forest, we could break your pact and you would be free for good."

Teagan put a hand to his wrist. She recalled the black ribbon that she had spotted briefly at the Games tied around his wrist there. Was that somehow related to his pact? "I'm not giving this up, not for you or anyone. Plenty of Faeries would kill to have the opportunity I've had. You can't imagine what I've been able to do with this. I've made a castle that should not be able to exist. I've transformed people into new forms of life. I've felt the very walls of this city quake when an attack comes. I even helped to turn the bloody forest into a slumbering one. Not even if you promised me love and affection for all eternity would I give up such a gift."

Stumbling, Talek put a hand to his lips, his face wet with tears. "Never," he muttered. "You would have never been so terrible to me before. This place is corrupt, and it's destroying you!"

Teagan stepped forward and cupped Talek's cheek with one hand. "Despite your insults and your silly obsessions, I will try to help you. I may not love you as I once did, but I do care about you. I don't want you to die over this. I can't promise anything, of course, but I'll do my best."

"That's not true," Talek said with a shake of his head. "You love me still. I saw it on that stage."

Teagan took the chair and left the cell. "It would be easier if you gave me more information to work with. If I could promise Madam Cloom that you weren't trying to start a rebellion or slaughter the city, I could perhaps ease your sentence."

"Don't you even hear yourself? Rebellions, slaughters, the fact that you must worry about such things is a clear sign of the danger you're in. If you're not careful, your pride will get you killed."

Teagan gave a heavy sigh, replacing the chair against the wall. "It's not my death I'm concerned about, love," he said, then turned and left down the hall. Talek sat in a back corner of his cell, dragging his chains with him. As Shaleigh and Colin followed Teagan out a few minutes later, she could still hear Talek's broken sobs echo against the stone walls.

ONLY THE TWO guards remained in the guard room when Colin and Shaleigh passed through. Now that the Captain had left, it was much easier for Colin to move through the shadows since the guards were too engrossed in their game to notice. Colin took the stairs on all fours, his furry hands and feet making no sound on the stone steps. The door at the top of the stairs had been left ajar, and he slipped through it easily. Shaleigh thought he would head to the Memorial Chamber again, but instead they headed for her room. Moving from each shadowy pool to dark corners, they passed unseen by the few guards still patrolling the halls.

When they reached her room, Shaleigh was glad to finally climb down from Colin's back. Her legs were stiff and her back sore, but mostly she wanted to get Colin's thoughts on what they had seen. He trilled a few notes on his silver flute and the room dimmed back down to its normal, bland hues.

"Have you ever seen him act like that?"

Colin stretched his back. "No, I've never seen him act like that. It was…bizarre." Shaleigh dropped down into a chair and Colin sat down opposite her with a strained expression. "I do think I've learned more about Master Teagan's love life than I ever wanted to know."

"Do you think Talek was right?" She asked, ignoring him. "About this pact destroying him?"

Colin shrugged. "I don't know, I never knew him before he came here." His face darkened. "But he's been vicious for as long as I've known him. Not always, mind you, but often enough that you know better than to cross him."

Shaleigh recalled how frank Teagan was when he told her he would be forced to kill her should she not attend the Games. The look on his face still brought a shudder. But she was just one of many Chosen, a small part of an endless line of potential reincarnations. Talek, on the other hand, was different. "I hope he doesn't kill him," she said, breaking the silence that filled the room.

"I know, me too. I know they're no longer close and all, but to have your lover killed just because—"

There was a knock at the door and Colin broke off mid-sentence. He jumped to his feet and fumbled for the flute around his neck even as the door squeaked open.

"There's no need to hide yourself, Colin," Teagan said in a flat voice as he stepped into the room.

A PROMISE

Colin stood frozen, his eyes wide and fingers trembling as he held the silver flute. Teagan gave him a cool smile before closing the door behind him. "Your skills have certainly improved, but I would appreciate it if you would not use them against me in the future. It insults me."

Colin gaped at him. "I mean—I didn't—we didn't—"

"It was my idea," Shaleigh said, drawing all eyes to her. "I made him do it."

Teagan arched an eyebrow. "Oh? That's rather unorthodox, but still quite effective." He was still steely from his conversation with Talek, apparently. "So, tell me, Shaleigh. Did you get Colin to sneak Talek into the city as well?"

"No, I had no idea he was going to come here," Shaleigh said as a lump formed in her throat. She had never considered what this might look like to Teagan. She met Colin's panicked gaze briefly and took a steadying breath. "I only met him in the forest. Him showing up at the Games completely took me by surprise." She thought it was probably best not to mention the day she had seen him in the Marketplace. Nobody had to know about that.

"It surprised us all," Teagan said with a dark expression. He hummed a quick tune and the fireplace came to life as he sat down across from her. He stared at her for a long moment, his fingers steepled, before he spoke again. "But you do have some affiliation with him."

She nodded. "He has saved my life...twice," she stated. "I may not know him well, but he has been kind to me. He and Mawr are the only ones here who haven't threatened me."

Colin pursed his lips and Teagan shifted in his seat as an uncomfortable silence filled the room.

"Are you going to kill him?" Colin asked, hunched and small on his chair. "Even with, you know, your history with him?"

Teagan sat back in his chair, his uncaring mask deflating. "He rendered Lieutenant Varg unconscious and we have no idea how long he's been lurking about the city." Teagan rubbed the bridge of his nose. "For all his pleas and ridiculous offers, he's given very little useful information. I'm not sure if he's merely being evasive or if he's really so obsessed with me that he can't see anything else." He closed his eyes and furrowed his brows and Shaleigh could see how heavily this weighed upon him.

"I think he's just hurt," Shaleigh offered. "You were cruel to him."

Teagan looked up at the ceiling. "Madam Cloom has requested I dispose of him. The Captain would be more than willing to do it, but Madam wants me to handle it directly." His voice broke slightly and he rose to stand by the window. Shaleigh exchanged a concerned look with Colin, but neither of them broke the pregnant silence. "She wants me to prove that I have cut off all ties to my old life. I was hoping I could persuade him to give me some information, to give her some reason to keep him alive, but he's reticent. I thought," he added, "a subtler method of disposal might be in order."

"What do you mean?" Shaleigh asked.

"He trusts you, doesn't he?" Teagan glanced back to her, his red hair gleaming in the sunlight. "He trusts you now far more than he does me."

Shaleigh didn't know what to say, having never considered Talek's opinion of her. "I...suppose so."

"I'm going to give you both an assignment, but you mustn't tell anyone."

Colin was on his feet in an instant. "Sir, we can't! Everyone is going to know who did it. They'll know it was me. You can't go against Madam Cloom's orders. That's the limit of your bond, you've said that a hundred times. I don't want you to—"

Teagan gave a thin smile. "Calm down, Colin. You've never gone against my wishes before, and technically we aren't disobeying her orders. She requested that I dispose of him, not kill him. This order can be fulfilled without any casualties if we are careful." He turned to look out the window. The afternoon sun sent long streaks of orange light across the city like the cuts of a knife. "You would be wrong to think that I chose to do this lightly. I was hoping he would give me something else to work with, I was hoping he would allow me to prove his innocence, but he didn't. This is our only alternative." He gave Colin a cold sidelong glance. "Don't make such accusations at me again, Colin."

Colin stiffened and gave a low bow, his ears folding back. "I'm sorry, sir. Please forgive me, it won't happen again."

It was strange to see Colin bend so quickly to Teagan's orders, especially knowing how much he questioned Teagan's decisions. It made her think of Talek's words about him being a glutton for power. Teagan didn't look like he accepted Colin's apologies, but he wore a thick mask. He could have assuaged Colin's worries without forcing an apology out of him. Talek, on the other hand, was very different. He was intent on questioning Teagan's orders, Teagan's decisions, Teagan's allegiances—and the more she saw how the High Faerie acted among his subordinates, the more she saw truth in Talek's words. Perhaps that was the real reason that Teagan couldn't kill him; it wasn't out of any affection or longing for a happy relationship, it was because Talek was one of the few people that Teagan couldn't order around.

"What do you want us to do?" Shaleigh asked, trying hard not to show her disgust.

Teagan pulled an iron key out of his pocket and stepped closer. "I want you to escort Talek out of my city." The key was cold as he dropped it into her palm. "Otherwise his execution will take place at midnight."

GETTING Talek free was the easy part of the plan. Getting him out of the city was a different story. Assuming that they could convince Talek to leave, they needed a way to get him out quickly without being seen. She doubted Colin could carry them both on his back. What she needed was a distraction. Fortunately, she knew someone who was a distraction everywhere he went.

Colin knew the city inside and out, so he knew exactly where the library was. Shaleigh wasn't sure if Mawr would even be there, but she knew that he would likely show up at some point. Located in the Garden district, near the High Castle but not quite in the Marketplace, the library was a massive structure. Stone pillars lined the front entrance in a way that reminded her of the library in Aife. The stoicism ended, though, once you stepped inside. The dark mahogany floor gleamed in the afternoon light, and in the center of the room was a statue that was so tall it loomed over everything else. The bookshelves stood at angles around the statue, arranged almost like layers of a flower petal around it, and Shaleigh had to get closer to get a good look. The statue was in the shape of a man she didn't recognize. He was sitting on a bench with tall stone flowers all around him. He had a book in his lap with a little boy and a little girl on either side of him. He was a heavier man with his hair pulled back in long dreadlocks. A thin pair of glasses lay low on the bridge of his nose and he wore a kind smile.

"Who is he?" she asked.

"Owain the Wise," Colin whispered at her side. "Perhaps the kindest of the original five magicians. He was a good friend of Master Cathal's, though he died during the battle against the Pello Pines. He was always speaking about some great ruined library in the south and insisted that there be a great one built here, but he didn't live to see it."

"You're a regular historian, aren't you?"

He shrugged. "If you weren't interested, then you shouldn't have asked."

"Oh, don't be like that. I'm joking with you. You've been moody ever since we talked with Teagan earlier. Are you okay?"

He folded his arms and his tail twitched in agitation. "I'm not being moody, I'm worried." He lowered his voice, his eyes darting around the room. "It's different slipping down there just to watch, but actually releasing him? I'm not a soldier, Shaleigh, I can't fight off guards."

"You won't have to. They won't even know we're there."

"We still have to get out with him, and I don't know how we're going to do that."

"That's why we're here. Come on, we've got to find Mawr."

They walked around the statue and looked down the different aisles of shelves, guessing there was no way they could possibly miss the enormous lion. The library was far larger than Shaleigh had expected, though. It was only after they had scoured the entire floor that she realized there were five floors in total to this place, and that didn't include the basement.

"If Mawr was here, we would see him," Colin said.

"Maybe we should ask someone."

She sighed and turned to the front desk. It seemed

rather silly to have to ask where a giant stone lion was. But the library was the only place she could imagine Mawr would be. He loved books, and now that he could actually see them, where else would he want to be?

"Excuse me," she asked an older woman with green-tipped ears and silver-framed spectacles who was sitting at the desk. "I'm looking for Mawr, he's a—"

She brightened and closed the book she was reading. "Oh, you're Mawr's friend!"

Shaleigh nodded.

"He's in the courtyard in the back. He's doing story time with the children," she said, standing up and moving around the desk. "Many of them were dropped off here while their parents attended the Games earlier. They're so violent; I wouldn't want my children to watch them either."

The woman led them to the back of the library and out a small door. If Shaleigh found the library to be beautiful, the courtyard was breathtaking. A metal trellis surrounded it, wound through with honeysuckle and ivy, giving the air a sweet, humid scent. A few finches were playing hide-and-seek amid the thick green foliage. Looking up, she saw that a pagoda stood above them that was thick with ivy and gave cool, dappled sunlight across the entire courtyard. A stone table sat in the middle, which she supposed was there for eating a picnic, perhaps, but the chairs had been pushed aside. Mawr used it as his pedestal, stretched out on it with a book held open between his paws and his golden glasses glinting in the dwindling sunlight. Children of all ages sat around him on the patio, and several adults too.

"Umm..." Colin stood in the doorway, staring into the courtyard with fear. She looped an arm around Colin's. "Come on, you'll be fine. Those kids don't seem to mind him."

But Colin pulled his furry arm away from her. "No, it's not Mawr. I didn't know there would be so many kids," he said, with wide eyes.

"What? You don't like children?"

"No, that's not it." He shook his head and backed away toward the opposite side of the courtyard where there was an open gate.

A curious little girl with pigtails stuck her head around the stone table. When her eyes landed on Colin, her whole face lit up.

"Kitty!" she screamed and more heads began poking up around the table.

"Oh crap..." Colin muttered.

Shaleigh couldn't hold back a laugh. Colin's ears went back in a pitiful plea. Then the girl with the pigtails shot up from her spot on the floor and hit Colin in a running tackle that almost knocked him to the ground.

"Oof!" Colin cracked an awkward smile. "Hi there, kid."

The girl with pigtails grabbed his tail and rubbed it against her face. "You're a soft little kitty, aren't you?"

Colin sighed. "Come on. Is that really necessary?"

More kids were heading his way, and Shaleigh used the moment to slip over to see Mawr, who was still blissfully unaware of the disruption. " 'I don't believe you're sick,' " Mawr read in a squeaky voice. " 'All you need is a good dose of sunshine. You only think you're sick.' "

Shaleigh put a hand on his mane between his shoulders and gave a rub. Mawr started kneading his paws, making gouges in the table, and broke into a rumbling purr. "Oh my," he said. "I can't concentrate when you're doing that, little one." He turned his big head to see her and his eyes went wide.

"Shaleigh!" he said with breathless excitement and turned to the handful of his remaining audience. "Please forgive me, everyone, but I have to step aside for just a moment. Don't worry, I'll be right back!" He picked up a bookmark in his teeth and laid it inside the book. The fact that most of the children had gone over to ogle Colin didn't bother him in the least, if he noticed it at all.

She led Mawr out of the courtyard and from inside she heard Colin say, "Don't be too long now, okay?" The desperation in his voice would almost be pitiful, if it wasn't so comical.

She and Mawr walked a good distance from the courtyard and the library. They needed privacy. She found an enormous birch tree whose initial trunk had split out into five sections, making it look like a hand had sprung out of the ground. She sat down on one of its thick branches and urged Mawr over. He kept looking over his shoulder, back to the courtyard.

"It's okay," she reassured. "We won't be long."

He turned back to her and gave her shoulder a gentle nudge with his chin. "I'm so glad to see you're alright. I was worried about you at the Games."

She wrapped her arms as best she could around his stone neck and gave him a hug. "I'm fine now. I'm glad you were there."

"That reminds me..." He pulled back and peered at her

through his golden spectacles. "Did you know that man that was with you was a Faerie?"

She shook her head.

"He's the one I was telling you about. He told me at the Games that I could come here to work, that he had set up a position for me. I was so excited, I thought he must run the library, you know? So, I went straight here and told Miss Manning at the front desk all about it. She said he's the High Faerie of this city." He jabbed her a bit harder, this time giving her a bruise.

"I didn't have a choice, Mawr. He's my captor here, kind of my guardian I guess. But look, I didn't come here for that. I need to ask a favor of you."

He pranced his stone paws on the ground. "Anything. You name it, and I'll find some way to do it."

She looked over his shoulder toward the courtyard again. No one had come out yet and she didn't see anyone nearby. "Colin and I are going to break someone out of the dungeons tonight."

"That sounds sneaky." He gave a wicked grin, "Wait, is it someone dangerous?"

"Eh..."

He narrowed his eyes. "It isn't that other Faerie from the Games, is it? The one everyone has been talking about?"

She held up her hands. "Look, he's really not so bad. He's just worried about his friend and made a mistake. Colin and I are going to free him, but we need your help to get him out of the city. I need you to make a distraction for us."

He clawed at the ground. "Shaleigh, I don't like you

spending so much time with Faeries! They're dangerous and fickle; you can't trust them."

She rubbed his cheek. "Look, all I need you to do is walk into the castle and make a fuss. Do something to get the guards attention, and then take your time leaving."

"But—but what if I lose my position at the library? I don't want to leave, Shaleigh, I like it here. Miss Manning is ever so sweet, and she said I could stay as long as I help them take care of the books. She said they might eventually get me a pedestal of my very own!"

"I don't think you have to worry about that. Teagan wouldn't let that happen."

Mawr's tail twitched back and forth as he gave his head a great shake. "Trusting a Faerie to help you save another Faerie. I don't like the sound of this. Are you sure we can trust them?"

"Look, you're my friend, aren't you?"

He nodded. "Of course I am."

"Well the other Faerie's name is Talek, and he's my friend too." Mawr tried to interrupt her. "Now hold on. He saved both our lives in the forest, didn't he?"

Mawr gave a deep sigh. "I guess so."

"I mean, I'm the reason you were in danger to begin with, but—"

"That wasn't really your fault though. You didn't want to be here, and who could blame you? Faeries with magic, wolves in the darkness." He looked up to the High Castle looming over everything in the distance. "And dangerous people everywhere. There isn't anything good here for you. Not for a human from the Human World."

She smiled and gave him another hug. "You're here. That's reason enough for me."

He put a heavy paw on her shoulder and rumbled with purrs. When she pulled away she saw dark, wet streaks falling down his stone cheeks. "Please be careful, Shaleigh. You're my best friend. I don't want you to get hurt."

"Me neither, which is why we're going to be so careful."

He gave a tearful nod and wiped at his cheeks.

"Now what do you have in mind for a good distraction?"

"Well," he sniffled. "In Aife we would have wondrous parties. They would last all night and the libraries would be lit up with dozens of candles. The finest wine was shipped in for those nights and everyone would dance. I thought maybe if I could pretend to have drunk some wine myself, maybe I would forget where I was, like they did."

She grinned. "That sounds like an excellent start."

"I FEEL SO RUFFLED..." Colin groaned. Once they got back to Shaleigh's room, he flopped down in the chair in front of the fireplace and didn't move for ten minutes. The only way she knew he wasn't asleep was because occasionally he would voice complaints. "There were so many of them. I think my ears are raw from getting rubbed by so many tiny fingers. I mean, it's not like they're made of velvet, you know? They're my ears."

Shaleigh chuckled but tried to focus on the splotchy

handwriting in front of her. When she asked Colin for a pen and a piece of paper, she hadn't expected all that she'd gotten. He'd laid out an ink well, a quill, and a roll of parchment paper in front of her, and all she could do was stare at it for a long minute. She was glad that she knew how to write in cursive, or it would have been even messier.

She considered asking Colin for assistance, but that seemed out of the question. He might occasionally answer her questions, but other than that, he was more interested in complaining right now. It was kind of eye-opening though; Colin's worst fear was a group of children.

While he groaned about his fur, Shaleigh made plans. It was easier when she had a place to put her thoughts down. They had decided to spring Talek at nine that evening. It was shortly after dinner, but still several hours before his scheduled execution, which hopefully caught the guards in a lull. Most of them would still be in the kitchens, Colin told her. They tended to take particularly long dinners when an execution was up, because the prep work and clean up always took a long time. The ones at night were even more rigid. Those were never done for entertainment. Mawr knew when to arrive, and she and Colin would have to be on their toes. When the guards left for Mawr's distraction, that was when they would move. The real difficulty would be getting out of the castle.

As Mawr finished up his distraction, they would stay at his side as he exited the front gates. Those doors were guarded at all hours, and there was no way Colin could creep it open without someone becoming suspicious.

Mawr's heavy steps would mask their own footfalls as they headed out of the city with Talek. It felt like a solid plan, but it still had a major hole.

They assumed Talek wanted them to save him. It seemed ridiculous not to want to be freed from the dungeons, but he was obviously depressed and seemed to have trouble thinking straight. Getting to Teagan was his goal, but after that, he didn't seem to know what to do. She wanted to help him, but Talek was resistant to any kind of authority. Even a human from a completely different world might be seen as an attempt to take him away from Teagan.

Someone knocked at the door, and she had to fight the urge to roll up the parchment to keep anyone from seeing her plans. That was fine when you were using a piece of wide-ruled paper and a ball point pen, but this ink was different. It smeared at just about anything. There was a powder she could sprinkle on top, but that would draw even more attention to her work. Instead Shaleigh got to her feet and stood so she was obscuring the parchment.

A short man entered, one of the servants based on his dress. "Excuse me, ma'am. Master Teagan wanted to make sure you had your dinner this evening, and—"

"No, we haven't had any food," Colin grumbled. "I thought you were trying to starve her or something."

The short man went bright red, "Oh no, sir! I believe we tried to bring something by earlier," he glanced to Shaleigh, "but you weren't in, ma'am."

"What difference does that make? Maybe she was in the bath."

"Colin!" Shaleigh couldn't believe him. He never acted like this. She had never seen him in such a foul mood.

The poor servant bowed, his face so red and words so quick that she thought he might pass out. "I'm-so-sorry-ma'am, we'll-get-something-up-quick!" He closed the door behind him as unobtrusively as he had entered.

She walked over to stand behind Colin's chair. He was laying back with his head against the cushion, staring at the ceiling. She leaned over him with a cross expression. "What's gotten into you? You're going to draw attention to us."

He sighed. "You're so calm about all this. I mean, I appreciate your confidence, but there's no way we're going to be lucky twice. Captain Briar nearly caught us last time. If she's down there..." He rubbed a hand over his eyes.

Colin's hesitancy surprised her. He was all boasts on the way down to the dungeons last time. Surely a group of school children didn't bother him that much. She sat down in the chair beside him.

"You did fine last time we went. What's the big deal?"

He gave a frightened chuckle and dragged his hand through his fur. "You really don't have any concept of how dangerous this is, do you?"

"Explain it to me then."

He stared at her for a moment before answering. "We're breaking a Faerie out of the dungeons. Not just any Faerie either, but one who has been masquerading in the streets of the Garden for who knows how long. That statue friend of yours was right. Faeries creep me out."

"First of all," she crossed her arms. "His name is Mawr.

Secondly, what is with this place and their hostility toward Faeries? You told me just the other day how much you appreciate Teagan's generosity to you. You said you see him as your mentor."

He nodded. "Almost like a really strict dad actually."

"Exactly. So, what's the big deal with Talek? You saw him in there. Did he seem like a dangerous Faerie to you?"

"No, but—"

"He's fast, yes, but he doesn't have magic like Teagan has. If you ask me, Madam Cloom and Teagan are far more dangerous. What's the worst he could do to you, run past you and out the door? He needs us to get out of here. Besides, I owe him. Mawr and I both owe him." She grinned and added, "Considering he helped to get me here, he kind of helped you too. This was where you were going to take me when you kidnapped me, right?"

Colin sighed and got to his feet. "Faeries don't do things like that, not without some other motive."

"Oh please," she snorted. "I haven't met a single person in this place who doesn't say one thing and do another. And besides, Teagan turned you into a stoatling, didn't he? What was his ulterior motive there?"

Colin's tail twitched and he let the question drop. Obviously, she had hit a nerve, but since Colin hadn't yet decided to back out on their plan, she must have hit on some truth too.

AFTER THEY ATE dinner and waited for the servant to take their plates, they decided to head down to the

Memorial Chamber. There was still half an hour before Mawr would begin his distraction, but they wanted to get there early just in case. The hallways were disturbingly empty, even more than earlier. If she hadn't just spoken to one of the servants, she would have thought the entire castle was empty. Colin ushered her into the Memorial Chamber and closed the door behind them.

"It's like a ghost town out there," he said with a frown.

"Any idea what's going on?"

"I'm not sure, I mean, they shouldn't still be searching for Faeries in the city. And I assume Master Teagan would summon me if there was an emergency."

She stretched her legs, preparing for the prolonged time she would be stuck on Colin's back. "Maybe he considers getting Talek out of here more of a priority than whatever else is going on."

"I guess."

She climbed onto his back and together they headed out toward the guard doors. There was more urgency to Colin's movements this time. He still moved between the shadowy pools in the hallway, but he didn't slide between them like before. If there had been anyone in the halls, they would have easily spotted them a handful of times. When he got to the door of the stairwell that led down to the dungeons, he seemed to have the patience of a kid in a candy store.

"Slow down," she whispered. "We need to take our time, remember?"

He crouched down near the doorway, his voice wavering. "I'm sorry, I guess I'm just nervous. It's bad enough we have to break a Faerie out of the dungeon, but the lack of guards around really bothers me."

"Just calm down, I'm with you still, okay? If there is some kind of ambush, you're not alone. I can always pull my weight with the whole reincarnation." She smirked.

He chuckled. "Be careful with that. It might not always work the way you think. Not everybody wants a new Madam in charge." He went down on all fours this time and started down the stairwell with far more caution. Shaleigh wrapped her legs around his waist just in case he had to leap to the ceiling. She had to admit, the lack of guards was getting to her too.

When they reached the bottom of the stairs, Colin poked his head around to check the numbers in the guard room, only to find it empty. "Something's wrong," Colin muttered, and Shaleigh agreed with him. The guards must have left in a hurry too, for a card game with three players had been completely forgotten, their hands dropped in their haste.

"What do you think happened?" She frowned, noticing a dagger had also been forgotten on the edge of the table. "Nothing violent, I hope."

"It looks like they left of their own will at least."

Colin gasped and darted across the room to a pool of shadows near the corridor to the cells. "Do you hear that?"

She had to hold her breath for a moment to hear over her panicked breathing, but she did finally hear a voice. A woman's voice lilted faintly from the hallway. "Let's go," Shaleigh whispered. "And this time, be careful!"

He nodded and crept down the sloped hall. The entire length of the area was dark, all except a torch that was lit at the far end near Talek's cell. As they got closer, she heard a thump that she didn't recognize, thick and muffled. Then it came again, and a man groaned with it. Her eyes went wide.

"Hurry, Colin."

He bounded forward on all fours but slowed as they reached the cell. Shaleigh couldn't believe what she saw.

"This would be far easier if you simply told me the truth," Captain Briar crooned as she walked around the cell. At her feet lay Talek. Shaleigh couldn't see his face very well, but he was shaking.

"Please," Talek whispered. "I don't know why the wolves are attacking. They have nothing to do with me."

"Don't give me that." She kicked him again, and Talek barely had time to pull his knees close to keep his stomach from getting hit. "It's too much of a coincidence! They come the very night you're to be slaughtered and they've been sniffing around the gates ever since nightfall, flinging themselves at it. Don't lie, Faerie, they come for you, don't they? Your little furry friends are coming to rescue you."

Shaleigh pulled away from Colin's shoulder only to have him pull her back. "Let me go in," she pleaded. "I've got to help him."

"No." He pulled her off his back but motioned for her to wait. "No, let me do it. You have no pull here." He took off the flute around his neck and put it around hers. Then he gave it a quick whistle. He became visible, but Shaleigh stayed in the strange shadowy form. He flashed her a brief, trying-to-be brave smile. "Stay hidden," he whispered. "I don't want her to do anything rash."

The cell had gone quiet other than the sounds of Talek's mumbled pleas.

"Who's there?" the Captain called. "Answer me. If I find out you've been spying on me, Madam Cloom will have your head!"

Colin put his hand on the hilt of the dagger he kept on his belt, then stepped forward. "You know, I may be wrong, but I'm pretty sure Teagan wouldn't appreciate you abusing his old lover."

"Colin," the Captain took a step back. "What are you doing down here?"

"Apparently, showing up in the nick of time." He glanced over to Talek, who was still curled up. "Did you know that there are no guards in the halls upstairs? Or even in the guard room back there?"

Captain Briar was pulling on her gloves again. "Of course not. We've had wolves at the gate all evening. I have guards at all exits to keep them at bay."

In the distance they heard the high-pitched whine of a horn sounding. The Captain's eyes went wide. "They've gotten through! How—"

Colin folded his arms. "Perhaps if the Captain of the Guards was down there, they wouldn't have been over-whelmed."

Captain Briar slammed the cell door closed and nearly knocked Colin to the ground as she pushed past him. "You're coming with me. You may be a terrible fighter, but we'll need your help if the wolves are in the city." She grabbed her sword from where it lay against the wall and stormed up the hall. "You had best not dally, Colin!"

"I wouldn't dream of it!" he called back and waited

until the Captain was out of sight. "Shaleigh? Are you still here?" he called softly.

She touched his arm and he put a hand over hers. "Good," he sighed in relief and put the key into her hand. "Meet me in the Memorial Chamber after you get him out, okay?"

"Will do," she said and gave his arm a squeeze.

"I'd better go. I don't think the Captain has much patience with me tonight." Before Shaleigh could ask him more, he bounded down the hall. She stood here, clutching the key in her hand and looking at the prone figure of Talek in the cell. Somehow this just became ten times more difficult.

~

WHEN SHALEIGH OPENED the cell door, Talek drew himself in again, waiting for the next blow. Unfortunately, it wasn't the first time she had approached someone who had been freshly beaten. She and Kaeja had stumbled upon a homeless man in an alleyway near an abandoned house downtown. At first, they had mistaken his cries for a mewling cat. She still remembered the blood that dribbled down his almost unrecognizable jaw.

Talek didn't look as bad off, but she had to approach him slowly. He might be in shock or have broken limbs. She had no idea what kind of damage the Captain had done to him, only that he was still in survival mode.

"Talek?" she whispered, "Talek, it's Shaleigh. I know you can't see me very well, but I've come to help you."

He peeked out between his arms with wide eyes. "Shaleigh?" he gasped. "You really are there, aren't you?"

When she got closer to him she could see that his clothes were torn in places, mostly along his calves where he had pulled up his knees to protect himself from the Captain's kicks. The sleeves of his shirt had been torn too, and dark splotches were visible on his pale skin. He would be sore for weeks at least, but she still didn't know if the damage went deeper.

She touched his arm and he jumped. "Shh, calm down. I'm going to get you out of here." She put an arm underneath his and tried to help him to his feet. This time he let her. "Take it slowly. Let me know if you think anything is busted."

He moaned as she helped him up, clutching at his midsection. The Captain must have gotten a strong hit in before he knew to protect himself. He hunched forward, unable to fully straighten, but at least he could stand on his own.

"I can't leave, Shaleigh. I can't leave without him."

"What?" He leaned heavily on her shoulder and she had to adjust her footing to keep from toppling over.

"Teagan, he needs me. I can't leave him in this place." A tear streaked down his dirty cheek. "I did this for him. If he isn't safe, then all of this, everything was for nothing. I can't do that, Shaleigh. I love him."

"I know, Talek, but they're going to kill you."

He shook his head. "I don't care. I'm not going anywhere without him."

She sighed. She should have expected this. Talek wasn't thinking straight, and looking at the conditions in which he was being kept, it wasn't terribly surprising. It didn't help that she sympathized with his mission. Being the High Faerie of the Garden was changing Teagan; already he was no longer the man Talek knew, but she couldn't tell Talek that. He had been through too much.

"He's going to say the same thing—that you need to leave. It isn't safe for you here."

"No," Talek shook his head in a jerky motion. "No, no, you don't understand. We need to break the bond. It's the only way to save him from this accursed place."

"But the Garden—"

"It'll get along just fine without him, trust me. I won't let him be destroyed by this place or by the witch that sits on the throne. Even Cathal wasn't the dictator that she is." He stared at her with pleading eyes in a face that had been dragged through the dirt. "Please, Shaleigh. You must help me save him."

She stared at him for a long moment. "What do I need to do?"

He gave a short nod and then flung his head forward. Leaning on Shaleigh he moved his fingers around against the back of his head until he began untying something.

"What are you—?"

"I had to hide it someplace safe, somewhere the guards would never look. They inspected everything on me: my boots, my gloves, even my pants; but they would never look here." He pulled out a tiny pair of silver scissors that had the smallest blades Shaleigh had ever seen. They had two large loops for fingers to go through. They were also almost the same color as Talek's hair too, so it would have been impossible to see them if you didn't know what you were looking for. He placed them in Shaleigh's hand.

"There's a black ribbon on his right wrist. Cut it with these, and the bond with that accursed witch will be broken forever. He'll be free to go home with me then, and we'll finally be able to live in peace." His eyes rolled as he teetered on his feet. Shaleigh was afraid he was going to pass out, but he shuddered against the urge. "Promise me, you'll do it, Shaleigh. Promise me."

"I'll do it," she whispered, slipping the scissors onto the necklace around her throat, so that it sat beside Colin's metal flute. "I promise."

"Thank you," he sighed and slumped against her. "We can go now. Thank you for helping him."

She gave him a small smile and slowly, step by step, they made their way out of the cell and up the long hallway. The stairs were more difficult, but without a single guard around, Talek was able to take his time. His midsection hurt him regularly and he kept having to take breaks. The damage on his legs and stomach hurt him more than any of the other injuries, and she wished she knew how to use those contraptions in the healer's room, with their colored glass and music. She could probably heal him in minutes, but all that was out of her reach. She could only be patient and help him along the way. She wasn't sure how she was going to get him out of the city though. He was visible, and she hadn't a clue how to use the flute Colin had left her. She wished she had paid more attention to the magical items that surrounded her. If she had embraced the world instead of fighting against it, maybe this would have been easier.

~

IT TOOK a while for Colin to catch up with the Captain. He reached her just as she reached the front gates of High Castle. Two soldiers were talking with her; one of them had a raw gash that had nearly taken off one of his eyebrows.

"None got inside," the wounded soldier reported. "We barricaded this door so they can't get in here. The rest were closed up earlier, so we should be secure for now."

"Have either of you seen Teagan?" she asked. The two soldiers exchanged a worried look and the Captain sighed. "Where was he last, do you know?"

"No, sir." The other soldier spoke in a wavering voice. "I thought I saw him near the kitchens, but he moves so quick sometimes, I—"

"It's not important. Stay put and inform me if he comes by here. Understood?"

They saluted. "Yes, sir!"

"Good. Colin, I'm glad you're here." It was strange the way she smiled at him. It was like she hadn't just been downstairs beating the snot out of that white-haired Faerie. "You'll be accompanying me." She drew her sword and requested that the gates be opened. "Close them again after we depart. Once the wolves are pushed back, I'll return." Her sword gleamed in the torchlight. "Make sure we have no breaches, soldiers."

They saluted her again as Colin stepped to her side. "Is that a good idea? I mean, if we open up the gates now, we could get overwhelmed ourselves." He looked around the hallway. There were only the four of them.

"High Castle has the best defenses in the Garden, but our citizens are boarded up in their homes and many of them are probably dead. I'm not going to leave my people to rot."

Colin considered pointing out that if she was so dedicated, she shouldn't have been downstairs beating the crud out of Talek while the city was at risk, but decided against it. Captain Briar was the leader here, and regardless of his opinions of her, she was quite effective in her position. Yes, she had a tendency to needlessly torture her prisoners, but most of her soldiers were keenly loyal to her for good reason.

It took two soldiers on either side to open the gate, but what lay beyond made the breath catch in Colin's throat. Skirmishes had broken out everywhere, and there was carnage in the streets. One soldier was face down in the mud, laying a few feet away from the open gates that led to the Slumbering Forest. Even from this distance, he could hear the man's cries. Another was defiantly shooting arrows into a shadowy wolf from the roof of a carriage. At first Colin wasn't sure why the soldier had chosen such a precarious position, but then he spotted the panicked faces of three children inside. Colin snarled.

He may not like the way children always bombarded him, but he felt pure anger at seeing those poor kids trapped. He couldn't just sit and wait for orders. He wasn't a soldier and wasn't even wearing any armor, but he could at least distract. Stoats and stoatlings were very good at distraction. Colin pulled his dagger off his belt and charged in, heedless of the Captain calling orders. He didn't have to follow her orders; she wasn't his boss.

When he got closer, he realized there were two wolves —one which the soldier was holding off with a dwindling supply of arrows, the other coming in from behind, as yet unspotted by the soldier. He could see the creature's orange eyes glowing through the cloudy windows of the carriage and the muffled cries of the children inside grew louder. The girl, who must have been the eldest, was trying to push the younger boys behind her in case the wolf got in.

Colin bit down on the blade of his dagger then sprinted forward on all fours. As he drew closer, he started zig-zagging side to side. The closer wolf turned and paused as though bewildered, its eyes tracking him back and forth in mute shock. It made a desperate swipe at him, but Colin dodged, the breeze ruffling the fur on his arm. Just as Colin was trying to find a way to get around the beast and to the other side of the carriage, an arrow erupted from the wolf's skull. Its orange eyes went wide as it fell to the ground. The soldier atop the carriage gave him a nod, only to cry out as the other wolf came from behind and stood on its haunches, its claws extended.

Colin slid underneath the carriage in a cloud of dust and knocked the wolf's legs out from under him. The wolf toppled to the ground, taking a moment to get his bearings, and that was the advantage the soldier needed. An arrow shot through the back of the wolf's neck; the beast gave a brief gurgle before going silent. Colin got to his feet. The children in the carriage were terrified, but he didn't have time to console them. He looked around at the streets of the Garden.

"Thank you, sir!" The soldier on top of the carriage removed his cap and wiped at his bald head.

"No problem," Colin replied, barely listening. There were too many of them. Captain Briar was fighting three on the bridge that led into the High Castle and there were six more on the streets, several eating the remains of the fallen.

A glass window broke off a small, wooden building and a wolf emerged head first. At first Colin thought it was leaping out until it landed in a heap. A gravelly voice cried out, "Stupid mutts!" Stepping awkwardly through the old storage house window was Graddic, holding a large metal pole that was for lighting streetlights.

"Graddic!" Colin called as he ran over.

The minotaur gave a heavy shake of his head, flinging off dirt and glass from his fur. He gave a deep laugh as he spotted Colin. "I should have known you'd be out here. Having a bit of sport yourself, eh?"

"There are people trapped everywhere. We have to get them out and away from the wolves."

Graddic rolled his eyes. "And where shall we take them exactly? The Garden is supposed to be a haven, right?"

Colin glared. "Yes, but it's not anymore. People are going to die if we don't get them out of here."

The minotaur pointed his metal staff to the front of the castle. "The last I heard, orders were to bring all citizens into High Castle. Is that not still the case?"

Colin looked over to the bridge to see Captain Briar slaying the last of the three wolves. The castle did seem the safest place to be, but Master Teagan was nowhere to be seen. Without his protection, it seemed foolish to rely on the castle's protection alone. Besides that, most of the soldiers were spread out across the city, and the Captain couldn't keep the wolves at bay by herself. Still, Graddic made a good point. Where else were they supposed to go? If High Castle was the safest stronghold in the land, then perhaps it was time to put its title to the test.

"Did you hear me, kid?" Graddic grunted, "Do we take them to the castle or not?"

"Sure," he sighed. "Do that. Use the carriages here and get people off the streets. Take anyone you can to the castle. Can you get any of the other minotaurs to help?"

"I can try," Graddic said. "But they don't like following orders much, not in a time like this, you understand. Can't say I do either, but they seem like good orders at least."

Why in the world did minotaurs have to be so difficult to work with? He hated to admit it, but he would rather be helping the Captain instead of trying to reason with a minotaur. Graddic was kinder than most, but he was just as stubborn as the rest of his kind.

A scream from behind tore Colin's attention away and he gasped in horror at the wave of wolves that had swarmed over the carriage of children he'd left behind. The soldier on top had been flung to the ground and three of the wolves were devouring him.

"Graddic..."

The minotaur tightened his grip on the metal pole in his hands and snarled. "Aye. I see them." Colin was about to follow him as the minotaur charged forward, but first turned to see Captain Briar on the bridge.

He cupped his hands around his mouth so she could hear him. "Captain!" She looked up from giving orders to four soldiers that now stood outside of the castle gates, and seeing what Colin was pointing at, gave a nod. She and two of the soldiers were making their way forward.

They might not be able to save the soldier, but perhaps they could help the children.

SHALEIGH AND TALEK climbed out of the stairwell. The first thing she noticed was that the halls of the castle were just as empty as they had been before; the emptiness made her uneasy. The footsteps of someone running echoed toward them and she ushered Talek into a small pool of shadow against the wall. She wasn't sure how well Colin's necklace would keep them hidden, but she couldn't help holding her breath as one of the servants ran around the corner at full speed. He stumbled once, but never glanced toward them before continuing down the hall. Talek sunk down to the floor to catch his breath. She held his hand firmly, to make sure they were both encompassed with the necklace's spell.

"What's going on?" she asked.

"Wolves are in the city. That's what the Captain said, at least." Talek gave a small shudder and Shaleigh crouched down beside him. She couldn't tell if he looked paler or not.

"Are you okay?"

"I'll live," he said with a weak smile. "Though I do doubt my eyes at times. Everything is brighter with you here. What sort of magic do you wield?"

"The special Colin kind. Don't ask me, I don't know anything about it."

He nodded, his eyes drifting to the flute around her throat. "It's probably one of Teagan's creations. I wonder what other strange things he's created in his time here."

"Come on. We've got to get you out of here." She helped him to his feet, noticing how much slower he was moving after their crawl up the long staircase. He was getting tired, and she couldn't blame him after the Captain's beating. She wished she and Colin had gone down to the dungeons an hour earlier.

Talek sucked in a breath and clutched at his midsection but waved away her concern when she turned towards him. "I'm fine. It's just better when I'm not moving, is all."

They walked slowly down the deserted hall, and Shaleigh was beginning to wonder if they were lost. She still hadn't seen the exit, certain they should have come across it by now. Perhaps she had gotten turned around after they left the dungeons. All the halls looked the same, and there were hardly any signs to help.

"Colin?" A voice whispered and she and Talek both jumped. "Are you Mister Colin?" The voice hissed again, and Shaleigh could hear the fear behind the words this time.

Talek was turning, looking around in confusion.

"Mawr?" Shaleigh asked, and at her voice the stone lion poked his head around the corner of the next hall. He motioned them over.

"I was going to make a distraction, like you asked, but I

couldn't find anyone to distract. They either run past me or are too busy to notice me."

"There's been a change in plans," Shaleigh told him. "Colin is with the Captain, so he won't be able to help. I have Talek though."

"Talek?" Mawr asked, his ears going back in fear.

"Yes," Talek said, letting go of her hand and stepping forward. "It's good to see you again, Mawr. You do remember me, don't you?"

The great stone lion pawed at the ground, digging great ruts into the floor. "Yes, I do. I'm sorry about running away from you like that. It wasn't very kind of me."

Talek chuckled. "No, but that's alright. I'm afraid I've grown accustomed to it." He glanced to Shaleigh. "I hope you haven't forgotten our agreement though."

"No, I know," she said. "I'm going to let Mawr take you out from here. I'm heading back in to finish it."

Talek turned his piercing gaze toward her. "Don't forget what you promised."

"Wait," Mawr stammered, looking between the two of them. "Shaleigh, you're not coming with us?"

"I'm sorry," she said. "I've got to finish something for Talek first." She wrapped her arms around his stone neck and hugged him. "As soon as I'm done though, I'm coming for you."

Mawr wiped at a tear. "I'm scared. There are all sorts of wolves out there." He sniffled, "And so many are dead. It reminds me of Aife when those great Pello Pines attacked."

Talek patted Mawr's shoulder. "I'll be with you. We'll get through them together."

"And I'll catch up as soon as I can, okay?" Shaleigh reassured.

"Alright." Mawr kneaded his paws on the ground again. "I'll try."

She turned to Talek. "Good luck. I'll be right behind you."

"Thank you again, Shaleigh. You have no idea how much this means to me."

Shaleigh gave him a hug and Talek stiffened as though in pain. She stepped back immediately, a blush staining her cheeks, "Sorry..."

His grimace turned into a tired smile. "It's alright. Hurry, while you have the chance."

She nodded and sprinted back down the hall the way she had come. As timid as Mawr was, he still had the courage to help, even with those terrible shadow wolves outside. She had considered giving them Colin's silver flute, but if she was going to get close to Teagan, she would need it. She just hoped Mawr could get Talek out without the Captain or the guards seeing him while she freed Teagan.

Even with Captain Briar and her guards at his side, the wolves were not in the least bit intimidated. In fact, as they moved closer, the beasts snorted and snickered at them. One of the larger wolves pushed itself onto its hind legs and stepped forward, its orange eyes gleaming.

The shadow wolves' bodies were lean and muscular with fur that was so dark, it was as if they grew shadow instead of fur. Of the ones that lingered in the darkness, all Colin could make out were their orange eyes and their wicked, sharp-toothed grins. Up on their hind legs, they were even more disturbing. Their long forelimbs hung far too low on their bodies, making them quite fast on all fours. Their barrel chests, made for their massive lungs, gave them disturbing proportions. Indeed, the rumors Colin had heard of them being the stuff of nightmares was an understatement. He hadn't gotten a good look at them when he was slicing through them earlier, but now he understood why so many feared them. The thought of these monsters slaughtering his old friend Finn in the darkness of the forest made a pit of remorse form in his stomach, but he pushed it away.

"What a terrible smell you have," the standing one quipped. "Very much like a rodent that eats its own dung."

Laughter rippled among them like a pack of hyenas. Colin stiffened. He hadn't realized they could talk. The ones he fought earlier had no voice, so he assumed they lacked intelligence. That, apparently, was not the case. There were at least twelve of them now. He could handle a couple here or there, but Colin had been on the losing side of enough fights to know they were outnumbered and outmatched.

"I wonder, Colin," Captain Briar's voice rang over their maddening laughter. "Do you think these animals will laugh so much when their insides are strewn about to steam on the ground?" She stepped up beside him, her sword held high and her eyes livid.

He cracked a smile. "I doubt it."

"Your kinsmen certainly didn't." She nodded toward the bridge, where bodies were piled like trash. "I've gutted three of you beasts already and my blade thirsts for more." She raised her voice and glanced over to the two guards on her other side. "Let us show them that they are but hares and foxes to us. Let us show them who the real wolves are here."

The standing wolf gave a low snarl and bared its sharp canines. "Kill them," it hissed.

In unison the other wolves lunged. Colin jerked back as one snapped its jaws only inches away from his face. Then he found himself dodging, leaping, ducking, and side-stepping at least four of the creatures. He swiped with his dagger, but they were quick and they seemed to anticipate his speed. They tried to close in around him, but he kept moving backwards to keep from being surrounded. He thought about confusing them like he had before but wasn't sure if it would work when they were in a frenzy, and he didn't have the space any longer. It didn't take long for them to herd him away from the Captain. With a careful leap, he tried to go over their heads to rejoin her. Normally it was hardly any trouble, but these wolves were clever. One of them sprang up to meet him, and he had to twist his body midair to keep from getting a limb caught in its open jaws. In his panic, he landed on his shoulder and a jolt of pain made him clench his teeth, but he got up and kept moving.

He was now not only separated from the Captain, but out of her sight as the wolves quickly circled him. The injury had stunned him just enough to give them time to close in. Pain was the price of speed, and the wolves used it to their advantage. No matter where he turned he had a wolf at his back, so he crouched down, ready to leap if given the chance. The first wolf lunged forward, and Colin slashed wildly at its face, panic turning his knife from the throat to the face, and one of its eyes burst with blood. It let out a hissing squeal and for a moment Colin felt rather good about himself, until the wolf from behind landed on him. His face was shoved into the gravel of the road and the heavy paws on his shoulders made it hard to breathe. The claws dug with expert efficiency into his shoulder where he'd been injured. He let out a loud cry, which brought forth a chorus of laughter from the three remaining wolves.

Their laughter was cut short and the weight on his back lifted. He got to his feet slowly, his shoulder protesting in pain, but he held his dagger up regardless as Captain Briar cut through a second wolf's snout. "Colin!" she cried, "Are you alright?"

"I am now," he gasped. He was shaking and disoriented. The Captain's blade was covered in blood, as was much of her armor. Even her face was splattered with it, despite the helmet keeping most of her head covered. The crimson made her look truly fierce in the dim light. She parried to the side of the third wolf's slash and cut off an ear. While the wolf howled in pain, she ended its suffering by impaling it through the throat.

"Good," she said as she freed her blade. "You held them off well. With a little more technique, I could make use of you in the force." She flashed him a wild smile. "That is, if being a Seeker doesn't work out."

Colin couldn't decide which was more disturbing, the wolves from the forest or the glee that seemed to take hold of the Captain on the battlefield. "Thank you, sir?"

She wiped the blade off on a red sash that hung from her waist. "Are you hurt?"

He shook his head, and she laughed.

"If you are, then you need to head back to the castle and get looked at. Take a break at least. No point in exhausting yourself early." She put a hand on his good shoulder, and in that moment the ruthless woman he had seen in the dungeons had been completely replaced by the inspiring leader who stood before him. It was as though spilling blood transformed her. All the vindictive words drained from her here, and every person who fought at her side became a younger sibling. It was easy to see how she came from royalty; the Briars were renowned for their abilities on the battlefield, but he also understood how they could be hated too.

"Maybe I should take a short break," he admitted. "Leave a few for me, won't you?"

She barked out a laugh at that. "Oh, there are plenty for both of us to slay, Colin. Don't you worry."

He headed to the front gates, stepping around the pile of dead shadow wolves which had become a sort of barricade. Two of the guards he had fought with were ushering the children from the carriage inside. All three of the kids had survived unscathed, despite the fact that the smallest boy was sobbing his eyes out.

One of the four soldiers who had helped with the pack of wolves, nodded to him. "Well fought there, sir."

"You too!" Colin smiled and slipped inside. Perhaps it wasn't just the Captain that was transformed in battle. Normally the soldiers and guards of the Garden barely acknowledged him, but put in a dire situation, they too lowered their defenses. Now that Colin was out of the fight, his could admit to himself how much his shoulder ached. He looked around to see where the Healers were hiding. That was when he saw them.

Straight ahead, at the highest point of the hall, just before it curved down out of sight, he saw two heads duck down quickly. Colin blinked. Surely that giant head hadn't been made of stone, and he couldn't have spotted the gleaming white hair of the most notorious prisoner in the city. Surely, they hadn't walked right up to the front gate and expected to be able to sneak out. Colin sighed and looked around to make sure he wasn't being seen. The work of Master Teagan's assistant was never finished.

Resisting the urge to crouch down on all fours, he trotted up and hunkered down between them. "What are you two doing?" he hissed in greeting.

"Trying to find a way out of here." Talek gave a weak smile. "I'm afraid we're having trouble."

Colin looked him up and down, noticing he looked even paler than he did back in the dungeon. His eyes were sunken and, even crouched down, he swayed back and forth. He was barely able to stay on his feet.

"You look terrible," Colin said with a frustrated sigh. "I wish we could get you to the Healers. I mean, they're just on the other side of that wall. That's where I was heading."

Talek gave a cold smile. "No one wishes that more than me, I assure you. However, I think I would be recognized almost before my stone friend here."

Mawr wasn't helping the situation. He kneaded his paws into the floor, his sharp claws making a maddening grinding noise. Colin glared at him. "Stop that. Are you trying to attract attention? I mean, if you want everyone in the castle to know you've been here, you're doing an excellent job by marking everything in the world."

The lion hung his head low. "Sorry."

Colin rolled his eyes. That lion was going to break his heart into pieces, either from nerves or cuteness. "What happened to Shaleigh?" He glanced around at the empty hall, "I assume she's not with you."

"No, she made me a promise; she had to go back to fulfill it."

"Okay," Colin sighed. "So where are you trying to get to? Outside of the gates to the Garden... Would that work?"

He gave a weak nod, "That should work. I can't go too far." He sat up a bit straighter, his words urgent. "I couldn't leave unless I knew this was taken care of. I would never forgive myself otherwise."

Colin cocked his head to the side. "What exactly was this promise?"

Talek pursed his lips. "I'm afraid I cannot say; however, I would still greatly appreciate your help."

Colin sighed and rubbed the fur on the back of his neck. "I guess it's none of my business. We just have to get you out of here." He looked to the front gate again, thinking of the two guards standing outside. "We could get you onto Mawr's back and I could walk him out. You keep your hair over your ears and they might not realize you're a Faerie."

"Yes, but—" Talek looked up to Mawr's back with a bleak expression and maybe even a little bit of fear in his eyes. "How?"

Colin nodded and stretched. "You let me help, that's how. I'm a little bruised and battered, but I can still do it."

"No," Talek blurted, then seemed to compose himself again. "I mean...I don't know if that's possible. He couldn't even carry me with his jaws earlier. I nearly passed out, I don't know if I can handle it." His voice grew a bit higher in pitch, and Colin saw where that fear from earlier came from. Getting jostled around by a giant stone lion probably didn't help him much. If he did have any internal injuries, that kind of movement would only aggravate them.

"Trust me, I can be careful." Colin winked, hoping to give him some reassurance. Talek's eyes went wide and he gave him a curious expression. It would normally be comical if they weren't in such a hurry. Talek blinked a few more times, then gave a curt nod.

"Great." Colin grinned wider. "Don't worry so much. I promise, I'll take good care of you, okay?"

Despite his words, the Faerie winced as Colin bent down to pick him up. He put one arm around his knees and his other arm beneath his shoulders. "Okay, lean back slowly." He said as kindly as he could. "Just fall into my arms."

Talek closed his eyes for a moment as though this annoyed him for some reason. It was at that moment that Colin wondered if he was grossed out by him. Some people had weird reactions to his physical appearance; perhaps Talek was a bit of an elitist who wasn't too keen on rubbing shoulders with a grimy stoatling. He pushed the thoughts aside. That probably had nothing to do with it. The only reason he thought that was because of the wolves' taunts, and the less power he gave those wolves the better. Talek leaned back against him and stiffened as his feet left the ground, bracing for the pain. He winced only for an instant then relaxed. He was stunned when he opened his eyes again.

"You good?" Colin asked, with a laugh.

Talek nodded and a flush came to his cheeks. Perhaps he was in more pain than Colin realized. Colin leapt onto

Mawr's back as carefully as he could, then laid the Faerie down with his shoulders elevated against the lion's mane. He tried to be as gentle as he could to prevent him from getting any more injuries. Since they weren't going to the Healers, he didn't want their escapee to pass out before they had even reached the Garden gates.

"You're not in any more pain, are you?" Colin inquired with a frown.

"No, I'm fine." Talek said without meeting his eyes. If he wasn't in pain, then maybe having to be carried around was a blow to his pride.

"Great." Colin gave a winning grin and dragged Talek's hair over his ears and part of his face. He looked rather ridiculous, but was good-natured about it at least, not that Talek had much room to complain. They either tried this, or he would get dragged back to his cell to serve as the Captain's personal punching bag until he was executed. Colin patted Mawr's side.

"Let's head to the front gate."

"What are we going to tell them though?" Mawr asked as he turned to peer at the guards around his glasses. "What if they're suspicious?"

"We have a patient who needs to reach a specialist in the Marketplace." Colin smiled at his own cleverness. "If they demand to follow, let them. Then we'll have some guards that can keep the wolves away. Once we shake them, we head to the main gates."

"I can't leave until Shaleigh has finished what she promised," Talek insisted in a muffled voice. It was funny to hear him try to be commanding with a wad of his own white hair covering his mouth.

"I hate to say it, but you don't get much of a choice in the matter, sunshine."

Talek sighed and Colin patted his shoulder. He hoped he found it reassuring and not insulting.

~

How in the world was she supposed to find Teagan? Her first instinct was to go to the flower garden in the gazebo that Teagan enjoyed so much. She hurried down the endless hall, trying to remember where she was in the castle and wishing she had asked if Mawr knew.

She came to an intersecting hall and skidded to a stop. The hallways all looked the same, with dark polished walls and colored glass windows, but this area felt familiar. It was an inclined hallway, and she remembered one direction led to the Healers and the other led down to the flower garden, but she couldn't remember which. She huffed, and chose at random, taking the decline.

As the hallway curved, she slowed down. She didn't care too much if she was seen in the halls by servants at this point, but she would have to sneak up on Teagan. He would resist his bond being cut. He was addicted to the power like Talek said after all. As voices filtered down the hall, she came to a complete stop.

"They do understand that this equipment isn't meant to be moved, don't they? I don't see why they can't bring the injured down here where we can treat them like normal patients." Franklin, one of the two obstinate doctors, was standing outside the door with a pile of scrolls in his arms.

Shaleigh had to stifle a gasp when she heard Lieutenant Varg's reply, "There are simply too many of them. Please, this is a matter of urgency. I ought to be outside where—"

"Where you can be injured even more," Franklin snapped. "Honestly, if we were expected to take on so many patients, the High Faerie should have trained more of us. It's an embarrassment that there are only two Healers in all of High Castle."

Shaleigh edged up to look around the bend in the hallway at the Healers' door. The Lieutenant stood outside with his arms crossed. "Perhaps he thought you two could handle it." He glanced toward Shaleigh and visibly stiffened. She pulled away and flattened herself against the wall, her heart pounding in her chest.

"Excuse me for a moment," the Lieutenant muttered, and she heard him approach. She edged along the wall to stop in one of the darker sections of the hallway, midway between two torches. It wasn't nearly as dark as the shadows that Colin had used in the dungeon before, but there were no other options.

Lieutenant Varg came around the bend, his sword glinting in the torchlight. Shaleigh clung to the wall and held her breath. She didn't have the fur clad feet that Colin did, so running away was out of the question. The Lieutenant had been knocked out at the Games, she recalled, but apparently it hadn't taken long to heal. He looked more than ready to hunt her down. She wrapped a hand around the hilt of her sword as the Lieutenant eyed the wall with keen eyes.

"I know you're here. I saw you. You'll make this easier

on both of us if you reveal yourself now." His eyes locked onto her position and Shaleigh felt the blood drain from her face.

"Please don't!" she whispered, not wanting the Healers down the hall to hear her.

The Lieutenant dropped his blade an inch, his face revealing his surprise.

"Shaleigh?"

"It's me. Colin lent me his flute so I can find Teagan, but I haven't seen him anywhere!"

"Master Teagan?" The Lieutenant narrowed his eyes and took a step closer to her. Shaleigh stepped away from him, nervous with the sword still aimed at her. "How do I know you really are Shaleigh? You could be some sort of shapeshifter, something that came inside with the wolves."

"Um," her mind went blank. She tried to think of anything about herself that he might know, but she only distantly knew the Lieutenant, and she had never spoken with him about her father or Kaeja. "I came in from the Slumbering Forest with Talek, the Faerie, and Mawr, the Living Statue."

He shook his head, lifting his sword higher. "Anyone with ears would know that."

"Oh crap, hang on!" She held her hands up, but the Lieutenant couldn't see them, and he was growing more suspicious by the second. "You were supposed to fight me earlier today at the Games, but you were knocked unconscious."

"Again, intruder, that is common knowledge. If you can't answer me, then I'm afraid—"

"No, wait! You had a locket. You were looking at it

when you were preparing for the Games. You said you didn't know who you were up against, but it was supposed to be a novice fighter. I think it was a picture of your family, of your wife and kids."

He froze and his hand relaxed on the hilt. "Go on."

"I couldn't see it very well, but—"

"What did they look like?"

"She has dark hair, maybe black or brown. The boys too, they have the same. There were two of them."

He sighed and shook his head. "By the gods, Shaleigh. I can't believe it's really you. Do you know how close I came to running you through?"

She leaned her head against the wall. "I—I believe it."

He sheathed his sword. "I'm sorry about that, but I had to be sure. There are strange rumors about, and I'm not sure who can be trusted."

"Colin will confirm that it's me. Mawr too. They're both outside."

He nodded. "So you need to reach Master Teagan?"

"Yes, but I got lost. I thought I was going to the flower garden."

The Lieutenant chuckled. "I don't know why you would even look there. Why would he be trimming flowers at a time like this?"

She gaped at him before huffing. "It seemed like a good idea at the time."

He shook his head. "He's probably up with Madam Cloom in the throne room, I'd assume. No one has seen him all evening, not since the wolves came through the gates. Let me get these Healers sorted out, then I'll escort you there myself."

"No, it's okay. People need you. Just tell me how to get there and I'll find it myself."

His brow scrunched up in confusion, "If you're sure..."

"Please, I'm in a hurry."

He studied her once more before nodding, "Alright then."

WHATEVER LUCK HAD TAKEN hold during his fight with the wolves earlier was quickly dwindling. The camaraderie that Colin had shared with the two soldiers at the gate had dissipated as soon as he went outside riding on top of a big, stone lion. Colin was beginning to wonder who he had angered that morning to deserve all this now.

"A specialist in the Marketplace?" The dark-skinned soldier asked slowly. "I thought the Healers could fix everything."

"Apparently not," Colin chuckled. "Look I don't mean to be rude, but we're kind of in a hurry. Thankfully Mawr's here to help me." He patted the stone lion's flank in appreciation. Mawr kneaded a paw into the bridge, then stopped when he realized what he was doing.

The other guard, a short woman with red cheeks, eyed Talek. "Does he have a name? He doesn't look familiar."

"He's too weak to talk, and he doesn't have any identification on him unfortunately; but that doesn't mean we deny him aid."

Talek gave a rattling moan. The dark-skinned guard put a hand on the woman's shoulder when she went to argue. "We'll let them go. There's enough to deal with without monitoring every person that leaves. It's intruders we're concerned about."

She nodded, but her eyes lingered on Talek all the same.

"Alright, thanks you two!" Colin urged Mawr forward, toward the gate entrance to the city. He wanted to put as much distance between them and the two soldiers as possible. Colin was also eyeing the streets for any sign of Captain Briar. She was the only weak point in this plan. She wouldn't be fooled by their stories, and she would recognize Talek in an instant. He didn't see her, but there was no telling when she might appear or what then she might do.

Pockets of wolves were everywhere. Fires had sprung up in some of the buildings, possibly from the streetlights being pulled down. The old storage house where Colin had found Graddic earlier was belching flames into the dark night, and the eyes of every wolf in the area seemed to catch in the firelight. Colin had counted at least six so far and wondered if the wolves had killed the Captain. Somehow that was far more terrifying than actually running into her.

"Colin..." Mawr whimpered. Colin realized they had come to a stop. There were four wolves at the gate that led to the Slumbering Forest, and he would wager that there would be even more outside of the city. He turned around to eye the other gate that led to the field for the Games, but it had collapsed. How had the wolves done that? They were strong, but they weren't that strong. At the entrance to the Marketplace, on the opposite side of High Castle, fire had spread to multiple shops and he could hear screams in the distance. That path was also out of the question.

"Damn it," Colin muttered.

"Which way?" Mawr pawed anxiously at the ground and Colin too was beginning to panic. At any moment the Captain could show up and demand answers with her bloody blade. At any moment Teagan could appear and wonder why in the world they were freeing the prisoner without using any sort of stealth to keep his old lover hidden. It had been a long time since Colin had failed, not since the time before he had been transformed into a stoatling. His change was supposed to give him an edge, an ability to put other Seekers to shame, but now, he realized how unprepared he was for this task.

From the Marketplace, the sound of breaking glass caught his attention, and the Captain climbed out through one of the fiery buildings, helping two elderly men escape the flames. She spotted Colin and he watched as her excitement transformed into suspicion. She started making her way toward them. A pair of wolves moved between them, but Colin doubted it would take her long to slay them.

"Crap!" he cried and slammed a hand against Mawr's side. A coldness filled his limbs and he pushed back the threatening tears. This wasn't how it was supposed to end.

"Which way, Colin?" Mawr urged again. The wolves at the gates had spotted them and were approaching. "How do we get out of here?"

"I don't know!" Colin said, his voice small while his heartbeat raged in his ears. In one night he had not only failed Master Teagan, but Shaleigh too, and here he thought he was an excellent Seeker. Perhaps in the simple task of kidnapping children with magic, but certainly not at any real assignment. If Captain Briar did get hold of them, Mawr would be seen as an accomplice. By dawn, Colin wasn't sure how many heads would roll for his blunder.

"To the Slumbering Forest," Talek hissed through his hair. "I can hide in the trees there. I know them."

"Are you sure?" Colin whispered, leaning down to hear him even as his eyes locked on the fierce Captain in the distance. "That's where the wolves are coming from. They could swarm you!"

"I know places where I can hide until the assault ends. I'll be safe there. Please. Just don't let them catch me."

There was desperation in his voice that Colin understood well. He didn't know what would happen to him and Mawr, but he could at least deliver Talek to safety. That was his mission after all, to get Talek out of the city. Colin nodded and swallowed down his terror. "Alright, Mawr. You heard him." He pulled out his dagger. "Let's try to make quick work of these wolves." Captain Briar had already dispatched one of the beasts. "We don't have much time."

With a deep, resounding growl, Mawr charged toward the four wolves in front of them. Colin was pretty sure one of them had its leg crushed under Mawr's foot, but another one rolled away in time. It was probably best not to tell Mawr though, the poor lion might never forgive himself. Two more had climbed onto Mawr's hind legs in preparation and latched onto Mawr's back as he charged past. Colin turned around and held out his dagger.

"Keep down," he said to Talek. "And hold on. It may get a bit bumpy."

It wasn't easy climbing up stone, especially when the stone was moving beneath you. One wolf had climbed up without a problem, but the other was still trying to get its hind legs up. Colin put his dagger between his teeth and went toward it on all fours to keep from losing his balance. The fumbling wolf looked up at him with wide, amber eyes as Colin pressed the knife to his throat.

"You sure you want to come up here? I think you would rather let go."

The wolf eyed the knife and looked up at Colin with a frightened stare.

"Come on, now. Don't be stupid."

With a small whimper, the wolf let go, falling to the ground, and narrowly avoiding Mawr's hind legs as it rolled away. Colin grinned. At least that one had some sense. Then he felt teeth dig into his injured shoulder. He screamed and fell flat onto Mawr's lower back.

"Are you okay?" Mawr asked, slowing his pace.

"Keep going!" he managed but it was hard to talk around the pain. "Don't stop, whatever you do." He flipped his body around, hoping to dislodge his arm, but the wolf didn't let go and merely bit down harder. Colin screamed again, reaching for the dagger he couldn't find. He grabbed the wolf's snout with one hand and punched at it with the other. He tried to push it away, but the wolf's jaws stayed locked. Once they closed, it was nearly impossible to open them again. He went limp as the pain consumed him, and heard the wolf hiss a laugh through its bloody teeth.

"Colin," Talek said in a cold voice. "I think you dropped this." Colin looked up in time to see Talek standing on Mawr's back with the dagger clutched in his hand. In a flash he moved forward and dug it deep into the wolf's throat before the creature could even react. Warm blood poured out and down Colin's arm, and finally the teeth let go of him. With an angry groan he shoved the body off and lay there panting against Mawr's cold back.

Talek crouched beside him, though he almost fell in the process. "I know that might not have been the wisest choice, but I had to do it. It was going to kill you."

"That's okay, I'm not too good about wise choices myself lately."

Colin spotted the gate moving away from them and realized they were on the bridge outside of the Garden, heading into the Slumbering Forest. How far was Mawr going to take them, exactly?

"Okay, that's good!" he called, but neither Mawr or Talek seemed to understand what he meant. "Mawr," he called. "Stop already!"

Obediently the lion came to an abrupt halt, and poor Talek would have fallen off if Colin hadn't caught him in time. The Faerie winced and groped at his midsection. Colin sighed, "Damn it, Mawr, I didn't mean that quick!"

"But—but Colin, there's—"

Colin lifted Talek quickly and leapt to the ground. His face was far paler and as soon as Colin released him, he curled up into a fetal position. "Look, not now, Mawr. He's in really bad shape." If only he had thought to bring some herbal droughts or at least a water skin with him, maybe that would have helped a little. Colin pushed the

Faerie's hair out of his face, but his eyes were squeezed shut. "I'm sorry, Talek. I don't have anything for you. Maybe I should go back and kidnap a Healer."

"That won't be necessary," a deep voice caught Colin's attention and he turned to look deeper into the woods. A man stood before them in a dark robe the color of the night sky. In one hand he held a gnarled stick that was as tall as him and gilded with a large, violet gem. A light seemed to emanate from it, as though it bore a candle inside. It was a common trick used by magicians, but something was different about this magic wielder. His robe was far heavier than the ones Colin had seen worn by traveling magicians, and of far better quality. Mawr backed away and crouched down behind Colin, as though he could even hope to hide his massive body behind Colin's tiny frame.

"Who are you?" Colin got to his feet, realizing with a glance that Talek no longer held his dagger.

"Oh, I doubt you'll have heard of me," the dark clad magician replied and gave a slow nod. "I am Keriam the Clever."

The breath caught in Colin's throat. "I know that name, though not the title." The magician narrowed his eyes. "I've heard of Keriam the Conceited or Keriam the Cruel, even—but I've never heard you described as the Clever."

Keriam clenched his jaw, which made the lines and flecks of purple in his gray skin catch the light.

"That was over two centuries ago," Colin said quickly. "How in the world are you still alive?"

Mawr whimpered, which did nothing to give Colin

any courage. He glanced down to Talek, who was still breathing heavy with his eyes closed tight. At least he was still conscious.

"The greatest wielders of magic do not let something as trivial as death take hold of them." Keriam laughed and it was as though the trees shuddered at the sound. "I waited until the time was right to strike."

"On the Garden, you mean." Colin's hands clenched into fists. "So, you're the one who unleashed the wolves."

"Yes." Keriam smiled and held out his hand. A wolf that Colin hadn't even seen in the shadows moved in to nuzzle its snout into his palm. "We have an understanding. And you," his gaze turned to Talek, "You are late."

"There was a slight change in plans," Talek grunted.

Colin looked down at him with wide eyes. "Wait, you're working with this guy?"

Talek cracked his eyes open to look up at Colin, but there was no smile on his lips.

"I ought to have let the Captain finish you off," Colin snarled.

Keriam gave a low, disturbing laugh and stepped forward. Mawr started backing away, as though no one would notice if he tip-toed back to the Garden. "There's no need to run," Keriam said in a smooth tone. "My friends have you surrounded."

Colin glanced around, unable to see anything except the trees and the darkness beyond.

"Oh, my apologies. I forget myself." The magician waved his hand and it was as though a shadowy veil was lifted from around them, revealing dozens of glinting amber eyes and snarling jaws.

Keriam crouched down beside Talek. "I know this probably isn't the best time to ask, my friend, but I must know if you are still dedicated."

The Faerie looked exhausted as he lay beside him, with his long white hair thrown about like a shredded cape. "We had a deal, didn't we?"

"Of course, but I will not be accused of misleading you." Keriam glanced to Colin. "Unlike your famed Cathal, I will not lie just to gain a Faerie's power."

Talek gave a weak nod. "You got me inside, but it was no good." He shook his head and stared at the ground as a tear fell down his cheek. "You were right, Teagan refused me."

"I am sorry to hear that," Keriam said in a sympathetic voice even though he was smiling. "I told you, the power he loves has him in its clutches."

"I know, I just thought… I hoped that perhaps…"

"He is a fickle man and certainly doesn't deserve your loyalty." He got to his feet with a groan. "But as you said, we had a deal. If he refused you once again, then I would provide my aid in exchange for your cooperation."

Talek stared up at him with tears in his eyes. "As long as Teagan is freed. That's all I want. If he doesn't want me, at least I'll know he isn't trapped anymore. "

"Once his bond is broken, he will come to no harm by my hand."

Talek narrowed his eyes. "And?"

Keriam gave a toothy grin. "Nor by any hand, claw, or paw that I control."

"I suppose that is the best I can ask for." Talek gave a shaky breath.

Something was about to happen, but Colin hadn't a clue what. He didn't know how this had anything to do with Cathal. He and Mawr needed to get away—now. He wasn't sure how they were going to do that exactly, but he had to try. While Keriam and Talek spoke, Colin saw where his dagger lay: underneath Talek's foot. All he had to do was get to it.

~

WITH LIEUTENANT VARG'S INSTRUCTIONS, it hadn't taken long to reach the throne room. The guards who usually stood watch were nowhere to be seen. Likely they had been called down to help on the front lines, protecting who they could on the streets. If the attacks were so urgent that Madam Cloom's guards would be summoned, why in the world was Teagan still up here?

At the top of the incline, Shaleigh took a moment to catch her breath. She didn't want the sound of her breathing to give away her presence. She caught the sweet smell of Madam Cloom's flowers and tensed. Inside she could hear Teagan and Madam Cloom talking. The doors were wide open, and the glass-domed room was dark except for a few candelabras that hung from the ceiling. Lightning lit up the sky in the distance; the storm would give her plenty of shadows to move in. She pulled off the scissors from the necklace around her throat and held them tight. The hard part would be getting close to Teagan.

He would be able to see her, just as he did in the dungeons with Colin. All it took was a glance. If she timed this right, if she used Madam Cloom as a distraction, she ought to be able to get close. She took a final deep breath before stepping into the throne room. The chamber had been bright during the day, with the windows letting in sunlight to expose every corner of the room, but now it was cloaked in darkness. The bundles of vines cast strange, amorphous shadows on the walls. Rain began hitting the glass windows above as the storm drew closer. She hoped it might muffle her footsteps.

"The wolves are only the start of something worse, I feel." Madam Cloom paced back and forth before her throne, her gray hair spilling down over her shoulders as though she had been roused early from bed. She looked more haggard than before; something about the way she crossed her arms close to her body and the nervousness of her steps spoke of more than weariness. She was terrified. "We've never seen them act like this before, have we?"

"No, Madam," Teagan said in an impatient voice. "They aren't normally organized at all; their attacks are typically more desperate, more random than this."

She gave a brief nod and continued her pacing.

Teagan rolled his shoulders and looked to one of the large windows that overlooked the city. "I'm letting some of the rain come through. It should help with the fires at least. There's just so much that needs doing. Let me go to the streets and help. What good I am doing here?"

"No," she said, her voice echoing across the ivy walls. "You are to stay here at my side. I won't have you running off. I've set up enough traps to smell one creeping up on me. The wolves are acting with purpose, so we know someone is giving them orders. The fact that the leader has yet to reveal herself is what concerns me. I wonder what she's waiting for..."

"She? You believe it to be Queen Mab?" Teagan chuckled. "I don't think she would have much interest in the Garden. She has never shown concern for my work here."

Madam Cloom shook her head. "Not for you, that other one."

Teagan's smile faded. Outside, a building collapsed and both turned to look. A fire had sprung up between multiple buildings, and the flames reached so high that several streets were fully illuminated. Teagan took a step forward and sheets of rain poured down on the flames as though a cloud had opened directly above them.

"Come now, it's not as though the Garden can burn to the ground, Teagan," Madam Cloom said impatiently. "Our enemy is trying to force us to make a move. Fortunately, they don't know who they're dealing with. I can wait all night if I must."

"All night..." Teagan's voice broke.

"Yes, all night!" she snapped. "All week if I must! You and I, Teagan, we're in this for the long race. I won't be dethroned by Queen Mab or anyone else who uses such loathsome creatures like shadow wolves to do their bidding!"

As Madam Cloom bellowed, Shaleigh couldn't look away from Teagan. He had tears in his eyes and his arms hung useless at his sides. Shaleigh pitied him. Here he was, the most powerful person in all the Garden, and yet he was told to stay put to protect one person. Out on the streets, another building burst into flames and Teagan winced. Talek had been absolutely right. Being in Madam Cloom's grip was killing him.

At the first sign of a threat, this woman didn't try to help her people or protect the city, she chose to protect herself like a coward. She holed herself up in the tallest tower with the strongest weapon she had and waited for the fires to burn out. Whatever doubt Shaleigh might have had in this dangerous request was quickly dwindling as the fires outside continued to spread. A crack of lightning from above made her heart skip a beat, and the boom of thunder afterward made the windows rattle. She didn't come here to watch, she reminded herself. She needed to act. She took a deep breath and tip-toed her way toward Teagan.

He had moved to the center of the room, drawn by pain and curiosity to the sight of the city—*his* city—below. Shaleigh could just glimpse the small bit of black ribbon beneath the white cuff of his right hand. If she could free him, if she could break him from this terrible curse, perhaps he could fix all of this. He wielded powerful magic. Putting out a few fires wouldn't take him any time. All she had to do was tear him from the cage Madam Cloom had locked him in.

"They need me," he said again. Shaleigh had never heard him sound so broken.

"No, they don't. I need you. Your part is to the ruler of the Garden, not to them. They merely make a living on my land." She came down the steps to stand beside him and looked out through the rain-streaked windows at the fires below. Her mouth was a thin line, her eyes impassive stones, the opposite of Teagan's obvious turmoil.

Shaleigh moved around behind her and slipped through the large gap she had left between her and Teagan. Perhaps he wouldn't hear her breathing with Madam Cloom so close. Perhaps he wouldn't hear her footfalls with the rain beating against the windows. Shaleigh kept her eyes locked on that thin sliver of ribbon on Teagan's right wrist and tried to calm her heart, which pounded in her ears. Teagan's hand twitched and she froze, expecting him to turn on her in rage, but he didn't move. It took her a moment to realize that he was trembling.

"Don't feel for them, Teagan, do you hear me?" Madam Cloom hissed at his side, "Don't feel for any of them. I order you not to."

"Yes, Madam," he answered in a calm voice. But his hands still trembled, and he clasped them tight behind him, as if ashamed of his emotion. The black ribbon hung down from his wrist only a tiny amount, but it was enough to put a single blade of the scissors through.

Shaleigh held her breath as she opened the scissors, then exhaled as she slipped the fragile ribbon between the blades, careful not to touch Teagan's skin. She had to act now. She had to do it before she lost the nerve and hoped that the scissors were sharp enough.

Shaleigh clenched the handles. The silver scissors bit through the fabric with ease. Teagan gasped and jerked away. He turned and stared right at her with pure shock.

"Shaleigh...what have you done?"

THE VIOLET EYE

*T*he rain came on suddenly, and with such ferocity, that for a moment Colin forgot that he was still within the boundaries of the Garden, with its pleasant showers and springtime temperatures. This rain felt cold, unrelenting—not the kind approved of by Madam Cloom.

Something had changed. Colin could feel it in the air and thrumming through the ground beneath his feet. He could sense it, like an electric charge, but he hadn't a clue where it came from. The creepy magician helped Talek to his feet, but he wasn't the cause. He must have felt it too, though, because he shook with a barking laugh that made Colin's fur stand on end.

"That would be the girl!" Keriam exclaimed, "Talek my friend, you have outdone yourself."

The white-haired Faerie beamed despite the fact he likely had broken ribs and had to lean on the magician's arm to keep from falling. "He's free," he whispered and stared to the sky. "He's finally free of her."

"Now for the contract," Keriam said, pulling a scroll out from his robes, which was promptly soaked by the rain. Why were they discussing contracts in the middle of a battle, here in the woods of all places? Colin couldn't make any sense of it. The shift in the air made him anxious, and the cold rain beating down from above wasn't helping. His dagger, that he spotted before at Talek's feet, was quickly getting pushed down into the mud. He could barely see the handle now. He needed a different plan of action. He backed up into Mawr, who was still cowering behind him.

"We have to make a run for it," Colin whispered, looking at all the wolves around them. He counted at least five, including the one at Keriam's side, but he was certain there were more in the shadows he couldn't see.

Mawr knew better than to talk. Even his whispers would grumble loud enough for the others to hear. Colin had to hope the wolves couldn't hear him. Mawr gave him a wide-eyed look that might have normally melted his determination if they weren't so desperate.

"I know, but if we stay here, we're dead."

"I accept," Talek said. He held out his arm and pulled up his sleeve.

Keriam flicked his wrist, and the contract transformed into a tiny violet ribbon, which he quickly tied around Talek's wrist. It reminded Colin of a wedding vow to bind two lovers together, but somehow, he doubted that was happening now. He had never heard of magicians using ribbons in their magic. The knot was tied and it sounded like an enormous bell was rung. It was so loud, that it felt as though someone had put it right next to his ears and struck it. The noise reverberated in his skull and Colin shouted as his head throbbed in pain. As the ringing slowly subsided, Colin made out another sound, and opened his eyes again. Talek was on the ground screaming.

Tendrils of purple flame moved beneath his skin and up his arm from where the ribbon rested. Keriam's mad laughter echoed amid the dark trees. Looking around Colin saw that the wolves had fled. Only the one at Keriam's side had stayed. Its eyes reflected terror—even it didn't know what was happening. Colin put a hand on Mawr's forearm, and they backed away together.

As the flames spread up to Talek's throat and began moving over his cheeks, something went wrong. The diminished ringing of the bell changed. It had been a crystal-clear note at first when it pounded into Colin's mind, but now it trembled along with Talek. Colin didn't understand it, but Keriam stopped laughing.

"Talek? What's wrong? What's happening?"

The white-haired Faerie wasn't hearing him, though. He screamed again and covered his face with his hands. Keriam crouched down at his side, his long robe dirtied from the mud.

"Answer me!" he demanded, but Talek didn't reply. Instead the Faerie's screams began to break into laughter. A cold chill went down Colin's back at the sound. His instincts were screaming at him to leave. Whatever magic was happening here had misfired, and there was no telling what could happen. Carefully Colin and Mawr took another step back, freezing when Keriam spun toward them.

"You two aren't going anywhere," Keriam snapped and leaned on his staff to stand as Talek twisted with laughter at his feet. He scowled down at the Faerie with a mixture of disgust and determination.

"What's wrong with him?" Mawr asked.

"It's the Madness," he spat. "I suppose he was too fragile for the binding. That won't nullify our contract though, will it, Talek?"

"No," the Faerie squeaked out through a chuckle, struggling to get to his feet.

Keriam sighed and grabbed his wrist, yanking him up to stand at his side. Talek was still injured, but he didn't even wince as Keriam forced him to his feet. There was something very wrong about him. It wasn't just that he was covered in mud and grime. He was distracted, and his head kept floating this way and that, as though seeing things they couldn't.

Keriam clenched his teeth. "Talek, I have a request to make of you."

Biting his lip to hold back a giggle, Talek turned to look at him, and Colin got a good look at his face. His right eye was now a luminescent violet, with tendrils of black that seemed to seep out from his pupil like a terrible infection.

"Talek?" Mawr asked in a tiny voice. "Are you alright?"

The Faerie gave a disturbing grin. "Oh yes, I'm fine. Everything is better now. Don't worry."

Colin didn't feel very reassured.

Keriam studied the Faerie hard. "First, I need you to heal your own wounds, can you do that?"

He nodded enthusiastically and clasped his hands over

his midsection. He closed his eyes for a minute and then took a deep breath. "What a good idea! I'm so glad you thought of it. I'd completely forgotten about those."

The magician smirked and added, "Next I need you to pay a visit to your friend."

His entire face brightened. "To see Teagan?"

Keriam nodded.

Talek bounced up and down on his toes. "Alright," He turned to leave, but Keriam put a hand to his shoulder. "I want you to bring Madam Cloom to me. Don't harm her though, not yet."

Colin tensed. They were going after Madam Cloom. He couldn't simply stand aside. As much as he disliked the woman, she was still the leader of the Garden. He still served her and Master Teagan. Working on impulse, Colin bounded forward, pulled his blade free from the mud, and grabbed the base of Keriam's staff. The magician hadn't expected it, and nearly fell to the ground. Colin bounded back to Mawr's side. For the first time in ages, Colin was grateful for his skill at stealing. He wasn't sure how powerful the magician's staff would be, but it was a distraction, at least. With the staff in one hand and the muddy knife in the other, he finally felt like he had the upper hand.

He leapt onto the lion's back and Mawr reared up as he turned around. They could see the eyes of the wolves all around them again, but Colin held the staff high, and the fear of that magic kept them at bay. Colin had forgotten how quick Mawr could move, and his tiny claws scraped against the lion's back as they hurried back toward the main gate of the Garden. They needed to get out of the woods, away from the trees where more wolves might be hiding. His heart leapt to his throat as the bridge came into view. He could see a few wolves fighting inside the gate. Yes, they might run into Captain Briar or even Master Teagan, but Colin didn't care anymore. All he had to do was show the staff to the Captain and tell her that Madam Cloom was in danger, and that would be enough.

They had almost reached the bridge when he caught a flash of white hair in the corner of his eye. Before he could turn around, he felt a powerful grip take hold of his hand with the dagger, then the blade pressed into his own throat. Another hand gripped hard onto his injured shoulder and Colin hissed against the flaring pain.

"Now do you really think my master would let you flee with his weapon of choice? Tell him to stop."

"Mawr," Colin choked, trying not to swallow so his Adam's apple wouldn't bob down against the blade. "Stop!"

Mawr slowly came to halt, stopping just underneath the front gates. "Colin?" He asked, trying to turn his large head around to see his own back.

"Such a good little pet," Talek whispered as he released Colin's injured shoulder and stroked his furry head instead.

"Why are you doing this?" Colin asked. His voice cracked and tears stung his eyes. This wasn't how it was supposed to end.

"You stole something that belongs to my master. I've been given orders to retrieve it and to punish you."

Colin glanced toward him, his gaze drawn to that violet eye with the blackness seeping from within.

"I could turn you into a toad, but that's a little cliché, is it not?" He reached forward and slid the staff out of Colin's grip. "Besides I think I like you as a stoatling. It suits you, being the quick, pathetic nuisance that you are. However, he did require a punishment..."

The knife left his throat, and Colin almost breathed a sigh of relief, but then Talek twirled the dagger in his fingers and it grew larger until it resembled a pike. Talek leaped quickly into the air, and Colin barely had the time to gasp before the blade pierced his leg. The blade was longer than his forearm now and it went straight through Colin's leg and dug into Mawr's back. Whatever material it was made of now was far stronger than any metal blade to be able to pierce stone.

Colin cried out as blood poured from the wound and soaked into Mawr's back. He felt Mawr's growls of pain as the big cat circled for a few moments before falling to the ground.

"Hang on, Mawr!" Colin groaned with eyes full of tears. He put both hands on the handle of his pike shaft and tried to pull it free, but Mawr let out a sad whimper. It was too deep. They were pinned together.

"Shaleigh...what have you done?" Teagan stared at her, his mouth agape. A silence fell over the room as the rain drummed against the windows.

The black ribbon fluttered to the floor like a dying butterfly, and as it touched the ground, a sound like the powerful strike of a gong reverberated through the room. The low pitch made her teeth rattle, her skull throb, and

Shaleigh covered her ears to block out the noise. Darkness closed in around her and for a moment she thought she was passing out.

Madam Cloom clutched at her head and spun around, her eyes fixed on Shaleigh. "What did you do?"

Teagan fell to the ground as the gong began to fade and Madam Cloom put a hand to his shoulder.

"You've broken it," Teagan panted, sounding like a lost child. "Why would you do such a thing?"

"She what?" Madam Cloom's low voice filled with rage.

"It's okay." Shaleigh pulled off the necklace and stuffed it into her pocket. Then she stepped closer to Teagan, trying to ignore Madam Cloom's vicious gaze. "You don't have to follow her orders anymore. You're free!"

She had expected him to be upset; he wouldn't want to lose so much power. It was for the best though, just like Talek had said. He might not appreciate it now, but he would eventually; he had no choice.

Teagan held his head with both hands, tangling his fingers in his red hair. "No, no, that's not how it works!"

Outside, the rain came down in torrents, hitting the windows so hard that it sounded like a tornado was headed toward them. The castle reverberated as though it might be ripped from the ground; it was a feeling Shaleigh recognized. It felt like a building standing on its last legs. It was similar to the occasional shifting that went through the old Ferris Factory regularly, but a jolt that was far more dangerous. High Castle was going to collapse, and soon.

Madam Cloom lost her balance and fell to the floor,

her nightgown splayed out around her like a cape. For an instant, Shaleigh almost went to her side. The old woman looked so frail as she sat there with her gray hair loose around her shoulders, her pale, thin arms holding her up. Madam Cloom's shoulders shook as though she was crying, but instead came laughter. It was a terrible and bitter sound—the combination of fear and apathy into a gut-wrenching train wreck that had no way to escape other than through that horrible, desperate laugh. It was the sound of someone who had nothing left to lose, and that frightened Shaleigh more than any shuddering building.

Shaleigh crouched down in front of Teagan so he could hear her over the noise. She put a hand on his, trying to seek out his face amid the tangle of hair and tears he had become, but Teagan kept his head down. "Didn't you hear me? I said she can't control you anymore. I know it's hard now, but—"

"Here I thought they had their sights on Teagan," Madam Cloom said in a shrill voice, glaring at Shaleigh with wild eyes. "How very clever! I never expected a waif like you to topple my kingdom."

Shaleigh got to her feet. "He couldn't be your slave forever! Now you can't use him to hurt anyone."

The old woman smiled as she made her way toward them. "You really are a naïve, foolish child. Go ahead, keep spouting all that nonsense. Keep believing every word of it. Let me guess—I bet they told you they would help you escape, didn't they? Said they would help you?"

Shaleigh gaped at her. How did she know so much about it? She glanced down to Teagan, but he still wouldn't look at her. Maybe the pact had meant more to him than she thought.

"How sweet." Madam Cloom grabbed hold of Shaleigh's jaw, digging her fingers into the soft flesh of her cheeks, and pulled down so that she had to crouch on one leg. Shaleigh was at eye level now with the woman, and staring into her crazed, bloodshot eyes.

"You cost me my throne. I had to *kill* for that. I had to *bleed* for it. Did you know that? Of course not," she chuckled, and her thin mouth curved into a cruel smile. "You live in a bubble where the only important thing to you is yourself and your wants." She shoved Shaleigh back so hard that she fell onto her butt. Shaleigh rubbed at her cheeks, a response already on her lips, but before she could utter a word, Madam Cloom backhanded her across the face. Pain erupted, and she squeezed her eyes shut against it. Instinctively she splayed out her arms to keep from hitting her face on the ground and tried to catch her breath.

"Who convinced you to do this?"

Shaleigh pushed herself back up. "What?"

The old woman gave a sick smile. "I'd rather not have to repeat myself. Who planted the seed in your mind, who gave you the tools, who told you what to do, child? Answer me!"

Shaleigh gaped at her. Teagan watched them both with a look of utter weariness. She hadn't thought about what she would do when she got to this point, Shaleigh realized. She had expected Teagan to be annoyed, but she certainly hadn't thought Madam Cloom would attack her like this. She didn't want Teagan or Talek in danger. "I don't know—"

"Of course you do." Madam Cloom lifted her hand again and Shaleigh winced in preparation for the strike.

"It was Talek, wasn't it?" Teagan asked as the castle shook again, this time groaning as though metal was straining. "He put you up to it, didn't he?"

Shaleigh nodded and Madam Cloom lowered her hand.

"I knew I should have beheaded him on stage. I knew he was more trouble than he was worth," the old woman said. She pointed a finger at Teagan, "It's your soft heart that did this."

He clenched his jaw.

"That's always been your weakness. You're always so—"

Every window along the wall smashed inward. The high-pitched shatter was quickly followed by the torrent of rain that drowned out all other sound. Shaleigh brought her arms up in reflex, but Teagan grabbed both women and leapt toward the throne. The wind howled around them as they skidded across the floor; the flowery vines shook, unraveling from their perches along the walls and their coral-colored petals flew about the room.

"So, here's where you've been hiding," Talek said as he stepped over shattered glass. The last Shaleigh had seen him, he had been barely able to stand up straight, but now he walked as though he had never been injured at all.

"Talek?" Shaleigh asked, confused, "What are you doing here?"

"Just carrying out my orders," he said with a crazed

smile.

Shaleigh started to ask what he meant, but then she saw his right eye. It glowed with a strange violet luminescence. Any question she had been about to ask died on her lips as she stared at that horrible, swirling eye.

"What in the world happened to you?" Teagan whispered as he got to his feet, dropping shards of glass to the floor.

A mixture of emotions seemed to pass over Talek's face all at once, something between panic, affection, and desperation. Finally, he settled on amusement, "It's nothing to worry about, Teagan." He lifted his right hand and displayed the violet ribbon that hung there. "I have a new master now."

Madam Cloom started to say something, but Teagan held out a hand to quiet her. To Shaleigh's surprise, she obeyed. Teagan took a step forward. "Who did you allow to bind you? I thought you were against such things." His gaze kept drifting over to the violet eye. "It's changed you."

"Yes, but you're free now, aren't you?" Talek asked, his sadness just visible beneath his cheerful facade. "You're no long bound by this woman's wicked whim." He pointed a finger at Madam Cloom, who had gotten to her feet, standing almost completely behind Teagan.

"If you wanted me to be freed," Teagan sighed, "this was not the way to do it."

"Then how was it to be done?" Talek's voice boomed across the throne room as the rain swept in behind him. Shaleigh had never seen him so angry. Even when Captain Briar was kicking him on the floor of his jail cell, he was nothing like this. "You were too fond of the power to let it go, weren't you?" Talek's voice cracked. "This, all of this, was just too tempting. And once you were here...well, you grew a taste for it." He broke into a snicker. "You grew to love this wretched Garden more than me." He howled with laughter but there were tears in his eyes.

Shaleigh took a step forward. "Talek, what happened to you?"

"Stay back," Teagan hissed. "It's the Madness."

Talek took a few deep breaths and wiped at his cheeks. "You left me for this bestial place. I don't see the appeal. Was it the power alone that stole you from me, that made you despise me, or was it something else?"

"Talek, honestly, I've never despised you..."

"Then was it something she did to make you hate me so?" Talek turned his gaze to Madam Cloom, who watched him as though he was a mad dog.

"Now Talek," she said in a wavering voice. "You understand I'm merely a steward here. I'm holding this place until Master Cathal's reincarnation returns. You can't blame me for—"

"Oh, I can blame you. Quite easily, really. You would have had me killed. You would have punished Teagan for helping me leave. You were even going to have Shaleigh murdered, weren't you? And look at her, she's not even an adult!"

Madam Cloom put on a sleek smile. "I think you've misjudged me, Talek. Perhaps if we could discuss this—"

"Liar." Talek stalked toward her, his white hair floating around his shoulders and his violet eye glowing in the darkened room. Madam Cloom clutched a hand around

Teagan's arm, hoping he could somehow protect her, but Shaleigh had broken that bond. It was in that moment that Shaleigh realized, if anything did happen to Madam Cloom, the responsibility would rest on her shoulders. She was the one who severed the ribbon and cut the bond.

"Now what were his orders again?" Talek mused, "Bring her or kill her? I simply can't recall!"

Madam Cloom was backing up the steps toward her throne, but Talek was close enough to touch her.

Shaleigh started toward them, not sure what she would do, but determined to do something. Teagan grabbed her shoulder and urged her back behind him.

"Talek is gripped in Madness, there's no telling what he is capable of. Don't get in his way."

Shaleigh held up the silver scissors so that he could see them, the ones that she had used to cut his bond. Teagan eyed them for a moment before clasping a hand over hers with a nervous eye to Talek. He shook his head as Talek advanced on Madam Cloom. Taking his warning and accepting it, Shaleigh slid them into the fold of her belt that held her scabbard. As much as she wanted to help, she had to trust that Teagan understood the dangers better than she did.

"I might be useful to your master," Madam Cloom implored. "I'm a strategist, some might say one of the best, and I can assure you that—"

Talek clasped a hand over the woman's mouth. "Shh, no more of that talk. No more lies, if you please." When he pulled his hand back, Madam Cloom's lips were stitching themselves together.

"Maaap!" she shrieked before her mouth was

completely folded over and her lips were gone. She tried to scream and felt her mouth in a panic.

Talek stepped back and turned to them again. "That's much better, is it not? I couldn't listen to any more of her vicious lies!"

Shaleigh couldn't breathe for a minute. Her lungs didn't want to obey. She watched helplessly as Madam Cloom collapsed to her knees and cried. The coral-colored petals scattered around her in mini whirlwinds. Shaleigh hadn't meant for this to happen. She hadn't meant to hurt anyone. All she had wanted was to fulfill her promise to Talek, free Teagan, and go home. She just wanted to help.

Talek suddenly crouched down in front of her, his violet eye studying her. "You have been a very dear friend to me, Shaleigh." He dragged a palm across her cheeks and the bruises that had formed there disappeared. Shaleigh stared at him, waiting for him to stitch her mouth closed next. Everything felt numb. "If you hadn't been here, I don't know what would have become of me." He smiled, and it reminded her of when she first saw him out in the Slumbering Forest, staring down from the trees, holding her camera in his hands.

"I just want to go home," she whispered.

"Home, yes," Talek muttered, his eyes rolling around the room as though seeing something she couldn't. The violet eye pulsed and the blackness seeped out from the center in tendrils. "I remember. I can send you there. Would you like that?"

She nodded, pushing away the guilt that tore at her. She knew she was responsible for all of this. How could she run away when she had been the unwitting corner-stone all along? She pushed it down, though, and forced herself not to look at Madam Cloom crying by her throne. The promise of seeing her father again was too tempting, the need to feel Kaeja hugging her was like a dream come true. The guilt would go away eventually. It couldn't last forever, right? She wiped at her nose and clutched her elbows tight. "I don't belong here."

"Shaleigh..." Teagan was standing stiff beside her, but if he was trying to tell her something, she had no idea what it could be. To be honest, she didn't care anymore. She was tired of messages behind words. All she wanted to do was go back home and forget that any of this ever happened.

"I know, child. Don't worry," Talek gently took her chin in his fingers. "I'll send you home." He took several steps back and closed his eyes. Then he started singing a cheerful song with playful lilts.

The room was getting brighter. At first, she thought that the sun was rising, but it was far too bright. It was like she was being swallowed by a camera flash. The rain thundered, relentless against the glass, drowning out any other noise. Soon she could barely make out the throne room or smell any hint of flowers. A hand wrapped around her wrist, and she looked up to see Teagan with his red hair whipping around in the wind. He said some-thing because she watched his lips move, but Shaleigh couldn't hear him.

"What are you doing?" she had to yell to be heard over the noise.

"Teagan, no!" Talek shrieked. He must have been

running toward them, a black shadow getting harder to see as the light grew brighter. His violet eye gleamed, his hand reaching out as though trying to grab hold of them, but then the room was gone and she and Teagan were alone in the white light.

BIRDS WERE SINGING. When was the last time she had heard those? Was it outside the library with Mawr? Or was it at the City of Aife when she was riding on their makeshift sled? Maybe it was back inside the Tree House with Kaeja. She hadn't realized she had closed her eyes until she opened them and saw the sky was a thick green canopy. She could see the fluttering shapes of birds as they darted from one tree to another and golden sunlight filtered down through the branches.

She put her hands down beside her and felt dirt and rocks against her fingertips. Had Talek done it? Had he sent her home? She pushed herself up and felt a weight fall from her arm. Teagan was lying beside her, his red hair all mussed around his face and his suit still wet from the rain.

"So it wasn't a dream," she whispered. Teagan was unconscious, but his breathing seemed steady. Shaleigh got to her feet and her head spun a little as she looked down to see a ring of white toadstools around where they had been lying. Each one was almost a foot tall with wide flat heads on top of skinny bodies.

She crouched down to examine one. "I think I know these." The realization made her heart race. But she had to stay calm. Even if she was back in her world, she had no idea where Talek had sent them. They could be halfway around the world for all she knew. She glanced down to Teagan before stepping carefully over the ring of toadstools. She considered waiting for him to wake, but she needed to know where they were first. She needed to find a road somewhere or maybe a house. Something to reassure her, something to appease the excitement growing in her chest.

"I'll be right back," she whispered to Teagan's form before heading into the trees. The forest was old; she could tell based on how few weeds and vines grew down on the ground compared to the thick canopy above. Occasionally she thought she saw animal tracks, but she couldn't identify them. Shaleigh knew buildings far better than she knew the woods. She kept checking behind her to make sure she didn't get lost. She wanted to make sure she could make it back to Teagan in case he needed her. She could only imagine how awkward it would be to explain should a pair of hikers or hunters stumble upon him.

The woods felt unending, but she couldn't bring herself to go back, not yet. That tightness in her chest was growing worse and the farther she went, the more nervous she became. She thought of all the dangerous places in the world they might have been left in, all the wild places, all the infectious diseases she might not be inoculated against. Then she spotted a concrete pillar.

Relief spread through her and she leaned against an old, knotted tree trunk. From behind she could hear Teagan calling her name, could hear him as he made his way toward her. Unlike her, he apparently didn't have any trouble navigating through the trees. She didn't reply as guilt tried to boil up within her again, but she pushed it away. It didn't matter anymore. She was back in her world, she was sure of it now.

"Shaleigh," Teagan hissed a few paces back. "Come here."

"It's alright," she said, swallowing a sob. "It's concrete. We have it all over the place in my world." She turned and headed toward the pillar.

"Shaleigh!"

Why was he so anxious? It was probably someone's house. All she had to do was make sure it was safe to approach. She stepped cautiously down a drainage ditch to reach a dirt road. Before she had even turned to face the pillar, Teagan was suddenly behind her. He wrapped an arm around her waist, intent to pull her back to the woods, but she fought him.

"Would you stop it already?" she cried.

"This is not your world!" Teagan hissed in her ear. "He sent us to *our* home, not yours. It was the Madness at work. We're in my homeland, ruled by Queen Mab!"

That was when Shaleigh saw the rest of the structure. What she had thought was concrete was actually stone. The pillar was one end of a rectangular stone arch, with holes cut into it. In each hole was a gleaming white human skull. There were maybe twelve of them in all.

Shaleigh couldn't even scream.

To be continued in:
Broken

ALSO BY MARLENA FRANK

The Stolen Series

Young adult, portal fantasy, faeries

Stolen

Broken

Chosen

The Wolves of Kanta Series

Young adult, dark fantasy, steampunk, werewolves

The She-Wolf of Kanta

The Blood of Kanta

The Hunters of Kanta

The Fury of Kanta

The Howl of Kanta

Standalones

Young adult, horror, sci-fi, dystopian

The Seeking

Short stories, horror, dark fantasy

The Impostor and Other Dark Tales

Ocean horror, weird, short story

Undertow

Weird western, werewolves, vampires, short story

Night Feeders

Mystery, film noir, humor, short story

The Mysterious Disappearance of Charlene Kerringer

The Blade Filled with Stars

A kingdom is under siege from a familiar enemy. Families and friends are pitted against each other without reason. Slaughter is imminent while the winged Queen Khafil soars overhead. Desperate and terrified, Anna works with her sister, Lilah, to summon aid from their mother's ancient spell book.

Determined to save their people, the sisters

summon Death to help them, but Death is not easily swayed. Neither of the sisters are prepared for the consequences.

Want a peek behind the scenes?
Want to preview my books before they get released?

Get exclusive access to book goodies, giveaways, and cover reveals by joining my mailing list. Not only will you get notified of all my new releases, you'll get an exclusive copy of The Blade Filled with Stars.

Subscribe to the Mailing List at:
http://marlenafrank.com/mailinglist/

Support Me On
Ko-fi

Follow me on Ko-Fi for regular updates on my writing progress.

Monthly subscribers get access to sneak peeks at stories way before anyone else. They also get access to cover reveals, monthly shout-outs on social media, and thanked by name in the acknowledgements in my books.

http://ko-fi.com/MarlenaFrank

ACKNOWLEDGMENTS

There are so many people to thank for this book. From my fellow Livejournal friends when I first started out to my fellow Camp Nanowrimo campers who cheered me on while writing multiple drafts. I want to thank my family for supporting me through this whole learning process and for helping me learn how to talk about myself and my books. A special thanks to my Aunt Charmaine for not only loving my work but sharing her love with others. She has been such an inspiration!

A big thanks goes out to my editors! Without their keen eyes and love for this book, it would never have been as clean and polished as it is. Trust me on that one. Their work is so very important and I appreciate every question they brought up and consistency mishap they found, even if it did have me face-palming at myself. A big thank you to my sister Kelley for updating the text on the cover for this edition and for helping me transition these books from small press to indie. Thank you all so much for bringing this book to life!

ABOUT THE AUTHOR

Marlena Frank is the author of young adult fantasy and horror novels, short stories, novellas, and book series. Many of her books have hit the bestseller charts, including her debut novel, Stolen. Her work has been praised by Readers' Favorite and featured in De Mode of Literature Magazine. Her stories have appeared in anthologies such as Emporium of Superstition, Catstruck!, Heroic Fantasy Quarterly, Georgia Gothic, and The Sirens Call ezine.

Although born in Tennessee, Marlena has spent most

of her life in Georgia. She lives with her sister and two spoiled adopted cats. She serves as the Vice President of the Atlanta Chapter of the Horror Writers Association, is an active member of the Science Fiction and Fantasy Writers Association, and is an avid member of the Atlanta cosplay community.

She is also an INFJ, a tea drinker, and a wildlife enthusiast.

Support her on Ko-Fi: ko-fi.com/MarlenaFrank